continued . . .

ALSO BY SHARON SHINN . . .

WRAPT IN CRYSTAL

"Shinn skillfully combines suspense, science fiction, and romance while posing thoughtful questions on worship, faith, and sacrifice."
—Booklist

"Taut, realistic police work, an involving love story, and a fetching backdrop . . . well up to Shinn's previous high standards."
—Kirkus Reviews

THE SHAPE-CHANGER'S WIFE
Selected by *Locus* as Best First Fantasy Novel

"A delightful world to escape into . . . Shinn has set out to create a sweet and beautiful story about love, magic, and honor and has proven that she can accomplish the task nobly, enjoyably, and well."
—Locus

"Ms. Shinn takes a traditional romance and wraps it in a fantasy . . . rousing." *—The Magazine of Fantasy and Science Fiction*

"The spellbinding Ms. Shinn writes with elegant imagination and a steely grace, bringing a remarkable freshness that will command a wide audience."
—Romantic Times

HEART OF GOLD

SHARON SHINN

ACE BOOKS, NEW YORK

THE BERKLEY PUBLISHING GROUP
Published by the Penguin Group
Penguin Group (USA) Inc.
375 Hudson Street, New York, New York 10014, USA
Penguin Group (Canada), 10 Alcorn Avenue, Toronto, Ontario M4V 3B2, Canada
(a division of Pearson Penguin Canada Inc.)
Penguin Books Ltd., 80 Strand, London WC2R 0RL, England
Penguin Group Ireland, 25 St. Stephen's Green, Dublin 2, Ireland (a division of Penguin Books Ltd.)
Penguin Group (Australia), 250 Camberwell Road, Camberwell, Victoria 3124, Australia
(a division of Pearson Australia Group Pty. Ltd.)
Penguin Books India Pvt. Ltd., 11 Community Centre, Panchsheel Park, New Delhi—110 017, India
Penguin Group (NZ), Cnr. Airborne and Rosedale Roads, Albany, Auckland 1310, New Zealand
(a division of Pearson New Zealand Ltd.)
Penguin Books (South Africa) (Pty.) Ltd., 24 Sturdee Avenue, Rosebank, Johannesburg 2196, South Africa

Penguin Books Ltd., Registered Offices: 80 Strand, London WC2R 0RL, England

This is a work of fiction. Names, characters, places, and incidents either are the product of the author's imagination or are used fictitiously, and any resemblance to actual persons, living or dead, business establishments, events, or locales is entirely coincidental.

HEART OF GOLD

An Ace Book / published by arrangement with the author

PRINTING HISTORY
Ace trade paperback edition / April 2000
Ace mass market edition / April 2001

Copyright © 2000 by Sharon Shinn.

ISBN: 0-441-00821-6

ACE
Ace Books are published by The Berkley Publishing Group,
a division of Penguin Group (USA) Inc.,
375 Hudson Street, New York, New York 10014.
ACE and the "A" design are trademarks belonging to Penguin Group (USA) Inc.

PRINTED IN THE UNITED STATES OF AMERICA

10 9 8 7 6 5 4 3 2

For Donna,
who wanted to marry Nolan

CHAPTER ONE

Nolan was nearly an hour late by the time he arrived at the Central Government Activities Complex, and even here his way was blocked. Throngs of tourists, lines of determined security guards, and pockets of news reporters clustered in front of every entrance to the huge red granite building that dominated the city skyline. Trying to be polite about it, Nolan edged his way past blueskin security forces, gulden spectators, and journalists of both races. This was one of the rare mornings he had to show an I.D. to enter the building.

"Name?" the guard questioned while he fumbled for his badge.

"Nolan Adelpho."

The guard checked a clipboard. "Adelpho. Indigo male," he muttered, marking off something on his sheet. "Reason for admittance to the Complex?"

Finally. In his left trouser pocket. Nolan pulled out his badge and handed it over. "I work at the Biolab."

The guard scrutinized the I.D., examined Nolan's face to make sure it matched, and waved him inside. Even the interior corridors were crowded, and the elevator was crammed with both indigo and gulden individuals. Nolan felt a sense of relief when he was finally able to disembark on the fourteenth floor—which, by eerie contrast, at first appeared totally deserted. Still, even the empty halls seemed electric with anticipation, and faint laughter floated to him from three rooms away.

"Hello?" he called out, trying to guess where everyone was.

"Here," someone shouted. "Melina's room."

He made his way through a maze of closed offices, open labs, and storage closets to the long, narrow room where Melina worked. About twenty people were pressed against the window, heads craned down to see the street below. As in the elevator, the company here was mixed—five indigo men, five indigo women, six gulden men, and a trio of albinos. The indigo presented a range of skin tones from the darkest navy to the palest sky blue, though they all had black hair of a similar rough texture. The gulden, on the other hand, were almost uniformly the same deep gold hue, though they sported a variety of hair color that was amazing to Nolan—blond, red, orange, brown, silver, and bronze. The whitemen, who kept to themselves at the far end of the window, were harder to distinguish one from the other. Even after working with three of them for five years, Nolan sometimes had trouble telling them apart.

Only Pakt turned to greet Nolan when he walked in the door. "You're earlier than I thought you'd be," he said with a grin. "I'd figured you couldn't make it for another hour."

"I was beginning to think that myself. The Centrifuge was so crowded that people were sharing ringcars with strangers. And once I got off at the gate, all the trolleys were packed. It was quicker to walk, so I did. What's going on?"

Pakt gestured at the window with one broad, golden palm. He was a big man, muscular, heavy-boned, and powerful; his tarnished-copper hair was long and a little wild but beginning to show gray. He radiated competence, self-confidence, health, and zest; and he was the first gulden man Nolan had ever spoken to in a real conversation. It had been quite a shock. Blueskin men were much more reserved than this.

"We're expecting Chay Zanlan to arrive any minute," Pakt said. "All the fools have lined up to gawk from the sidelines. You'd think there'd never been a gulden man set foot in the city before."

"Chay Zanlan never has, has he?" asked Melina, briefly turning away from the window. "Not that I remember."

"Yes, he came to Jex's graduation from City College," said Colt, another gulden. "But that was ten years ago or more."

"And the spectacle was just as grand," Pakt added. "You don't remember it because you were living on your mama's farm, learning the finer points of cruelty, bigotry, and the subjugation of men."

Melina favored him with one bright, impudent glance. "And learning them well," she said before turning her attention back to the parade below. She was a high-caste blueskin with incredibly fine cobalt skin and the blackest imaginable hair, which she kept trimmed so close to the scalp that the shape of her skull showed through. In her mid-twenties, she was the youngest engineer in the lab—and the most outrageous. Pakt, her supervisor, constantly needled her about her patrician background, and she would enthusiastically enter verbal battle with him at a moment's notice. Everyone adored her, Pakt included.

"So is he actually here?" Nolan asked, stepping forward and pushing between Melina and Colt to look out the window. All he could see were mobs of security forces and throngs of people pressing against a yellow cordon. "I don't think I'd recognize him if I saw him."

"Can't tell one gulden from another," Colt said lazily. Like Pakt, he was a strongly built guldman, though younger, slimmer, and more athletic. His hair was a metallic yellow, shoulder length, and always carefully groomed. Nolan liked him, but Colt made him just a little nervous. As if some day Colt's sardonic calm would explode into ferocity over some insult so slight Nolan would not be able to reconstruct it.

"Well, Chay Zanlan's got bright red hair, and yours is a sickly blond, so that's how I tell *you* two apart," Melina answered instantly. "Otherwise, you know, you're dead ringers."

"Chay Zanlan also has a more regal bearing than our friend Colt," Pakt said, earning a sideways smile from the other guldman.

"At any rate, Chay Zanlan appears to be nowhere on the streets," Melina said. "When is he supposed to arrive, anyway?"

Others at the window offered their guesses. "By now, I thought."

"I heard noon."

"He probably came in last night, but they kept it a secret."

"Well, how much longer can we stand here looking out the window and wondering?" Melina asked.

"No longer, I hope," drawled a new voice from the doorway, and in one convulsive movement, they all turned to face the speaker. Cerisa Daylen stood there unsmiling, her long black hair pulled back severely from her aristocratic face, her long thin fingers tapping against her crossed arms. Every inch of her bespoke her Higher Hundred heritage, from her rich blueskin tone to her contemptuous expression. She was head of the lab, the most gifted biologist of their century, and every one of them hated her without reservation.

"Time to go back to work," Pakt said in a pleasant voice, and everyone except Melina sidled for the door. Cerisa stepped to one side to allow them room to pass, but she kept her reproving gaze on Pakt. The guldman smiled back at her, unimpressed.

"It's a special event," he said. "Everyone wants to see."

"There's a plague killing children in the albino slums," she answered without inflection. "I'd say that's a little more important than watching Chay Zanlan disrupt an entire city."

"Indeed it is," Pakt answered. "And we're all working on it. And we'll let you know the instant we discover anything worth reporting."

If Cerisa made a reply to that, Nolan didn't hear it, having escaped far enough to shut out the sound of voices. He was inside his own lab in moments, a pristine, orderly environment that smelled of chemicals, books, and electronics.

Technically, the job of isolating the albino virus would fall to Hiram, one of the other blueskin researchers, but all of them would try their hand at it until someone came up with a vaccine or a cure. That had been Cerisa Daylen's great breakthrough, twenty years ago: a cure for a virulent disease that had scarred, damaged, or killed indigo and albino children for decades. Mysteriously, the *corrigio* plague had had no effect on the gulden race, not even in milder symptoms. Cerisa Daylen had made her name on that discovery, but it was only one of many of her contributions to medical research. She had concocted a variety of antibiotics to combat a wide array of major and minor illnesses, she had led the battle for universal and mandatory inoculations against specific diseases—and she had fought for the continued funding and operation of the Biolab.

Nolan had first come across her work in the journals he studied back in-country, when he was still convincing his mother that he wanted to become a biologist. He had read everything he could find about Cerisa Daylen, studied her experiments, replicated them as best he could in the inferior conditions of his homemade lab. When his scientific test scores outpulled those of every student in every upper school in-country, male and female, his mother reluctantly agreed to let him study medical research at Inrhio State University. Upon graduation, he applied in secret to Cerisa Daylen, asking for admittance into her talented group of researchers. As far as he knew, no one who had not attended City College had ever been chosen for such an exalted position.

He had been shocked when he received her letter. "Come to me no later than next month. We have a lab ready for you and work piled up. If your mother objects, I will persuade her." He had made no mention of his mother in his letter of application, but Cerisa Daylen, of course, was bone and offspring of that select, unyielding, tradition-bound indigo matriarchy. She would know without being told how reluctant any woman would be to send her son off to such questionable work in the city.

Indeed, Nolan was positive that only the fact that Cerisa was a Higher Hundred indigo woman permitted him to be at the Biolab today. Had she been a mid-caste woman or even a high-caste man, his mother would have refused to allow him to go. Had the lab been run by a gulden of any rank or gender, the move would have been out of the question.

So Cerisa Daylen had been his heroine, until he actually met her. Then, like everyone else who worked for her, he hated her, resented her, rebelled against her, and learned from her every single day.

In the past five years, she had allowed Nolan to develop his own area of expertise, which was, rather unexpectedly, the gulden immune system. He had first become intrigued by it when studying Cerisa Daylen's papers on the *corrigio* plague which only affected the white and blue races. Why not the gulden? What was different about their bodies and their blood? There were hundreds of other diseases to which they were susceptible; why not this one?

He had conducted thousands of experiments to answer just these questions, and he had been the one to discover two potent antibiotics that shut down ill-natured bacteria that favored the elderly gulden. To date it was his proudest accomplishment.

Though he had not shared the news with his mother. Indiscriminately saving the lives of guldmen would not be something she considered a particular mark of achievement. In any case, she was merely counting the days till he came back to Inrhio and married his fiancée, Leesa, when all the world, as far as she was concerned, would be back in its proper orbit and continuing on its preordained course.

But that would not be for some time yet. Not today, at any rate. Nolan shut himself into his office, flicked on his computer, and began the new day's chores.

During lunch hour, most of them crammed back into Melina's office to watch the street theater again. As far as they could tell, Chay Zanlan had not yet arrived, or else the crowds on the street were hanging around hoping for a glimpse of him when he reemerged.

"So why exactly is he here?" Melina asked, directing the question at Pakt. She, Nolan, Colt, Pakt, and a blueskin woman named Varella were sitting around her desk, sharing food and idle conversation. The others kept watch at the window.

"To visit his son, Jex, who is in jail," Pakt said, stating the obvious with exaggerated patience. They all knew Jex Zanlan was in jail. He had been arrested three months ago after setting off a bomb that had destroyed a medical compound near the West Two gate of the Centrifuge.

"And a damn good thing Jex Zanlan *is* in jail," Melina retorted. "But does Chay Zanlan expect to negotiate his release with Ariana Bayless?"

"Ultimately," Pakt said. "But I think Mayor Bayless and her council will make him sweat it out a little longer."

"Why would she ever release him?" Varella asked. She was a paler, frailer version of Melina, not as smart, not as beautiful, not as lively. But likable nonetheless, Nolan always thought.

"This gives her more leverage over Chay Zanlan than she's ever had, and she's within her rights to keep him. I mean, he *did* try to blow up the building."

"Exactly. So if she gives him up, she'll be able to expect a powerful return gift from Chay," Pakt said.

"And any number of gifts spring to mind," Colt added. "Foremost being rights to the Carbonnier Extension."

"But not far behind is her desire to add a new ring to the Centrifuge," Pakt said. "Chay could make her a gift of the construction stone, since it's quarried in Geldricht. For that, Ariana Bayless just might release Jex Zanlan."

Melina was shaking her head. "I will never understand politics," she said. "How you can balance lives against commerce will always elude me. I could never make such a bargain."

"Fortunately, Ariana Bayless is not so squeamish," Pakt said dryly. "Chay, I am sure, is counting on it."

"You keep calling him 'Chay,' " Varella said a little irritably. "Do you actually *know* him?"

Colt was grinning. "It's a gulden habit," he said. "We have a very personal stake in our leader. We like to feel we could walk up to him any day and have a serious conversation with him, man to man."

Melina gave Varella a significant look. "Not *woman* to man, you'll notice."

Colt gave an exaggerated shrug and spoke in an arrogant tone that was meant to annoy. "No gulden woman, no matter how schooled, would ever know as much as her husband, her brother, or her father."

"Whereas my husband, brother, *and* father, all sitting together in one room, pooling their limited intellectual resources, would never have the ability to make a worthwhile decision in Inrhio," Melina said loftily.

Pakt sent an amused sideways glance at Nolan. "Poor emasculated fools," he said. "Letting their women cut them off at the balls."

Nolan smiled back a little uncertainly. He was clearly the outsider in this group, the only member of the team who did not come from a racial or sexual power base. In Inrhio, women controlled the wealth, the land, the succession—everything. Inheritances passed through the hands of the mother; she chose who her daughters would marry and bargained with her neighboring matriarchs for brides for her sons.

In Geldricht, though, it was the men who had absolute power. The women were, as far as Nolan had been able to observe, shamefully abused and degraded. He could not imagine what honor accrued to a man who beat his wife or mistreated his children. Among the indigo, although the matriarchy controlled the pattern of life, men were cherished and valued. And children were considered a treasure past price.

"Not emasculated," Nolan said gallantly, "gratefully admitted to a wide circle of fascinating and elegant women."

The women cooed and clapped their hands; the men were loudly derisive. Melina patted him on the shoulder. "Does Leesa know what a sweet boy you are? Does she appreciate you?"

Colt pointed at Nolan. "What's to appreciate? He's exactly as he was bred to be by you and all the rest of you women. He's no different from any other downtrodden blueskin man I've ever met."

"Well, if you think that, you haven't met that many indigo boys," Varella murmured, and Melina added a heartfelt "so true." Varella added, "Nolan *is* sweet, you know. A lot of the blueskins back in-country are—agreeable, let's say—but there's something special about Nolan. He means it when he says things like that."

"No one could mean it," Colt informed her.

Nolan turned to Pakt. "This happens to me all the time. People talk about me when I'm sitting right here."

"Doesn't happen to me," Pakt said with a grin. "I guess I'm a little harder to overlook."

"Harder to like," Melina said.

"But then, you don't much like any man," Pakt responded, "no matter what his color or attitude."

Melina laughed. For the past six months, she had been living with a female lover, a jahla girl, as the indigo called it. Varella, Nolan, and the other blueskins had treated the news with the mild, courteous interest they showed in the rotating love lives of all their fellow workers, but the guldmen had been repelled and outraged. Melina and Colt had had a huge fight about it, in fact, a screaming match that had made stupefied coworkers come running down the halls in time to see Melina hit Colt in the chest with her balled-up fist. To which Colt had replied with a slap across her face that sent her stumbling four feet back into the wall. Pakt had dashed between them before either could strike again, muscling Colt back toward the door, holding Melina off with one imperious hand.

"You—will—*not*," he had stated in the dead-cold fury they had all learned to fear, "move—or speak—either one of you!— until I say you may. Nolan! Clear everyone out of here. Shut the door behind you. You two. Sit. I said *sit*."

And that was all any of the rest of them had been privileged to witness, though they milled about in the halls for the next half hour, whispering over what they had overheard.

It still astonished Nolan that anyone could care one way or the other if one woman chose to love another. Among the indigo, jahla girls were common; even married women often preferred the company of a jahla partner, relying on their husbands only for financial advantages, social connections, biological contributions to pregnancy, and, sometimes, companionship.

On the other hand, Nolan was revolted at the male homosexuality he had heard of among the guldmen. The only proper object of love for a man or a woman, or so he had learned from the cradle, was a woman. For a man to love another man was unthinkable, gruesome, actually sickening. He did not know any homosexual guldmen, of course; he did not think he would be able to force himself to look such a man in the face.

He might work up the nerve to ask Pakt about it some day. Pakt was the most broad-minded person Nolan had ever come across, male, female, blue, gold, or white. If Pakt could not explain society to him, no one could, for Pakt understood everything and everyone.

Pakt had calmed down Colt and Melina on that violent day, though it had been weeks before the two were reconciled enough to speak civilly to each other. Even now there was an edge between them much of the time, a pointed banter that was not nearly as playful as the teasing that Pakt and Melina tossed to each other. Yes, Nolan was sure of it, one day Colt would explode, and there would be no telling how far that destructive blast would blow them all.

"I like men," Melina was saying now to Pakt. "Not you and *Colt*, of course, but some men. Nolan."

"Hiram," Colt said with a sneer. Hiram was a small, nervous, and apologetic light-skinned indigo; he was difficult even for the other blueskins to love.

"I can tolerate Hiram," Melina said calmly. "There are men I like better. And I don't *only* like indigo men, though I have to admit they make more sense to me than you two wild creatures."

Colt leaned forward. "Because we're *real* men, and you can't make us fit into your dainty little patterns," he breathed.

"Colt," she said coolly, "have no fear. No one in the world would be fool enough to try to make you over. So relax. You are safe from me."

The others laughed. Colt drew back, looking annoyed. Before anyone else could speak, there was a shout from across the room.

"Look! There he is! There he is!"

The five of them bounded to their feet and ran to the window. A phalanx of bodies was exiting from the building and onto the street. It appeared to be a tight, human wall of security around one central figure, and it was difficult to make out anything of the ruler from this elevation and angle. Nolan got an impression of height and mass—a big man, this Chay Zanlan, bigger than Pakt, with thick shoulders and broad thighs—topped by a crown of fiery red hair. The gulden ruler was dressed in bright colors, as were his attendants, and their loose tunics snapped gaily around them as they strode by.

Moments later, a second cadre of officials emerged. This time, they were all blueskins, dressed in black and white and wearing their formal clan colors in sashes and shawls. Ariana Bayless was in the center of the group, taller than all the other women and most of the men, her blue-black hair glinting like mica in the afternoon sun. She was speaking to one woman as she walked, reaching a hand out to another woman who offered her a briefcase, and gesturing impatiently to a man who trailed behind her, obviously trying to snare her attention. *Newsman*, Nolan thought. *Asking how the conference went.*

"Well, things appear to be going smoothly enough," Nolan commented.

Only Pakt appeared to have overheard, for the guldman raised an eyebrow at him. "They haven't killed each other yet, at any rate," he said. "But there's a lot of room left for trouble."

"What do you mean?"

"How would you feel if you were negotiating for your sister's life with Cerisa Daylen? Because Ariana Bayless comes from the same mold, and it's not a friendly one."

"If she gave her word," Nolan said slowly. He had not previously considered this; he'd had no cause to picture himself feinting with either the head of the Biolab or the mayor of the city. "She would honor it."

Pakt was nodding. "To the letter," he said.

"Well, then," Nolan said, and shrugged. He turned back to the window, but the crowd had dispersed; there was nothing left to see.

That turned out to be the last of the excitement for the day. Even the trip home on the Centrifuge that night was less eventful. As always, there was a big crowd at the North Zero gate, the stop closest to both the Complex and the entertainment district. Unlike this morning, however, commuters were not sharing ringcars with strangers, so the line moved slowly. Nolan had a long wait on the inside of the gate and stared unseeingly at the vast, curved walls of the Centrifuge unfolding to either side of him.

Finally, a ringcar pulled up before him, and its driver left the vehicle. Nolan climbed into the small, spherical cocoon, all metal and glass on the outside, merely a bench and a set of hand controls inside. He pulled the rudder to the left, and the car glided into the entry lane, the middle of the three traffic levels. As soon as the lane above him cleared out, he pulled the rudder back and angled upward, increasing his speed with a squeeze of his hand. The great stone hallway of the Centrifuge unrolled before him, honey yellow, filled with a bee's hive of scurrying shapes, curving to the left in a continuous unbroken circle. The gates flashed by on his right, and he skimmed along in the highest lane until he reached his own. Then he dropped to the middle level, pulled up at the gate, and exited onto the street. From there, he took a slow, lumbering bus to his own neighborhood.

It was the fashionable district for indigo bachelors. Nearly everyone on the bus was dressed in clothes remarkably similar to Nolan's, and they all lived in apartment buildings that he easily could have mistaken for his own. A few miles away were the expensive multistory houses where the Higher Hundred families lived when they were in the city, but for an unmarried blueskin man, this was the only acceptable place to live.

There was a small pile of mail awaiting Nolan outside the door to his apartment. Bills; a letter from his mother; the fashion magazine he subscribed to, though he rarely read it. And a note from Leesa. He opened that first.

As he read, he absently toyed with the medallion he wore, a disk stamped with Leesa's clan device, which she had given him the day they became engaged. Her handwriting was large, looped, and lazy. Every time he read it, he imagined her speaking in her usual languid, unimpassioned tones, and he automatically slowed the pace at which he consumed her words.

"Nolan: Is it as hot in the city as it is in-country? Today Bettahelia and I did nothing but sit on the porch drinking lemonade and watching the wind move the grass in the field. We didn't even speak more than five sentences to each other, and she was with me the entire day. I think her visit has gone on too long, but I've been too fatigued to tell her so. Maybe she will leave by the end of the week.

"Did I tell you I have business in the city in two weeks? Some boring investment trouble that mother wants me to see to personally. As long as I have to make the trip, though, I may as well stay a few days. With you, of course, unless there's some sly bachelor reason you don't want me in your quarters. Or if you can't bother to clean them, then I'll stay in a hotel. But of course I'd rather be with you.

"Corzehia is planning to be in the city for the rest of the summer, so I'm going to write her, as well. She's having some big party that I think we can go to. Otherwise, you'll have to think of entertainments for me. I'll try to be easy to amuse.

"I'll let you know when I'm to arrive. Put your lips to the paper right under my signature—that's where I've left you a kiss. Analeesa"

Nolan read the letter a second time, then dutifully pressed his mouth to Leesa's name. She wrote him at least once a week, letters much like this one, with little information, light humor, and easy affection. He wrote her back at least as often, though sometimes he was at a loss as to what to say. She cared very little about his job, though she always assured him she was pleased to hear how well he was doing. When he had formulated the gulden antibiotics and had reported Cerisa's praise, Leesa had sent him a finely embroidered shirt as a celebratory gift. And yet, he could scarcely give her a day-by-day account of his activities at the lab; she could not possibly understand his pursuit and attack of cells and tissues. So news about the lab was minimal.

And he did not have much to tell her about his social life. A few times a week, he played curfball with men in the neighboring building, and sometimes they met to play cards or go for dinner. Now and then he lingered in the city after closing hours to attend the theater with Hiram or Melina. These events he could mention to Leesa, but he could hardly recount a stroke-by-stroke description of his curfball game or an item-by-item dissection of his meal. And she had no interest in the theater, so he rarely bothered to give her long reviews of these nights.

And he had never mentioned the fact that he had, more than once, gone with his fellow employees to Pakt's house for a meal and a convivial evening. It would not have occurred to Leesa that there were any circumstances under which an indigo man would have social dealings with a guldman—would walk into his house, sit at his table, eat his food. She could scarcely comprehend the fact that Nolan worked in harmony with half a dozen gulden men, and she had literally refused to acknowledge that a guldman could be his superior in the workplace. She would have disbelieved him if he had told her he had gone to Pakt's house for dinner and enjoyed himself very much.

Before he had come to the city, Nolan would have been just as shocked to think he could have enjoyed such an event. Before he had come to the city, Nolan had seen maybe a dozen gulden in his life, and he had always had to restrain himself from staring. It was not polite to gawk at someone strange, inferior, and unfortunate, his mother had drilled into him. The courteous thing to do would be to act as if you did not notice such a person's defects, did not realize that his gold skin and fair hair doomed him to a life of misery and worthlessness. Treat any gulden you encounter (though there were not many in-country and almost none in the lush lands where the Higher Hundred had their estates) with the cheerful compassion you would give to a mute child, an injured dog, a feebleminded old man. And never let him realize how terribly sorry you feel for him.

His mother, of course, was widely considered to be the most broad-minded of women. Most of the other indigo matriarchs— and their spouses—could not bring themselves to speak of the gulden with such tolerance. Although the ultimate *gilder* insult was used sparingly, virtually every other term of opprobrium was casually applied to members of the gulden race. A guldman was a thing to sometimes fear, always revile, and certainly avoid.

So when Nolan came to the city, he was astonished. Not only did gulden walk the city streets as if they had every right to be there, they ate in blueskin restaurants and patronized blueskin shops, and no one questioned them as long as they had the cash to pay their way. They could be found in any profession, though they tended toward the more scientific and mechanical pursuits; they were engineers, chemists, architects. They were also lawyers, restaurateurs, political appointees—in short, they were everywhere.

The albinos, too, were far more visible than they had ever been in Inrhio. In-country, the whitefolk routinely held menial positions—gardener, nursemaid, chauffeur—although the very high-caste indigo preferred to hire low-caste blueskins for those positions if they could. Nolan's mother had often said a good albino housekeeper was worth any salary she wished to charge, and she would trust an albino man with any job around the house. But she had warned her children against trying to make friends with the whitefolk. They were trustworthy, but they were still foreign.

But in the city it was a different story. The albinos kept

mostly to themselves in small enclaves in the northern and western edges of the city. Here, however, they were not just domestic helpers but acute businessmen, running affluent shops that catered to the whims of guldmen and blueskins alike. They led tidy, quiet lives and mingled freely with the other two races, causing no dissension.

Unlike the gulden, who—it seemed to Nolan—caused dissension everywhere. Sudden violence seemed to swirl around the gulden like a windswept aureole of danger. One man would kill another, suddenly, for no reason, in the middle of the street in the middle of the day. And, Nolan couldn't count how many news stories he had heard of gulden children slaughtered in the women's ghetto on the west edge of town. It was always some gulden male on a rampage, come to the city specifically for the purpose of hunting down this particular woman and her hapless clutch of children.

Ariana Bayless had decided long ago that gulden crimes against gulden residents should be judged and punished by peers. So the city officials did little to curtail these acts of violence. Gulden men and gulden ways; that was no business of indigo lawmakers.

None of it made any sense to Nolan. But he did not have to understand the gulden. He merely had to coexist with them, as civilly as possible, until his abbreviated life in the city was done. And then he would return in-country, marry Leesa, and live the life he had been destined for. And that, he was very sure, was a life that would hold no surprises.

CHAPTER TWO

Kit stood at the balcony of the eleventh-story window and watched night unfold over the city. Even she had to admit that it was very picturesque, and she was not fond of the city. But the city, which was serious and workaday during daylight hours, took on a playful mood as night fell. The double row of white lights that outlined the Centrifuge made a great endless loop around the buildings; the multicolored lamps of the entertainment district fluttered like tossed glitter. The moving headlights of trolleys and trucks wove among the stationary beacons, and the undying flame on top of the Complex scrawled its brilliant, varied comments against the deepening black of the sky.

The Complex where Jex Zanlan was being held prisoner. She had not seen him in two weeks, and she had missed him so much that she thought she might go mad. Even now, she wanted to vault from the balcony and follow that fiery beacon to her lover's side. She wrapped her hands tightly around the railing and forced herself to focus on the contrasting colors, the blue of her fingers cool against the warm bronze of the bar. She stared so hard that the textures melted together, her fingers became metal and the railing itself became liquid and insubstantial.

Sereva's voice came from inside the double doors that led to the balcony. "Kitrini? What are you doing out there? Come on in before you catch cold."

"I'm just watching the city lights come up."

Sereva had come to the doors to take her own look at the city lights. "Well, don't stand so close to the railing. You'll fall and break your neck. And how would I explain that to Granmama?"

Kit couldn't help grinning, but she obligingly stepped away from the balcony and past Sereva into the office. "She would hardly be surprised. She expects me to come to a bad end, anyway."

"Everyone expects you to come to a bad end," Sereva said absently. She had returned to her desk and was bending over to look through papers in a file, frowning down at whatever the words or figures told her. "Granmama is just hoping it will not happen while you're living with her."

"Oh, well, make no mistake, I am closer to desperate suicide than I have ever been," Kit said. "Living with that woman! Every day it's a lecture about something. A remark I've made, a color I've worn, the fact that she glimpsed me from the window speaking to some guldwoman I passed on the street—because that won't *do*, you know, Sereva, it might encourage the poor misbegotten mistreated fool to think she actually has a friend among the blueshis—"

Sereva straightened to stare at her. "*Kitrini!* Don't you ever say such a word! No wonder Granmama worries about you—"

Kit shrugged impatiently and begin pacing around the room. *Blueshi* was the ultimate gulden insult that could be leveled at an indigo, although, frankly, Kit had always liked the sort of lilting twist to the word and would have used it all the time if it wasn't considered so vulgar. She knew what the "shi" suffix meant in the gulden tongue, though, and her ethics prevented her from encouraging verbal violence, so she restricted herself. Unless she was seriously ruffled.

"What I'm saying is, we grate on each other night and day. I go out of my way to avoid her—and in that ancestral *mansion* you would think it would be easy—but she's decided I've come home to her to reform. I do my best to be meek and sweet-tempered when I'm around her, but we all know I'm *not* meek and sweet-tempered. It's wearing on me."

"She only wants what's best for you. She only wants you to be well and happy."

Kit flung herself into a chair and stared at her cousin. After her father had died, Sereva was the only family member Kit could honestly say she liked. Of course, she had had no dealings with her father's relatives, for they had cast him off before she was born. It was her mother's family she had to contend with, Granmama especially. Lorimela Candachi had shown every sign of trying to reclaim her granddaughter, replacing the daughter she had lost to a mid-caste indigo boy nearly thirty years ago. The fact that Kit had no wish to be reclaimed did not deter Granmama at all.

"She does *not* care if I am well or happy," Kit replied, speaking each word with precision. "What she wants is to indoctrinate me. She wants me to be just like her. And like you, and like every other Candachi woman in the history of Inrhio."

"I'm happy to hear you rate me so highly," Sereva said. "I'm glad you think I'm just as good as every other blueskin woman that you despise so much."

Kit grinned slightly. "Well, you *are* just as bad as the rest of them. You're a high-caste indigo woman with a well-run ancestral estate, a handpicked husband, and an unshakable belief that the world goes on exactly as it should. Why should I think you're any different from the rest?"

"Because I put up with you," Sereva answered a little curtly. "That ought to earn me a little credit in your eyes."

Kit's expression softened. "Oh, it does. To tell you the truth, I've never understood why you do put up with me. I can't be an easy friend for someone like you to have."

Sereva slung her briefcase strap over her shoulder and flicked off the overhead lamp. Instantly, darkness leapt inside the room, crouched at their feet and looked around. The moving lights of traffic made flowing, uncertain patterns on the pale walls. Sereva took three swift steps to her cousin's side, and Kit rose quickly to her feet.

"You're not my friend," Sereva said. "You're my family. I would love you no matter what you did. No matter how much I hated it. And, just in case you judge her too harshly, that's one of the lessons I learned from Granmama, along with how to run a vast estate and how to behave in a room of mixed races. I love you, and she loves you, and even though you're not one of us, you're one of *ours*. And someday maybe you'll live long enough to appreciate that."

"I appreciate it," Kit said a little gruffly, feeling strangely chastised and slightly defensive. "It just suffocates me sometimes. I haven't changed, Sereva, just because I'm living with Granmama here in the city. I'm still my father's daughter. I haven't suddenly grown respectable."

Sereva laughed and reached for the door. Light from the hallway showed her face genuinely amused. "And I wouldn't expect it," she said. "You will continue to astound us all, I'm sure. I have no illusions about that."

They stepped into the hall, took the elevator to the basement garage, and climbed into Sereva's waiting limousine. The driver, an indigo boy whose mother worked on Sereva's estates, nodded at them shyly. "Good evening, *hela* Candachi," he greeted Sereva with the courtesy title, then repeated it for Kit.

"Good evening," Kit replied, climbing in.

"Yes, good evening, Simon," Sereva said. "Take us home, please."

Simon put the car in motion and it purred forward out of the garage. Kit, who was used to relying on public transportation, had to remind herself sternly that she did not endorse or enjoy the privileges of the rich. "It might take a while," Simon said over his shoulder in an apologetic voice. "Traffic is still terrible because of Chay Zanlan's visit."

Sereva made a small *tsk*ing sound of annoyance, then shrugged and smiled. "Well, I suppose we're not the only ones inconvenienced for the pleasure of Chay Zanlan," she said.

"No, indeed," Kit agreed suavely. "Delays on the Centrifuge were hours long this morning, and I'm sure they're just as bad tonight."

Sereva shuddered slightly. "The Centrifuge. I can't imagine how you can actually ride that thing every day—"

"I like it. I like to see how fast I can go and make the other cars get out of my way."

"Don't even tell me. I don't want to picture you risking your life in that stupid way."

Kit laughed. "Well, the Centrifuge is pretty safe. I think it's been three years since anyone died in the tunnels."

"Just the same. Maybe you should stay at my house for a few days and ride into the city with me. Until everything gets back to normal."

"When Chay leaves?" Kit asked, stressing the ruler's name.

Sereva turned her head to eye Kit in the flashing, changing lights of the passing buildings. Then she touched a control panel at her fingertips, and the security window went up between Simon and the passenger's compartment.

"Have you actually seen him?" Sereva asked quietly.

Kit's eyebrows rose. "Chay? I think he has a lot more important people to visit while he's here than me."

"Does he know you're in the city?"

Kit looked out the window. "I imagine he does."

"Does he know how to get in touch with you?"

Kit looked back at her cousin with some irritation. "I suppose so! Why? Why do you think he would want to get in touch with me? I don't have any information for him. I can't tell him how to get Jex out of prison. I can't explain to him how to deal with Ariana Bayless. He doesn't need me."

"I know he's fond of you," Sereva continued in that same quiet voice. "I thought perhaps he might find it restful to see a friendly face. This can't be a pleasant journey for him."

Kit was looking out the window again. "He's less fond of me these days than he used to be," she said, her voice low. "I don't think I'll be approaching him while he's here."

And that was all they said on the subject, but Kit had to give Sereva a little credit; Granmama would not have acknowledged Chay Zanlan's presence in the city, let alone the fact that Kit knew him. Let alone the fact that Kit loved his son, Jex. But Granmama indeed was aware of all these disgraceful facts. Kit knew she considered that one more black mark to be scrawled next to Anton Solvano's name, that he had taken his daughter with him into Geldricht and there lived among the gulden as an equal and a friend. Granmama was able to lay at the father's door all blame for the daughter's wayward behavior.

"Well, at any rate, you're welcome to stay with me a few days," Sereva said. "It would be a good excuse to get out of Granmama's house for a while. And I'd be happy to have you."

It was a kind invitation and a thoughtful change of subject.

Kit smiled over at her cousin in the dark. "Let's see how well dinner goes first," she said with a laugh. "And then we'll talk about extended visits."

But dinner, as they had both expected, was fine. Sereva's husband, Jayson, was there, of course, and her two sons. Impossible to dislike any of them, even on moral grounds, though in the past Kit had tried. Jayson was a pleasant, vague, unalarming scholar who could not possibly rouse anyone's antagonism, and the boys were delightful. Aged ten and twelve, Marcus and Bascom were well-behaved, well-spoken, courteous, and bright, and for some strange reason, they adored Kit.

"Kitrini! Kitrini!" Marcus exclaimed when she sauntered through the door. "Do you want to see what I learned in school today? I can draw a—a conical!"

Kit glanced questioningly at Sereva. "Cone?" Sereva guessed. "He's in a geometry class."

"I'd love to see it," Kit told him. Bascom was standing patiently beside her, waiting for her to acknowledge him, so she smiled down at him. Not too far down; he was growing at a shocking rate. "Yes?" she encouraged him with a smile.

"After the meal is over, would you play a game with me?" he asked in a formal voice. "I have several to choose from, so you can select the one that interests you most."

It was all she could do to keep from breaking into laughter. He spoke so seriously and with such care. "Yes, I'd be happy to," she said. "But don't think I'll let you win just because you're one of my two favorite nephews."

"Actually, I'm not really a nephew," Bascom said, his brow furrowing as he tried to decide exactly what she was. "Because you're not my mother's sister."

Kit waved a hand. "Close enough. We'll pretend. I'll even let you pick the game."

Jayson wandered up to his wife to kiss her on the cheek. "They have been talking all day about Kitrini's arrival," he remarked. "You would think it was the high holidays. You'll have to come visit with us more often."

Sereva led the way to the family dining room, a much more cozy place than the huge, elegant chamber where they did their grand entertaining. She poured drinks for herself and Jayson, but Kit shook her head. "In fact," Sereva said, sipping a liqueur, "I've been trying to convince Kitrini to come stay with us a few days. Maybe if she thinks the boys will like it, she'll be more inclined to accept."

Kit smiled. "You make it sound like I dread the prospect. I just don't want to get in the way."

"Oh, no. You couldn't get in the way here," Jayson said earnestly. "There's too much room to stumble over anyone."

"Well," said Kit, "it sounds tempting."

Dinner itself was lively. Marcus insisted on sitting next to Kit, but Bascom sat directly across from her and pelted her with questions during most of the meal. Did you know that the average lifespan of a blueskin male was five years longer than a blueskin female? Did you know that in general, gulden men weighed fifteen pounds more than indigo men of comparable height? Did you know that Centrifuge ringcars were designed to achieve a maximum speed of one hundred miles per hour but that due to high traffic volume in the tunnels most cars rarely made it to half that rate?

"Let me guess," Kit said, laughing again. "Science is your favorite subject in school."

"I'm in the advanced class," he said proudly. "And I have the highest scores! Even higher than Marrina Boswen."

Kit glanced at Sereva. "An old nemesis, I take it."

Sereva nodded. "She's the smartest girl in his class. She always has been. And you know, generally, the boys aren't as good at math and science as the girls are. So we've both been pleased at how well Bascom's doing."

"And where did he pick up this ability?" Kit asked. "Since neither his father nor his mother is particularly good at the sciences."

"Well, I've always been terrific at math, but biology and chemistry and all that—" Sereva rolled her eyes. "Too boring. Maybe he picked it up from one of his grandmothers. They say some things skip generations."

Jayson was shaking his head. "It didn't skip over from my family," he said. "We were all born with literary inclinations, even the girls. One of my sisters is a historian in her spare time, and the other is a poet. So Bascom seems to have developed these amazing abilities all on his own."

"Which makes us even prouder of him," Sereva said, smiling at her eldest son.

It had all been quite lighthearted over the meal but later, as Kit and Sereva sat in the library together, the talk became a bit more serious.

"Actually, Jayson and I had a little argument about Bascom just the other day," Sereva told Kit. She was sipping another drink, and Kit had consented to a glass of wine. She was feeling sleepy after the rich meal, but she knew she didn't have to bother to keep alert for the trip home; Simon would take her in the limousine.

"An argument? About what?"

"This science class, in fact. Bascom wants to sign up for the advanced class next year, too, and Jayson sees no reason he should. Thinks it's all a waste of time and energy, since Bascom will never end up going on to City College or pursuing a degree in—in—medical science or something like that."

Kit weighed her words before speaking. It all seemed obvious to her, but she was in a blueskin stronghold now, and here a specific set of rules applied. "If he was interested in studying medical science—or something—wouldn't you encourage him?" she asked.

Sereva sighed and rested her mouth on the rim of her glass for a moment. She stared at the rug on the floor between them. "That's so hard to say for certain," she answered at last, taking another swallow then setting the glass down. "If he was a girl— yes, of course I'd encourage him. I'd want him to strive as hard as he could, be the best scientist in the city. But as it is . . . In another ten years, he'll just marry some high-caste girl and move back in-country, and what good will it have done him to get all that specialized schooling? Jayson's right, it would just waste his time and energy. And it might—I don't know—make him more unhappy to have acquired all that knowledge if he never gets a chance to use it. I don't want to open up doors that might later be shut in his face."

Listen to yourself! Kit wanted to scream. *Listen to every sad, repressive syllable you're saying!* But anger was no way to win this argument. "Well, and he might not prove to have any real aptitude for medical biology," she said in a casual voice. "It's pretty hard to tell about a twelve-year-old. But do you think there's no chance that he might want to pursue a career of his own? There are a lot of blueskin men working in the city. If Bascom really wants to try his hand at some profession—"

Sereva nodded unhappily. "I know. And that's what we had the fight about. I just can't stand the thought that Bascom won't be able to have everything he wants. If he wants to go to City College, then I say, he can go. If he wants to work for a few years before he gets married, then, yes, I'd agree to that, too. Why shouldn't he? Who would it hurt? Jayson was shocked. No one in his family has ever done anything except own land and write philosophy. He thinks it's demeaning and cheap to follow a profession. He even—well. Let's just say he made me furious by belittling Bascom's high scores. I was—I was *suffused* with anger. To see this excited little boy sharing his great achievement with his father and have his father *laugh* at him. I won't have an attitude like that in my house, and so I told him. We will encourage Bascom in whatever he wants to do, because he's our son and we love him. And so I told Jayson."

It was one of the longest, most tangled, and most impassioned speeches Kit had ever heard her cousin give. No wonder, though; here, wrapped up in the tight swaddling of filial love, were all the painful issues of the day, issues about gender and heritage and how society valued an individual's contribution to its greater good. Even unconventional people were wrestling with some of the same questions, and Sereva was not used to having to challenge her most basic assumptions.

"You've got time, after all," Kit said neutrally. "He's only twelve. In a few years, you may see so many blueskin men taking on jobs in the city that it will seem like the right thing for everyone to do. But if you hold him back now—"

"I know! Exactly! He'll lose his advantage, he'll lose his initiative, and then he won't even have a chance to show us how good he could be! The strange thing is, I don't think this decision would be nearly so hard if he was my daughter instead of my son. I even think—if *one* of them had been a girl—I would have spent most of my energy deciding how to direct her. But

I can't stand the thought that my children won't have the same chances as Yasmina Boswen's girls. Bascom's as smart as Marrina. And I won't hold him back." She smiled a little painfully over at her cousin. "So you see, you're not the only rebel in the family."

"I won't tell Granmama," Kit said, returning the smile. "It would do her in. And just for the record, I'm proud of you."

"Not exactly a comfort to have *you* on my side," Sereva said, but she laughed.

Kit laughed back. "Someday it will be," she said. "Just wait and see."

So that was the evening, which lasted much longer than Kit was accustomed to. It was close to midnight before they finalized plans for Kit to return the following day, carrying enough luggage to see her through a week. Then Sereva bundled her into the limousine and adjured Simon to drive extremely carefully. Not that there was far to go. For Sereva, for Granmama, for any respectable blueskin matron, there was only one neighborhood in which to locate the town house, and that was a small enough district that, in daylight, Kit wouldn't have minded making the trek on foot. But now, in the dark and full of food and wine, she was just as glad to be spared the effort. She snuggled deep into the plush leather of the seat and drowsed until Simon pulled up before her grandmother's house.

"Thank you," she made a point of saying as she climbed from the car. All the street-level lights were on in the four-story house, and before Kit could put a hand to the door, it was opened by a blueskin servant. There was no hour of the night or day when there was not some footman on duty to attend to any emergencies or sudden whims of the residents. At first, Kit had found this a little disconcerting, but she had grown to like the idea that, no matter how wakeful and isolated she might feel, even in the middle of the night, somewhere in the mansion was another soul alert and ready to spring to her aid.

"Good evening, Patrin," she said to the young man at the door.

"Good evening, *hela*," he replied.

"I assume my grandmother is asleep?"

"Not quite yet," he said, a shade of regret in his well-trained voice. "She indicated that she wished to wait up for you."

Kit grimaced. "Oh, joy. All right. I'll go right up."

So she climbed up two flights of stairs to the suites where her grandmother lived. Some of the more modern city homes had been built with elevators, but Granmama, a hard-core traditionalist, would have no such contemporary devices in her home. Instead, a lovingly maintained wooden staircase curved up all four flights of the house, even into the servants' quarters on the upper level. Granmama never asked for anyone's help climbing those two flights, either, and she probably made the trip five times a day. The exercise must be what kept her in such fearsomely good health, Kit thought. She herself was just a little winded by the time she made the landing on the third floor.

The door to her grandmother's suite was closed, but a spray of light spilled out over the threshold. Kit waited till she had caught her breath, then knocked lightly on the door. "Granmama? Patrin said you wanted to see me when I came home."

"Yes, yes, come in," was the impatient invitation from inside the room. Kit opened the door and stepped in.

Her grandmother's sitting room was the most beautiful room in a truly elegant home. Each of the five high windows was draped with pale green linen; the ivory wallpaper was patterned with ivied trellises. The furniture was upholstered in emerald-colored damask and carefully arranged over a luminous hardwood floor. Potted plants and cut flowers were set on tiers of wrought-iron stands, so that the room was filled with the scent and color of living beauty. Everywhere were reminders that this was a woman tied to the land, who derived her wealth, her strength, and her sense of time from the regulated seasons of nature.

That woman was seated in a huge, overstuffed armchair, almost lost in a gold satin robe and the contours of the chair itself. She was small-boned and delicate, and anyone who did not know her would think she was frail. Her skin, once a cobalt so deep it had appeared almost ebony, had lightened over time to a soft, washed denim; her black hair had turned a vivid white. A stranger would have thought he beheld a woman whose intensity and will had been slowly drained by the inexorable leeching of age; but he would have been mistaken.

"Good evening, Granmama," Kit said formally. "If I'd known you would be waiting for me, I would have come sooner."

"If I had grown tired of waiting for you, I would have gone to bed," was the dry reply. "Sit down. Talk to me. You look tired."

Kit smiled and seated herself on the divan closest to her grandmother. "It's Sereva's wine. I'm not used to drinking anything so deceptive and potent."

"It's good for you," her grandmother responded instantly. "Wine clears the mind and settles the systems. Good wine, anyway. Bad wine rots your stomach."

"Well, then my stomach is probably a sieve by now."

"How's that boy of hers? Bascom? She told me she'd enrolled him in some special class."

Kit hadn't expected to be drawn into this debate quite so quickly. "Yes, an advanced science class. He seems to enjoy it."

Granmama made a slight sniff of annoyance. "Waste of time. If he enjoys it, fine, let him have his fun. No use to him to know all that scientific nonsense once he's living in-country."

"That's years away," Kit said neutrally. "Who knows what will happen in the next ten years?"

"*I* know," Granmama said instantly. "I was at the Lansdon estate last time I was in-country. Jeretta Lansdon had her little granddaughter there—daughter of what's his name, her second boy. Now *that* would be a good match. I'd been thinking about Kellisia Faremen's daughter, because she's got the bloodlines *and* the beauty, but there's something about the girl I don't quite like. Too soft, I think that's it. Too easily swayed by someone else's opinion. That's a dangerous trait, and you can always spot it early."

"Granmama, she's only fourteen, if she's the one I'm thinking of."

"That's her. And she might do yet. But Jeretta's daughter just appealed to me. I'm thinking she might be the one."

"And she's how old?"

"Eight this spring."

"And Bascom is twelve? Granmama, they're *children*. How can you consider pairing them up when they aren't even *people* yet? You talk like you're planning to breed a couple of dogs."

Granmama turned the full force of an icy stare in Kit's direction. Most of the indigo had dark eyes, brown or black; only a handful, the descendants of the most uncorrupted bloodlines, had blue eyes. Granmama's were a startling layered turquoise flecked with chips of granite; they appeared to be lit from behind by an unwavering torch.

"Marriage among the Higher Hundred can never be left to chance," she said in a calm, measured voice. "There is too much at stake. Do you know how much property Sereva owns outright, property that came to her through her mother and through her marriage settlement? Neither Bascom nor Marcus can inherit that land. Unless they marry, and marry well, all that property goes to the daughters of a second cousin of mine who married a mid-caste boy and squandered her life. I've only met her daughters a few times, and let me tell you, I will scheme and matchmake until the day I die to prevent either one of them from inheriting an acre of my mother's land. And if that means Bascom *and* Marcus must be betrothed before they turn thirteen, so be it. It is the way of our world, and it is a good way."

Kit knew she shouldn't, but she couldn't help herself. "Land—isn't there anything else you think of? Anything else you care about?" she demanded. "Is a piece of property more valuable to you than the happiness of a human being?"

"The land is all that lasts. The land is the only thing that links us, one generation to the next, and keeps us safe," her grandmother declared in a steely voice. "Is it more important than happiness? Of course it is. Whoever was happy more than a few days together at a time? Whoever truly knew what would make him happy? Are you happy? You think you're such a rebel, you think you're so free, but I've seen you sobbing when you thought I wasn't looking, and you wouldn't be in this house at this moment if you had any other place to go. And you're going to hold your life up as an example? If your father had left you to me to raise when your mother died, do you think you would be happier than you are now? I know the answer to that one. You'd be just like your cousin Sereva, and she's a good girl, calm and content. Wouldn't you rather be like her some days than the person you are now?"

This was why it was dangerous to quarrel with her grandmother, not because it made her so angry but because Granmama's blunt, sledgehammer arguments sometimes made a brutal sort of sense. Oh, no doubt, reared side by side with her cousin, Kit would have been as much like Sereva as a twin. She would have willingly married the man of her grandmother's choice, thoughtfully undertaken the management of her estates, and unquestioningly followed the dictates of a culture bound by tradition. And—hard to refute this point—she would almost certainly be less miserable than she was now.

But. "I am not Sereva, and I was not brought up as she was," Kit answered calmly. "I was raised to ask questions, to see that the world has more elemental laws than the rules of the Higher Hundred. You say a boy cannot study science or become a mathematician. I say, why not? What makes your traditions more worthwhile than a single man's desires? What has made you the only woman in the world who knows what is right and what is wrong?"

"They are not my laws. They are not my opinions. They are the truths and customs that have evolved over a hundred generations. Do you think you are the first fiery young girl to rail against some practice that she thought was archaic and restrictive? We have these customs, we have these laws, because they protect a way of life that the majority of us value. If we bent and changed for every fleeting whim of young girls like you, we would have no society worth handing down from mother to daughter. We would have no land, no possessions, no wealth. And you would have nothing to rail against. Would you like that better?"

Kit jumped to her feet, unable to sit still a second longer. She was filled with a liquid protest that seemed half fury and half despair, and she did not know how to articulate any of it. "I think you could be more open to change and yet not lose all those possessions you prize so much—yes, I do think that," she said rapidly. "I think you could say, 'I don't want to lose my land, but I want my great-grandson to be happy. I want him to have every opportunity I would give his sister if he had one.'

You could say, 'This I must keep, but this I am willing to examine and perhaps cast aside.' You could say—"

"I could, but I will not," Granmama said, interrupting again.
"Because I do not believe any of those things. Once you compromise your values, you begin to lose ground. The things that
matter to you get worn away—or wrested away. You must fight
every day to hold on to what matters. And you will see. I am
right. Ask Bascom, forty years from now, when he is married
and living on his wife's estates and sees how good his life has
been. I will not be here, but you will. Ask him then what he
regrets, and I can tell you now what the answer will be. He will
regret nothing."

He will regret all of it, Kit thought, but she did not say so.
How could she be sure? How could Granmama? "I won't have
to ask him," she said over her shoulder, because she had come
to a halt looking out one of the curtained windows. "Because
you will surprise everyone if you do not live forever. You can
ask him yourself."

Granmama was tricked into a laugh. "Then in forty years, I
will ask you the same question. And I will expect an honest
reply."

Kit smiled at the green draperies, then pivoted to share the
smile with her grandmother. "Agreed," she said, crossing the
room to kiss the old lady on the cheek. "Good night, *hela* Candachi. I will spar with you in the morning."

"And in the evening as well."

One hand on the door, Kit paused. "No—not in the evening.
I've told Sereva I will come spend a few days at her house."

Granmama nodded. "That will be good for both of you. Tell
her to invite me to dinner one night while you are there."

"All right. I will. Good night."

And she escaped from the lovely, suffocating room. If only
it were as easy to escape from the suffocating life that her grandmother was determined to have her live.

CHAPTER THREE

Kit was awake with the dawn, and ready to leave the house thirty minutes later. As always, she wasted little time on her appearance. That, of course, was more a rebellion against the gulden than the indigo, for among the guldwomen, elaborate dress and cosmetics were essential; only a beautiful woman would attract a virile man. There were detailed, torturous rituals the unmarried women went through every day to make themselves look desirable. Not until she had come to the city had Kit ever seen the bare face of a gulden woman.

Kit herself only bothered with a quick shower and throwing on the most casual of clothes. The most tedious part of her toilette consisted in toweling dry the thick, unmanageable mane of black curls and then, once she'd run a comb through it, clipping back the whole mass at the nape of her neck.

She would really be much happier with the closely cropped cut she had seen on many of the most fashionable city girls, but she couldn't bring herself to chop off her hair. Her father had always admired it, that was one reason; but Jex had always adored it, had loved to bury his face in the rioting black curls and wrap them around his fingers. She could not forgo those memories, so she lived with the inconvenience. She pulled her hair back and sauntered from the house.

After a short wait, she hopped onto the nearest shuttle to the

Centrifuge. It was crowded, as it was every morning, but nothing like the way it had been yesterday upon Chay's arrival. She caught a ringcar within ten minutes, and took off fast.

She loved the Centrifuge. Loved it. She knew she was exactly the type of driver who shouldn't be allowed in the tunnels, but she couldn't help herself. Every time she climbed into one of the ringcars, she felt a rising, guilty sense of excitement that she could not resist. She would slip instantly into the upper lane and accelerate as fast as the traffic would permit, and she would swoop into the middle and even the slow, lower lanes if it would allow her to zip by someone in the upper level who was moving too slowly. Other times, she would merely ride as close as she dared to whatever slowpoke was blocking her way, and more often than not the driver would dip into the center lane to let her pass. They weren't all gracious about this; more than once she saw angry faces turned her way from the windows of the other cars, and just as often a furiously gesturing hand. She didn't care. She knew she was rude, and she didn't care. She knew she was dangerous, and she didn't care. She loved the Centrifuge, and she craved its speed.

Once in the city, of course, she was more sedate. She could either take the trolley or go on foot to her destination, and either way, the pace was slow. Once she exited the Centrifuge at the West Zero gate, the distance was not far, and she often elected to walk it, though even she was a little nervous from time to time in this neighborhood.

When she had come back to the city six months ago, she had had no clear idea what she would do with herself. She had degrees from City College in anthropology, linguistics, and history, but she had no interest in teaching rich young indigo girls about the origins of their race and the peculiarities of their language. She could have taken a job at one of the city museums, but she was too restless to tiptoe down the quiet halls and spend all day in reverence over objects from the past. She needed to do something with meaning, something that would give her life some value. These days, it seemed to have so little.

So she went to the charity bank on the west edge of the city, outside the loop of the Centrifuge, and offered her services. They were wary of her there in the Lost City, of course—she looked every inch the blueskin heiress and she knew it—but her father's name bought her instant recognition and a grudging tolerance. "Tell me what you need done," she had said to the old gulden woman named Del who ran the place. "I can help you."

And help them she had. The charity bank was multipurpose and greatly overburdened. It served as a school for the poorest children in the neighborhood, a food pantry for those who could not buy their own, a medical center for the sick, a shelter for shivering gulden women straight in from the mountains who had nowhere to go for safety and were often in fear for their lives. It was a place where there were only women and children, and even the boys, once they had begun to gain their teenage height and lose their childlike voices, were viewed with suspicion. There was a tumbledown community center a few blocks away, built for just such a troublesome group: transplanted gulden boys who did not know the ways of the city and had been ripped from the ways of Geldricht.

It was hard to know what would happen to these boys, for, in terms of population percentage, there were very few of them, and this was really only the first generation that had been brought up in the city. As gulden men in Geldricht, of course, they would be reared as kings; they were strong voices in their ancestral households from the time they were very young. A gulden man had absolute power over his wife and, if she was unmarried, his sister—and, if she was widowed and he was over twelve, his mother. It was a right so basic, a law so inherent, that even women who had run to the city when their sons were infants watched their boys fearfully as they began to grow to adulthood. What buried trigger, what race memory, would remind these young men that they were the lords and these women merely chattels? No city guldwoman taught her son these principles, of course, at least not deliberately, but somehow the knowledge seemed to be there, instinctual and fully formed. As a boy edged to manhood, he changed. Kit had seen it. So had the women of the ghetto.

And so they sent the boys to the community center and worried about what would happen next.

Some of the young men, of course, took jobs in the city,

drifted into the more affluent gulden neighborhoods, tried to make a life for themselves that had nothing to do with their heritage. Some of them continued to hang around in the women's ghetto, aimless and angry and harder by the year to control. Some packed their possessions and boarded the train for Gold Mountain, to seek their fathers and their fortunes. Most of them were never heard from again.

They were better off staying in the city. Their mothers tried to tell them that. But these were men who had somehow divined that their mothers' opinions did not matter much in the world they came from, the world in which they belonged; and they were determined to discover what they were worth in the only sphere worth inhabiting. And so they left the ghetto, and they never returned.

Kit had spent some energy trying to convince Del and the other women that they should make a huge effort to reclaim these gulden boys. Inculcated with a whole new set of beliefs and perceptions, she argued, these city guldmen could reshape the history of the race. They could be taught to value their mothers, cherish their sisters, consider their wives their equals, and disdain their forefathers. To this end, she had said, what was needed was not a dilapidated gymnasium where the gulden teens could work off their aggressions in unsupervised sports, but a school, a cultural center, a place where they could learn and grow. She was willing to draft the plans and look for the instructors. She was willing to set the curriculum and teach the classes herself.

But Del did not agree and the other women did not comprehend, and so her words were wasted. Besides, they wanted to use her for other work. Fund-raising, for instance. She was a blueskin; she could approach the indigo corporations and ask for money. She could wheedle for concessions from the utility companies who did not understand why so many of the guldwomen's bills were paid late or not at all. She could recruit highly trained indigo doctors who felt enough compassion to donate their time and services to the poorly equipped clinic. She could be their conduit to all that indigo wealth.

And so she had done it. Uncomplainingly, though at first with a certain degree of embarrassment. It was begging, after all, even though her cause was noble and she was not begging for herself. She had enlisted Sereva's help, because her cousin had not spent half her life in Geldricht, as Kit had. Sereva knew who among the indigo were philanthropists and crusaders. She knew who had a genuinely kind heart and who could be moved by appeals to *noblesse oblige*.

In fact, Kit was surprised at how many indigo women were eager to help their unfortunate sisters, how many gave generously of both personal and corporate funds. When she considered it, she realized that, in this particular instance, gender superseded race. The blueskin women were appalled at the lives of their gulden counterparts. If a loaf of bread, a hefty check, or a pile of used clothing (scarcely worn and good as new) could transform the hapless, helpless, fearful guldwomen into strong, independent, righteous members of society—well, then, they were glad to give what they had. It was the least they could do. And they felt proud of themselves once they'd done it.

It was a start. There was so much more to be done that sometimes Kit could hardly bear it. But a start.

This morning, when she arrived at the charity bank, there was a small mob of women standing outside the double doors, huddled close together but not speaking. They were all dressed in the city drab that the ghetto women affected. In Geldricht, they wore a medley of bright colors, rich blues and hand-dyed green and scarlet. Here, khaki and olive and tan. They did not like to draw attention to themselves; they had no joy in color anymore. And their gold skin, like their clothing, seemed to fade and lighten under the city sun, till their rich complexions were a pasty beige and their lovely flaming hair showed no life or brilliance at all.

Today, the group outside the charity bank seemed even paler and more colorless than ever. Kit counted about fifty women, more than could usually be found here at this hour, all wrapped in fear and silence. "What is it? What's happened?" she asked in goldtongue as she strode up to them. No one answered her. A few looked away.

There were a few women here she knew, and she planted herself before the nearest one. "Shan, what's going on?" Kit demanded. "Why is everyone here?"

Shan reluctantly met her eyes. "They see troubles," she said in that elliptical singsong so prevalent among the gulden. It was as though their conversation had nothing to do with themselves; they could tell the most intimate story as if it were a myth about some long-dead ancestor. "They see such sadness."

"What happened?" Kit said. Even though long experience told her it was impossible to rush a gulden telling a sensitive story, Kit tried to hurry her to the point. "Was there another murder?"

"A woman and her three girls, could it be they are dead? Oldest boy, they say, not to be found."

Kit briefly shut her eyes. So a young man had killed his mother and sisters. It was a frequent tale. "Who was killed?" she asked.

"Some woman come to the city to be safe."

"What was her name? Did you know her?"

"Her name was Mish. She was here only three or four weeks."

Mish. Not a name Kit recognized, but there were so many women here she didn't know. So many women here. "And her oldest son is missing? Does anyone know where he might be found?"

"With his father, they are saying."

"Back in Geldricht?"

"This young man's father, he has come to the city to visit."

Kit frowned, trying to follow. "Mish's husband is in the city? Did he come to the district looking for her?"

"No one I know has seen this man nearby."

It was the most frustrating conversation imaginable, but Kit tried to hold on to her patience. She had had countless conversations like this over the years—conversations that were even less productive than this one, in fact. "Why do you think Mish's husband is here if you haven't seen him?"

"Wouldn't you come to the city with Chay Zanlan if Chay Zanlan was your uncle and a man you greatly admired?"

So Mish had been married to one of Chay's nephews. And enlightened though Chay assuredly was, many of his relatives were as traditional and fierce as the feudal clan leaders of a hundred years ago. "What is his name, do you know?" she asked sharply. "This man who was married to Mish?"

"Girt Zanlan," Shan said flatly.

Kit nodded. She had met Girt Zanlan a dozen times, a brawny, stupid, brutal man who embodied every quality, good or bad, that could be assigned to the gulden. Chay had never seemed to trust him, though he kept Girt around—mostly, Kit had always thought, to intimidate blueskin ambassadors who were unsure of how to negotiate with the gulden. Jex had always spoken of his cousin with a mix of affection and derision, but he was not above using the man's clan loyalty when he needed something risky accomplished. Girt was just the sort of father who would inspire a lost, angry young ghetto boy to an act of savagery. Girt would probably even take his son back, after such an act. Girt would consider it noble.

But. "I can't believe it of Chay," Kit said, shaking her head. "He would not encourage such a thing. Chay has spoken out against the slaughters again and again."

Shan shrugged. "Mish is dead. The boy is gone. Girt is in the city. Those are the pieces. Work the puzzle any way you wish."

Kit nodded again and turned away. She felt sick and exhausted, and the day had just begun. She slipped past the crowd of women and into the building, thinking that perhaps Del would have more information for her. But the stooped, pale, white-haired woman merely looked as weary and heartsick as Kit felt.

"Who knows why this happened?" she said when Kit found her and demanded explanations. "I cannot blame Chay or Girt or even the boy. He did what he was taught. Mish should have left him behind when she came to the city."

"It's surely not *her* fault," Kit said. "If there is blame here, it is not hers."

Del shrugged. "There is no blame. There is only tragedy and sorrow. Not even you can come up with a way to solve that."

Kit swallowed a retort. Del—all of them—seemed to believe that she considered herself practically omnipotent, armed with the answers that would save the world. The truth was, she so often felt confused, overwhelmed, and hopeless that she couldn't imagine she would ever be able to help anyone. She must act more confident than she felt, she supposed. She must exude that indigo arrogance like a perfume from her skin.

"Very well, then. What is done, is done. Is there anything I can do now to ease or aid anyone?"

"There is that new restaurant in the city. You said you would go there."

Kit nodded, trying to stave off a wave of bitterness. Such a pointless activity—now—after such an event. The last thing she felt like doing was going into the city and soliciting more donations. Though Del had seemed quite hopeful about the possibilities here. It was an unlikely joint venture between an indigo capitalist and a gulden cook, and it was designed to attract wealthy patrons of all the major races. The food was supposed to be fabulous, and the clientele had already included everyone from Ariana Bayless to the richest guldmen in the city. Del thought it was possible that the restaurant owners would be willing to donate their leftover food every day to the charity bank, an idea that had seemed meritorious to Kit when she heard of it. But now . . .

"Of course. Today? There is such turmoil here—"

Del shrugged again. "And what is it you can do about such turmoil? In the city, I think, they do not notice that the ghetto women are suffering. Unless we tell them. You said you would tell them."

"I'll tell them," Kit said on a sigh. "I'll be back sometime today."

So she was, fairly soon, back on the Centrifuge, going three-quarters of the way around the city to the North Zero gate. The express trolley to the Complex took her close to her destination, but she still had a walk ahead of her to the restaurant. Not a bad thing. She needed a bit of brisk exercise to clear her mind of its sudden black depression.

Though it was hard to walk as quickly as she would like; the streets were far more crowded than usual. *Chay,* she thought, as she noted all the extra security forces on every corner. *The police and the gawkers. It'll take me forever just to cross the street.*

But eventually, pushing through tourists and guards, she made her way to the restaurant. It was chic, small, decorated with a mix of Higher Hundred heraldry and gulden craftwork. Even at this morning hour, the aromas seeping out from the kitchen were varied and delicious. Kit stopped the first employee she saw and asked to be taken to an owner.

"You have a complaint?" the young woman asked. She was lowcaste blueskin but well-educated, Kit thought; she seemed both deferential and confident.

"Not at all. A request. I work for a charity, and we were hoping to interest your owners in our work."

"I'll see if Dort is available."

Dort. The curt one-syllable name nearly always indicated a gulden; the hard final consonant usually signalled a male. Not always, of course, Chay being the most famous example. *Not to mention Kit,* she thought wryly. But of course only her father called her Kit. And Jex. And the other gulden. To the blueskins, she was Kitrini. Only rarely would Sereva or her other family members call her by any other name.

In a few moments, she was joined by a middle-aged, sharp-eyed gulden man who was trying to size her up with one quick glance and failing. Kit smiled to herself. He was smart enough not to make the obvious assumption—*high-caste blueskin, I must curry her favor*—and businessman enough to be ready to listen.

"Good morning, *hela*," he said graciously enough. "I'm willing to hear about your charitable requests. But I must tell you that now is not a good time for me. Our tables are reserved for luncheon, and my entire staff is quite busy."

"May I take five minutes to state my case? Or should I return some other day? Tomorrow perhaps?"

"If you can tell me quickly, I will hear the outline and then ask you back later in the week for details."

"I am with the charity bank in the women's ghetto on the west side of town," Kit said baldly. "You may have heard of us. We have many corporate sponsors and many individual contributors as well. We thought you might be willing to help us out."

Dort shrugged. "We're a new business. We are not yet certain of our profits."

Kit nodded. "Of course not. But at the end of the day, if there is food that you would throw away because you have not sold it and cannot save it for the next day, we would be glad to take that food off your hands. We would send someone to collect it.

A few loaves of bread or a pile of fruit. Whatever you happened to have."

Dort looked intrigued but, as he glanced at his watch, harassed as well. "It is an interesting proposition, *hela*," he said. "If we could mention this charity in some of our advertising—"

"We would hope you would do so," Kit said quickly. "That benefits us as well and puts our name before others who might wish to become benefactors."

"I'll mention it to my partner," he said. "If he agrees—"

"When should I come back to hear your answer?"

"Three mornings from now. I will know by then."

"You're kind. I'll see you then."

"And your name, *hela*? In case my partner asks."

A name his blueskin partner was sure to recognize even if Dort did not. Kit did not even allow her muscles to tense as she replied, "Kitrini Solvano Candachi." Her own name, her father's, her mother's. Dort's eyes widened involuntarily, but he wiped the look away quickly.

"And so I shall tell him," he said. "In three days, then."

Kit had just stepped outside the door when she realized she would not be making much progress anytime soon. The streets on both sides of the restaurant were being cordoned off, and a wall of mixed-race security forces blocked her escape in any direction. On her left, she could see a slow cavalcade moving up the street. It took her a moment to realize who must be at the heart of that mass of bodies, though she recognized the tourists and the reporters and the guards who circled around it.

"Chay," she said aloud, and waited at the door for the procession to pass.

Except that it did not pass. It came her way, slowed even more, and turned toward the restaurant in one chattering lump. She was squeezed back to the brick of the wall, pushed off the walkway by a blueskin guard who was shouting orders into a handheld communicator and gesturing widely as if to sweep the air clean with his palms. She hopped to get her footing on the rocky ground and tried not to elbow the other unfortunates who had been shoved off the sidewalk next to her.

And then, like the others, she craned her neck and peered

around people's heads to try to catch a glimpse of the infamous visitor. There was Ariana Bayless, no mistaking that severe blue face and regal bearing. There was Ariana's favorite council-woman, whose name escaped Kit at the moment. And there—yes, it was Girt, as blond and stupid as ever.

And beside him, big and golden and ropy with power, strode Chay Zanlan. He was dressed in a ceremonial tunic, a richly embroidered green silk, but his powerful arms were bare and the breadth of his chest was in no way disguised by the cut of the cloth. His bushy red hair was streaked with gray, his face was lined with every one of his sixty-some years, but there was nothing feeble or infirm about him. He was taller than Ariana Bayless by a least a head. As always, he used that height to his advantage, staring imperiously at the crowd around him with a gaze fearsome enough to make the most ardent stalker slink back.

A gaze that snagged on Kit's face and brought those roving gray eyes to a standstill. Chay halted, and the entourage around him came to a sloppy stop. "What—?" "Who—?" "Is there a problem?" his escort murmured, but Chay ignored them all and pushed past his bodyguards to come face-to-face with Kit.

She had straightened against the wall as soon as he noticed her, but she made no move to meet him halfway. They had not parted on the best of terms. She would not go running to him now.

"Kit," he said, when they were only a couple of feet apart. The crowd around them was breathlessly silent to listen; they might have been actors in a beloved play. "I did not know you were in the city."

She stared back at him, not knowing what he was thinking, if he hated her or if he still loved her. "For about six months now."

"Staying where?"

"With my grandmother."

"Have they allowed you to see Jex?"

She nodded, for a moment wordless. It was over Jex that they had argued, she and this man who had been as dear to her as her own father. "From time to time. And you? Have they let you see him?"

"Twice. He appears to be treated well enough."

"I believe he is. Though you would be wise—" She paused, bit her lip, and switched to goldtongue. "Not to trust easy promises this woman makes you."

He smiled, that wide, feral grin that Jex had inherited. "I will not," he said, speaking still in the indigo language. "I am not free at the moment, or I would invite you to join us for lunch."

"Thank you for the offer, but I am not free to join you anyway," she said. "I do not expect you to have time for me while you are here."

"But soon," he said. "You must visit when I am back in Geldricht."

She nodded again, once more unsure of what to say. He gave her a short bow of farewell—an act of high courtesy, though most people in the crowd would not know that—and turned back to his companions. The whole lot of them shuffled into the restaurant, speaking in low voices and now and then glancing back at Kit.

She remained where she stood, held in place by the pressure of the crowd and the sense of hundreds of eyes trained upon her. She kept her head high and her gaze focused slightly above the crowd, but she knew people were staring at her, whispering and wondering. As soon as she could, she elbowed her way through the dissipating mob, trying not to make eye contact with anyone, blue or gold. She was almost on the street again, almost clear of the throng, when she caught one low-voiced exchange between two gulden men standing nearby.

"Who did you say that was?" the first asked.

And the second replied, "That's Kit Candachi. Anton Solvano's daughter and Jex Zanlan's blueshi mistress."

CHAPTER FOUR

The day had started well at the Biolab, but quickly turned nasty. In the morning, they had all gathered in Melina's office again to see what they could glimpse of Chay Zanlan's comings and goings. They felt free to do so since Cerisa would be gone for the day. The rumor was, though Nolan could scarcely credit it, that Ariana Bayless had invited Cerisa to join the select group that was socializing with the gulden king. True, Cerisa and Ariana were great friends (the same woman mysteriously split in two, Pakt often said darkly); and Cerisa was one of the most sought-after dinner guests in the city, since she had an impeccable lineage and an impressive career. But she was hardly famed for her small talk and sociability. Though perhaps, when one was entertaining a hostile ambassador, that was not the point.

Nonetheless, she was gone, and they all felt a carnival mood of freedom lift their spirits. They sat at the window; they told jokes. Varella lofted wads of paper at Hiram, hitting him in the head. Colt bent over Melina, his white-blond hair drifting over her shaved head, and whispered something that made her laugh till she cried. Nolan stood near the back of the room, idly discussing rental property with Sochin, a blueskin who lived in his neighborhood and wanted to be rid of his roommate.

And then suddenly there was a scream of fury, and Melina was pummeling Colt with both hands. He drew back his hand

and hit her so hard she rammed into the windowpane. The room became an instant melee, bodies pushing between the combatants, Varella shrieking like a hysterical child, Melina thrashing in the arms of those who sought to hold her back. None of the blueskins wanted to attempt to restrain Colt, but after that one terrific blow, he made no move to touch Melina again. The guldmen surrounded him, edging him back toward the door, but even they didn't lay a hand on him. His face was a study in sullen scorn. He looked as though he could burst into slow, uncontrollable flame at any moment.

Pakt dashed into the room, took in the scene with one glance, and grabbed Colt by the arm with more nerve than the rest of them had mustered. "My office. Now," snapped the senior guldman, and Colt wrenched his arm away. "Melina. You, too."

"I'll kill him," she panted.

Nolan spoke to Pakt in a low voice. "I'd separate them for now."

Pakt frowned at him. Colt had melted from the room, and everyone else was concentrating on Melina. "What happened? What was said?" Pakt demanded.

Nolan gestured his ignorance. "I didn't hear it. But she was screaming and beating on him, and he walloped her so hard she might be hurt. I wouldn't put them together anytime soon."

Pakt nodded, still frowning. "Does she need a doctor?"

"I'll find out."

Pakt left. Nolan pushed his way through the other technicians to Melina's side. Varella was cradling the dark head against her shoulder, but Melina's tears looked more like rage than pain.

"Let me see her," Nolan said, and Varella pulled back. Melina lifted her head and let Nolan examine her cheek and scalp. There was a huge welt across her face and a lump under the hairline, but no blood. Nothing irreparable. "Pakt wants to know if you need a doctor."

"I need a gun," she said in a wild voice.

"I think you're all right," Nolan said, ignoring that comment. "What did he say to you? Pakt will ask."

"Gilder trash," Melina said viciously under her breath. Even Varella looked shocked. "I wouldn't repeat it if it would save my grandmother from hanging."

"Your grandmother's dead," Nolan said calmly. "You can say anything you like."

Varella smothered another gasp, and Melina actually gave a weak laugh. "But I am too much of a lady."

"What do you want me to tell Pakt?"

"I'll tell him myself," she said haughtily, "when he gets that gilderman out of his office."

"Say it again," Nolan said, "and I'll hit you myself."

Now Varella was affronted. "How dare you," she said coldly. "Even to joke about violence to an indigo woman."

But Melina was watching him with those wide, intelligent eyes. They understood each other absolutely; they always had. They came from a background so similar as to almost make them brother and sister. "No, he's right," she said slowly. "I *am* too much of a lady. Nothing excuses such language. I would not want to shame my mother."

"Or yourself," Nolan added. "So tell the truth, when you tell Pakt your side of the story. Colt won't lie, you know, even if he's the one to blame. He never lies."

"Pakt will side with Colt no matter what he says," Varella said.

Nolan shook his head. Melina was still watching him. "What Pakt wants is harmony," he said. "And he'll do what it takes to keep Colt in line. But not if this was something Melina started."

"I didn't—"

"Well, one of you said something."

Melina lifted her chin. "He insulted me. And Julitta."

Ah, the cultural gulf again. Not much Pakt could do to solve that. "What did you say about Julitta?" Nolan wanted to know, but he guessed the answer before she spoke.

Melina twirled the end of a new silver chain, showing off the pendant at the end. A stylized arrangement of color and pattern; it must be Julitta's family heraldry. "I showed him my necklace. How was I supposed to know—"

Nolan held up both hands for silence, for peace. "Tell it to Pakt," he said. "But I think he'll say you should have known."

"And does *that* mean," Varella burst out, "that Melina should have to pretend? Conceal? Live a lie just to make *Colt* happy? A gulden boy? Who cares what he thinks, anyway?"

Right; she was entirely right; and even if Colt loathed Melina's arrangements, who had appointed him judge of her actions? And yet it seemed to Nolan that if peace between races was to be maintained, some circumspection might be called for on both sides. In this, his training warred with his ingrained desire to avoid strife. Why should an indigo woman have to make concessions to a gulden man? He was not the philosopher who could answer that.

"Talk to Pakt," he said again. "I'll go tell him you don't need a doctor."

So that little incident had set the tone for the rest of the day and, naturally, none of them could talk of anything else. And—naturally—conversation broke down entirely along racial lines, the gulden gathering together in Colt's office, the blueskins in Melina's or Varella's labs. The albinos stayed in their own rooms, working without recourse to gossip. Normally, there was an easy camaraderie among all three races in the Biolab. They shared with each other a knowledge so esoteric that anyone else who understood it became an instant kinsman. This had made them comrades if not actual friends—though the relationships seldom extended beyond the confines of the building.

And this unsettling disturbance was likely to make them strangers to each other for a day or two within the familiar walls.

Nolan, Hiram, Sochin, and another blueskin named Felder all left for a late lunch together when the indigo women declined to join them. At a nearby restaurant, they sat at a table near the window and watched the city walk by.

"I'll tell you, though, something should be done about Colt," Sochin said. He was the newest member of their group, a fine-featured, dark-skinned, high-caste thirty-year-old who had never spent an hour in the presence of a guldman until he walked into Biolab eight months ago. "A man like that shouldn't even be allowed to *speak* to a woman like Melina."

"Well," said Nolan, but Felder overrode him. Felder had been a city man a little longer than Nolan had, but he still bore the unmistakable stamp of in-country aristocracy.

"I hope Melina plans to talk to Cerisa about this," Felder said warmly. "Because you can't count on Pakt to do it, and she ought to know."

"A blow like that! He should be arrested," Sochin said.

"At least fired," Hiram agreed.

"She hit him first," Nolan reminded them. Three pairs of unfriendly eyes swung his way. "Well, she did."

"Because he said something unpardonable," Felder said in a starchy voice.

"Did you hear him?" Nolan asked mildly. "What did he say?"

"If *she* considered it unpardonable, that's good enough for me," Sochin said. The other two agreed.

"I like Melina as much as anybody does, but she's not above teasing somebody when she knows he can't take it," Nolan said stubbornly. "I've seen her bait Colt before. So have you."

Sochin spread his hands in a gesture that indicated an inarguable case. "Her prerogative," he said. "She's an indigo woman. Her word is law."

"Well," Nolan said again, but again Felder interrupted with some passion.

"At no time, under no circumstances, is violence against a blueskin woman tolerable! And perpetrated by a guldman—ten years ago that would mean instant death! Forget having him fired! He deserves to die!"

Nolan looked at him seriously. "You can't mean that."

"I do mean it! If he had hit my mother or my sister, I would have killed him myself."

"I think Melina can take care of herself," Nolan said.

"Well, she'd better tell Cerisa. Or I'll do it," Felder said.

"And my guess is that Pakt would like to handle this without Cerisa's interference," Nolan added.

"Pakt!" Sochin snorted. Nolan gave him a level look.

"You have a problem with Pakt, too?" Nolan asked gently.

Sochin looked away. Even Felder shrugged. "Pakt's all right for a guldman," Felder answered. "But he's a guldman. He doesn't see things the way we do. And you know he'll take Colt's side."

"I think Pakt is pretty fair," Nolan said.

Hiram spoke up unexpectedly. He was the most quiet and submissive of the lot, and the others could sometimes forget he was even present. "I like Pakt," Hiram said. "And he likes Melina. I don't think he'll let Colt off so easy."

"Well, if I don't like the way he handles this, I'm going to Cerisa," Felder said.

Things seemed to calm down a little after that, bravado spent and honor satisfied. Talk turned inevitably to work matters, a new drug Hiram was working on, a slippery virus that Felder had been examining. Nolan let his mind wander, idly watching the passersby, blue, gold, white, in endless variety and profusion. His eyes were on the pageantry before him, but his mind was on Melina, when Felder suddenly exclaimed, "Look at that! Revolting."

"What?" Hiram asked, and Felder pointed. Nolan's eyes automatically sharpened on the view outside the window. Felder was slamming his palm against the table in disgust.

"How can he do it? Look at him, he's got to be mid-caste, looks respectable enough—"

"Well, she looks clean, anyway," Sochin said with a smothered laugh.

"Clean is not the issue. Self-respect is the issue. A—a basic human decency, a basic understanding of what is allowable and what is not—"

What he was ranting about was a mixed race couple standing hand in hand a few yards from their window. The man, as Felder had noted, appeared to be a perfectly ordinary middle-aged blueskin; the woman was a gulden girl some years his junior. She wore the flashy clothes and elaborately coiffed hair that branded her a prostitute, but the expression on her face looked warmer and more tragic than the profession usually demanded.

"She looks like a nice person," Hiram offered when there was a break in the tirade. "Maybe he's just lonely."

"A man doesn't get that lonely. Not a blueskin man," Felder said.

Sochin was laughing. "Oh, come on now. You've never seen one of those gilt girls walking by, her face all made up and one of those tight, tight skirts on, and wondered just what it might be like? You're lying if you say you haven't."

"I haven't," Felder said stiffly.

"I have," Hiram said.

Sochin nodded. "Of course you have. My first day in the city, I saw one of those girls, and I thought, 'Whoa, now! That's a package you can't buy in-country, and I wouldn't mind taking it out and trying it on for size.' "

"I trust you never did," Felder said.

Sochin shrugged. "Not yet, but why shouldn't I? What would it hurt? It's not like messing with some low-caste indigo girl who thinks you're going to marry her because you've felt her up behind her mother's barn. The gilt girls know how the land lies. They don't want your precious bloodline, anyway. All they want's your money. That's a bargain that makes sense."

"Do you suppose it's any different," Hiram asked, "with a gulden woman? Do you think they're—well—the same?"

Sochin was laughing again. "All women are the same. All men are the same. Makes it easy to tell apart the sexes."

There was more in this vein, but Nolan tried to tune it out. He didn't know which he found more offensive, Felder's self-righteous prejudice or Sochin's sly leering. Whenever he saw one of those so-called gilt girls working the richer districts of town, he was washed with a fierce and unexpected sadness. Those pale faces seemed overburdened, not enhanced, by the careful cosmetics; the bright, cheap clothes reminded him of the items a child would dress her dolls in. He always tried to avoid making eye contact with such women, but now and then he had been caught unawares, approached, and made an offer. Twice he had given the girls money and hurried away before they could question or thank him. He had been sure neither Leesa nor his mother would approve.

"What about you, Nolan? You fantasize about the gulden whores? Or are you like Felder here, you think they should be whipped off the streets and locked up for good?"

Nolan rose to his feet and tossed a few bills on the table to cover his portion of the meal. "I think it's too bad when an unfortunate gulden girl has to make money from pleasing a prick like you," he replied coolly. "I've got things to do. I'll see you later."

So that left a fairly silent party behind him; and, once back at the Biolab, he discovered that silence had descended upon the offices as well. All the others were working in a solitary state in their own labs, and no one looked up as he passed door after door.

He was checking on Melina, but she was nowhere to be found. He hesitated, then sought out Pakt, who was alone in his own office, studying something under a microscope.

"Pakt," Nolan said quietly, and the big guldman looked up. He was wearing a neutral expression, and Nolan kept his voice formal. "I was wondering if Melina was all right, but I can't find her. Do you know where she is?"

"I sent her home for the day. And Colt. For today and to-morrow, in fact. As far as I can tell, they were equally at fault, but I can't tolerate such behavior from either of them. From any of you."

Nolan nodded. "I understand. Some of the others—" he paused, feeling disloyal, and plunged on. "Some of them are pretty upset."

Pakt nodded and ran a hand through his copper hair. "That's true on both sides of the color line," he said gravely. "That's why I sent each of them home. I cannot allow this to recur or get out of hand. And I'm not going to play favorites."

"Are you going to tell Cerisa?"

"I'll have to. If she finds out from someone besides me, it will create distrust between us, and I can't do my job without Cerisa's trust. But she won't want to know the details as long as everything's under control."

"Melina might go to Cerisa, you know. If she's mad enough."

"She might. I don't think she will. And Colt certainly won't."

Nolan knew he should leave, but Pakt's voice had grown friendlier the longer they spoke, and he had questions only Pakt could answer. "Why does he care, anyway?" he burst out, step-ping a little deeper into the room. "Colt? Why does he care who Melina takes for a lover? Nobody pays any attention to all of his women, though he seems to have hundreds of them."

"Hardly hundreds," Pakt said, sounding a little amused. "But Colt certainly does like to play the field."

"So? How can he set himself up to judge somebody else?"

Pakt sighed a little and settled himself back in his chair. He motioned Nolan forward with one hand, so Nolan took the seat opposite Pakt's lab table. "Colt's completely a product of his upbringing. As is Melina, as are you, as are we all. His upbring-ing tells him there is something repugnant and even dishonorable about one woman taking another as a lover. It would not happen in his own society, not at all, not ever. He can't accept it. He can't even overlook it."

"But there's nothing wrong with it. I know a lot of women—my sister, even—"

"Please. I don't want those details. I have to admit, my emotions side with Colt on this one, even though my brain tells me it is an irrational prejudice brought about by a cultural schism. But I don't like to think about it."

"But among the gulden, there are men who—well, what the men do with each other is even worse than what the women do!" Nolan burst out.

Pakt smiled faintly. "Now, to me, a male homosexual is an understandable and acceptable individual. Many of them are the orphans, the young men with no father or uncle to take them in. But many of them are the most powerful clan leaders in Geldricht, who do anything they choose and dare anyone to question them."

Nolan felt queasy at the very images the talk conjured up, but he continued to listen; he wanted to understand. "Why would it be like that," he asked, "jahlas among the indigo and—and whatever you call those men among the gulden?"

Pakt shrugged and spread his hands. "The anthropologist Anton Solvano said that women are always drawn to power. Among the indigo, the women have the power, and among the gulden, it's men. Those with the power have the women."

Nolan was fascinated but still unsure. "And men? What are they drawn to?"

Pakt laughed. "The availability of sex. If it were not such a cultural taboo, believe me, you would have homosexuals among the indigo. Indigo men profess to despise all guldwomen, but who are the customers for the gulden whores? Most of them are blueskins, did you know that? They're drawn by the availability of sexual favors. But blueskin whores don't entertain gulden men. Even a low-caste blue-skin woman has more prestige than a guldman, and a woman does not engage below her station. First law of the species."

Now Nolan's head was beginning to ache. "The law of the indigo species?"

Pakt smiled. "No, you innocent, the human species. A woman who mates with an inferior produces inferior children. They will not be as strong, as big, as intelligent as their cousins and rivals. Therefore, they will not be able to win the most attractive and fertile women of the next generation, and eventually the bloodline thins out and vanishes. All human behavior can be traced back to the biological imperatives. Most of it, anyway."

"And men's desire for sex?"

Pakt flung his arms out over his desk. "Procreate everywhere! Produce hundreds of sons! Make sure your lineage never dies out!"

"Well, but if a man is taking another man as his lover—"

Pakt laughed again. "True, no children will result. At times the biological impulse gets cross-wired. But it's always in there working."

Nolan thought a moment, sighed, and pushed himself to his feet. "I don't know. You might be right. But my life seems more controlled by outside forces than anything ticking inside my head."

"Well, yes, when culture reinforces biology, your destiny can seem pretty inescapable. Even so, the individual will sometimes surprise you. More often than you think."

The rest of the day passed calmly enough, though there was still little interaction among the races—indeed, among anyone. They all kept to their own offices, working diligently. Nolan spared a thought to regret that Cerisa was gone this day and so did not have a chance to observe how industrious they all had become.

And the next two days, though Cerisa was among them again, she might as well have been absent. She locked herself in her lab and did not emerge even for lunch. Melina and Colt returned that second day, each of them appearing both chastened and defiant, and, like the others, confined themselves to their workspaces. Nolan noticed that Melina was no longer wearing her lover's necklace, though she was wearing a shirt whose collar was embroidered with Julitta's family colors. He guessed that Colt was not conversant enough with the heraldry of the midcaste indigo to recognize the symbolism of that pattern. In any case, the guldman did not react to the provocation.

The afternoon of her second day back, Nolan stopped by Melina's office and asked her to lunch. "That would be fun," she said in her usual decisive manner, and so they left the building together, chatting idly. Over the meal, they talked mostly of their work, but conversation gradually turned to more personal topics.

"So. I saw you talking with Colt this morning. Have you two smoothed things over?" Nolan asked cautiously.

She laughed and rolled her eyes. "Yes. You know we fight all the time, and we never stay mad at each other for long. In some ways, he's my best friend at the lab. We're so much alike."

"You and *Colt*?" Nolan said incredulously. "Alike?"

She nodded vigorously. "Oh yes! We're both the oldest in our families, and we each have four sisters and brothers, so there's a lot of pressure there to do well and set a good example. My mother would be so mortified if I came to the city and didn't do something distinctive with my life. And Colt's father—he's told me his father would disinherit him. Which means even more to the gulden than it does to us," she added thoughtfully. "For us, it means losing money and land and—well, prestige. A place in the community. For them, it means losing family, becoming—I think he called it a ghost. Someone who is no longer alive. I didn't quite understand it. But I knew what he meant."

"I don't think you're alike at all."

She laughed again. "Oh, we *are*! We were both brought up to believe we're the most important person in the room and everyone should do whatever we say, whether or not we say it nicely. The only reason Colt doesn't completely lord it over everyone else in the lab is Pakt—because he was brought up to respect the dominant male. And the only reason *I'm* bearable is Cerisa. Same reason."

"You and Pakt," Nolan said, shaking his head. "You make it all sound so complicated. Like there's more going on than just a few individuals in a room."

"There's always more going on than that," she said wryly.

Nolan wasn't sure how to reply to that, but there was never any need to strain for conversation with Melina. "How's Leesa?" she asked a few minutes later. "Are you going to see her anytime soon?"

He nodded. "As a matter of fact, she's coming to the city in a couple of days. Business, she says, but I think she really wants to attend Corzehia Mallin's big event."

"Oh, are you going to be there? Good! You can meet Julitta. We've been invited, of course. I think even Cerisa will be there."

Nolan grimaced. "I thought she'd been invited, but I was hoping she wouldn't go. The crowd will be a little young for her, won't it?"

"Actually, I think Corzehia's invited everyone—all the Higher Hundred in the city. So you'll have to come in formal dress. Which I know you love."

"Anything to impress Cerisa," he said, and she laughed again.

They headed back to the Complex together, but Melina veered off to stop at a public news monitor. He waited a moment while she scanned the screen, her finger on the "hard copy" button in case she wanted a record of anything.

"What are you looking for?" he asked when he got bored.

She shrugged. "Just looking for news of the day. Go on, I'll catch up with you later."

He nodded and strolled on down the sidewalk till he came to the nearest entrance of the Complex. It was on the far side of the building in relation to the Biolab, closest to the government offices, a region that was somewhat unfamiliar to him. He wondered where Jex Zanlan was being held—in this quarter of the building, he thought, but undoubtedly not on the ground floor—and whether Chay Zanlan was anywhere in the vicinity. Probably not. Most likely, all the diplomats were out lunching with Ariana Bayless and the gulden king. In fact, these corridors seemed almost deserted.

Which was why the lone figure, sitting on the marble floor with her head in her hands in a pose of absolute dejection, caught his attention. She was a blueskin, though he could tell little about her caste from her clothing or her hidden face, and she looked as though she could weep until the world ended.

Unthinking, Nolan crossed the smooth stone in a few quick strides and put a hesitant hand to her shoulder. "*Hela*?" he said in a soft voice. "Can I help you? Can I get you anything?"

At his touch, her head had jerked up, and as he spoke, she scrambled to her feet. *High-caste* was his first thought, before he registered the wild, almost frightened look on her face. "Are you all right?" he asked more urgently.

She backed a step away from him and tried to push her heavy hair from her forehead. Her hands were shaking and the deep color of her face seemed bleached and insufficient. Nonetheless, there was something regal about her, something that scorned him for even presuming to aid her.

"Yes. I'm fine. Just go on."

His training urged him to obey her curt words, but his compassion made him linger. "I can take you to a doctor if you need help. Or I can fetch you a glass of water—"

"I'm fine," she said even more sharply. The color had returned to her cheeks on a wave of anger or embarrassment; she seemed to grow calmer and more assured as he stood and watched. "Thank you. You're quite kind. But please leave me."

Well, she seemed capable of speech and motion, and she clearly did not want him nearby, so he nodded once and turned away. He had only gone a few yards down the echoing hallway when quick footsteps hurried up behind him, and Melina fell in step beside him.

"What were you saying to *her*?" she asked incredulously. "I didn't know you knew her."

"I don't," he replied, surprised. "She was sitting all hunched up on the floor. I thought something was wrong and went over to offer her help. Which she didn't want. Why? Who is she?"

"Anton Solvano's daughter," Melina responded. "The disgrace of the Candachi family."

Even Nolan had heard of renegade blueskin anthropologist Anton Solvano; in fact, Pakt had mentioned the name just the other day. "She's a disgrace because she's Solvano's daughter? That's not really her fault, is it?"

"That isn't, no. But she's also chosen to become Jex Zanlan's mistress."

Nolan couldn't help himself; he pivoted on one foot to look back at the girl who had huddled so miserably on the floor. But she was nowhere in sight. "That's incredible," he said.

Melina shrugged. "True, though. She never makes an attempt to deny it. They say her family is completely mortified by the situation, but they haven't disinherited her. Yet. Which you have to give them credit for, because surely the temptation must be strong."

Nolan resumed walking toward the lab, Melina beside him. "Guess she won't be at Corzehia's ball, though," he said.

Melina laughed so hard she almost couldn't catch her breath. "No," she said at last, "I guess she won't."

Two days later, she told him more about Kitrini Candachi. They were drinking their first cups of coffee in Melina's office and celebrating the calm that had descended upon the city with Chay Zanlan's departure. The thought of Chay Zanlan had reminded Nolan of Jex, which had reminded him of the dark, despairing woman he had spoken to so briefly.

"Tell me about her," he said to Melina. "How did she even get to know Jex Zanlan?"

"What do you know about the Solvanos? Her father and her grandfather?"

"Not much. I think they're mid-caste or high-caste but not Higher Hundred. They did some famous studies in anthropology."

"Right. Well, her grandfather, Casen Solvano, was this brilliant but sort of demented scholar who went off to live with the gulden when he was a young man. This was fifty or sixty years ago, you understand, when the city was maybe a third of the size it is now. There were very few gulden in the city, and most of them were the engineering specialists who had only agreed to come in because they were paid a great deal of money. The gulden built the city, you know—the indigo didn't have the technology for it. The gulden were the architects and the engineers, and that's what really gave them a foothold in the city."

"This is like talking to Pakt," Nolan said. "Always some kind of history lesson."

"Well, you asked."

"I asked about her."

"Right. Well, so there had been almost no contact between the two races since the indigo drove the gulden out of the valley two hundred years ago. So the fact that Casen Solvano went off to study the gulden was this amazingly shocking thing. He would resurface every few years and give anthropological papers on 'The Lifestyle of the Gulden Tribe' and things like that. Then he'd disappear again. He was considered a nutcase, but he was actually pretty valuable because he brokered some of the deals between races that got more of the city built. There's a plaza named after him somewhere on the west edge of the city. I've never been there."

"So then, this girl," Nolan said patiently. "Kitrini? Is that her name?"

Melina nodded. "Solvano had a son named Anton—who took his father's name, by the way, not his mother's, though I've never been too clear on what kind of strange woman he could convince to marry him. Probably some low-caste girl willing to take any husband. But this Anton, he was like some wild man. He was practically brought up among the gulden—I heard some story that he never saw his grandmother's land till he was ten years old. They sent him to City College, and he blew away all their test scores. I mean, he was brilliant, but he was totally lunatic. He started agitating for the admission of gulden to City College, and for equal rights in the city for guldmen and guldwomen. Until Anton Solvano came around, you know, the gulden couldn't own property in the city. They still can't own it in-country, of course, and I don't expect that will ever change. But he did a lot for the gulden within the city limits."

Melina took a sip of her coffee while Nolan waited impatiently. "Like his father," she continued, "he had studied anthropology, and he produced all these really inflammatory papers about the differences between the indigo and the gulden. I mean, pretty brutal assessments of the indigo, calling them a primitive matriarchal feudal system and questioning all sorts of inheritance laws that had been in existence for centuries. Most people tried to ignore him but he did have an impact, and all sorts of debate groups were started to discuss some of his observations." Melina smiled. "Anton Solvano is probably the reason you're here in the city today. He called the female-dominated blueskin society barbaric, inefficient, and repressive, and he made a lot of young men his age start questioning their roles in their mothers' houses."

"And then he had this daughter," Nolan prompted.

"And then he got married to Roetta Candachi," Melina obligingly went on. "Which was something of a scandal for the Candachis, as you might guess. I mean, they don't come any purer than the Candachi. Roetta, they say, was completely headstrong—not to be held by love or honor, as my grandmother would say. They married, and had a daughter within a year."

"Kitrini."

"Kitrini. So of course old Lorimela Candachi was pretty happy about that, though she already had another granddaughter. What's her name—Sereva, that's it. She's a couple years older than Kitrini. Anyway, everything seemed fine, everyone expected Anton to settle down and become more normal—and then his wife died. And he took his daughter and went back to Gold Mountain."

"Why did Lorimela Candachi allow that?"

Melina smiled. "I don't think he asked her. One day, they were just gone. I guess Kitrini was four or five by then. And for the next twenty years, she spent most of her life in Geldricht, and only a few months of the year with her mother's family. So you would have to guess she's not your ordinary blueskin girl."

"Have you ever met her?"

Melina shook her head. "The Candachis live pretty far upcountry, not at all close to my mother's estates. They haven't come my way much, though Lorimela Candachi would recognize me if she saw me on the street, and I've met Sereva a few times. Lorimela is a bitch, but I like Sereva."

Now Nolan smiled at the casual epithet. "You shouldn't speak so slightingly of your high-caste elders."

Melina laughed. "Well, you know what I mean. My grandmother's the same way—so's yours, probably. Lays down the law absolutely, expects everyone to obey every word she says. Completely inflexible. Completely unwilling to entertain a new thought. I know, I know, they're the ones who have made Inrhio the prosperous country it is today, but you can't have a conversation with one of them without wanting to run screaming from the room."

"So Kitrini grew up in Geldricht, and met the ruler's son, and fell in love with him. And didn't know any better," Nolan said thoughtfully, "because she hadn't had a mother to tell her how to behave."

"And her father was hardly a role model."

"It still seems incredible," Nolan said. "I mean, except for the gilt girls, you never see an indigo with a gulden. And I've never seen an indigo woman with a gulden man. Not ever."

"Well, and you wonder how long Lorimela Candachi will let this go on. Kitrini's living at her house right now. Surely the old lady has some influence over her."

"So tell me," Nolan said. "How do you know so much about these Solvanos? I've heard the names, of course, but I didn't know half that stuff."

Melina grinned. "My dad knew Anton Solvano at City College. My dad was in the first class of men that were allowed in the university, and I guess they were all fairly close. And I think they all found Anton Solvano pretty amazing. But I don't think they stayed in touch much after Anton moved back to Geldricht."

"Where is he now? Solvano?"

"Died a few years back."

"Did your dad go to the funeral?"

Melina shook her head, her eyes wide with more revelations. "He was buried on Gold Mountain. Well, of course, none of the indigo would attend such an event. I don't even think the Solvanos went."

"And Kitrini? What happened to her then?"

"I think she stayed in Geldricht until just a few months ago. I know Lorimela Candachi put a lot of effort into trying to make her come home. I don't know why she decided to return when she did."

"To see Jex in jail," Nolan suggested.

"He's only been here a month. She came back a while before that. Who knows? As I said, I've never met her, so I wouldn't know why she would do anything. But she sure is interesting."

"I would think," Nolan said cautiously, "that she'd be ostracized. I'm amazed that her grandmother hasn't cut her off. But with an upbringing like that—even if she wasn't involved with Jex Zanlan, I would think the rest of the Higher Hundred would pretend she doesn't even exist."

Melina nodded seriously. "I think some of them do."

"I mean," he said awkwardly, "Leesa. I can't imagine that

she'd ever allow somebody like Kitrini Candachi to walk through her mother's door. She's very traditional."

"I'm not sure *my* mother would welcome Kitrini Candachi, so you don't need to apologize for Leesa," Melina said gently.

"But—you seem pretty forgiving," he went on, still feeling clumsy and confused, but wanting to know. "Why is that?"

"I'm a city girl," Melina said softly. She glanced briefly out at the crowded skyline visible from her window. "Don't get me wrong, I'm as blue as they come. I'm going to marry a man of my mother's choosing and run the land the way my ancestors have run it for thousands of years, and I'm going to give my daughters every advantage my heritage allows. But . . . Living in the city changes you. It shows you that life can be different from the way you were always taught. It makes you a little less quick to judge."

"My mother would never understand how I could feel so much respect for Pakt," Nolan said.

Melina nodded. "And my mother would never believe that I could be friends with Colt. Actually *like* him, want to hear what he has to say, and trust his opinion. On some matters, anyway. So this is what the city has done for us."

Nolan attempted a smile. "Ruined us for the lives we were born for."

"No, no, no," Melina said swiftly. "Made us part of the vanguard of change."

"Our society will not change," Nolan scoffed. "The blueskin world? It will go on for centuries as it has always gone on."

"You're wrong about that," Melina said seriously. "Change may come slowly, but it will come. And it's people like us who will allow it to happen."

But Melina's words rang hollow not three days later, when there was an incident over at the Carbonnier Extension. This was a strip of semi-mountainous land that had always belonged to the gulden. But then, the valley that contained the city, a hundred years ago, belonged to the gulden, and so had the rocky but arable miles of farmland that extended for a hundred miles to the east of the city.

The indigo had gradually but implacably taken over that land, decade by decade, crowding the gulden back farther and farther toward the Katlin Divide and up to the edge of the Varho Sea. The battle for the valley had been protracted and bloody, and the gulden ruler of that time had vowed that the indigo would never advance another acre into gulden territory. In fact, treaties signed twenty years ago had spelled out that very provision: Here the indigo property ends, here the gulden land begins.

That was before the city had grown so crowded; that was before agreements with two continents four thousand miles away had turned the city into a trade center with an urgent need for growth. Hence, Ariana Bayless and her colleagues had commandeered a tract of land "for development" about fifteen miles west of the city. It was small by standards of indigo imperialism in the past, but it was still an unauthorized annexation; and Chay Zanlan had made it clear that he was not about to allow it tamely.

Negotiations between indigo and gulden had been heated, but cooled somewhat when Ariana Bayless began offering money for the land she had at first just blithely overtaken. Chay had seemed willing to entertain proposals, but many of the other gulden clan chiefs had expressed outrage and hostility at the idea of giving up another square foot of land to the indigo raiders, even for a hefty price. No one had protested more vehemently than Jex Zanlan, whose bombing of the medical center had been in protest of the plans for the Carbonnier Extension.

Even after Jex was imprisoned, there had been disturbances over the land marked for expansion—two minor explosions and one fairly spectacular brawl between indigo laborers and gulden protestors. No one had been seriously hurt in any of these instances. The rebels seemed more interested in drawing attention than inciting widespread violence. Though that didn't make them any more popular.

This time, the incident was a little more serious. It occurred on a day when several high-level city officials went to tour the construction site, bringing maps and timetables of their own to compare against the progress made so far. Two members of the delegation were from Ariana Bayless's office. They were joined by bankers, city planners, and news reporters.

And while they were touring the only completed building at the construction site, they were firebombed.

As the wood and stone of the building melted into ecstatic flame, indigo workers dashed for the conflagration and sent out calls to the city for emergency help. But the guldmen who had thrown the bomb raced out past the blazing structure to prevent rescuers from reaching the scene. There was a sudden and bloody struggle in the muddy ground under construction. Cinders and burning splinters drifted over the heads of the shouting combatants while the fire leapt and writhed nearby. The gulden had strength and skill on their side, but the indigo had numbers, which were shortly reinforced. Screaming sirens heralded the approach of city security, and most of the gulden scattered at the sound. The one who remained was facedown in a shallow ditch, and upon examination, he proved to be dead.

The construction office itself had been engulfed in flames so hungry that the building had been totally consumed. Most of the mayor's delegation had managed to scramble to safety when the first explosions bloomed into fire. When the security forces arrived and accounts were being taken, it was learned that one of the bankers and one of Ariana Bayless's assistants were missing. Volunteers cautiously entered the smoking shell of the building and began searching through the wreckage. The banker was found, unconscious, pinned under a fallen beam and almost unrecognizable with soot. She was freed and carried to safety.

Ariana Bayless's aide was not so lucky. She appeared to have died of smoke inhalation, for there were only minor burns on her chest and none of her clothes had been charred away. When her body was discovered, the other delegate from the mayor's office, a young man fresh up from the country, grew so upset he had to be sedated. The other representatives appeared to be incapacitated by shock.

News of the tragedy seemed to sweep through the city like a treacherous storm. It had occurred a little after noon; by two P.M., there was no one in the whole city who had not heard the details. Work at the Biolab halted completely, as all the blueskins huddled together in Melina's office and the guldmen found themselves standing silently in Pakt's. Violence between races had been a common thing generations ago, but Ariana Bayless and the mayor before her had enacted and maintained strict laws of nonaggression. There were bitter words, sometimes, and quick, hot arguments in the streets; but no guldman had died at the hands of an indigo vigilante in ten years, and certainly no blueskin had been killed by a gulden man in that same length of time.

Response from Ariana Bayless's office came down within a few hours. Curfew for all gulden males lasting from sunset to dawn every day until further notice. Any gulden male in company with more than one other gulden male would be subject to arrest or interrogation. Any gulden male within two miles of the Carbonnier Extension subject to arrest or interrogation. Conditions to be in force until further notice.

"This is bad," Melina whispered as, with the other technicians, she watched Ariana make her announcement over a tiny news screen Pakt kept in his office. The albinos and the guldmen had joined them, though they had all unconsciously gathered into groups divided by race. "This is only going to make things worse."

"This is what you'd expect from lying blueshi women who don't respect treaties and then blame others for breaking the peace," Colt said in a hard voice. Varella turned toward him angrily, but Pakt stepped forward, practically shoving Colt aside.

"Don't," Pakt said sharply. "If it means we have no conversation between races at all, I don't want to hear a single insult, not even the smallest joke. Do you all understand me? Colt? Do you understand me?"

Colt stared back at him, defiant and angry, but nodded slowly. Pakt looked over at the indigo women. "Varella? Melina? I want civility in this office, do you hear me?"

"If *he* doesn't keep needling everybody," Varella burst out.

Melina elbowed her in the ribs. "Be quiet," she said to Varella, and then to Pakt, "We hear you. What do we do if somebody tries to start an argument?"

"Bring it to me. At the first word, bring it to me. All of you. You don't want trouble to come to Cerisa's ears no matter who you are."

"All right," Melina said.

"All right," Pakt echoed her. "Now. Everybody back to their

offices. No gathering around gossiping. It'll just make things worse. If I see any two of you talking together for more than a few minutes, I'm going to break it up. For as long as the curfew lasts. We all just need to do our jobs, and try to get through this."

Silence followed his words. No one knew what to say or who to look at. Then Melina shrugged, nodded, and walked out the door. The blueskins followed her, the albinos behind them, and the guldmen in the rear. Nolan hurried to his office, head down, thoughts spinning through his brain in a rushed, unsettled whirl. This was bad, as Melina had said. But it seemed a sloppy misstep on a ladder suspended over terrors. All his instincts screamed that somehow it could all get worse.

CHAPTER FIVE

When Kit got the message from Jex, she felt her heart start its stupid, painful pounding; her breath instantly felt sharp and spiny in her lungs. She had not expected to be allowed to see him while Chay was in town. What few hours he would be allotted for visitors must surely go to his father—that only made sense—and so she had steeled herself to the knowledge that she would not see him again for a week at least, maybe two. His captors were capricious. They had no discernible schedule of visitation.

But here was the note in his usual peremptory hand, telling her to come to his prison that afternoon, for he had been granted an hour. She could hardly think. An hour. What should she wear, what picture could she make to sustain him through the bitter, colorless days of his confinement? She must return to her grandmother's, where her few fancy clothes were stored. Sereva's, where she had stayed the past few nights, held only her drab workaday outfits, and those clearly would not do.

"I must leave for a few hours," she told Del, for the note had come to her at the charity bank. "I'll be back this afternoon."

The guldwoman nodded indifferently and went back to her financial accounts. Kit could not shake off the feeling that Del did not care one way or another if this high-caste blueskin ever again stepped across the threshold into her line of vision. It was discouraging. Kit wanted so much to make a difference, enact dramatic changes in the lives of the suffering city gulden, and as far as she could tell, none of them even noticed her presence—or if they did, viewed her with an exhausted suspicion.

But she would change all that. Surely with time, persistence, and victories, she would be able to make some small difference in their lives.

Her thoughts slid most traitorously from her virtuous work among the women to a frank desire merely to see Jex's face again. Her anticipation was so intense that it hurt; she felt her cheeks go taut with want. And even seeing him, even being allowed to touch his hand, would not be enough for her, though it was all she could have of him today. It had been six months since she had made love to Jex Zanlan, and every single day she had missed that great, simple pleasure.

Patrin greeted her at her grandmother's door, and she made rare use of one of her aristocratic privileges. "Could you have my grandmother's limousine ready to take me to the city in fifteen minutes?" she asked him.

He nodded. "Certainly, *hela*."

"Thank you," she answered, already bounding up the stairs.

Jex's favorite color was red, but it made Kit's cobalt skin look garish and overbright. Instead she dressed in a sunny yellow pantsuit, with a high collar that unfolded around her face like the petals of a proud flower, and a multicolored belt that accented her slim waist. She slipped on a dozen gold bracelets, all of them gifts from Jex or his father, and twisted her hands to make them chime together. She bothered, just this once, just for Jex, to make up her face with rouge and eye color, darkening her lashes, arching her brows, hollowing out the curve of her cheeks. She scorned the practice, she despised the women who felt they had to adorn themselves to attract a man, but Jex would appreciate the effort, she knew. She wanted to be beautiful for Jex.

The car was waiting for her when she ran back downstairs. During the whole drive to the city, all she could do was think of Jex. She had loved him for almost as long as she could remember. He was the embodiment of the gulden ideal: the lordly young prince, handsome, charming, self-assured, dangerous. He had been a man groomed for power, and it made him lethal and irresistible; just the turn of his head betrayed his utter self-confidence, his cool knowledge of his worth. All the gulden girls were mad for him, and Kit was as besotted as the rest.

But she had not showed it at first. When he came to visit his mothers and sisters in the women's quarters of the Zanlan palace, when Kit happened to be there, she would ignore him. She would read magazines until he was done teasing his sisters. She would watch the news monitors while he debated family matters with his mother. On the state occasions when Chay invited Kit and her father to banquets and festivals, she would give Jex the required formal greeting and then go stand in the back of the crowd. She would not gaze at him doe-eyed like all those other girls. She was too proud for that.

But Jex Zanlan was a man drawn to the unattainable and piqued by the extraordinary. He began to include her in conversations when he visited the women of his family; he asked her questions until she responded. And then his face went blank in astonishment when she fired off one of her father's radical theories or offered him her own analysis of some political event that had transpired on Gold Mountain. She caught his attention. And when Jex Zanlan focused his attention on a person or an idea, everything else faded away.

They became lovers the summer she was twenty-one. She had resisted that long because she knew, it was so obvious, that once she surrendered to the inferno of her infatuation for Jex Zanlan, she would be consumed. She would melt into a blue puddle of ecstasy and desire. And it was also obvious—impossible to avoid knowing—that they were meant for lives with anyone but each other. He was the gulden heir and fated to take some carefully chosen pureblood as his wife. She was a strange, displaced foreign woman, born to a hostile race, with no real position in his society and only a tenuous one in her own. They could be lovers, but not for long. Whatever they meant to each other now would one day be erased by the inexorable demands of their conflicting worlds.

Perhaps it was that which made Kit cling to Jex all the more tightly as the years progressed and their ideologies began to force them apart as surely as their heritage did. She had strongly disapproved of his trips to the city and his bitter protests staged in the crowded streets. She had been profoundly shocked when she learned of the bomb set at the medical building, an exploit he passionately defended. She deplored his action—but she understood his motive—and whatever he did, she could not unlove him. He was Jex. Half the cells in her body seemed inscribed with his name. The gravitational pull that drew her to his side seemed stronger than the one that anchored her to the world.

And she had not seen him in weeks and weeks. And she was on her way to see him now.

She was nervous and unsteady as she stepped from the car and hurried up the stone steps to the Complex. She went through the high-ceilinged corridors, up the creaking elevator to the fifth floor, and showed her identification card to the guard outside the door. She was a Candachi, her grandmother would say; every man, woman, and child in the city should recognize her face, there should be no need for picture I.D.s. But Ariana Bayless had done away with that special privilege for the Higher Hundred ten years ago, and it was one of the few things the mayor had done that Kit actually approved of. Make them all equal in the eyes of the law, blueskin, guldman, and albino. The first step to true parity.

"Kitrini Candachi," she said to the guard, reinforcing her name, trying not to sound breathless. He was a blueskin, as all the Complex security forces were, and he looked disgusted at her request for admittance to Jex Zanlan's cell. But she was authorized, and he let her in.

"Cell" was the wrong word, of course; it was a plush apartment, two rooms as well as a bathing chamber, and it offered a wide variety of comforts. There were chairs, sofas, mirrors, books, and news screens, as well as a small kitchen area holding a selection of food. Kit had even been here when Jex served her liquor left over from a dinner meeting he'd had the day before with some of the city officials. There were no windows, of course, and a guard outside, and to someone with Jex's expansive, impatient temperament, lack of freedom was almost equivalent to death; but Kit had been to real prisons, and she could not help thinking he was being very well-treated.

He had been reading when she stepped through the door, but he flung himself to his feet at her entrance. "Kit," he said and crossed the room in a few strides. The kiss was comprehensive and bruising. She felt her body break against his, her flesh tear across his, and yet it was not enough. She wanted to be closer, inside him, curled around his beating heart, protected by the canopy of his ribs.

When he broke apart from her as violently as he had embraced her, she felt a deep and wrenching sense of loss. It was always this way on their short visits. She would have been happy merely to sit beside him, pressed against his body while his arm crushed her against him, saying nothing for the full duration of her stay. But Jex was too restless. He was not a man to snuggle and coo for love.

"Have you seen my father?" he demanded, pacing the room. She took a few steps forward, for she had only advanced a couple of feet into the room. "He was here yesterday, lecturing me."

"No—well, on the street for five minutes, if that counts," she said, trying to still her protesting heart. She needed him to love her, but he needed her for a sounding board, a sieve that would sift apart his anger; that had often been true. "What did he say to you?"

He laughed shortly and tossed up his hands. He moved through the apartment like a fallen angel across unsanctified ground—graceful, feral, and lawless. His skin was the color of apricot, and his hair raged with the hues of flame, and he did not belong in this place, and it could not hold him. Kit watched him and felt again that rogue desire.

"He was furious about the medical building, for one thing. As of course I knew he would be! It was nothing but the same argument between us. I say he does not do enough to force back the blueshi bastards. He says I endanger everything with my wild tactics. If that was all he had to say, I wish he would have stayed home."

"I think he came to discuss you with Ariana Bayless and see how he could get you freed from here."

He had thrown himself against the wall and now stared at her moodily. Even from across the room, his eyes were an electric green, snapping with lights from those interior fuses. "He did not seem to think Ariana Bayless was in any hurry to let me go."

And did you think she would be? Kit wanted to cry. *Did you think you could attack her city, endanger her people, dare her to punish you, and then find her eager to set you back on her streets again?* She understood Jex Zanlan right down to his toes, oh yes, and she knew what fevers drove him to shake his fist in the collective indigo face and scream out against injustice. But she could not agree with his methods and had said so. And received the full force of his fury in her turn. So she had learned to be careful about when she challenged him, though it cost her something to hold her tongue.

"Did he think he would be able to make a deal with her at all?" she asked neutrally instead.

"A deal," he said scornfully. "The *deal* he should be making is telling her there will never be peace in this city until the indigo abandon all plans for this so-called Carbonnier Extension. What he should be telling her is, no matter what dire punishment she flings down on my head, the gulden will not yield another scrap of land to blueskin imperialism. He shouldn't be making a deal for my freedom. He should be forcing her to withdraw her armies from gulden land."

"I don't think they're armies," Kit said. "I think they're construction workers."

"An advancing army all the same," he said, and pushed himself restlessly away from the wall. Kit dropped to a seat on one of the chairs and watched him stalk through the room.

"So what else did your father say?" she asked, when it appeared he had no other conversation to offer.

"We didn't talk long. I told him that Hecht and Shate had been to see me—"

"Hecht and Shate!" she exclaimed. "When did you see them?"

He shrugged irritably. "Last week, when I had a visitor's pass. What I didn't tell him was—"

"You had a visitor's pass last week?" she interrupted. "But I thought—I hadn't seen you for so long, I thought you hadn't been given any passes at all!"

"No, not until last week," he agreed.

"But—Hecht and Shate!" she repeated. She still could not

believe it. "I thought if you only had one pass a week, you would send for me. I thought—Jex, I worry about you so much, I think about you all the time, I think, 'Oh, if I can only see him an hour a week, then I can live on that.' But you had the hour and you spent it with—with Hecht and—"

"Oh, spare me the tantrum!" he exploded, ramming away from one wall to practically plow into another. "Hecht and Shate can carry on my business for me while I'm stuck in here, which is something you can't do, and wouldn't if you could! Of course I had to see them! What can you do for me? You can't get me out of here, and you won't talk strategies with me, and you won't even fuck me while there's a camera in the wall, which—" He turned to shout at the discreet round eye sitting at the highest edge of the ceiling moulding in the corner facing the door. "Which there still is, isn't there, Ariana Bayless? You watching the films every night, you stupid blueshi bitch? Would you like to see me fucking my girlfriend?"

He was laughing as he turned back to Kit, and he bounded to her side to pull her to her feet. "Now, that might just be worth it, a chance to turn the mayor's face bright red instead of blue. Are you game, Kitrini? Want to help me give old Ariana Bayless a show?"

She was so shocked that for a minute she stood rigid in his arms, and then she shoved him away furiously when he tried to kiss her. He was still laughing, though he stumbled a little as she sent him backward. "Oh, come on," he said. "It'll be fun."

She was so upset, so angry, so hurt that she was actually in tears. "How could you?" she choked out. "Talk about such a thing—joke about such a thing—even think about making love to me as a way to revolt Ariana Bayless—"

"Well, I admit that would be my primary motive, but I think I could enjoy some secondary benefits as well," he said, coming closer again, dropping his voice into amorous accents. "It's been a long time, and I surely do miss holding on to you."

His arms were around her again, once more he bent to kiss her. This time she hit him in the chest as hard as she could and scrambled away before he could react. His smile changed in an instant to a snarl. "You might not want to play, but you better be careful how you say no," he said in a low voice.

She was trembling now; she felt the loose wobble in her knees and arms and shoulders. "I thought you wanted to be with me," she said, and even the words sounded pitiful and shaky. "I thought you loved me."

Again, he threw his hands in the air; it was his frequent expression of exasperation at the ridiculous, incomprehensible world around him. "What does that have to do with anything? Why are you fighting with me? All I did—"

"All you did!" she exclaimed. She heard the shrill note in her voice, but she couldn't erase it. Her words tumbled out disordered and incoherent. "All you did was want to see anybody except me—and tell me I don't have anything to offer you— and then insult me by—by—How can you treat somebody you love that way? How can you treat anybody that way?"

He raised his hands again and turned his back. "Fine. If that's how you feel, don't come back and see me again."

She ran for the door before he could realize she was headed out. Her tears nearly blinded her. She tripped once and heard him turn to watch her. "Kit—" he said, but she had reached the door and flung it open.

"It's how I feel, so don't ask me back," she said over her shoulder and stumbled across the threshold practically into the arms of the astonished guard.

Jex called her name again, but if he had any other words to offer, they were cut off by the door closing. Kit was running out of the room, running down the hallway, running down the deserted marble stairs because she could not bear the wait at the elevator door. She was sobbing so hard she could not draw breath. At one point, she had to come to a dead halt on the stairwell—bent half double like a woman pummeled in the stomach—and try to force the air in her lungs. She could not take a deep breath, and the short shallow sips of air would not give her enough to live on. She didn't want to live. She wanted to curl up right here and die.

More slowly, she continued her descent, clinging to the bannister for both support and guidance, since her eyes were blinded by tears. What would she do, where could she go, what possible small fragment of her life had any meaning if she could not love Jex and be loved by him in turn? She had not felt so abandoned or adrift since the day her father died. That was the day she had known, in her blood cells and her bones, that the world was an empty place echoing with ghostly winds. But nothing could have prepared her for the shock and devastation she felt now.

She stumbled down the stairwell and stood for a moment in the great, empty hallway, unable to think or move. She had told Patrin to come back for her in an hour, and of course she had been with Jex only ten or fifteen minutes. She must be here when he returned—and anyway, she did not think she could, in her present state, negotiate the streets or the trolleys or the Centrifuge. She must find someplace to sit, to collect her thoughts, to regain her strength.

There was nowhere. She didn't care. She staggered toward the nearest wall, laid her back against it, and slowly sank to the floor. Drawing her knees toward her chin, she put her face down and let herself sob.

How could he have done such things, how could he have said them? She had been shocked first at his cavalier announcement that he had chosen to visit with his friends instead of her—something incomprehensible to her. Had she been the one in prison, she would have schemed and lived for another minute with Jex, to the exclusion of any other human being, she would have counted the minutes, crammed the hours with activity just to make them fly past. How could he wish to see anyone else? Where did she fall on his list of imperatives and desires?

And then—and then—The unpardonable joke, the parody of love . . . That he could think it, say it, seem to mean it . . . She could not get her mind around it. She could not believe it had happened. She could not imagine forgiving someone who had made such an offer.

She could not imagine her life without the great luminous excitement that was her heart whenever she thought of Jex.

She did not know how to walk back from this point. She did not know how to move forward. Her blood screamed in her veins, dragged its nails across the interior walls of her arteries. She ground her cheeks against her knees and wept, and knew there was no hope or comfort in this world.

The voice startled her as much as the touch on her shoulder.

A man had come up to her so quietly she had not heard his approach. "*Hela*? Can I help you? Can I get you anything?"

Surprise for the moment dried her tears, gave her enough strength to jump gracelessly to her feet. She stared at him, noting nothing but the blue skin and the sweetness of the nondescript face. His voice became more insistent. "Are you all right?"

No, I'm dying, I'm betrayed, there is no love in the world at all, she found herself thinking, but she could not say such lunatic things. She had to pull herself together, show that iron will that she had inherited, surely, from her grandmother, though her grandmother would not have been in just this situation no matter how oddly the world turned. As coldly as she could, she said, "Yes. I'm fine. Just go on."

He was high-caste; no doubt about it. She recognized the medallion against his shirt and the formality of his clothes, but even had he been dressed in gulden rags, there would have been no mistaking the breeding in his face, his voice, and his expression. She had always had a quick contempt for most of the indigo men she had met; they had all seemed—compared to the virile, volatile gulden—ineffectual and tame. But there was a gentleness to them, or at least to this one, that was in stark contrast to the violence of mood she had just left behind. And a certain kindness that appeared almost stubborn, for he still would not leave.

"I can take you to a doctor if you need help. Or I can fetch you a glass of water—"

"I'm fine," she said, interrupting. She could not allow him to succor her. What kind of end would that be to this horrific day? She had no need of help from chance-met indigo men. She did not even like them. "Thank you," she said austerely. "You're quite kind. But please leave me."

He seemed reluctant, but he responded to the note of command in her voice and turned away. She remained upright, propped against the wall, learning that she had remembered, during this exchange, the proper way to breathe. She watched him walk away, saw him joined in a few moments by a blueskin woman who glanced back at Kit with knowing, scandalized eyes. Fine; let them gossip about her. She cared little about what the Higher Hundred thought of her antics. She did not belong to them—would not go to them even if they invited her.

But she did not belong with the gulden either—or not with the gulden she had loved her whole life. That much seemed plain. Slowly, because her legs would no longer hold her, she collapsed to the floor again and laid her cheek across her up-drawn knees. But this time she did not cry. She would wait here till Patrin returned, but she would not cry.

Sereva commented that night on her unusual quietness, but Kit had regained enough poise to merely shrug. This was not some-thing she could discuss with Sereva, with anyone. She had in-herited self-control from her Candachi forebears and learned silence from the gulden matrons. She knew how to keep her own counsel and guard her sorrows.

Two days later, she returned to her grandmother's house, where it was even easier to brood in secret. She still had not decided what to do, what to say to Jex if she ever saw him again (though surely she would; surely this cold stone that had become her heart would thaw and flutter again). She moved through the days automatically, thoughtlessly, and shut down her interior vision because she could not bear the view.

Two days after the debacle at the Complex, a note came for her at the charity bank. She knew before she opened it that it was from Jex, and her heart began that painful, noisy pounding that made it hard for her to hear. "Thank you," she said to the courier who had brought it, and took it to a corner of the room where she could face the wall in case she could not school her expression.

The note was brief. "I have an hour visitor's pass for tomor-row at noon," Jex had written in bluetongue. "Come see me." There was no apology. There was no word of affection. No indication that they had quarreled and needed repair.

She found a pen on Del's desk. "I can't," she wrote on the outside of the note, and signed it. "Could you take this back to Jex?" she said to the courier in a colorless voice. "Thank you."

And she worked the rest of the day blindly, bloodlessly, feel-ing the heavens rage soundlessly about her head. Del asked her once if she was feeling all right ("Many women, some times of the month, they grow dizzy and strange" was in fact the guldwomen's comment), but she replied that she was fine.

When she returned to her grandmother's that night, she went straight to the bathroom and began to vomit. She was sick for the next two hours, until one of the servants found her and discovered she had a fever. Her grandmother, the last person Kit would have chosen to see right then, was interrupted at her dinner and brought into Kit's room.

"Let me see, let me see," the old woman murmured, laying cool hands on her granddaughter's forehead and patting the hot flesh along her throat and collarbone. The fierce blue eyes stared down at Kit, boring through the forehead to investigate the brain. No one would be able to guess what the sickness actually was, Kit thought, least of all her grandmother, but the old woman's eyes narrowed and her head snapped up.

"Bring me some of that miraleaf potion. In the blue bottle in my room," Granmama said to one of the hovering servants. In minutes, Kit was being urged to drink a mixture of miraleaf and hot tea, and for a moment she thought she would start throwing up again. But soon enough, she felt her whole body relax. She had not even realized how tense she was until she felt the knotted muscles grow lax and compliant. Her eyes closed against the onslaught of her grandmother's gaze, and she could not open them again. She could not think or grieve. She slept.

She slept nearly two days straight, waking only at intervals when someone brought her food, water, or more of the miraleaf potion. *This is pointless. Nothing will heal me*, she thought once as she obediently sipped another glass of the mixture, and yet each time she woke she felt a little less despairing. It occurred to her to wonder how her grandmother knew how to diagnose and cure the most severe forms of heartache. It would not have been a skill she would have attributed to Lorimela Candachi.

The third day when she woke, she felt light-headed but functional. Her body was stiff from too much sleep, and her eyes felt unaccustomed to vision, taking in everything as if it were new, but she felt somehow refreshed and made over. Her heart still hurt with an actual pain and her thoughts skittered away from examining, again, her last scene with Jex and the note of refusal she had sent him a few days ago. She still could not imagine either how to repair the breach or how to exist without him. But at least now she felt that she had the strength to consider her options.

Her grandmother bustled in, attired in full formal dress and obviously on her way to some event. "Well, you look halfway human again," was the acerbic greeting. "Do you think you might be getting up someday? The servants would like to clean your room."

Kit sat up in bed and noticed that she did not feel dizzy. "Yes, I was just thinking that I'd like a change of scenery," she said, her own voice cool and light. "What in the world have you been dosing me with? It's some kind of miracle drug, I think."

Her grandmother laughed shortly. "Miraleaf. Grows wild in Inrhio. It's a cure for exhaustion and all sorts of ills. When I was a young girl, my mother and grandmother spent one month every summer harvesting it and boiling it down for medicine. None of those fancy drugs they've come up with at Cerisa Daylen's Biolab have ever worked half so well."

"Well, it certainly worked for me. I'm glad you thought of it."

"I'm glad you're better."

"You look nice," Kit said. "Are you going off to a party or something?"

Her grandmother snorted. "Hardly. A funeral."

Kit's eyebrows rose. "Who died?"

"A woman in Ariana Bayless's office." Her grandmother was watching her with those clear eyes, gauging her reactions, what she knew, what she felt. Automatically, Kit felt her face grow impassive. "She was with a delegation down at the Carbonnier Extension yesterday when a bomb went off."

But this was too terrible to withstand the neutral expression. "A bomb—a gulden bomb?" Kit stammered.

"So it would appear," her grandmother said dryly. "Since a guldman was killed in the fracas that followed."

"Oh, how dreadful," Kit murmured, feeling all of a sudden as nauseated as she had two days ago. "This is terrible."

"Couldn't agree more," her grandmother said briskly. "I'll tell you all about it when I get back. Now get up and have some breakfast, and I'll see you in a little while."

But as soon as the door closed behind her grandmother, Kit lay back down again, sick and shaking. She knew now why Jex had wanted to see Hecht and Shate, and everything was even worse than she had realized.

CHAPTER SIX

When Leesa arrived, all of Nolan's senses seemed to change. He noticed things he had overlooked before, forgot about things that, while she was in-country, seemed a part of his unchanging daily routine. Cleanliness, that was one variable. He was ordinarily a neat man, but Leesa was fastidious, and so the first instant she walked through his door, he spotted the dust castles in the corner and the stains on the carpet. Scent, that was another. The air inside the apartment seemed stale and flat, but Leesa's hair smelled like lavender and camomile, perfumes he would not even have been able to name a day ago but which now reminded him of the ingredients in his sister's soaps and shampoos.

"Sorry," was the first word out of his mouth as he ushered her in. "It's a little messier than I remembered."

Leesa strolled in with her usual unconscious grace, like a statue that had deigned to step down from its marble base, and trailed absolution behind her. "Oh, it's just fine," she said. "That's new, isn't it? That chair? What else have you gotten since I was here last?"

"When were you here last?" he said, because he couldn't remember. She gave him a brief minatory look which told him he should not have forgotten. "Oh, right, three months ago," he said hastily. "Well, the chair. That painting by the kitchen door. Some pillows in the bedroom."

She wandered over to inspect the painting, a small oil showing the city skyline by a subtle sunset. He had bought it one afternoon at an art festival held outside the Complex, and Melina had admired it. Leesa did not. "I don't think it's very good," she pronounced. "Was this a student artist?"

"Probably. I didn't ask," Nolan said. "I got it at a street fair. I liked the colors."

She turned and smiled at him. "Naturally you should buy anything you like," she said. "There will always be rooms in our house that are just yours, and you can fill every wall with pictures and colors that I can't stand."

He smiled. "That's very generous of you."

She was laughing. "The public rooms, however, the rooms that people will actually *see*, those I insist on decorating exactly how I choose."

"Well, of course," he said with heavy gallantry. "You're the one with the exquisite taste."

She pirouetted again, giving the whole room one comprehensive glance, then crossed to the sofa. Sitting down, she patted the cushion beside her. "Come talk to me," she said in a voice that was half plaintive, half commanding. "You write such short letters, I never feel as if I know what's going on in your life."

Obediently, he sat beside her, taking her hand because he knew she liked these casual gestures of affection. "Sometimes I think my life would sound strange but uninteresting to you," he said.

"Strange, maybe, but how could it be uninteresting?" she protested. "I want to know everything that happens to you. I hate it that you're so far away. So tell me. All of it."

"Well, let's see. The big excitement last week, of course, was Chay Zanlan's visit to the city. That had everybody worked up."

"Yes? And did you see him?"

"Only from the window. We couldn't tell much, except that he looks really tall. Cerisa actually got to meet him, but of course the rest of us didn't, and since Cerisa never *talks* to any of us, I don't know what she thought of him."

"And then there was a bombing, I heard," she said. "That must have been exciting, too."

"Well, exciting in a sort of terrible way," Nolan replied. "And it's created a lot of tension in the city. There's still an after-dark curfew for gulden men, and they resent it, of course, and don't think they should be punished for the behavior of a few terrorists. It's made working conditions at the office a little tense."

"You work with gulden men?" she said, her eyes wide.

"Sure. I thought you knew that."

"Well, I knew you said they were there at the lab . . . I mean, I thought they were janitors or something."

He was pretty sure he had mentioned Pakt before, maybe even Colt; was it possible he had neglected to specify race and rank? "No, they're scientists, just like me. Pretty good ones, too."

"But you're better," she said.

He laughed. "I'm not better than Pakt. He's pretty amazing. He can look over any compilation of data—just the data, not even the experiments set up under the microscope—and show you where you've gone wrong. Everybody in the lab respects Pakt."

"But he's a guldman?"

"Well, yes."

She arched her eyebrows but forbore to make any of the comments obviously circling in her brain. This was her idea of broadmindedness. "So what are you working on right now?" she asked. "What project?"

"A sort of generic antibiotic that will destroy any number of bacteria that attack the gulden," he said calmly, anticipating her reaction. "I haven't actually tested it in the field, but in the lab it's one hundred percent effective."

She was trying hard to keep an encouraging, pleasant expression on her face, but bewilderment and a certain repulsion were trying to work their way through. "An antibiotic that only helps the gulden?" she repeated. "That's what you're working on?"

He nodded. "It could have incredible consequences if it really works. There's a lot of disease, especially in the Lost City—"

"The what?"

"The part of town where the impoverished guldwomen live with their children. Bad health and living conditions there, so there's a lot of illness."

She looked more puzzled and incredulous with every word.

"But—Nolan—why do you *care* if these guldwomen are sick? I mean—of course we should help everybody if we *can*, but shouldn't you be working on some other kind of medication? You know, something to help the indigo when they're sick? Wouldn't that be more valuable?"

He shouldn't even feel this great swoop of anger. This was Leesa, he had known what her reaction would be. He shouldn't even have told her what project he had under way; he had known she would be baffled and dismayed. "Maybe, but there are other people working on indigo cures," he said as gently as he could. "I seem to have a particular talent for understanding the gulden cells. And it gives me a great deal of—" He hesitated and discarded the word *pleasure*. "Of pride to be able to produce something that will alleviate suffering in another human being. No matter who that human being is."

"Well, of course, I didn't mean to belittle your work," she said, though the words rang somewhat false. "I'm very impressed with your abilities, you know that. It's just that—I would think, with all your skills and your intelligence, you would be working on something just a little more—important, I guess." She gave him a smile that was intended to be soothing, for she must realize her words had ruffled him a little, and then she laughed self-consciously. "And now I'm not sure exactly what I'm going to tell my mother! She keeps asking me what it is you're doing, and I felt so guilty that I didn't really know. But I'm not sure she'll be too enthusiastic when I tell her."

Oh, he was sure she wouldn't be. He could picture her, the majestic Brentitia Corova, having all her high-born indigo friends over for drinks, trying to explain what it was her prospective son-in-law did for a living. No wonder Leesa seemed so ill at ease; she was asking for her mother, not herself, and his answers seemed even more radical, judged by that standard. "Just tell her I'm working on drugs that will cure serious infectious diseases," Nolan said. "That should please her."

Leesa bestowed a radiant smile upon him. "Of course! That's perfect! It sounds quite wonderful when you put it that way."

He gave her a teasing smile in return, though his heart was a little heavy. Though his heart was unsurprised. "So," he said, "do you think she'll still respect me enough to allow you to marry me?"

But Leesa answered him seriously. "Yes," she said, "I think she still will be able to respect you when I tell her that."

Nolan felt his smile grow a little twisted, but he did not think Leesa noticed. In fact, her next words were on a completely different subject. She had apparently forgotten that her plan was to find out everything about his life. "Did I tell you?" she said, her voice taking on a lilt of excitement. "My grandmother has decided to give up her Chabbedon property. Well, it's just gotten to be too much for her—the house is huge, and the grounds are so extensive that she can't possibly keep track of everything. So she's moving in with my mother at the end of the year."

"Chabbedon," Nolan repeated. "That's one of the ones your mother is to inherit, isn't it? And Corfelo goes to your aunt."

Leesa nodded. She was almost bouncing where she sat, and her black eyes snapped with delight. "Yes, and of course Mother has always planned to leave Chabbedon to me. So she told me, if I want, we can move in there as soon as my grandmother moves out! That's this year, Nolan! I thought we'd have to wait at least another year before the Hayden property was ready. And Chabbedon! It's always been my favorite house."

Nolan felt his bones curl inward and his muscles spike with chill. This year! To be back in-country so soon! "Yes, it's a beautiful place. I can't remember why, but I remember that your family and mine all spent one summer there when my sister and I were little."

"That's when your mother was remodeling your house," said Leesa. She was two years older than, Nolan, and she never forgot anything—none of the details of her life, none of the details of his. "And my father had been sick, and my mother wanted us to be away so we didn't all get infected. So she brought all of us to Chabbedon and invited your family so she wouldn't get bored. I thought it was a wonderful summer. Which makes it even more perfect that Chabbedon will be our first home together."

He had been betrothed to Leesa since he was fourteen; he had expected to marry her, been delighted at the prospect of marrying her, since he was old enough to understand what it meant. She was beautiful, educated, gracious, and sweet-tempered, and any indigo man in or out of the Higher Hundred would envy him. So why did he feel this depression, this sense of loss, this moment's brief spasm of protest? "We must marry before we live together," he said, attempting both a smile and a light tone. "Did you have a timetable for that as well?"

"Yes. We can have a winter wedding at Chabbedon, itself—probably a month or two after my grandmother leaves. I'll need a little time to change the furnishings—at least in our private rooms. The main rooms have antiques that have been in the family since my grandmother's mother was born—I don't think we'll want to part with those. But in our bedrooms—well, you know, she's an old lady! All this fussy lace and heavy pieces of dark old wood. I know we want something a little more modern to live with every day. Although—" She paused, inspected him, and gave him a little-girl smile. "Although perhaps there are some colors and fabrics and furniture styles that you would prefer over others?" she said in a conciliatory voice. "And perhaps I shouldn't go wild just ordering the sorts of things *I* like?"

"Oh, you've remembered the sunset picture on the wall," he said, managing to smile back. "And you don't see how it will fit in with all your decorating schemes."

She scooted over to nestle against him, tucking her free hand under his arm and laying her black, black hair against his shoulder. "I just want to make sure you're happy," she said into the weave of his shirt. "You seem so far away sometimes. I'm not always certain you want the same things I want anymore."

He could not help his sudden look of surprise, for that much insight he had not expected from Leesa, but fortunately she could not see his face. He kissed her on the back of the head. "Of course I'll be happy," he said. "I'm always happy when I'm with you."

They stayed in that first evening, cooking together in the small kitchen, eating by candlelight at the cramped dining room table. Leesa spent most of the meal recounting for him stories of her recent social life—who she had visited, what her sister had done, what his sister had said, the betrothals, the inheritances, the big and small details of their families and their friends. Nolan listened and commented but was not required to talk much, so he did not. Mostly, he watched the shades and colors of Leesa's face by the flickering light, and thought about her.

He could not remember a time he had not known her. Their mothers were best friends and had planned, since the children were born, to marry them off at a suitable time. That had been common knowledge between them and among their friends, but Nolan could still recall the afternoon, fifteen years ago, when the formal announcement was made. Their parents had held a joint lawn party, overflowing with expensive meats and rich pastries and an extraordinary assortment of wines; there must have been two hundred people in attendance. He and Leesa and their parents had stood in a small circle at the head of the salad table while Leesa's mother told the assembled aristocracy how her daughter and Margo Adelpho's son had been promised to each other in marriage. Everyone had clapped madly, and Nolan had been ready to die.

He had been a thin and awkward youth, sensitive and shy; the concept of marriage to anyone, particularly someone like Leesa, made him almost painfully sick. Leesa, at sixteen, had been lovely, with that sculpted blue face, fine flyaway hair, and legs so long she could never find trousers to fit, so she always wore filmy, floating skirts which gave her even more grace and motion. It was impossible to imagine touching such a goddess, let alone engaging in any intimacy with her. He was not of her sphere.

But Leesa at sixteen had also been kindhearted, unaffected, and eager to please, and she had, after all, known him her whole life. She found a minute, in the press of all those people and their waterfall of congratulations, to seek Nolan out where he had hidden himself behind the serving tent. The instant he had seen her, he had dropped his china plate and spilled his wine, and his face, his whole body, had reddened with mortification.

"Leesa—you—that is—isn't there someone your mother wants to introduce you to?" were the only stammered words he could think to utter.

But she had laughed, and come close enough to squeeze his arm, and bent to retrieve his dishes. "I know. It seems pretty awful now," she said in the most sympathetic of voices. "But I think you'll be happier about it in a couple of years."

"No, I—of course I'm *happy*," he had said, stuttering again, but she had burst out laughing and kissed him suddenly on the cheek.

"Don't even think about it," she advised. "We'll just be friends like we've always been friends. You'll see. It won't be so terrible."

And in fact, for the next four years it was just that—the same friendship they had always had, though tinged with a certain inescapable knowledge of the future. In fact, that knowledge had deepened their friendship, to the point where they told each other things they told no one else. She repeated to him her rare, bitter fights with her mother; he confided in her his desire to go to Inrhio State University. She described her ineradicable fear of the horrors of childbirth. He confessed, at the age of eighteen, that he was still a virgin.

"Oh, I hoped so," was her reply, although he knew (for she had told him) that she was not. "I always wanted you to be all mine, but of course I know that a lot of men—well, Mother says it's to be expected, especially with all those low-caste girls working out at the processing facilities. And I wasn't going to be angry with you if you—but I'm glad you didn't."

"Well, I just—I wanted you to know because I didn't want you to be disappointed," he said in a rush. Disappointing a bride was a murky concept to Nolan, but one he had heard spoken of with great disapproval by his father and some of his older friends, and he did not want to be guilty of such a sin.

She had given him one of those sweet, soul-deep smiles and put her hand to his cheek. "I don't think you'd ever disappoint me, Nolan," she said in a low voice. "But we can see that you get a little practice."

They both lived on estates of a thousand acres. There were unused rooms in the mansions of each of their homes, any number of dairy houses, barns, outbuildings, and cottages that were empty at least some of the time. They had no problem finding privacy, and they were old enough to be able to dictate the uses of their time. That summer they met each other three or four times a week, on her family's property or on his, and taught each other the finer points of love. Nolan had not believed how such a simple thing could assume such importance. During that summer, he could not stop thinking of her, could not stop replaying in his head the details of their last encounter. He was eighteen, and few physical pleasures had come his way—certainly none that so engrossed his whole body and rerouted all the circuits in his brain. He became obsessed with her, this girl he had known his whole life. He did not have a thought, waking or sleeping, that was not tinged by her cobalt skin and midnight hair. If he could not see her, he suffered. If he could not touch her, the flesh of his entire body tightened and grew anxious; to meet her in a roomful of people, when he could not even take her hand, was torture. He could see no possibility of recovery from such a divine and lunatic state.

That fever lasted nearly two full years, and when it burned past its highest pitch, a great warmth still remained with him. For her part, Leesa had never seemed quite as stirred by their lovemaking sessions as he was, though she had obviously enjoyed them. But she had had more on her mind that past year. She had been spending a great deal of time with her mother, learning more about management of the vast estates, and she had been deeply involved in her social circle of young women. Love with Nolan had not been her only priority; she had other things to preoccupy her.

And eventually, so did he. He finished his classes at Inrhio State University and was invited to join Cerisa Daylen's team of scientists. He was sad to leave Leesa but excited about the opportunities before him, impatient to begin this new, surely brief, phase of his life. They had not been too unhappy at their parting because they knew they would see each other frequently, she coming to the city for visits, he returning often for family events. And within a few years, of course, they would be married and never need to part again.

Nolan's five-year stint in the city had changed him more than he expected—more than Leesa realized, though apparently she had sensed more of his transmogrification than he had thought. It was not that it had lessened his affection for his family or his fiancée—not exactly—it was just that he had seen how different life could be. It had not occurred to him, till he began working in the city, that any man might live a life unbounded by women—that a man could live, work, eat, entertain himself, distinguish himself, or destroy himself, without the guidance and commentary of a mother, sister, cousin, aunt, or wife. He had never seen it happen before. At first, he had pitied the old bachelors he had spotted in the city apartments, alone, unloved, living untethered lives; but gradually the existence began to appeal to him more and more. He would not want such a life, not really, but it was not as miserable as it had first appeared.

The city had changed him in other ways, too—or changed some of his desires. More than once, he had caught himself watching Melina and wishing Leesa were a bit more like her— bolder, more aggressive, more vivid. Oh, Melina was not so unique—high-couraged, outspoken blueskin girls were common as weeds in a garden—and Leesa was just as sure of herself as Nolan could wish. But there was a spark to Melina, a universal flame, that caught fire at any human kindling. She loved the whole world, everyone in it; nothing bored her or seemed beneath her attention. Leesa was not so adventurous and would not view that as a fault on her part. She would disapprove of Melina's passions, frown at her excesses. She would not consider them torches to throw her own straitened world into bright relief.

But that was Melina, and this was Leesa, and it was Leesa to whom Nolan had been betrothed. And she was an openhearted girl, and he loved her, and the course of his life was set, anyway. No stray wishes or comparisons could change that.

Leesa was to be in town four days, and Nolan had arranged to be off from work for two of them. Accordingly, he spent most of that time squiring her around the city, taking her to her favorite shopping venues and the best new restaurants, escorting her to concerts and the theater. She did not like the Centrifuge, so he hired a limousine and a driver, and they toured around town in style.

The central event of those four days, of course, was the party at Corzehia Mallin's to which the whole world had been invited—or at least, that portion of the world which was composed of Higher Hundred scions currently residing in the city. Leesa had spent one whole day shopping for a dress to wear to this event, though she had brought two with her just in case she wasn't able to find anything she liked. Nolan made a point of admiring her purchase every time she asked him if he didn't think it was the most beautiful gown ever, but frankly he wouldn't have been able to describe it five minutes after he glanced away. Fashion was not his forte.

Of course, he too would go in formal dress to this party, but for men it was much simpler: black trousers of extremely fine fabric, a white shirt of washed silk, form-fitting boots, and the latest hairstyle. Naturally, the shirt would have the subtle collar embroidery of his family's heraldry—and equally of course, he would be wearing the medallion Leesa had given him the day they became engaged. But the outfit would not vary much from the attire he wore every day, except that the cut of the clothes would be fancier and the materials would be grander.

Leesa dressed slowly and carefully, and when she emerged, Nolan made a great show of admiring her. It was not hard to do; she was truly a beautiful girl. The dress (he remembered now) was blue, but a carefully selected shade that perfectly matched the tones of her skin, so that its swirls and folds seemed to be an extension of her long neck and graceful arms. She had pulled her silky hair into a complicated knot woven with sapphires and silver, and she wore a flat silver necklace hung with matching gems. She had done something impressive with cosmetics, because her face looked glamorous and smoky, and her eyes were as dark as the night sky.

"Don't you look wonderful," he enthused, taking her arm and turning her this way and that. "I like your hair that way! That really is a spectacular gown. How did you get so pretty?"

She laughed, not quite believing him, but liking the compliments anyway. "Well, I do think I look nice, but no one will notice me once Aliria Carvon arrives," she said, laying her hand on his bent arm and mincing out the door beside him.

"Why? What's she going to wear?"

Leesa shook her head. "Who knows? It's always something outrageous. Don't you remember the last party at my mother's house? Aliria was wearing this incredible red dress and dark, dark makeup. Most of us can't wear red because it clashes with our skin tones, but she was able to pull it off. She looked like a gilt girl, of course, but I suppose that was the point. People certainly noticed her."

He was surprised to hear her use the slang phrase but let it pass. "Well, no matter how shocking her dress, she won't be as adorable as you," he said in a comforting voice, and she laughed again.

The drive to Corzehia's was not far, for she lived in the fashionable indigo district just east of Nolan's neighborhood, but the traffic was amazing. Every limo in the city must have been pressed into service, Nolan thought, for the wide streets were jammed with the long sleek cars, and they all appeared to be heading to the same address. Nolan considered this a fair augury of the evening's tedium, but Leesa was so excited she actually squirmed in her seat.

"I haven't been to a party in so long," she said. "Isn't this fun?"

Finally, they were before the house, on the sidewalk, at the door, being admitted by a triple set of hostesses who must be Corzehia and her mother and sister. Nolan only knew Corzehia vaguely and the rest of her family not at all, but apparently they were familiar with him.

"Oh, and you're Nolan Adelpho!" the older of the three women greeted him, taking his hand in a very firm grip. "The scientist, isn't that right? When are you two planning to be married?"

"Soon, I think," Nolan said, giving her his politest smile. It was not up to him to supply dates and details; Leesa's privilege, if she chose to exercise it.

"Tell her not to wait too long now," she admonished. "Corzehia got married last year, and she was telling me just yesterday that she wished she hadn't waited even that long. Your Leesa's a prize, now. I hope you realize that."

"I do," he said, and smiled, and moved on.

They were in a mob of people working their way slowly down a long hallway toward the main ballroom. Leesa either knew everyone in their immediate vicinity or recognized their heraldry, because before they had made it to the threshold, she had exchanged light conversation with all the women within hailing distance. Nolan couldn't count the number of times he heard the phrase, "Oh, that's *Nolan*." He couldn't tell if the voices were pleased, disappointed, or merely exclamatory.

Eventually their passageway emptied into the main room of the house, a ballroom-sized chamber festooned with the sky blue and grass green plaid of Corzehia's family colors. The room was large enough to comfortably swallow the crowd and open its doors for more. Glancing around, Nolan estimated that perhaps two hundred people were already there—and the evening was early.

"Do we hold court or do we mingle?" he asked, for it was never clear to him why some people seemed to take up stations in a room such as this while others made the rounds. Apparently, Leesa had no such doubts. She gave him a look of reproof and replied, "We mingle."

So for the next hour they traveled slowly around the great room, pausing to talk to this prominent indigo matron and that self-assured heiress. Nolan knew only a fraction of the people there, though all of their family names were familiar to him, so Leesa spent much of the time whispering gossip and background information to him as they approached or departed from each cluster of guests. When Evelina Margosa said, "Oh, *you're* Nolan" to him, he was tempted to reply, "Oh, *you're* the girl who left two husbands in six months." But he was incapable of such casual cruelty, so he merely smiled.

As far as he was concerned, the only really enjoyable conversation was the brief one they had with Melina and her jahla girl, Julitta. This time he was the one to make introductions, for Leesa had never met the women, and he watched curiously to see how his friend and his fiancée would interact. But it was conventional talk—they instantly began discussing what friends they had in common, where their estates lay, and some of the places they had traveled. Nolan turned his attention to Julitta.

"So are you having a good time?" he asked, since he couldn't think of anything else to say. She gave him a nervous smile and glanced around the room as if she couldn't quite believe she was in it.

"I'm trying to," was her soft-voiced reply. "But I don't know anybody here, and I'm not sure what to say to them."

He did a quick second assessment of her face and clothes. Yes, he thought he had remembered correctly: mid-caste girl, not used to this scale of grandeur. She was pretty, in a mild, unalarming way; she looked eager to please but rather uncertain. Melina had not done her any favors by bringing her here.

"Well, this is the worst of it," he said in a bracing voice. "Pretty soon the dancing will start, so most of the socializing will move to the sidelines. And eventually they'll serve a buffet dinner, so that will give you something to do with your hands. And of course no one will expect you to talk while you're eating, so make sure you get a big plate of food."

She laughed, but she looked more grateful than amused. "Will they allow me to dance with Melina?" she asked. "It would be fine at one of my mother's parties, but here—"

But here, no; she had guessed correctly. "Ah. Well. Perhaps not," Nolan said. "I'll dance with you, though. Do you like to dance?"

She nodded. "Oh yes! And I'm really a pretty good dancer, because I had lessons, so you won't need to be embarrassed."

"I wouldn't be embarrassed," he said gently.

Julitta glanced at Leesa. "But will your fiancée mind? I wouldn't want—"

Nolan smiled. "I'll be lucky if she has time for one dance with me," he said. "She knows everyone in the room."

"So does Melina."

"What?" said Melina, catching her name. "What awful things are you telling her about me, Nolan?"

"I told her that I would dance with her because you would be too selfish to bother to find her partners," was his prompt reply.

"Oh, good," said Melina. "Because I'm going to have to dance at least once with Corzehia's brother, and I know Mora Ellison will want me to dance with her son. I don't want Julitta to be bored."

"Bored? Here? Not possible," he said. Melina laughed, but Leesa only nodded.

"Have you seen Cerisa?" Melina asked him, and he shook his head. "She's over there on the other side of the door. She'd probably like it if you introduced Leesa to her."

"I can't imagine why. She doesn't ever like it when I talk to her."

"This is different. Trust me. It'll make her happy."

"A real treat for Leesa," he said, his eyes on his fiancée's face. She wasn't listening to him; she was making polite but apparently kind conversation with the shy Julitta.

Melina leaned closer. "And did you see? Over there, by that horrible pot of blue roses? It's Kitrini Candachi."

He could not help it; he stared. "I thought you said—"

Melina nodded. "She came with her cousin. So far people have been polite—at least I haven't noticed anyone ignoring her completely. But look at her! She looks as though she's been scheduled for execution. She must be having a miserable time. I'm going to talk to her as soon as I have a chance."

"She's probably not too friendly," he warned, remembering his brief conversation with her in the halls of the Complex.

Melina gave him a brilliant smile. "That's all right," she said. "I'm friendly enough for two."

Shortly after that, Leesa and Nolan moved on, continuing their circuit around the room. Nolan did not want to, but he heeded Melina's advice and directed Leesa over to where the head of the Biolab was standing.

"Good evening, Nolan," Cerisa greeted him with all her usual cool poise. She was dressed in a silver gown and appeared to have been sprinkled with diamonds; she glittered coldly and with infinite self-possession. "Melina told me she thought you might be here tonight."

Nolan made the introductions and was gratified when Cerisa held out her hand. She disliked casual contact, even on social occasions. But Leesa, of course, was her equal in bloodline and breeding, and that was something Cerisa would respect.

"Your Nolan is quite a gifted scientist," Cerisa said to Leesa. "I have often been impressed by his ability to think through a problem and come up with an unusual solution."

Leesa looked unreasonably pleased, but she did not, as Nolan half-expected, demand "*Really?*" Instead, she said, "I know so little about his work that it's hard for me to understand how talented he is."

"Oh, he's talented," Cerisa said. "But now that I've met you,

I can see why he's determined to leave my offices for your estates when the time comes. You're quite a lovely young lady."

Another smile from Leesa, this one a little coy. She was used to being admired by older women; she was quite a favorite with her mother's friends. "Thank you," she said tranquilly. "But I'd rather hear praise of Nolan."

Cerisa actually laughed, something Nolan did not remember ever witnessing before. "Well, he's invented two drugs that between them have saved about two thousand lives," she said. "That's an impressive statistic to take home to your mother's social circle."

"And it will mean so much more to them because it's come from you," Leesa said. "They've all heard of you, of course. My mother mentions your name every time the subject of Nolan's work comes up."

Cerisa smiled, a somewhat wolfish expression on that haughty face. Nolan hoped suddenly that Melina had not subjected Julitta to a similar interview; she would not fare nearly so well as Leesa. "Well, you can tell them that my opinion of Nolan is the highest," she said. "And that I will be sorry to see him go."

Even Nolan could tell that comment signalled the end of the audience, so he murmured indistinguishable words of farewell and ushered Leesa away. She was positively glowing, which annoyed him just a little; he knew she was thinking how delighted her mother would be with Cerisa's comments, and it irritated him that Cerisa's words carried more weight than his own.

"Well, I can see you enjoyed that," he said, a slight edge to his voice, but she missed it.

"Oh, she's an old hag—worse than my grandmother!—but I was glad to hear her say such nice things about you," Leesa said merrily. "Weren't you?"

"She's never said anything like them to my face, so I suppose I suspect her motives," he said dryly.

"Her motives? What could those be?" she asked in an innocent voice.

He smiled down at her. "To please a pretty girl? You have a charming smile. Maybe she just wanted to see it."

"Don't be ridiculous," Leesa said, but she was smiling, too.

"She's just the kind who can't praise someone to his face. No doubt she's been waiting a long time to find a way to tell you how much she values you."

Nolan glanced briefly around the room. "So are we done here? Haven't we spoken to just about everyone in the room?"

Leesa nodded, gesturing to the far end of the chamber where a small orchestra had just finished setting up. "I think it's time for the music to begin," she said. "Will you dance with me at least once or twice before I go off and do my social duty?"

"I'd rather dance with you all night, but yes," he replied. "I'll take whatever time you can spare."

"Silly," she said, and slipped into his arms just as the music started. It was an old song, a formal dance; they had learned it together when they were eight and ten. Nolan could not remember the number of times they had performed it together since then.

Dancing with Leesa was like listening to his breathing or counting his heartbeat. He could do it unconsciously unless he was paying attention. Her arms, lightly laid on his shoulders, felt as familiar as his own bones. Her shape could have been his shadow, so nearly did it match him. He never danced well with any other partner, although he could do his part creditably. Only with Leesa did he exhibit any grace, and that was because he borrowed it all from her.

"One more?" he asked, when the first number ended, and she broke into a smile and nodded. The second dance was much like the first, though a little faster, a little more modern. Leesa was slightly breathless as the music came to an end, and so he squeezed her tight a moment to accentuate her condition.

"Stop it!" she gasped, laughing, and pushed him away. "If you aren't good, there won't be any more dances for you."

"My last chance," he said. "Who will your next partner be?"

She turned from him to view the crowd now disentangling on the dance floor. "I think—" she said, and then abruptly stopped speaking. As did everyone else. Profound and shocked silence fell over the room as if tragedy had suddenly walked through the door.

What had in fact just entered the room was a sight even more appalling—a fashionable young indigo woman clad in a gold dress, her dark hair spiked with artificial swatches of blonde. Her skirt was cut away in front so that her fine knees peeked out of the sliced fabric; the sleeveless bodice showed off the shape and color of her arms. Those were transgressions enough, but nobody noticed them. Nobody saw the vivid color of her dress or the brassy style of her hair. All eyes were fixed on her escort.

A gulden man.

He looked to be about twenty-five, maybe a little older, in the absolute pinnacle and prime of manhood. He was easily the tallest man in the room, visibly well-muscled, moving forward with all the unconscious insolence of an athlete at the highest pitch of training. He wore some kind of flowing multicolored tunic belted over tight-fitting trousers, but his arms were bare, and his broad chest showed through the open buttons at his collar. His hair was a deep bronze, wickedly alive in the thousand lights of the room. The smooth amber of his skin exactly matched the hue of the woman's gown.

"Let me guess," Nolan murmured in Leesa's ear. "This must be the notorious Aliria Carvon."

But there was no answer from Leesa. He saw her eyes dart around the room, though the rest of her body was immobile, saw her assimilate the looks of horror and condemnation on the faces of the other women in the assembly. No one stepped forward to greet the new arrivals. No one appeared to speak, either to her partner or to her friends nearby. No one changed position by so much as an inch while the silence held and Aliria and her escort stood at the head of the room and, like the others, waited.

And then the orchestra struck up the opening bars to yet another dance number. And Leesa melted back into Nolan's arms without a word of explanation. And all the other women returned to the dance floor in the embrace of their last partners, and they all acted as if not a single thing had changed.

What? Nolan wanted to demand. *What happens now? You can hardly ignore someone you've known your entire life.* But perhaps that was exactly what Leesa intended to do. Perhaps that was what they all intended to do. There was a code that every woman in the room understood, and it would govern all their behavior. They had telegraphed it from face to face in those few fleet moments while the orchestra rustled and the guests postured at the door. And it was inviolable, universal, and cruel, and Aliria Carvon had tested it too far.

When this third dance ended, Leesa spoke as if no great social cataclysm had occurred just ten minutes before. "Try to amuse yourself as best you can," she said, patting him on the cheek as if he were a child. "I'll catch up with you in an hour or so."

"Well," he said, but she had twirled away. A few minutes later he saw her in the arms of a thin, nervous, awkward young man who must be the son or brother of someone who mattered. He would not be able to keep track of her progress for the rest of the evening, this he knew from long experience. It might be time to seek out Melina's friend or sample the refreshments.

But before setting out on either of those quests, he took a moment to look for Aliria Carvon and her ill-chosen guest. No longer standing proud and alone at the entrance, they had joined the others on the floor and were moving with a sinuous grace through the patterns of the latest dance. Aliria was gazing up at her partner, laughing as if he had just said something amusing. He was staring down at her with a peculiar and somewhat unnerving intensity, and he did not look as if he had just made a clever remark. The other couples around them took care not to come too close. Aliria and the guldman danced in a small deliberate bubble of privacy and may as well have been embracing in the unobserved seclusion of her home.

Nolan pushed his way slowly through the crowd, nodding to the people he recognized, hoping he would not accidentally encounter Cerisa again. He had been here less than two hours, and already he was wishing the evening was over. He was relieved when he finally spotted Julitta, standing quite alone under the shadow of some impossibly contorted greenhouse plant.

"I see my prophecy came true," he greeted her. "Melina has abandoned you."

She seemed grateful to see him and gave a friendly smile. "She did warn me before we arrived. But I thought it would be fun anyway."

"And has it been?"

"Not quite as much as I'd hoped."

He nodded. "It never is."

"Things are—livelier at the parties at my mother's house. Not so much politeness and strict decorum."

"Has she taken you in-country yet? This is relaxed compared to some of the formal events there."

Julitta shook her head, the expression on her face somewhat alarmed. "No, but her sister's engagement ball is set for next fall, and she already asked me—"

Nolan laughed. "Oh, you should go. Just once. Just to see what it's like. Stories to tell your granddaughters twenty years from now."

Julitta wrinkled her nose. She did not have quite the delicacy of bone structure that marked Melina, Leesa, all these Higher Hundred girls, but Nolan liked her quirky brows and wide mouth. "I guess this is why our mothers tell us not to date outside our caste."

"Ah, no harm in the dating," Nolan said. "The real heartache's in the marrying. I like Melina. She'll be good to you."

"While she's around," Julitta answered in a low voice, so low that Nolan thought perhaps he had not heard her right. But he did not want to investigate; already this conversation was leading him into matters a little more personal than he liked to explore.

"So! Are you still willing to dance with me?" he said, his voice just a shade too hearty.

"Oh, yes, please! I thought maybe you'd changed your mind."

He was not used to blueskin girls who were so retiring and self-deprecatory. It made him the slightest bit uncomfortable. "No, of course not. I warn you, though, I'm not a very good dancer unless I'm dancing with Leesa. So be patient with me."

She gave him that small, grateful smile again, and put out her arms for his embrace. "I'm sure you're wonderful," she said, and allowed him to lead her onto the floor.

In fact, they made a passable pair, probably because they were both trying so hard not to take a misstep. Her face was furrowed in concentration, so Nolan quickly gave up any attempts at conversation, but that was fine, too. He was not good at small talk with strange women, though this one demanded less of him than almost any partner he'd had.

When the music ended, she gave him a dimpling smile that

lent her a momentary radiance. "That was fun!" she exclaimed. "Thank you so much!"

He laughed and could not help but feel flattered. "Well, I enjoyed it, too," he said. "Would you like another?"

"Oh, *yes*," she breathed, and made him laugh again. Really, this was almost too easy; none of Leesa's friends had ever relished any dance with him this much.

"Well, then," he said, and took her back in his arms.

They danced the next three numbers together, Nolan enjoying himself more and more as the evening progressed. Julitta's naïveté was surprisingly refreshing, and she made no effort to disguise any of her reactions. If she liked the music, she said so. If she thought someone nearby had said something rude, she looked up expressively at Nolan and allowed herself to smile. She thought the food was exquisite. She pointed out the dresses that she liked best (including Leesa's). She even admired the topiary, though she had some doubts about the blue roses.

"But I'm sure they're very fashionable," she added hastily. "I just don't think my mother would like them in her house."

She even had decided opinions on Aliria Carvon and her unexpected guest. For she and Nolan, like everyone else in the room, had kept a surreptitious eye on these late arrivals during the past two hours, and watched as Aliria seemed to grow more and more repentant of her outrageous act.

"She's going to dump him," Julitta said to Nolan after their second dance together. "Watch her."

"She can't. It would be too rude. She brought him here, and he doesn't know a soul in the room."

"She will. She's overstepped, and she knows it, and she'll do anything to get back in the fold."

Nolan glanced down at her curiously, for that sounded like the voice of bitter experience. "Well, I'm sure she's sorry, but—"

"Watch her," Julitta said again.

Sure enough, twice in the next hour, Aliria left the guldman standing alone on the fringes of the room while she paused to chat with reluctant friends. Aliria never seemed less than animated and talkative, but the women she spoke to made cool and brief replies. Each time she left him, the guldman stood where he had been placed, arms folded across his chest, eyes impassively watching the crowd that made every attempt not to look at him.

"I wonder what he's thinking," Nolan said once.

"How to punish her," was Julitta's soft reply.

That had caught Nolan completely by surprise. He glanced down at her again. "Really? If I were in his situation, I would be wishing I could die or grow invisible."

She smiled a little sadly. "That's what you or I would be thinking. But a guldman has his own honor."

Nolan caught himself before he said "Really?" again, and tried to imagine Colt in such a situation. Yes, definitely, he would not melt quietly into the wallpaper. Thinking about Colt here made Nolan a little nervous.

"Maybe someone should get him out of here before something happens," he said.

Julitta shrugged. "Maybe."

But Aliria was not ready to abandon her companion yet. She returned to him after the second extended absence, smiling up at him as if she had great news. The cool, considering look on his face did not change. He allowed her to lead him to the buffet table, and they picked among the offerings for their midnight meal. No one sat at their table while they dined. The guldman ate with a hearty appetite, but Aliria merely played with her food and seemed to lose some of that gaiety she had striven for all evening.

"She's going to dump him," Julitta sang in Nolan's ear. "Not very long now."

Indeed, half an hour later, as they watched, Aliria touched the guldman on the shoulder as if to signal that she would be gone for only a moment, and then strolled over to a group of young women on the other side of the room. For a moment or two, the indigo women stood reserved and judgmental, listening to some low-voiced commentary or plea; and then suddenly their blue bodies closed around the errant noblewoman, and she was locked in their protective circle. Almost immediately, Nolan lost sight of her flame-frosted hair and vibrant gown. Had she been swallowed up or had she voluntarily plunged back into that pure ocean of indigo heritage? Nolan wondered. He noted without surprise that Leesa was standing in the group that had reclaimed Aliria. He saw her blue dress, the color of her skin, indistinguishable from the hands and arms and faces of the women that surrounded her, so that they all seemed to meld together, all become a part of Leesa as he watched from across the ballroom. Into this primal vat of indigo heiresses Aliria Carvon had slipped without a ripple.

"Told you," Julitta said.

"Yes, but what about the guldman?"

"Maybe he'll just go home."

But she did not believe it, and, still thinking of Colt, neither did Nolan. No one else in the room seemed to give him a second thought. He stood by the pot of blue roses, arms still crossed on his chest, hooded eyes still watching the assembled company, and seemed to grow more fierce and more silent as the next hour passed. Perhaps he thought this was another one of Aliria's brief separations and that the indigo girl would return to him with some light apology and a request for another dance. Perhaps, as Julitta thought, he was thinking of revenge.

And then, as Nolan continued to watch, another amazing thing happened—something even more amazing than the daring act that had brought this guldman through the door to begin with. A blueskin woman shook herself free from the indifferent crowd, approached the gulden man, and put her hand on his arm in a gesture of affection or supplication. There was—although the whole crowd had appeared oblivious to the man's existence just a moment before—a collective holding of breath, a dumbfounded moment of silence into which the orchestra's brisk music made a brassy intrusion. The guldman nodded once, sharply, and swept the blueskin onto the floor for the dance.

Julitta was shaking her head, disbelieving. "That cannot have just happened," she said. "Who in the world could she be?"

But just then the figure of the dance turned the couple around, and Nolan could see the woman's face. Oh, she was as proud and defiant as any indigo heiress; she was a daughter of the

Higher Hundred who would not be intimidated by scandal, insult, or ostracism.

Nolan's voice was low and just a little admiring. "Kitrini Candachi," he replied.

CHAPTER SEVEN

The last thing in the world that Kit wanted to do—literally the last, coming even after walking naked through the Complex during the noon lunch break—was attend some awful party at Corzehia Mallin's. She had declined the invitation when Sereva first asked her to go and declined again when her grandmother made it clear that she would like Kit to attend the event. It was only Sereva's flare of anger, two days before the party, that made Kit grudgingly change her mind.

"Do you suppose it costs Granmama nothing to keep you beside her, odd and disgraced? Do you realize how many women just like her would have refused to take you in when you returned to the city? You may despise her way of life, you may scorn everything she believes in, but you owe her something, after all. It would please her to see you make the smallest effort to take your rightful place in society. Would it hurt you so much to attend one party? Would it kill you to smile and make polite conversation? She's an old lady, Kit. How would it compromise you to try to make her happy?"

And there was no good response to that argument for, put in human rather than sociological terms, Kit's refusal was nothing but rude. She suspected that Sereva and her grandmother had secondary motives for getting her out of the house, as well, hoping that a little activity would nudge her from her depression.

She had tried to conceal her low spirits. She had been gracious and responsive when anyone spoke to her, and she had even managed to initiate a conversation or two on her own. They were not deceived, of course. She was heartbroken, and that was something it was impossible to hide. But their manners forbade them to comment.

She had not seen Jex, would not see Jex, had not been importuned by Jex. The world was over. She might as well go to this wretched ball.

Sereva and Granmama had tertiary motives as well for sending her to Corzehia's party, Kit realized later. Unattached indigo males were rare in the Higher Hundred—most were paired off before they were twenty—but there were still a few decent matches to be made, to third and fourth sons, widowers, and recalcitrant young bachelors who had for some reason ruptured their engagements and were living defiantly on their own. Of the three categories, Kit was sure she would prefer someone from the third. No well-bred, well-mannered, compliant, bloodless blueskin boy would do for her.

As if any blueskin man could suit her. Or she him. She was as unlikely to make a match among the Higher Hundred as she was to wake up one morning and find her cobalt skin dyed alabaster. Cruel though he was, indifferent though he now appeared to be, she would love Jex Zanlan till she died, and that was the end of it.

But she had agreed to go to this stupid party, and so she may as well appear to advantage.

She allowed Sereva to dress her in a gown of embroidered white. She wore her grandmother's triple rope of pearls, and pearl bracelets so wide and stiff that she found it hard to bend her wrists. They had arrayed themselves at Sereva's house but stopped by Granmama's to show themselves off to the old woman before they left for the party. Granmama, to Kit's astonishment, appeared for a moment as if she might cry.

"You look like your mother," Granmama said, fingering the stiff folds of the gown in an uncharacteristic moment of sentimentality. "White was her favorite color."

"Sereva picked it out," Kit said awkwardly.

"It's just the right thing," her grandmother said, nodding vigorously and seeming to toss aside the tears. "Perfect color for you. How are your shoes? Comfortable? You'll want to dance, you know."

Kit made a face. "So Sereva tells me. She's made Bascom practice with me all week, but he's much better than I am."

"She has a natural grace," Sereva interposed. "She'll do fine."

"And where's Jayson?" Granmama wanted to know.

Sereva laughed. "He declined the enchantment of the evening, as he put it. I know he hates these sorts of things, so I let him stay home. Just this once."

They took Sereva's limousine to the house not six blocks away. The street was so thick with sleek automobiles that they could have walked in less time, though they would have ruined their elegant thin-soled shoes.

"Is there anybody here I should particularly know?" Kit asked. "So I don't embarrass myself?"

"Well, the hostess of course, but she'll be at the door. And her mother. I'll introduce them to you. The others—you ought to recognize the family names of the Higher Hundred. Be nice to them."

"I'll be nice to everyone," Kit replied. Thinking, *To anyone who bothers to speak to me at all.*

Inside, it was even worse than she could have imagined, a huge festive room crammed with people. Everything about the assembly seemed false to Kit—the proportions of the room, the colors of the flowers, the smiles, the voices. A congregation of hypocrites, she thought. Rich, smug, lethal hypocrites. She wished again she had not agreed to come.

Sereva escorted her through the crowd, stopping now and then to make introductions and exchange quick, gossipy comments. Kit endeavored to keep a polite expression on her face and did not trouble to attempt conversation except in direst necessity.

As when: "Oh, you're Lorimela Candachi's granddaughter! Have you met my cousin Emron? He works in the city, too, don't you Emron?"

"Yes, in the law offices just inside the Complex. I take it you're a city commuter, too?"

Then the desperate reply, for Sereva had not schooled her in this, and surely none of these people would be impressed that she worked in the gulden women's ghetto: "Yes, I'm involved in some social charities. How long have you been in the city?"

"Oh, let's see, not quite two years now. Minus the time I've gone back in-country, of course."

"My aunt can't stand to have him gone too long, you know."

"As a mother, I can perfectly understand that." Sereva's voice.

Emron again. "I have bachelor's quarters around the South Zero exit. I suppose you're somewhere a little more upscale?"

"Oh yes, I live with my grandmother. Not far from here, actually. But I still like to take the Centrifuge into work."

Uneasy laughter from everyone. "*Do* you?" Emron said. "It's so rare that I see indigo women in the ringcars."

"I like them," Kit said, and could think of nothing else to say. But Sereva changed the subject smoothly, and Kit was not required to speak another word, and soon enough they moved on.

And had, essentially, the same conversation with a dozen others. It was beyond dull, it was horrifying, and even Sereva's whispered commentary couldn't spice it up enough to be tolerable.

"Now Emron, he was betrothed to a Twellin girl, but she wouldn't marry him. Says she won't marry anyone, and she's got her jahla girl installed with her on this remote piece of property that she inherited when her grandmother died. Such an awkward thing to have happened, because he's a nice young man."

"A little vacuous, I thought."

"Kit! Well, nobody really scintillates at events like this. But his cousin says he's very bright. You might like him."

"I like everybody," Kit said mildly.

Sereva made a ladylike sniff.

Eventually, the music started, and to Kit's surprise Emron wended his way to her side and invited her to dance. She accepted politely and did her part with all the grace she could muster, which was enough to keep them from crashing into other partners on the floor. There was little requirement to converse, which was a blessing, so Kit was actually grateful when

Emron suggested a second dance. It was a way to kill another ten or fifteen minutes.

When he returned her to Sereva's side, her cousin wanted to know everything Emron had said to her. "I think it was 'Would you dance with me once more?' and 'That was very pleasant,' " Kit recounted. "Neither of us appear to be talkers."

"Well, he's a nice man," Sereva said again. "Maybe I should have him and his cousin over to dinner one evening."

The whole possibility that she could ever be married off to some eligible blueskin beau, discarded though he may have been by someone far more desirable, seemed so remote to Kit that she didn't even protest. Instead, she wanted to know exactly what information she was allowed to give out about her current employment. "What I meant to ask you," she began, but did not have a chance to finish her sentence. The whole room grew taut with incredulity; the force of three hundred stares turned Kit's head toward the door.

"Oh, no," she said involuntarily.

"Unbelievable," Sereva breathed. "Aliria Carvon is wild as they come, but what an insult to Corzehia!"

"That poor man," Kit said.

She received Sereva's scorching look. "That poor *man*? What is he doing here? How dare he walk into a house like this?"

"How dare *he*—" For a moment, Kit's anger was so hot that she felt it sizzle past all her bones. She paused, pressed her lips together, tried to be rational. "*She* invited him. How would it have occurred to him to come here on his own? How could she do such a cruel thing?"

Sereva waved her hands as if to say, *I don't want to argue about this*. "This is real trouble," she said in a worried voice. "I can't imagine—This will ruin the whole evening for Corzehia."

"Maybe they'll leave early," Kit said.

"That would be best."

But the miscast couple stayed for the next hour, and the next. Everyone watched them even when they appeared not to. Even as Kit's hand was solicited for three more dances by young men whose names she could not recall, she could not completely drag her attention away from the gulden man and the indigo woman.

How had he learned these indigo dances? For these were not performed in Geldricht. Aliria Carvon must have taught him over the past week or so; she must have been planning to bring him to the party for some time. Which made her actions now even more reprehensible.

Kit felt herself growing more and more tense as Aliria Carvon spent less and less time with her consort. She knew the temper of gulden men. They did not like to be ignored or ridiculed, and they were unlikely to take either action lightly. But what would he do, could he do, in an indigo stronghold such as this? He could make a scene, of course, but there were plenty of servants to throw him out and prevent him from growing violent.

But she watched him watching Aliria Carvon, and she grew afraid.

"I wouldn't worry too much about Aliria if I were you," said a voice in her ear, and she looked up to find herself accosted by a young woman with a friendly smile and an intelligent expression. "She lives to be outrageous. The party wouldn't be any fun for her if people weren't talking about her when it was over."

"They might be talking about her corpse," Kit said shortly. "That wouldn't be much fun for her either."

The woman turned to survey the guldman, once more standing alone on the edge of the room. "I don't doubt that he'd love to strangle her, but I can't imagine he'd have the chance."

"More likely to cut her throat," Kit said coldly. "He could do it faster than she could draw breath to scream."

The blueskin turned back to survey Kit with interest. She wore her hair cut close to her scalp and jewelry from a jahla lover, so she clearly considered herself both fashionable and rebellious. But Kit was not impressed. Her Higher Hundred breeding molded her cheekbones and settled across her shoulders like a shawl; this was not a woman who strayed too far from the common road. "To slit her throat," the woman said, "he'd have to be armed. And surely, at an event like this—"

"He's got a knife," Kit said. "I guarantee it."

"Maybe somebody should warn Aliria, then."

"I think that would be an excellent idea."

The woman held out her hand. "I'm Melina Lurio, by the

way," she said. "You weren't introduced to me when you came in, but I know your cousin by sight."

"Kitrini Candachi."

Melina smiled, an unexpectedly engaging expression. "Yes, I knew that," she admitted. "I thought it was awfully brave of you to come here."

"It feels more stupid than brave."

"But you've done so well! Emron Vermer is something of a catch, you know. He doesn't have any sisters, so all his mother's property will go to his wife."

Kit could not help staring in indignation until she caught Melina's laughing expression. A joke. "My cousin Sereva is already planning to invite him to dinner."

"I can't tell you the number of eligible men I've been introduced to in the past three years," said Melina. "All completely insufferable, although I know that someday I'll have to marry. I keep waiting to find the least offensive of the lot before I agree to anything. Actually, I'd probably marry Nolan if he'd have me. I can't imagine anyone easier."

"Nolan?" Kit asked politely.

"Oh, a man I work with."

Ah, not only a jahla but a career woman. Perhaps Melina was a bit more outrageous than Kit had thought. "And where do you work?"

"The Biolab. I'm a research scientist. Working on discovering cures to all the worst diseases of mankind, although so far we've just managed to isolate a few viruses here and there. But it's wonderful work. I don't know that I'll ever be able to give it up."

"Then don't. Marry this Nolan and stay in the city your whole life."

"Nolan's betrothed."

"Well, someone just like him, then." Kit could hear the boredom creeping into her voice and hoped Melina didn't notice. But how could she possibly care about the lives of these total strangers?

Melina grinned again; oh yes, she had noticed the boredom. "Good plan," she said. "I'll keep my eyes open. Well, it was charming to meet you. I hope you're able to enjoy the rest of the evening." And with a few more casual words, she left.

Sereva returned moments later, apologizing for abandoning Kit so long, and swept her off to the dinner buffet. They were joined by Emron Vermer and his cousin, so there was more torturous talk that led eventually to the dinner invitation. Which was quickly accepted. Kit kept her gaze on her plate so her combination of panic and disbelief could not shine out from her eyes. Worse and worse. She would be engaged to the man before the evening was ended, and she had not yet said more than a hundred words to him.

Nor would she, if she could help it.

Sereva murmured some excuse, and left Kit with the Vermers at the dinner table. But this Kit could not allow. "I'm sorry," she said with a wide false smile. "There's something I need to take care of." And she jumped to her feet and hurried back into the ballroom to look for the least accessible corner in which to hide herself. She would stay here half hidden by a towering topiary plant for the rest of the night, if need be. She was not exchanging one more word with Emron Vermer.

In a few minutes, her eyes were drawn back to the gulden man, standing as solitary as she but far more visibly at the edge of the ballroom. His eyes were on a knot of indigo women a few feet away from Kit, and his look was coolly assessing. Kit spared a minute to glance at that small group—yes, that appeared to be the miscreant Aliria safely folded into their midst—and then turned her eyes back to the gulden man. He seemed completely unaware of anyone else in the room. He might have been in one of the rough forested tracts on the boundary of Geldricht, stalking wild boar for his evening meal, so completely was his attention focused on his prey. As Kit watched, he gave a short, swift twist of his right wrist.

And invisibly shook a dagger into his hand.

Without thinking, Kit stepped from her concealment and glided across the room, dodging past dancing couples without seeing them. He would wait a moment more, plot his route across the room, she had a minute, maybe two . . . Once he was set in motion, there would be no deterring him. He would dart across the floor so swiftly no one would see him move . . .

Her hand on his arm made him start so suddenly she thought

he would bury the dagger in her throat. The blazing gold eyes fixed on her almost unseeingly; it took him thirty seconds to cool his rage enough to take in anyone, anything, except Aliria Carvon.

"Don't," she said in a low voice. "If you kill her, they will kill you. For absolute certain."

He was still seething, but he had calmed just enough to take in fresh details. The shape of her face, for instance, which so many guldmen knew; the fact that she was speaking in gold-tongue. "Anton Solvano's daughter," he said, and she nodded. Every indigo identified her by her mother's bloodline, every gulden by her father's name. He added, "And that might be a surprising thing, that the child of such a man would care about the fate of such a woman."

Ah, he was using the elliptical, impenetrable dialect; he planned to be difficult. "More surprising that I care about the fate of a guldman fool enough to allow himself to be tricked into such a situation," she retorted, for the direct attack was all that would catch his attention at this stage of his fury. "How could you allow yourself to be brought here? Couldn't you guess what reception awaited you?"

"A man with honor expects honor," he said. "A man who does not receive honor expresses his displeasure."

"Of course you cannot just walk out of here," she said, thinking rapidly. "I understand that. That would shame you."

"There is no shame in a quick death," he said.

"It is stupid to die for a blueshi whim," she said starkly, and that caught his full attention. "There is shame in being stupid."

"It would be interesting," he said in an idle voice, "to know what such a woman values."

"She values her place in her society. She values her reputation," Kit said. She could not come straight out and make the suggestion; he would never do what a woman told him. But at least he was listening. He would let her words spark his own imagination. "She would not want to stand naked before her friends and live to remember her mortification."

"A guldman is proud of his body and not afraid to show it to the world," he said now.

"Well, a blueskin woman is not. She hides that more faithfully than you would hide your father's secrets."

He actually smiled—a ferocious expression, true, but still a smile. "It would be good," he said, "to make the blueshi women relax from all thoughts of danger."

"Perhaps if you danced," Kit said.

He nodded once and shook his dagger back into its hidden sheath. Without asking permission, he put his arms around her and pulled her onto the dance floor. Nothing like dancing with the polite indigo men, not this; he held her hard against his body and tugged her any way he chose. As he had done when he danced with Aliria, he bent his eyes unwaveringly on his partner's face, but Kit could tell he was straining all his senses to gauge the crowd around them. Surely everyone was staring at them. She did not have the heart to look. Surely Sereva would never speak to her again.

On the bright side, Emron would no doubt rethink that invitation to dinner.

There was no need to attempt conversation. They had nothing to talk about and the gulden was, though he appeared oblivious, tracking Aliria's movement within the crowd. Kit concentrated on keeping a pleasant, unconcerned look upon her face. *Dancing with a gulden man at an indigo ball. Oh, of course, I do this every day. An ordinary occurrence.* What could she possibly tell Sereva? That, she supposed, depended on whether or not Aliria Carvon was alive when the gulden left the room.

She lifted her eyes briefly to his face, wondering who he was and how he had met the blueskin girl. Not a city man; no gulden who had been in the metropolis more than a month would have accepted such an invitation. Perhaps he had come in Chay's train and stayed on to see the big town. If he had been part of Chay Zanlan's retinue, Aliria Carvon could have met him at any of a dozen functions. For all Kit knew, Aliria worked in the mayor's office and had spent the past two weeks in this man's company, squiring him to elegant dinners, entertaining him while their bosses talked politics, seeing him at his best and most dangerous—

The gulden wrenched free of Kit, spun on one heel and flung himself a few paces away. Dizzy and thrown off balance, Kit missed most of the motion but heard the single frenzied cry followed by hoarse screams of outrage and a general crashing and stomping throughout the room. She righted herself and whirled around, taking in sights and details: the gulden man sprinting for the door, outstretched hands and blocking bodies powerless to stop him; the roomful of shocked aristocrats, staring, pointing, and covering their mouths with their hands; and Aliria Carvon, stripped of her golden gown, standing naked and shrieking in the center of the fashionable ballroom.

It had not occurred to Kit that she might become a heroine. Half the partygoers, it seemed, flocked instantly to Aliria's side, but the other half surged around her, calling out questions and expressing their fury. Kit felt swamped and panicked, and looked around desperately for Sereva. Who broke through the crowd moments later to sweep Kit into an embrace.

"Oh, honey, what happened, what did he say to you, are you all right?" Sereva demanded in one breathless sentence. "Why did you go dance with him like that, I was so worried—"

"I thought he might—I wanted to distract him," Kit said, stumbling over the words. Sereva was shaking her or—no, that was her own treacherous body, trembling with a fever ague. "He had a dagger, I thought he might hurt Aliria—"

"A dagger!" "A knife!" "The gulden had a dagger?" The cries and questions swept around the circle hemming them in. One voice rose a little more clearly than the others. "Did you see this dagger?"

Kit nodded but addressed her reply to Sereva. "I saw him shake it into his hand. That's why I went over to him. I thought if I could just get his attention, someone might get Aliria safely from the room—"

Sereva clutched her more closely; it was hard to breathe. "Oh, my brave girl!" her cousin murmured into her neck. "Weren't you afraid?"

Actually, yes. "A little," Kit admitted. "But he wasn't really focused on me."

She heard fragments of talk as her story was circulated among the onlookers, and there was an entirely unexpected murmur of approval that drifted back. "Quick thinking!" "There's a smart girl." "It's that Candachi, isn't it? Solvano's daughter?" Then, more ominously, "And he just strolled out the door! That's not right! Someone better notify Ariana Bayless. A gulden man attacking a woman right here in an indigo house—!"

"Damn guldman's got to be brought to justice. Now, before he gets too far—send out a search party—"

Kit freed herself from her cousin's arms and surveyed the crowd, trying to discover who was talking. The last two had been male voices, but everybody in the crowd looked wrathful.

"You won't find him," she said quietly. "He'll probably go straight back to Geldricht tonight."

One of the men snorted. He was a short effete man with pale blue skin and lackluster hair. "He'll stay to brag to his gilder friends how he insulted an indigo queen."

Kit's voice cut through the small chorus of agreement. "He's gone," she said decisively. "And if you bring in the wrong guldman for punishment, can you guess what kind of trouble you'd raise in the city?"

That created an uneasy stir in the crowd. Kit pressed her advantage. "Would you recognize him, if he was brought to you tonight in the company with three other gulden men? I don't think so."

"But surely you would," said a hawk-faced older woman with a low, commanding voice. "You danced with him for ten minutes."

Kit took a deep breath and loosed it on a lie. "I don't think so," she said. "I was too nervous to take in too many details."

"Aliria, then," the woman said. "Surely she could identify him."

Everyone agreed loudly with that, seeming relieved and purposeful at the thought of some definite action. "We'll tell Ariana Bayless in the morning." "Yes, Ariana's the one to handle this." Kit hesitated, opened her mouth, then said nothing. It didn't matter, anyway. The guldman, she was sure, had already put himself beyond their reach. He had satisfied his honor and shamed the indigo girl. Now he would retreat to Gold Mountain and shun the city the rest of his days.

"At any rate, all's well now," one of the men said. That pronouncement too won its supporters, and the crowd around Kit began to dissipate. But not before a round dozen stepped forward to pat Kit on the back, or reach for her hand, and tell her again how brave she was, how foresighted, a remarkable girl, splendid. She was numb with the night's many twists and turns, its public events and dark undercurrents. She shook their hands, accepted their thanks, and with her eyes begged Sereva to take her home.

Worse was to follow. Worse by Kit's standards, anyway. Having become a heroine, she must now be lionized. Emron Vermer was not the only indigo to come calling at her grandmother's during the next few days. She was visited by no less than twenty of the brightest lights in indigo society, all of whom had been present at the ball, all of whom raved about her quick actions and ready wit. Fortunately, she was not required to say much during these sessions, since she couldn't think of a clever or witty remark to save her life. But her grandmother presided over all of the visits, glowing with a fierce satisfaction, and she was able to make all the necessary Candachi contributions to the conversations.

Even Aliria Carvon came to offer careless thanks, seeming much less chastened than Kit would have expected. "I thought it would be more fun than it was to dance with a gulden man," Aliria said in such a disappointed voice that Kit could hardly keep from staring. Then the heiress laughed, shook her head, and laid a restless hand briefly on Kit's arm. "But I find myself hoping you're around the next time I decide to be outrageous. I do believe I have you to thank for saving my life."

But the Higher Hundred, it turned out, were not the only ones to approve of Kit's dramatic intervention. The day after Aliria came to call, a note came to Kit at the charity bank in the Lost City.

From Jex.

Cursing herself and her giddy heart, Kit opened the letter with fingers that trembled. They had not communicated since she had returned his last summons with a curt negative. She had not been able to convince herself that she would never see him again; she had not been able to forget he was alive, in the city, a few miles distant. Three times—she was humiliated to realize she could not stop herself—she had gone to the Complex merely to walk past it, to assure herself that it was still standing and that Jex, therefore, must still be whole and breathing. And yet he would never send for her, she knew this. And she could not forgive him. And so there was no hope and, in the whole world, no joy at all.

But here. A note from Jex. And it said: "Come to me today. I need to see you. Please." She stared, read it again, and a third time. She had never heard Jex utter the word *please*. She had not thought it was in his vocabulary. It was possible, she thought, her brain idly toying with this concept while her body turned to fire and her heart went yapping against her ribs, it was possible that she had never heard a guldman use the word. Only the timid and fearful guldwomen were ever reduced to begging. And Jex had written it out with his usual bold stroke, and it meant in his hand what it meant in anybody's, and of course she would go to him. There was simply no question.

Twenty minutes later, she was in a ringcar, breaking all speed records as she dipped and snaked through traffic in the Centrifuge. One car wobbled and nearly skidded into the curved wall as she darted around it with scarcely enough room to spare. The driver, an older indigo man whose white hair contrasted sharply with his blue skin, stared out at her, aghast and terrified. Remorse made Kit slow down sharply and drive with more care. She did not want to kill herself, after all, before she saw Jex one more time.

Still, she was so eager that she could have outrun the trolley (which moved more slowly, she was sure, than a crippled man on his knees), and she had to force herself to await the elevator at the Complex rather than racing up the stairs. She wanted to appear before Jex with at least a shred of dignity, a semblance of calm.

The same sour guard admitted her with the same obvious disapproval, and she stepped into Jex's apartment, trying not to hold a hand to her anxious heart. He was waiting by the door. It had not even shut behind her before he took her into a crushing embrace.

"Kit! Marvelous! Brilliant and honorable and unexpected all

at once! I could never have forgiven myself if Clent had come to harm. He would be dead by now if it wasn't for you."

She struggled to pull back just far enough to see his face. She didn't want to free herself from those demanding arms, oh no. "You know him, then? What's his name—Clent?"

Jex kissed her on the mouth, then continued kissing her right through his next words. "Yes. He came to town—with my father. I know him from Geldricht, and he—mmm, I've missed you—he wanted to stay. Hecht put him up. I don't know where he—mmm—met this blueshi bitch."

"No one told me. I can't imagine why she would have *thought* of inviting him to this party, and why he would actually go—"

"I told him he should. I thought he would intimidate them. So—if something had happened to him—the fault would have been all mine. Except for you—for you—for you—!"

He tightened his arms again, flattening her against his chest and covering her face with kisses. She couldn't breathe, she couldn't even protest, and she felt a moment's physical panic. Something would break, her bones would snap in his hold . . . She tried to choke out a plea, but his arms loosened of their own accord, and she drew two long, hard breaths.

"Intimidate them," were her first gasping words. "Intimidate the *indigo*? On their own territory? Jex, what were you thinking?"

"Bad idea. I realize that now. As soon as he started telling me the story, I couldn't believe he'd gotten out alive. And then, he told me how you had come to his rescue—"

She couldn't help a weak laugh. Her ribs still hurt. "Funny, the indigo all think I came to Aliria's rescue."

"And I was so proud of you! And I had to thank you myself! And tell you how much I've missed you. And ask you if you've missed me."

"Of course I've missed you," she said in a low voice, but had no time to add anything else, for he kissed her again. Part of her mind wanted to protest, to slow him down, to say, *What about the explosion at the Carbonnier Extension? What about the quarrel we had last time I was here? How much do I really matter to you, and do you care about this stupid Clent more than you care about me?* But she could not think, she could not speak, she could not be anything except almost painfully elated to be in his arms again, existing through his kiss. How had she survived a day without this, how had she survived an hour?

"Look," he said, drawing her farther into the room, for they had stood all this time not two inches from the door. "Look. Don't you think this will work? I'll turn on music, it will drown out any noise. Isn't this clever? Say you'll stay."

And she had, perforce, to turn her head and discover what he was talking about. Even so, it took her a minute to assimilate the significance of the furniture pushed together in the center of the room, a bed quilt thrown over the sofa and the back of the chair to form a tent over a pile of rugs on the floor.

"No one will see us," he said, his voice urgent, his hands upon her body more urgent still. "I'll turn up the music. No one will hear us. Oh, Kit, I want you so much—I can't put it in words—I need you—"

Lovers, here in Ariana Bayless's prison, huddling under a makeshift shelter. She should be horrified, she should be offended, but she had missed his body more than she would miss sunlight if she were buried alive. She turned back to his embrace, strained upward to invite his kiss, and gave her silent consent to the seduction.

They kissed till their bodies were fused, then broke apart, breathless and laughing. Jex reached for the laces on her shirt, but she pushed him away. "No—the cameras—" she said, so he guided her toward the tented furniture and they crawled beneath the blanket. There was almost no room. Giggling and squirming, they kicked off their shoes, pulled off their own clothes, came together naked in the filtered light of the overhead canopy. She was shocked, as she was always shocked, by the gleaming incandescence of his body, almost phosphorescent against the rich, matte surfaces of her own. When he laid his hand against her cheek, she imagined the effect of a lamp held against her skin, lighting up the interior cavities of her skull, giving it an inky luminescence of its own.

"I love you," she said, flinging herself against him, clinging to that golden body with the length of her own so that it passed its ardent light through every knot of muscle, every hollow bone. She could feel herself catch fire, feel her midnight colors pale and scatter before his blaze. "Oh, Jex, I love you, more than anything else in the world."

An hour later, she left the Complex in a state of near-total disorientation. Part of it was the sheer dissolution of self she felt every time she made love to Jex. The first time it had happened, she had felt dazed for a week. She had been unable to tell how much of that was physical, how much emotional; he left her always feeling as if a cataclysm had erupted inside her head, disrupting her balance, changing the molecules of her skin.

But part of it, this time at least, was a niggling, worrisome tendril of dissatisfaction, an inability to overlook completely some of the omissions of this assignment. He had never said he loved her, that was one thing. Of course, it was something Jex rarely said, but still, under these circumstances, it would seem appropriate—in fact, essential. He had seemed more concerned with Clent's fate than her own, that was the second problem; and he had still never apologized for the hateful words that caused the rift in the first place. He seemed oblivious to the fact that he should feel remorse. He seemed to think that the fact that he wanted her should be enough for her.

And for so long it had been. Maybe it still was. Clearly, there was no one among the indigo who could enchant her the way Jex had. She had met the best of them a week ago, and not one of them had moved her to anything except boredom and disdain. Jex was careless always, cruel sometimes, calculating in many ways, but he had a passion for life so furious that it could not help but ignite fires in everyone around him. It was impossible to stand beside him and be indifferent. Long ago, Kit had given up trying.

So he was flawed, but she loved him, and the rupture between them was healed. She could not help smiling, sometimes actually laughing aloud, as she made the long dreary trek back by trolley to the Centrifuge station. Granmama would wonder what had made her so light-hearted. Sereva would guess, and would rage in silence. But there was no help for it. She loved Jex, and he loved her.

The Centrifuge was crowded. She had paid no attention to the passing of time, but this was the homeward hour, when the city's workers left their daytime jobs and flocked back to their houses and apartments. She had to wait thirty minutes for a ringcar. The tunnels were so jammed she could not travel at her usual speeds. Indeed, traffic slowed so much each time they approached a gate that at times she felt lucky to be moving forward at all. Things would only get worse as they neared the South Zero and South One gates, where most of the indigo commuters would exit. If she could think of an alternate way home, she would pull over at one of the West gates and take a surface route out of the city.

But the pace picked up a little as she cleared West Four, and she was able to lift into the upper lane, where she increased her speed. The driver before her was riding so close to the tail of the car in front of him that any sudden slowdown would send him careening into it. Kit eased up on the throttle; she did not want to be part of a pileup. Cars were packed in so tightly there was no room to maneuver. One vehicle spinning out of control would take a dozen or so with it.

She slowed still more as she passed South Zero and dipped to the middle lane, weaving a little to try to get ahead of a cautious driver. Actually, if she dropped to the bottom level, speeded up, and darted back upward, she might be able to—

The tunnels before her blossomed into an orange panorama of fire. She saw the colors before she heard the explosion. The world was nothing but a rage of scarlet dotted with spinning black shapes—ringcars tossed backward by the force of a powerful blast. Even before the first ringcar barreled backward into hers, she felt her vehicle buck and shudder from the shock waves, and she fought the controls to keep it steady. Everywhere around her was the slam and screech of metal hitting stone and metal. She felt a hundred small collisions as ringcars from above and behind knocked into hers and in turn were hit by others. That was all a matter of seconds; then a ringcar before her came hurtling backward, red with fire, black with smoke, and plowed into her car. Her body smashed sideways into the wall; her neck seemed to snap in two. Another collision rammed her against the opposite wall—and then another and another, until she was too hurt and dizzy to count. The heat was impossible. She couldn't breathe. Her right arm felt both leaden and tortured.

Had she broken it? She couldn't twist her head far enough to take a look.

Then behind her, the second explosion went off. She felt it, though she could not turn her head to view it. There was nothing she could do. Oddly, she felt no fear, no panic, nothing but an irresistible lassitude. She closed her eyes and thought how easy it would be to fall asleep.

CHAPTER EIGHT

Leesa left the morning after the ball. Just as Nolan had felt his perceptions alter when she arrived, so did he feel them realign the day that she packed up her belongings and departed. What confused him was wondering what was reality—the world as colored by Leesa or the world viewed through his own lens. For surely the world itself was unvarying, unchanged. He was the one going through permutations.

She had been reluctant to leave because, she said, "All the best gossip will come after I've gone! Let me know the instant you hear anything about Aliria. Corzehia has promised to write, but she's so unfaithful, and I must know everything that happens."

"You could stay another few days," Nolan offered. "I'd be more than happy to keep you."

She laughed. "No, I've been gone too long as it is. Mother will be completely disorganized without me. But you can come in-country anytime to visit me. The spring holidays, maybe. That would be nice."

"That *would* be nice," Nolan agreed, thinking with a moment's longing of the unbroken green vistas of his mother's land. It had been months and months since he'd been back, and the sound of Leesa's voice had the uncanny ability to make him, briefly at least, fiercely homesick. "I'll check with Pakt. Maybe I can get some time off."

"I hope so," she said, and kissed him good-bye once more. They were standing on the street outside his apartment, and her mother's traveling car waited. The driver was an ancient blue-skin, schooled in patience. They could kiss as long as they liked. "I miss you, and I'm not even out of the city. Good-bye. Take care of yourself."

"I miss you more," he said. "Travel safely."

And she had left, and he had taken the Centrifuge to work, and all his perceptions were off. He had to drive slowly, in the bottom lane, for most of the trip, because he did not trust his reflexes in the upper levels. He had not piloted a ringcar since Leesa arrived in town five days ago; he was out of practice. But it was more than that. It had something to do with the fact that Analeesa Corova did not like the ringcars, considered them dirty and noisy and probably dangerous, so that this morning Nolan could not be comfortable and skillful in the Centrifuge as he usually was. He exited at the North Zero gate and ran for the trolley, then looked around and realized that he shared its seats and aisles with albinos, gulden, and indigo of every caste, and this made his skin prickle and his bones attempt to retract into the cavities of his skeleton. He walked the final short distance from the trolley stop to the Complex and felt a marveling, incredulous distaste at the fact that he brushed shoulders with men and women of every race, purchased goods from the same vendors, breathed from the same compressed cubic feet of air. How could this be? They were foreign and inferior; how had he come to overlook, even tolerate, their presence for so long?

Once he stepped inside the Biolab, the feeling for a few hours actually intensified. He made no effort to join the informal morning gathering in Melina's office. He couldn't think how he would answer if Pakt or Colt or one of the other gulden addressed him. But the world seemed strange, askew, even as he sat in his own office playing with familiar figures on his computer screen. What was he doing here, what did these numbers mean, and even if he deciphered them, how had he materially benefited the world? Why was he here in the city when everything of any worth or value was several hundred miles distant, living a far more gracious life?

He kept himself locked in his office the whole morning, laboriously going over old formulas just for the comfort of their familiarity. Eventually, some of the symmetry and intractability of the numbers gave him back a measure of security; these were equations that would not change, that held true no matter how they were influenced by outside factors and new variables. Their core values remained intact. They could shift to new places, new formulas, and mean exactly the same thing.

Melina came for him at lunchtime, stepping quietly into the room and shutting the door behind her. For a second, her clipped hair and lively expression looked wrong to him, out of place, but in a moment Leesa's superimposed image faded. "Good morning," Nolan said formally. "What's going on?"

"Nothing. I just came in to chat. You've been working awfully hard, and everyone just wanted to make sure you were all right."

Nolan raised his eyebrows in surprise. He had forgotten there were other people in the world who might wonder about him. "Oh. Yes. I'm just a little behind here, and I thought I'd try to catch up—"

Melina crossed the room and took a seat close to his, leaning forward to peer at him. "Is Leesa still here?" she asked.

"No, she left this morning."

Melina leaned back in her chair. "Ah. I know. It's a strange feeling, isn't it? When my mother comes in for a visit, I have to take a vacation day after she leaves. I walk around from place to place, reminding myself why I love the city. And I won't let Julitta come over till I'm back to normal. Otherwise, I say things that hurt her feelings."

Nolan stared at her, bringing her fine face into sharper focus. "How can they do that to us?" he asked at last. "What kind of indigo magic is it?"

"Pakt would call it the spell of heritage," Melina said. "Those of us who live in the city have contravened all the social, political, and cthnic laws wc wcrc taught from childhood. Anything you learn that young has a sort of mystical hold on you. It's hard to shake off." She paused, thought of something, and gave a light laugh. "Did you ever have any low-caste servants working for you? Girls from the swamplands where they have those atrocious nasal accents?"

"Yes," said Nolan. "But my mother only hired the ones who had a more cultivated speech. There were vocal coaches, I know, who made a living training low-caste girls to speak like high-caste servants."

"Exactly," Melina said, nodding. "Ours could talk like the Higher Hundred, too. We had one woman who had been employed by my mother since she was about fifteen. She spoke more beautifully than I could. But I happened to be nearby once when her sister and her cousin came up to visit her, both of them talking with that awful swampland accent. In less than a minute, Lelia was talking exactly like them—same inflection, same word choice, same intonation. It was amazing. And I think you and I do the same thing when we're back with our birth culture. We pick up the accent. We revert."

"This seems to go a little deeper than speech," Nolan said.

Melina smiled. "It was a metaphor, silly boy. Of course it goes deeper than speech. But you're also smarter than Lelia, and you can see what's happening to you. And you can make an effort not to alienate your coworkers who wonder why you've suddenly become a snob."

That made Nolan look over at her sharply. "I didn't mean—"

"Relax. I told everyone you were missing your girlfriend. But that doesn't mean they won't notice if the only one you talk to is your blueskin social equal."

"Well. Right. What can I—"

She came to her feet. "We ordered sandwiches to eat in my office. I ordered one for you, and the food's on the way. Will you join us?"

"Of course," Nolan said, standing as well. "Just do what you can to make sure I'm not rude to anyone else."

She laid a mock fist against his cheek. "I'll whop you on the head," she said affectionately. "Is that subtle enough for you?"

"Yes, thank you. I'm sure no one else will notice."

Everyone but Cerisa was in Melina's office. Colt and Hiram had managed to pry open two of the windows, so a shredded breath of the fresh spring breeze was able to curl through the stuffy room. The mingled smells of bread, meat, cheese, and onions made Nolan realize how hungry he was.

"Hey, the hermit's come out to join us," Colt greeted him with his usual edged voice. "Have you decided we're good enough company for you after all?"

Nolan gave a faint smile. "Sorry," he said. "Leesa left this morning, and I guess I'm sort of daydreaming."

"Nothing like food to take your mind off the lack of sex," Colt said, and Melina burst out laughing. Nolan felt a moment's shocked outrage sparkle down his spine, but when he saw Pakt's grin, he managed a weak smile of his own.

"I don't know," Nolan said. "It would have to be pretty damn good food."

"And this isn't," Melina said, handing him a sandwich, "but it will have to do."

"So tell me," Pakt said, pulling up a chair. As usual, the two gulden men, Melina, and Nolan had fallen into a small closed group while the others held their own conversations around them. It struck Nolan as strange that this should seem so familiar, these three friends, these three mismatched cohorts. "Melina tells me you were both at this famous ball last night. What really did happen with the guldman?"

Nolan shot him a quick, uneasy glance, and then looked over at Colt. Pakt seemed genuinely interested; Colt appeared more suspicious.

"How did you hear about that already?" Melina demanded.

"Word travels fast," Colt said tightly.

Melina shook her head in wonder. "Well. I don't want to say anything that riles you, but he was the last person any of the indigo expected to see there. And I know Aliria Carvon was merely trying to be shocking, but I think she really was being deliberately cruel, because she should have known that the last place he would be treated with any civility would be a Higher Hundred ball. He didn't belong there, and the whole evening became awkward because he was there."

"I agree he didn't belong," Pakt said. "But having brought him there, didn't she at least owe him some courtesy? As I heard the tale, she abandoned him the minute they came through the door."

"An hour or so after they arrived," Melina corrected. "But yes, she abandoned him. And yes, she treated him badly. And I for one think she got what she deserved."

"Hardly," Colt said in a low voice. "What she deserved was to be killed for deliberate dishonor."

"An old code," Pakt said to him in a gentle voice. "Even in Geldricht, a death over a dishonorable deed is no longer considered honorable in itself."

"It is by some," Colt said.

"I don't know about Geldricht," Melina said, "but in the city, if he'd murdered that girl, he'd have been dead himself inside of fifteen minutes. Would that have made you any happier?"

Colt gave her a quick frowning look, for he plainly did not like the question restated in that way. "I would not have been pleased with that outcome, but nothing about the story pleases me," he said curtly. "She should not have exposed him to humiliation that way."

"I agree. She's a bitch. But he agreed to go with her, and he must have known he wouldn't be welcome there. What were *his* motives? Did he think he'd be able to humiliate the Higher Hundred just by showing up at the door? That's what I think. Which makes me think he may have gotten a little of what he deserved, too."

"He in good faith accepted an invitation extended by a woman he presumed to be honorable," Colt said coldly. "If he—"

"If *I* invited you to my mother's house for the spring holidays," Melina interrupted, "would you go with me? Knowing what you know about my mother, and my family—and me? Wouldn't you wonder why I'd invited you? Wouldn't you think I only brought you along to create a stir in my mother's house? Wouldn't that give you a moment's pause?"

Colt looked stormy for a moment and then broke into an unexpected, though somewhat alarming, smile. "If I went to your mother's house," he said, "she and her sisters would run screaming through the doors, shouting 'Barbarian!' 'Savage!' 'Save yourselves!' " Colt said disdainfully. "Even if I came with you clinging to my arm."

"Exactly," Melina said. "So why would this guldman expect anything different? He didn't. He knew what he was in for, and he went anyway. I blame Aliria, but I wonder about him."

"It's the curfew," Pakt said quietly.

"What?" the other three said in unison.

"The curfew," Pakt repeated. "It's made all the young guld-men edgy. Spoiling for a fight. I think he was looking forward to having a chance to disrupt an indigo household. I'm just glad it didn't turn more violent than it did, or we'd be seeing a lot worse than the curfew. We'd be seeing arrests and executions."

"Surely not," Melina said.

Pakt nodded. "It happened twelve years ago. An altercation on the street. Who knows who said what first? But the indigo girl claimed that the guldman touched her hand. Touched her hand, mind you—he didn't strike her or hurt her in any way. She screamed assault, and twenty guldmen were rounded up. She chose one at random, for even she admitted she couldn't identify this man she called her 'attacker.' She picked a man, and he was put to death."

"I don't believe it," Melina said.

"Ask Cerisa," Pakt said. "It was her daughter."

There was a long moment of silence, while the blueskins con-templated their sandwiches, unable to take another bite, and the guldmen reviewed the bitter past. Melina was the first to re-cover, shaking her head as if to dislodge a clinging ghost. "But that was twelve years ago," she said. "So much has changed since then."

"Has it?" Colt said.

"We have made progress, certainly," Pakt said. "But there is no true equality between races. I have lived long enough to wonder if there ever will be. Not in my lifetime, I'm afraid."

"And a guldman may still be arrested for taking a woman by the hand," Nolan said. "We've all seen that. But I don't think he'd be executed. Not today."

"I want to see the day when he isn't even arrested," Colt said. "I want to see the day when it doesn't matter."

"You'll see the day when it happens," Melina said, in the quietest voice any of them had heard from her. She reached out and laid her fine blue palm over Colt's large gold hand. None of the rest of them moved; Colt stared at her, unblinking. "But perhaps there won't ever come a day when it doesn't matter."

• • •

The next day's lunch was less eventful, and only involved Nolan and Melina. The topic was again the contretemps at Corzehia's ball, since word of the incident had spread throughout the city. Ariana Bayless's response had been to extend the curfew by a week—although, to give her credit, she did issue a statement saying that any indigo caught baiting a gulden would be subject to swift arrest.

"Trying to be neutral," Melina said, reading over the accounts in the news. She had requested hard copies from both a gulden monitor and an indigo one, saying that was the only way to get a true perspective on events in the city. "But she can't help but appear to favor the blueskins."

Nolan had browsed through the gulden news, utterly fascinated. He had never before had occasion to glance at a gulden monitor, let alone pay for a hard copy to read the pages at leisure. He was surprised to find it printed in dual languages and illustrated with clever, colorful graphics.

"Why do they print it in two languages?" he asked Melina. "Don't all the gulden speak goldtongue?"

"I think it's a political thing," she said, glancing up from her own reading. "Proving to any blueskin who takes the trouble to read their news that they can be fair and accurate reporters."

"Yes, but, unless we could actually read goldtongue as well, we wouldn't know if the translation is accurate," Nolan pointed out.

Melina laughed. "True. I'll have to ask Colt. Maybe they're not so respectable after all."

She returned to her reading, so Nolan continued thumbing through his hard copy. Some of the articles merely repeated the city news, of the day, but others reflected a totally different lifestyle than the one he knew. There were listings of athletic and academic accomplishments, in sports and subjects Nolan had never heard of; there were recipes given with ingredients he could not even pronounce. A small box in the corner of the third page noted "Dishonors done," and gave names and offenses committed by one gulden against another. Nolan read them all, wholly engrossed. Insulted on the street. Word disbelieved. Father mentioned with disrespect. Clan dishonored. A second column across from the offenses listed the status of the event: "settled" or "pending." Details were not given.

He kept reading, learning how to make a tolerable red fabric dye from the inferior pigments sold in city stores, and then how to grow some exotic flowering plant in the imperfect lowland climate. He was all the way to the last page of the printout before he got to the small news item about another death in the gulden prison. He knew nothing about the gulden jail except that it was twice the size of the indigo one, so he read the brief article from start to finish.

"Huh," he said, as he came to the end. "That's strange."

"I know," Melina said absently. "Those recipes. Even if you could figure out how to make it, you wouldn't want to eat it."

"No," Nolan said. "There have been a handful of unexplained deaths at the gulden jail. They think maybe there's a virus or something."

Now Melina looked up again. "A handful? How many?"

"Well, four for sure and one that might have been a virus or might have been the result of a stab wound. The guy was sick before he got knifed," Nolan explained.

Melina rolled her eyes. "Well, four people, that's not an epidemic. I'm sure Cerisa's watching it, though. Any more people die, she'll probably send one of us in."

"You think she knows about it?"

"Cerisa knows everything. She reads the gulden monitors every day. It's where I picked up the habit."

"I wonder if—" Nolan began, but he didn't have a chance to finish the thought. They were hailed by a lovely indigo woman with waist-length black hair and enormous blue eyes. Melina jumped to her feet to give the newcomer a hug and make quick introductions. Nolan smiled politely, but prepared to depart without attempting to make conversation.

"I'll tell Pakt you'll be a few minutes late," he said to Melina. "See you back at the lab."

He meant to ask Colt or Pakt about the translations in the newspaper, but he never got a chance. When he returned to the office, Varella and Hiram and Sochin were huddled together, gazing fearfully down the hall toward Cerisa's closed door. Nolan could catch the sound of raised voices but no distinct words.

"What is it? What's wrong?" he demanded.

"Something to do with Colt," Varella said. "Cerisa's furious."

"Is Pakt in there, too?"

"Yes, but he didn't look too happy either."

They knew nothing more by the time Melina returned, ten minutes later, but on her advice they all scattered to their own offices before Cerisa found them eavesdropping in the hall. So none of them could see exactly what happened when Cerisa's door was flung open and angry footsteps went stomping down the hall. They heard Pakt call out, "No, wait!" and they heard the cool, liquid tones of Cerisa's voice saying, "Don't even try to stop him."

And they all caught Colt's voice, raised for the whole lab to hear, eerily calm and freighted with the singsong malevolence of a curse: "Dishonor to you. Dishonor to your family. May you be punished according to your crimes."

Then more footsteps, quieter this time, and the sound of the outer door opening and falling shut. And then silence.

They had all been afraid to leave their offices for the rest of the day. Dread hung over the lab, seeped in under the closed doors, wound around their uneasy fingers, and made them clumsy at their keyboards. They all listened for the sound of Cerisa leaving, but the sound did not come, and so they felt tied to their own desks and computers until the final hour of the day. In silence, they left their offices, traded glances in the halls, and shrugged to indicate that they had no news. Even Melina, who could glean information from the most casually dropped word, could not guess what had transpired.

"Tomorrow," she whispered to Nolan as they exited from the building. "Come early. We'll ask Pakt."

And so the next morning, Nolan arrived an hour early, to find Melina ahead of him by five minutes. Pakt was not in his office yet, but neither was Cerisa, so they settled themselves in Pakt's chairs and waited.

"It must be bad," Nolan said. "I don't know much about it, but that dishonor thing sounded terrible."

Melina nodded. "I don't know much about it, either. I think it's the worst thing you can wish on somebody."

"Will Pakt tell us?"

"I don't know."

But Pakt, when he arrived a few minutes later, merely nodded when he saw them sitting in his office. The big guldman looked exhausted, his pale skin stretched and blotchy, his copper hair barely combed. It occurred to Nolan to wonder how old Pakt was. Today, he looked eighty. Normally he looked twenty-five years younger. It must be even worse than he and Melina suspected.

"Is she here?" were Pakt's first words. Melina shook her head. "All right. What do you know? What did you hear?"

"Nothing. Except that bit about dishonor," Melina said.

"That's the least of it," Pakt said.

"Well, tell us. If you can."

Pakt dropped heavily into his own chair behind his desk and rubbed his big hand across his forehead. "Cerisa caught Colt going to visit Jex Zanlan," he said.

"Oh, no," Melina said.

"How did she catch him?" Nolan asked.

"Apparently, she had some suspicion that Colt had been to see Jex before. She briefed the guard, and she monitored Colt's lunch hours. She was up there yesterday when Colt dropped by for a visit."

"I suppose that's the end of Colt, then," Melina murmured.

Nolan was wholly confused. "What? So what? Why does she care who visits Jex Zanlan? What's it to her?"

Melina shot him a pitying look; Pakt regarded him somberly. "Jex Zanlan is a known criminal, incarcerated for crimes against the city. Colt is a city employee, and city employees are not allowed to fraternize with felons. If you didn't know that, you should."

"I don't know any felons," Nolan said. "But if I did—I still don't get it. I didn't even know Colt was friends with Jex Zanlan."

"He wasn't," Melina said briefly. "I asked him that once, a few months back. He'd never met him."

"But then—" Nolan felt a nightmarish incomprehension; none of this made sense.

"Jex Zanlan is a terrorist," Melina said in a patient voice. "He and his friends have already blown up at least two buildings, though they've never proved he had anything to do with the fire at the Carbonnier Extension. If Colt never knew him before, he only knows him now by association. He's made friends with Jex's terrorist friends living in the city. Is that the way it goes, Pakt?"

Pakt nodded. "That's the way Cerisa sees it. Frankly, I can't read it any other way myself."

"And if he only knows Jex through these terrorist friends," Melina continued, her voice growing smaller and softer, "what reason could he have for visiting Jex in prison? What information could he have been trying to pass to Chay Zanlan's son?"

Nolan spread his hands, a gesture of ignorance. "I can't imagine! What information? What could Colt know that would matter to Jex—or anyone?"

"It doesn't matter what he actually knows or doesn't know," Pakt said in a slow, hurt voice. "The point is, he's a city employee. He works for a confidante of the mayor. He could have overheard anything, at any time, that would be valuable information to a terrorist and devastating to the city. Whatever reason he had for trying to meet with Jex Zanlan, innocent or not, cannot in fact be innocent, because he is capable of doing real damage just by what he knows."

"He's been fired," Melina said suddenly.

"Yes."

"And you agree with Cerisa," she added.

"Yes," Pakt said. "I do."

"Then he won't—he won't ever be back here," Nolan said, still trying to take it in. "He's gone. We won't see him again."

"I will try to see him," Pakt said. "But I doubt I'll be successful. I was in the room with Cerisa, and I backed everything she said."

Melina suddenly looked frightened. "That curse, as he left— that thing about dishonor—was he saying it to *you*?"

Pakt shook his head. "I don't believe so. But it's possible. I will watch my step very carefully in the next few weeks, in any case."

"Will he—what exactly did it mean?" Melina asked. "Will he try to harm you—or something?"

Pakt shook his head again. He looked even more tired than before. "It was not a challenge to defend my honor—or for Cerisa to defend hers. It was more of a—a statement, a notice to the fates that here walks an unprotected soul." At their matching looks of confusion, Pakt explained. "A man or woman walks through the world defended by his honor. Whatever ill befalls him, if he still has his honor, he cannot be materially harmed. But once his honor is flawed, he has no shield—nothing can deflect from him the tribulations and disgraces that float freely around us every day, looking for a place to settle. Colt was merely pointing out to the universe at large that Cerisa—and, perhaps, I—can be destroyed by some petty trial. I don't believe he will make the attempt to destroy us."

"This is terrible," Melina said. "This is worse than I thought."

"What happens now?" Nolan asked.

"We hire a new technician," Pakt said.

"No, I meant—what happens to Colt? Will he return to his mother's home?"

"His father's house," Pakt corrected. "No, I don't believe so. He has skills, and there are other labs in the city. There's a gulden pharmacy near the West Two gate that could use a man with Colt's ability. I don't see him going back to Geldricht."

"What about Cerisa?" Melina asked. "Is she upset?"

"Furious, yes. Upset? I don't think so. Not about losing Colt. She doesn't really like guldmen."

"She doesn't like any of us," Melina said.

"She hired Colt when there was a quota on. And, make no mistake, he was the best candidate we interviewed. But there's no quota on now, and I'd bet you my father's reputation that she hired an indigo to replace him."

"But there are three other guldmen here," Melina said. "Even if she's going by quotas, she *has* hired fairly."

"She'd get rid of us all if she could do it," Pakt said.

"Even you?" Nolan asked.

Pakt smiled, an expression that was an odd mixture of sadness and anger. "Especially me," he said.

• • •

Naturally, no one talked of anything else for the rest of the day, though the conversations were whispered and tended to break down along race lines. Cerisa, who had been absent much of the past few days, was very much in evidence, saying little to any of them but making sure they marked her presence. As soon as she appeared, they all melted back into their offices to try and continue the hopeless task of concentrating on their projects. Nolan, for his part, accomplished nothing useful the entire day.

As the quitting hour rolled around, Melina appeared in his office. "Are you busy tomorrow night?" she asked.

"I don't think so. Why?"

"I want you to come with me."

"Come with you where?" he replied suspiciously.

"To see Colt."

"To see—" Nolan stared at her. "That can't be a good idea."

Melina shrugged. "That's what Pakt said. Will you come?"

"I don't even know where he lives."

"I got his address from Dade."

"Do you know how to find it?"

"It's somewhere off West One."

"West *One*! Not once in my life have I ever exited there."

"I know. Me either. Will you come?"

"What if I won't?"

She shrugged. "I'll go by myself."

"You can't do that!"

"Well, I will."

"Why don't you just let Pakt go? He said he would."

"Because Colt put a curse on Pakt, and he didn't put one on you and me. Because it's important that we show him that we haven't abandoned him. Because he's a friend of ours."

"I don't know that I'd actually consider him a friend," Nolan said slowly. "I don't know that he actually likes either of us."

She shrugged again. "Fine," she said, and left before Nolan could say another word.

He left without speaking to her again. During the trip home (which seemed longer than usual this night), he could think of nothing else. There was no reason, of course, they should not go to the gulden residential districts off of West One. Those were not areas particularly known for violence, and, like other parts of the city, they were regularly patroled by security forces. And yet—it was the heart of gulden territory within the city. It would be like traveling to a foreign land.

Where the natives were not particularly well-disposed toward visitors.

But he could not let Melina go there alone. Even Leesa would tell him that. And Melina, of course, knew it.

At work the next day, he made no attempt to talk to her, and she only nodded neutrally when she passed him in the hall. He took his lunch with Varella and Hiram (naturally they talked about Colt; there was no other topic), then spent the afternoon going over some of his recent formulas with Pakt. He was in his own office straightening his desk as the final hour of the day passed, and Melina appeared in his doorway.

"Ready?" she asked.

"Just let me turn off my computer," he said. And that was all the discussion they had on the topic.

They took the trolley to the Centrifuge, arguing over who would pilot the ringcar. Melina wanted to be the driver, but Nolan had ridden with her in the past and refused to do it again. She was—like all the indigo women who bothered to use the Centrifuge—a reckless and inconsiderate driver, and he told her so.

"I'm no worse than anyone else," she said impatiently.

"You're worse than I am," he said. "And I'm not getting in the car with you. If you want to drive, you can take your own ringcar, and I'll take the one that comes right after."

She was annoyed but ultimately acquiesced. "Well, I'm driving on the way back," she said. Nolan merely shrugged.

The trip from North Zero to West One was relatively quick, despite heavy traffic; but then, it was only about half the distance of Nolan's normal commute. Nolan felt a strange sense of uneasy excitement overtake him as he maneuvered the craft to the unfamiliar gate. It was ridiculous, he knew, but he half-expected to step through the door onto another planet, ridged with unknown red mountains and lit by an aqueous sun. How could a place only a few miles from his own home seem so foreign and fraught with danger?

Melina had jumped to the curb before the ringcar had come

to a complete halt. Nolan climbed out without bothering to reprimand her, and glanced around him. Same arched stone doorway, same apron of asphalt on the interior side of the gate. As far as he could tell, same hazy sunlight on the other side of the door, a light gradually fading to dusk. The only difference between West One and South Zero was that here, every single commuter besides the two of them was a gulden male.

And they were drawing no little attention.

No one approached them or questioned them, however, and Melina made her way through the crowd at her usual brisk pace. Force of habit, or perhaps surprise, induced the guldmen to fall back for her, but all of them watched her pass and then looked appraisingly at Nolan.

She emerged into the twilight and looked around. "Now, we're supposed to take the Elmtree shuttle, Dade said."

"They have shuttles here?" Nolan asked before he could stop himself.

Melina gave him a look of supreme irritation. "Of *course* they have shuttles here! Nolan, we haven't even left the city limits! Why would you think we'd suddenly wandered into a wasteland?"

"I just—I've never been—oh, never mind."

The bus arrived five minutes later. Elmtree was apparently a popular route, for a crowd of gulden men scrambled for the bus as soon as it pulled to the curb. Luck had positioned the blueskins in just the right spot; they were among the first to board. Nolan's eyes went immediately to the back of the shuttle, where twenty or thirty gulden women were crammed together in seats that were clearly meant to accommodate about half their number. The benches up front, he guessed, must have been left empty for the men.

Melina, oblivious, headed for the first unoccupied seats and sat down. "I think," Nolan began, but she grabbed him by the wrist and pulled him down next to her. "I think women are supposed to sit in the back," he whispered in her ear.

"Nonsense," she said aloud. "It's a public conveyance, and I can sit anywhere I choose."

The rest of the seats filled rapidly, and about a dozen men remained standing in the aisles, wrapping their hands around chrome rails. The bus lurched forward, and Nolan was thrown against Melina. He righted himself quickly and took a furtive glance around.

No one was actually staring at them, though he would have sworn all eyes were turned in their direction. A few of the riders glanced his way, took a few moments to consider Melina, then returned their attention to their printouts or their conversations. Yet every nerve in Nolan's body screamed its awareness that he did not belong here. He felt like a foreign particle introduced to a host body that had begun to marshal all its resources to throw him out.

"We should be on the shuttle fifteen minutes or so," Melina said. She was looking out the window, apparently watching for landmarks, for every once in a while she nodded. "We want to get off at Cloverton."

"And then what?"

"And then we walk."

"How far?" Nolan asked nervously.

"A few blocks. I don't think the exercise will be too much for you."

"I just thought—it's going to be dark soon, and—"

She turned to give him a malicious smile. "Just think how dark it will be when we come back this way," she said.

Which made his stomach lurch with apprehension. He did not know why he felt so certain they would be lucky to return from this adventure alive.

"Here it is," she said suddenly and jumped to her feet. Nolan scrambled up beside her and began excusing himself as he edged through the press of guldmen. Everyone politely squeezed back to allow him and Melina room to disembark. Surely it was his imagination that one of them pantomimed a quick kick to his backside.

"Well, isn't this pretty!" Melina exclaimed, pausing a moment on the street corner to survey the scenery. Nolan, who had spent the whole ride watching the action on the interior, now caught his first glimpse of a gulden neighborhood. It stopped him in his tracks.

Instead of the stark blacks, whites, and grays of his own district, here the buildings wore festive pastel hues on their painted brick, on their draped awnings, on the flags and signboards and shutters that decorated their exteriors. There were plants and flowers everywhere, climbing up trellises, pouring out of hanging baskets, peering out from the windows of houses and retail shops. Every storefront featured a fountain of varying complexity, and the sound of splashing water murmured up and down the street.

"Well, I think I like this much better than the neighborhood where I live," Melina said.

"You don't think it's a little—inelegant? Overdone?" Nolan asked.

"No, I think it's cheerful."

"You'd get tired of it after a while."

"Well, I don't suppose we'll be here long enough to find out."

"Which way now?"

She pointed. "North on Cloverton. To number 1811."

They walked slowly down the street, Nolan at least trying not to gawk. Melina frankly looked about her, lifting her arm to point to views she found particularly intriguing. Nolan hoped no one was watching from the windows, indignant at the blue-skins sightseeing through their neighborhood. The few other pedestrians they encountered tended to be young men, apparently heading home from work, and older women shepherding flocks of children down the sidewalk. They saw no young women out walking alone. They saw no couples.

"Is there a curfew for girls?" Melina wondered.

"I don't know. You see gulden women in the city all the time."

"Older women," Melina said thoughtfully. "We'll have to ask Pakt."

It was about an hour before true dark by the time they arrived at number 1811. The midsized house was small by indigo standards, but comfortable-looking nonetheless, and certainly respectable enough for the locale. It was painted with colorful stripes of sky blue, pale orange and yellow, and its slanted roof was copper tile. Out front played a small fountain in the shape of a lily whose petals narrowed into streams of water.

"Not the sort of place I would imagine Colt coming from," Melina said under her breath. "But I rather like it."

"Does he live here alone?"

"I didn't ask. I wouldn't think so. Let's see who's home."

The woman who answered the door was a tall, beautiful, tawny-skinned woman about Melina's age. She had the longest, thickest gold hair that Nolan had ever seen and eyes the color of amber. She looked terrified to see them. She seemed to want to crouch behind the door to hide as much of herself as possible, and her flustered greeting was incomprehensible.

Melina stepped forward and spoke in her usual brisk voice. "I'm Melina Lurio, this is Nolan Adelpho. We come from the Biolab in the city. Is Colt here?"

The woman stared at them, her eyes growing even wider. Her hands appeared to tighten on the edge of the door. "Colt?" she repeated and then asked a question in an unfamiliar language.

"Oh, for heaven's sake, she can't speak bluetongue," Melina said, her voice a mix of frustration and disbelief. "How can anybody live in this city and not bother to learn the language?"

"Maybe she never ventures out of the neighborhood," Nolan said. "Maybe she's just moved here."

"What do you suppose she is to Colt? Sister? Wife? Lover?"

"He doesn't have a wife. As far as I know."

"I suppose it doesn't matter what her connection to him is. Listen, young lady," Melina said. She switched to a slow, emphatic tone of voice and asked a question in a set of words Nolan could not understand.

"I didn't know you spoke goldtongue!" he exclaimed.

"I don't. Just enough to ask if anyone here speaks our language. I had to learn a few phrases when I did a summer internship at a clinic in the Lost City. I can say some other choice words, too, like 'fever' and 'broken bone,' but I don't think any of those will help us now."

The gulden woman had nodded vigorously and replied at length in her own language, but Melina flung up a hand to cut her off. She repeated her request and then assumed an impatient, imperious pose. The woman spoke again, a little more briefly, then disappeared into the recesses of the house.

"Is she coming back?" Nolan asked.

"I have no idea."

But she did return, less than five minutes later, followed by a boy who appeared to be about fourteen. He was tall and gangly, awkward for his height; his face looked incomplete, as if he had not yet mastered all its expressions. But there was an indefinable arrogance to his carriage, an incipient self-assurance that made it clear he couldn't imagine what blueskins were doing at his door and he hoped he would not have to deal with them for long.

"Can you speak bluetongue?" Melina demanded.

He looked down at her out of mint-green eyes and visibly wondered at her manners. "There is a woman at my door speaking the indigo language," he said, pronouncing the words with a perfect accent. "Is that why I was called here?"

Oh, yes. Nolan had forgotten. This was the way an uncooperative gulden would always speak to an impatient blueskin, in the most roundabout, indirect fashion imaginable. At the lab, they were all too busy to indulge in such affectations, though Nolan had heard Colt and Dade and even Pakt use such oblique commentaries when they were dealing with vendors or security officers or anyone else who had raised their ire. The practice nearly drove the efficient Melina mad; she could not stand any senseless waste of time.

"Yes. To interpret for me. I am Melina, this is Nolan, we're friends of Colt's. Is he here?"

"Strange to think that a guldman might have friends among the indigo," the boy replied.

"Strange but true. We've come to offer him help—anything he might need. Can you tell him we're here?"

"With such a commotion at the door, anyone within would know there are visitors."

Melina digested that a moment in silence. "You mean he's *not* here? Will he be coming home anytime soon?"

The boy looked up at the sky as if gauging time. The saffron twilight had deepened to an opaque blue; filmy curtains of night seemed to hang suspended between each of the neighborhood houses. "Wherever a guldman is now, he will most likely stay till dawn," was the unhelpful reply.

"What? He's not coming home? Is that what you mean?"

Nolan touched her on the arm to catch her attention. He thought she might be ready to grab the boy and give him a good hard shake. Bad idea, though. "Curfew," Nolan said briefly. "If Colt's not home now, he can't come in after dark."

"Damn. I forgot. A wasted trip, then."

"Not if the point was to let Colt know you were worried about him."

"I wanted to talk to him. I wanted to see his face."

Nolan addressed the boy. "Can we leave him a note? Can you bring us something to write with?"

The boy didn't seem to be able to come up with any oblique way to say "yes" to that, so he nodded and ducked away from the door. Melina paced back and forth on the narrow porch, more agitated than Nolan had expected.

"Don't be so upset," he said. "You couldn't do anything for him even if you saw him face-to-face. He might not even be pleased to see you. Did you think of that?"

"Of course I thought of that! He'd probably throw us out in the street if he saw us! It's just that—I'm worried about him. He can't come to me if he needs something. And I'm just afraid—he'll do something stupid. I wanted to tell him not to."

"He's Colt," Nolan said. "He'll do whatever he wants."

The boy reappeared a few minutes later with several sheets of paper and a couple of pens. Clearly, he thought each of the visitors might have something to communicate to Colt. Nolan took a page and a pen and wondered blankly what he might write to the guldman. He had never considered Colt a friend and rarely even an ally. He was always a little on edge around the gulden man, afraid to make some unwary remark that would fire the combustibles that appeared to lie, ready mixed, just beneath the surface of the golden skin. And yet Colt was an integral part of Nolan's life in the city, one of its colors, textures, sounds, delights, trials, foreign frightening elements that had become, over time, part of the pastiche Nolan had grown to love. He could not imagine the lab without Colt. It would seem wrong, a chemical formula that would not combine. The loss of Colt would trigger some malfunction that would throw something else out of synch, and eventually the whole place would fall into chaos and disorder.

Melina was hastily scrawling out a long message; she seemed to have no trouble deciding what to say. But Colt had touchy notions of honor and pride, and Nolan did not want to run afoul of those by any expressions of sympathy or offers of aid. It was pointless to ask Colt to keep in touch—he wouldn't—and anyway, what could they possibly talk about if they attempted a social meeting? So Nolan braced his paper against the front of the house and wrote only, "We miss you already. Nolan" and folded up the paper.

Melina was just adding her signature to her message, and soon enough the young guldman was accepting both their notes. "Now, you'll give this to him as soon as you see him, won't you?" Melina said sternly. "It's very important. You *will* see him again, won't you? He'll come back here tomorrow or the next day, won't he?"

"A man always returns to his home," the boy replied. Melina seemed satisfied with that, but it made Nolan wonder. This might not be Colt's home after all; and then who would be poring over their notes the instant they were gone?

"Well, thanks. Really. You've been helpful," Melina said, and even Nolan was not sure if she was sincere or sarcastic. "I guess we'll be going now."

"Then go," the boy said, and closed the door on them before they could say another word.

"Well! That was an interesting cross-cultural adventure!" Melina said as they stepped onto the street, back in the direction of Elmtree. It was true dark now, and the only illumination came from the houses themselves—and that was directed more inward than out. Indeed, the gaily colored buildings seemed like nothing so much as oversized lanterns laid down on either side of the road. Nolan stepped carefully. Melina, of course, strode on without once looking at her feet. "That boy! Could he have been less helpful? Whoever taught them to talk that way?"

"Maybe that's not how they talk to each other in goldtongue. Or maybe it is. All that honor stuff. Maybe they phrase things so indirectly to avoid offending anyone."

Melina snorted. "Ridiculous way to behave. Never get anything accomplished. Pakt and Colt never talk like that."

"Pakt and Colt know how to get along in the blueskin world," Nolan said. Or at least Pakt did. Whether or not Colt had really learned the trick was yet to be seen.

The trip back seemed longer than the trip out, mostly because of the dark. They had arrived at Cloverton before it occurred to either of them to wonder if buses would be running after dark—particularly now, with the curfew in place. In fact, since most drivers were guldmen, the answer was probably "no," which meant they faced a long, dreary trudge ahead of them.

"Well, nothing to do but start walking," Melina said after they had waited on the corner for a few minutes and seen no other traffic. The retail stores at the intersection had all been closed for the day, so there was no shopkeeper to ask for information, and the only souls who appeared to be out at this hour were young children playing in their own yards. The guldmen, it appeared, were obeying the curfew; and the guldwomen, or so they had guessed, were not out much anyway. Therefore, they were on their own.

"It would have been nice if Dade had mentioned this little transportation problem," Melina grumbled as she stumbled once over an obstruction in the road. "I might have timed our visit a little differently if I'd known the shuttles weren't running."

"He probably didn't think you'd really come."

"I'm beginning to wish I hadn't. How far do you think it is to the Centrifuge?"

"Five miles. Maybe less. Take us about an hour and a half."

But they had not walked more than fifteen minutes down Elmtree when Nolan heard the lumbering, sighing wheeze of a big vehicle coming up behind him. He spun around and began waving his arms before Melina had even caught the sound. It might be too dark for the driver to see them, but Nolan hoped his white shirt would reflect some of the nearby light—and sure enough, much to his relief, the bus groaned to a halt beside them in the road.

"Thank goodness you saw us," Melina exclaimed, hopping aboard. The driver was a gulden woman who looked to be in her late fifties; no curfew on her. There were no other passengers. "We weren't even sure there'd be a bus out this time of night."

The woman merely nodded, clearly not understanding a word. "Centrifuge?" Nolan asked, pointing straight down Elmtree. She nodded twice, repeating the word back to him. He was washed with a complex mix of relief, exhaustion, elation, and guilt (he was ecstatic to be getting out of this neighborhood, the quicker the better, but he felt bad about the intensity of the emotion). They were on the road to home.

He took a seat across the aisle from Melina, for he had nothing to say to her in bluetongue, goldtongue, or charade. This time, he watched the neighborhood unfolding outside his window, noting how the houses grew smaller and more dilapidated the closer they drew to the Centrifuge. He would have been truly alarmed to be passing through this district on foot as the night grew blacker around them.

But now they were delivered, safely and rapidly, to their destination, and soon they were in the familiar confines of the Centrifuge, albeit at an unknown gate. There was even a car awaiting them.

"You go to South Zero, right?" Melina said, letting him precede her so he could take the controls. "I'm South One. Let's just share this one, and I'll drop you off."

"Sounds good," he said, and pulled away from the curb. That was all they said to each other until they made brief good-byes at South Zero, and Nolan was finally on his way home.

And that day had been strange enough, but the next day was even stranger. Pakt had called an afternoon meeting that kept them all in the lab an hour past their usual closing time. Hiram and Varella, squirming in their seats, made no attempt to hide their disapproval of such a use of their time. They had barely wrapped up their discussion when they heard a faint "boom!" echoing through the mazelike baffles of the city's skyscrapers. They all looked at each other in bewilderment.

"Did anybody else hear that?" Hiram asked.

"Was it inside? Outside? It sounded so far away."

"Was it an explosion?"

"I can't see anything out the window."

"Wait! That was another one! I could feel it!"

"What direction did it come from?"

"West, I think."

"No, south."

"Could it have been something important?"

Almost as if in answer, the city began to wail with sirens, originating from police posts all over the city but converging toward one central spot. "Turn on the monitor," Pakt said suddenly. "I think this is bad."

So they hurried into Pakt's office and turned on his little monitor and huddled around it in silence until a shaken indigo broadcaster appeared on screen, interrupting an everyday program.

"We've just learned there's been a series of explosions near the South Zero exit of the Centrifuge," the reporter said in an unsteady voice. "Medical and police units are on the way. At this time, we don't know how extensive the damage is or how many people have been hurt. Officials are closing the Centrifuge immediately, leaving thousands of commuters stranded, in the city and in the tunnels themselves. We'll be back with more news when we have it."

The screen went blank, then returned to its scheduled picture. They were left staring at each other, drenched in horror. "The *Centrifuge*," Varella said, but there was nothing any of them could add in elaboration. No one needed to point out that, without Pakt's impromptu meeting, nearly all of them would have been in the Centrifuge at that exact moment, heading into the scene of the blast. If the explosion had been fatal, Pakt had just saved all of their lives.

CHAPTER NINE

At first, Kit was embarrassed that she had fallen unconscious. She had been trained in basic first aid; she could have been of some help as the medics fought through the smoke and rubble to find the broken bodies in the downed cars. Then she learned that, of the three hundred men and women caught in the explosions, only thirteen had survived. Then she felt lucky.

These were the emotions that came to visit her over the next twelve hours, when her mind was clear and she could actually think. The hour she had spent on the tunnel floor, semiconscious and bleeding in her crumpled car, was pretty much a blur, and the following hours of rescue and medical attention were hard to reconstruct coherently. They had taken her to the gulden hospital, that she remembered, because it was closest and because the two other survivors they had recovered at that time were both guldmen. The pain had made it hard to focus as they wheeled her through the neat, bright corridors, but she did notice that nearly all the faces peering down at her were gold. It confused her; she thought she was somehow back in Geldricht, that the explosion had catapulted her across the Katlin Divide and into the territory with which she was most familiar.

"Is Chay here?" she asked one of the attendants, causing him to look down at her strangely and check her temperature. "Is Jex?"

"Do we have an I.D. on this one?" the doctor asked someone striding along behind him. He spoke bluetongue, so he must have thought she was conscious enough to understand him. "We're going to need to notify relatives."

"I'm checking her handbag right now. Looks like—Candachi. Might not have relatives in the city, though. Sounds high-caste."

The doctor was gazing at her again, clearly impressed or at least informed. He knew who she was. "Oh, she's got people in the city," he said softly. "She's Anton Solvano's daughter."

"Who?"

He shook his head. "Never mind."

She drifted off again as they began to examine her, though she had the impression they badly wanted her to stay awake and talk to them. It seemed like minutes later, but was probably hours, that she woke to find Sereva in the room, speaking in a calm voice with the physician. "How soon can I take her home?" Sereva was asking. "How soon can I get her to a doctor?"

"*Hela*, I am a doctor," was the edged response.

"I mean—I'm sorry—but I'd rather have my own doctor see her."

"Have as many doctors see her as you'd like. She has a concussion, a sprained wrist, a twisted ankle, a possible broken rib, and she is about the luckiest woman in the city. I don't want her moved for twenty-four hours, because I don't like the way she keeps passing out, but after that, if she's no worse, you can take her to any medical facility you choose. But she's not leaving here tonight."

"But—" Sereva looked around fearfully, as if afraid to find mold growing on the walls and insects feeding on the patients. "But she can't stay here."

"I assure you, my staff and I are fully capable of setting the broken bones and monitoring the pulse rates of even the most select heiress of the Higher Hundred," the doctor replied in an icy voice. "And judging by the vaccination scar she has on her left arm, she's spent some time in a gulden clinic before this. That's a shot they only give in Geldricht, for a fever you can't catch here. I don't think Anton Solvano's daughter will suffer at my hands."

It was the longest, most direct speech Kit remembered hearing from a gulden addressing a difficult indigo, and it made her appreciate the doctor even more. She wanted to say so to Sereva but she couldn't make the muscles of her mouth work. It was too much trouble; she went back to sleep.

When she woke, it was somewhere past midnight, and Sereva was sleeping in a chair by her bed. Kit was a mass of aches and bruises. Her brain seemed to be holding its breath inside her skull, trying to puff itself up so large that it burst through the bone. The whole left side of her body throbbed in time with her heartbeat; her arm was cocooned in something soft and clumsy. Her head hurt so much that it was hard to think clearly, but at least her thoughts felt as if they could be forced into some kind of order.

"Sereva," she called and had to repeat the name twice before her cousin stirred. Then, instantly, Sereva was on her feet and bending over the bed.

"Kitrini! You're awake! How are you feeling?"

"Awful. I hurt all over. I'm not even sure what happened."

"There were a couple of explosions in the Centrifuge this afternoon. Hundreds of people killed. Only a few of you got out alive. They sent a message to Granmama and it—Kit, she actually fainted. I think she's so much frailer than we realize. I didn't know if I should stay with her or come to you, but Jayson's with her, and he called a while ago to say she's fine now. But you! You were so pale and crazy when I came in. You didn't recognize me—you didn't speak to me—"

"I recognized you." But now a new pain was settling in over Kit's chest, weaving itself through the warp of her ribs and troubling her breathing. "You said—explosions in the tunnel? Caused by—what?"

"They don't know yet. Could have been some electrical malfunction, I heard."

"Or it could have been a bomb. Bombs."

"Maybe, but that's too horrible to think about."

Kit knew she would be unable to think of anything else. "When will they know? Are they investigating? Did they shut down the tunnels?"

"Oh, yes, the Centrifuge is closed for the next week at least. There's a two-mile section between South Zero and One that's completely caved in. Nobody knows how long it will take to repair. Ariana Bayless is already trying to figure out how to route commuter traffic into the city. They're offering incentives to workers to stay in the city at special hotel rates, and they're planning to overhaul all these old buses that haven't run for years. It's going to be a mess."

It was Jex. Surely not. Surely, not even Jex would blow up hundreds of people during the commuting hour, just to make a point, just to infuriate Ariana Bayless? *It was Jex.* He was not so cruel, so reckless, so prodigal with others' lives. *It was Jex.* But she had just left his arms, and he knew she would be taking the Centrifuge home. He loved her; he would not have sent her into such danger without a warning, would not have allowed her to leave him blithely to steer straight into certain carnage. *It was Jex. It was Jex. It was Jex.*

Sereva was still talking, nervously, as if she couldn't stop herself. "I can't imagine why they brought you here, but that arrogant doctor—or whatever he is, I'm sure he doesn't have an actual degree—he wouldn't let me move you to a real hospital. So I said, then I'll have to stay, I'm not leaving her there alone all night with people who can't be trusted to care for her—"

"The gulden have superb medical training facilities on Gold Mountain," Kit said faintly. Her brain squeezed against her skull with an insistent pressure; surely her head was about to shatter. "They produce marvelous doctors."

"Well—maybe for their own kind—everybody knows that their blood is just a little different from ours—"

"It is," Kit agreed. She closed her eyes, hoping to ease the pain a little. "It's weaker. More vulnerable to disease. But their bones are stronger. Other than that—not much difference."

"You may say that," Sereva said, "but I don't believe it." She may have added more, but Kit did not hear it. She curled in upon herself, trying to ease both the pressure in her head and the pressure on her heart, and fell asleep once more.

In the morning, except for a nagging headache and a leaden pain throughout the left half of her body, Kit felt relatively normal. Clear-headed, at least. She was hungry, though when they brought her food, it suddenly did not seem like a good idea to eat it. However, when a nurse told her she couldn't go home till she'd kept food down for at least six hours, she ate about half the meal, and she actually felt better for it. Late in the afternoon, a gulden doctor came in to examine her—not the one from the night before—and pronounced her well enough to leave.

"But I'd have her checked by her own doctor in a day or so," he advised. Sereva answered with a sniff and a look that meant *I certainly intend to!* but Kit smiled at him warmly and thanked him and the hospital staff for their care. They took a limo to Sereva's, for Granmama did not feel well enough to watch the invalid, and the boys came rushing out to help her to the door.

"Here, Kitrini, lean on me! I'm so strong!" Bascom exclaimed, tugging her arm over his shoulder and putting a hand at her waist.

"Kitrini, you look terrible!" Marcus informed her, dancing before them up the wide walk. "What's a concussion? Does it hurt? Will your brain burst open?"

Kit laughed weakly. "I don't *think* my brain will burst open, but I wouldn't swear to it at this point. Bascom, a little slower, please? My ankle hurts."

But eventually she was ensconced in the room she had claimed a few weeks ago, pillows behind her back, under her foot, and under her elbow. Bascom was volunteering to sleep on the floor outside her door in case she became wakeful during the night, and Marcus said he would be happy to stay home from school all week to amuse her.

"I don't think either of those sacrifices will be necessary, thank you very much, but you might check in with her every once in a while to see if she needs anything," their mother told them. Her voice was stern, but she was smiling, and she reached out a hand to play with Marcus's long, tangled hair. "She should be up and on her feet very soon."

"I'll have to send a note to Del and tell her I won't be in for a while," Kit said, sinking back into the pillows. Ah, this was heaven after the flat mattresses and severe pillows of the hospital.

"Who's Del?" Sereva asked.

"The woman who runs the charity bank."

"All right. Anyone else I should contact for you?"

Jex. If he had not set the bombs, he surely would have heard about them, and he knew when she had left the Complex. He would be frantic, wondering if she was hurt or dead, cursing himself for not keeping her there an hour longer, half an hour— fifteen minutes would have saved her from the blast—

"No," she said, closing her eyes against every imaginable kind of pain. "No one else needs to know."

The next two days passed quietly, almost pleasantly, with Sereva and her family going to elaborate lengths to make sure Kit was comfortable, well-fed, and entertained. Granmama came to visit, looking, as Sereva had said, so fragile and old that Kit wanted to jump from the bed and ease her into a chair. Her skin looked dull and faded, exposed overlong to sun or some other impossibly stressful element; her coiled white hair seemed thinner, more brittle. But her intense blue eyes were bright as ever, and her spirit seemed completely undaunted.

"Haven't you caused me enough worry already?" the old lady asked as soon as Marcus and Bascom had helped her settle in. "Now you have to go soaring through explosions? What's the matter with you? Don't you have any sense at all?"

Marcus and Bascom stood riveted with shock, but Kit burst out laughing. "You're right, Granmama, I had a concussion just to upset you. I hope it worked."

The old lady shook a finger at her. "Trying to send me off before my time. Think you're going to inherit all my property. One more trick like this and you'll be out of the will forever."

"I thought I was out of the will, anyway. I *hoped* I was! Leave it all to Sereva. She's a much better steward than I am."

"Well, I would, if she'd bothered to have a daughter. Now, maybe if these two young rascals marry well, I'll give their brides some tidy property. Only if I like the girls, though."

Bascom was listening closely, but Marcus had wandered over to the window and picked up a discarded book. Bascom said, "That's a long way off, Granmama. I won't marry for years and years, and Marcus—"

Now he was the one to have a finger pointed in his direction.

"I'm already making plans for you, young man! It's never too early to pick out the proper girl. You keep that in mind. You marry a girl your great-grandmother likes, you can have a nice piece of land. Any of my estates you like the best? Hey? You've been to them all. Which do you like?"

"Granmama, he's just a boy—" Kit murmured, but Bascom had come closer, a considering frown on his face.

"Well, my father always says Govedere is the most profitable of your lands, but I think Munetrun is my favorite," he said seriously. "I like the house the best. It's not as grand as Govedere, but I feel happy when I'm there. And I like the land. It's so wild. I feel like you could go live there and no one would come bother you for years."

Granmama was smiling oddly, but she kept her voice gruff. "And that's what you want? To live tucked away somewhere completely isolated from the rest of the world?"

"Sometimes," he admitted. "The city's so crowded. Sometimes, I can't concentrate. Sometimes, I just want to get away from everybody."

"Well, Munetrun's the place for that," Granmama said, and now she allowed her smile to grow. "That's where your great-grandfather and I lived when we were first married. I've always loved that estate. Doesn't earn a damn dollar, of course, and it takes so long to get there that you've practically aged a year before you arrive, but that's the place I'd choose, too. Not that you'll get it. Fairenen or Glosadel is more like what I'd bestow on your bride—but only if I like her."

"And I would be happy to have either of those, Granmama," Bascom said, so seriously that both Kit and the old lady started laughing.

"So you shall, then," Granmama said in delight, "so you shall."

Kit was up and walking on the third day, though she was cautious about putting weight on her left foot, and her first expedition tired her more than she would have believed possible. Sereva's doctor had come twice and pronounced her well on the way to mending, though he warned her to watch for headaches and come instantly to see him if any became too intense. When she asked him what limitation she should put on her activity, he smiled somewhat sardonically and said, "You'll know." Which had proved to be true.

Late in the afternoon of that third day, while the boys were still in school, Sereva was at the office, and Jayson had left on errands, a maid came to find Kit in her bedroom.

"*Hela*, there are people here to see you," the girl said. She spoke so oddly that Kit felt a sudden flush of alarm. There had been any number of visitors in the past few days—Emron Vermer and his cousin, Aliria, Carvon, even Corzehia Mallin and her husband—all bringing flowers and condolences to the downed heroine. Kit had told Sereva that she absolutely refused to see any of them, so Sereva had merely carried reports of Kit's condition to her well-wishers. But none of the servants would seem so unnerved at the arrival of more of these high-caste callers.

"What kind of people, Catie?" Kit asked.

"They say they're from the mayor's office. They look like security officers."

Ah. Kit had not expected this, but she should have—in fact, she was surprised it had taken so long. "Well, bring them up to see me. And bring us all some kind of refreshments. Be polite."

"Of course, *hela*."

A few minutes later, Catie had opened Kit's bedroom door to show in a man and a woman dressed in the shapeless khaki uniforms of the city police. Kit had managed to arrange herself on a quilted chair so they didn't find her lying helplessly on her bed, and she graciously indicated that they could seat themselves on a small sofa nearby. They complied, glancing around the room with expressions that were meant to be blank. Kit could read them, though: These were low-caste indigo unused to the luxuries of the Higher Hundred, and they were awed.

Something in her favor. One of the few things. She must be careful.

"I'm Kitrini Candachi," she introduced herself, though they knew damn well who she was. "Won't you tell me your names?"

"I'm Hoyla Davit, and this is Berkin Star," the woman said. She was middle-aged, somewhat paunchy, with skin so dark that the folds of her neck looked painted on in black. Her fingers were broad and stubby, but her arms, even enclosed in the form-less cotton, looked powerful. "We're investigating the explosion in the Centrifuge that occurred four days ago."

"I thought you might be. Have you figured out yet what caused it?"

"We're not certain yet, but it seems unlikely to have been an accident or an electrical malfunction."

"So—you think it was—a bomb or something like that."

"It's too early to say, *hela*. Maybe you can help us fill in some of the gaps."

Kit took a deep breath. "If I can. What do you want to know?"

"Tell us what happened when you were in the tunnels."

"I had just passed the South Zero gate when I saw a bright orange light in front of me. I didn't even realize what it was at first, until the other ringcars started tumbling back. Then all the cars started smashing together, then there was another explosion behind me and more cars started crashing into each other. I didn't actually see either of the explosions. They seemed to be about a minute apart, but I kind of lost my sense of time. They could have been seconds apart, or ten minutes. I just couldn't tell."

"And you've had a concussion, we hear, so your memory might not be perfect."

"Well, there are parts of that night that I don't recall."

"What's the next thing you remember?"

"Mmm—I guess when the medics came and started digging me out. But that's pretty hazy. The next thing I remember clearly is waking up at the hospital."

Hoyla Davit gave her one close sharp look. "The gulden hospital, wasn't it?"

"Yes."

"Why were you taken there?"

Kit felt her eyes widen in unfeigned surprise. "I don't know. I suppose it was the nearest—"

"You didn't ask to be taken there? As a preference?"

"Well, no—I didn't mind, of course, but I didn't choose the hospital. I was unconscious at the time, Officer."

Hoyla Davit nodded. Her partner all this while had said noth-ing. He looked to be about thirty years old, well-built and stupid.

Kit could not help that ridiculous childhood rhyme from singing through her head: *A woman has the brains/A man has the muscle/A woman holds the reins/Till a man wants to tussle.* Who had taught her that? Surely no one in Geldricht. She gave her head an infinitesimal shake. Concussion or no, she must concentrate; she must understand what was going on here.

Hoyla Davit was speaking again. "When you entered the Centrifuge, where were you coming from?"

"I'd been in the city. Running errands," Kit said, trying to keep her voice casual. It was hard when her chest suddenly constricted and her lungs could not take in enough air to support her words.

"Do you remember exactly what errands you were running?"

She manufactured a lie on the spot. "Well, I'd stopped at my bank—I'd gone by a restaurant to try and solicit donations for the charity bank where I work—I'd gone to visit a friend—"

"What friend?" The question pounced out.

Kit raised her eyebrows. "And why exactly is it you need to know?" she asked in the haughtiest Granmama tone she could manage.

"And why exactly would you be reluctant to tell?"

"It seems to me," Kit said, still in that supercilious tone, "that no friend I would visit in the city could have any relation to explosions in the Centrifuge—which, as I understand it, is what you're here investigating?"

"Unless that friend was Jex Zanlan," Hoyla Davit said.

So they knew. Of course they knew. The guard at the gate had recognized her name, her face; and hadn't there been cameras trained on them the whole time she was in Jex's prison? In his prison, making love to him under the thin shield of blankets and furniture. Worse and worse and worse.

"Jex was one of the people I visited that day," she said calmly. "Why?"

"Jex Zanlan is a known terrorist who has been responsible for several acts of violence recently committed in this city," said Hoyla Davit. "If we discover that the explosives were deliberately set, Jex Zanlan is the first person we will look to."

"He's in jail," Kit said. "How could he set off any bombs?"

"That's a stupid question, *hela,*" Hoyla Davit said softly.

"Not as stupid as some of the questions you've been asking me."

"Then answer this one. Did Jex Zanlan tell you of any plans he'd made to sabotage the Centrifuge that day?"

Kit leaned forward and, dropping the hauteur, infused her voice with cold passion. "If Jex Zanlan or *anyone* had told me of plans to blow up the Centrifuge, I would have been in Ariana Bayless's office faster than you could call my name. And, believe me, Officer, if anyone had warned me that the Centrifuge was about to be bombed to pieces, I would have walked home sooner than board a ringcar and try to beat the explosion to my gate."

Hoyla was unimpressed. "You might have been misinformed. He might have told you the explosions were planned for later in the week. You might have felt safe."

"That doesn't seem very likely, either," Kit said boldly. "I'm sure you've heard gossip about my—relationship—with Jex Zanlan."

"You're his lover," Hoyla Davit said flatly.

"That being the case," Kit said, "why in the world do you think he would have allowed me to enter the Centrifuge that night if he knew a bomb had been planted?"

"He might have thought you planned to take a limo home."

"He knows I never do."

"He might not have noticed the time."

"A man planning murder surely is paying attention to the clock," Kit said.

Berkin Star stirred and for the first time spoke. "He might have wanted you dead in the tunnels," he said in a nasal, swamp-country accent. "Might have wanted to be shed of you altogether."

Kit stared at him; Hoyla stared at him; every mirror, window, knob, and painting seemed to grow eyes and focus them on Berkin Star's unmoved face. Kit knew her expression was one of furious outrage, but the words had landed against her stomach with the force of a killing blow. *Could it be true? Not possible. Could it be true? Could it be true?*

Jex had called her there that day after weeks of silence. He was always granted a pass that lasted roughly an hour, and he had told her when to arrive. He had started no argument that would have sent her sooner from the room; he had made no move to keep her when she prepared to leave. He knew her route, he knew her habits, he knew her exit. If he also knew the timing of the bomb . . .

This was ice in her veins; this was the arctic season of the heart. She could not even ponder these things and continue to exist.

"Officer," she said, and the winter in her blood chilled her voice to zero. "I will consider that remark unsaid."

Hoyla Davit clearly realized that they had lost any chance they might have had of wringing admissions from this miscreant. She heaved her big body upright and, with a glance at her partner, jerked him to his feet as well. "All right, *hela*, I can see you don't have anything left to tell us. If you remember something, you can find us over at the Complex. Always be glad to hear from you—if your concussion clears up, you know, and something else occurs to you. Thanks for your time."

Kit did not even rise to see them to the door. She heard the servant Catie approach them in the hallway, heard the murmur of their voices fading as they descended the stairwell. She merely sat where they had left her, a statue of ice, afraid for Jex, afraid for herself.

When Sereva returned that night, she found Kit packing. "Kitrini! What are you—? Sit down right this minute! What do you think you're doing?"

"Leaving. I don't know that it will be any better at Granmama's. Maybe I should get an apartment in the city. If anyone will rent to me."

Sereva pulled at her shoulder, pushed her away from the bed where her piles of clothing lay. "Sit down! Talk to me! What in the world's wrong with you?"

Kit hobbled back to the chair she had occupied during the police interrogation. "I had a visit today from two officers of the law. Asking about the explosions. Asking about where I'd been earlier that day. Asking me if I knew anything about the bombs—if they were in fact bombs, which so far has not been established."

Sereva sank to the couch facing her, her expression troubled. "But—what could you possibly know?"

"I was visiting Jex that afternoon," Kit said baldly. "And they know it. And they think he told me about the bomb. And that he set it."

Sereva paled. "Oh, Kit—do you think that's true?"

"That he knew about it? I think it's possible. It's not true that he told *me*, because—well, I would have done something, told somebody, I never would have— But that's not what matters right now. What matters is that if these officers think I'm implicated, Ariana Bayless thinks I'm implicated. And what she knows, every high-caste blueskin in the city will eventually know. And that means you can't possibly keep me in this house. You'll be completely ostracized. It might be too late already. Sereva, I'm sorry, I never would have meant for this to happen—"

"Will you shut up?" Sereva demanded fiercely. "Do you think I will throw you out of my house *now*—when you're sick and hurt and accused and alone? How dare you say that to me? Anybody with any sense and reason must realize you wouldn't go headlong into a bombing you knew about! No one will believe you were involved in this! And even if they did, even if the evidence was piled up against you, how can you believe I would throw you out? How can you hurt me like that?"

"Sereva—I'm sorry—I'm just trying to protect you," Kit stammered. "No matter what the truth is, the rumors will stick to me, and those rumors will hurt you. The truth is, I was with Jex that day. Whatever else they suspect about me, that they will know for certain. And that's almost as bad, in their eyes, as conspiring to blow up the city. I can't stay here. But I'm not sure where to go."

"Well, if you leave me, it will be when you're well enough to move," Sereva said so firmly that Kit was taken aback. "If you leave me, it won't be while you're in trouble. Now you get back in bed while I put all your things away, and I don't want to hear another word about it."

She was too tired to argue—tonight, anyway. She knew she was right; she knew she could not stay here and taint Sereva's reputation, harm her nephews' chances to make advantageous marriages. She must leave, and soon. But she was too tired. She was too heartsick. Tomorrow, or the day after. She would be strong enough then.

But she did not actually leave the house for another two days, and that was in response to a summons from Jex.

It came in the morning, carried by Shan from the charity bank, who stood on the front porch and would not even step into the hallway when Catie dubiously invited her in. Kit limped down the stairs, clinging to the bannister, because this was not an event she had expected any more than Catie had: a guld-woman calling at an indigo door.

"Yes, Shan, what is it?" Kit said, hopping out onto the porch. "What's happened?"

Shan glanced at her and looked back down at her feet as if even Kit's common face was too glorious to look at in this setting. She was dressed in the usual gray drab of the ghetto women, but her long curly hair was held back with a red ribbon that gave her a somewhat festive air. "While the indigo lady is not with us, news comes sometimes, and letters," Shan replied in a low, almost inaudible murmur.

"You have news? What's happened?"

"And perhaps it is not the place of the gulden to track through the property of the indigo. But perhaps the letters are urgent."

"Wait—you've gotten letters for me? At the charity bank?"

Shan nodded. "Three of them. It is hard to know what might be important."

"Did you bring the letters with you? May I have them?"

Shan handed them over, three slim folded sheafs of paper. Kit felt her heart swell up to fill her entire rib cage. Messages from Jex. "When did these arrive?" she whispered.

"The days are hard to tell apart," Shan replied. "But this morning I saw one of the letters in Del's hand."

The Centrifuge had been damaged six days ago; two of these could have lain unopened at the charity bank all this time. If Jex had written to inquire about her safety, he must be mad with worry by now.

"Thank you for bringing them to me," Kit said, keeping her voice gentle. She knew Del well enough to guess that the older woman would have let the letters lie there till the city burned around her. Shan must have lobbied heavily for the right to do this task. "How can I show my appreciation? Will you allow me to send you back in a limousine?"

"Feet serve me well," Shan said, turning to go without any more conversation. "No thanks required."

"Shan—" Kit called after her, but the guldwoman was already on her way, walking through the strange, fabulous neighborhood with her head down to avoid catching a glimpse of seductive marvels. Kit watched her a moment in silence, then slumped down to the porch and ripped open the envelopes, one by one.

By chance, she read the most recent one first. "I have an hour's visitation today at three. Come if you are well enough. If not, write. I must know you are well." Which sounded anxious but hardly frantic.

She opened the other two in order. The first one said, "Kit— Were you in the explosion? If you went straight home, you must have been. I cannot have visitors for another few days, but send me a note to reassure me." Ah, that sounded alarmed; that was, for Jex, a tone of unreasonable concern. The second, written two days later, was actually calmer: "I have heard that you were harmed but alive. Gulden doctors spread that news to my friends. What a relief! If you are not too hurt, write me."

She had not written, of course, and he had become worried enough to write her a third time, to ask after her health yet again. And he wanted to see her. Today. In five hours' time.

She should not go. Wracked with doubt and horror as she was, terrified at the thought that he might have planned the explosion—convinced as she was that he was capable of it, whether he was responsible for this one or not—how could she consider going to him, how could she long, so suddenly and so violently, for one more moment in the catastrophic sun of his presence? But the brief words of invitation woke an irresistible, primitive desire in her muscles and bones. She could feel the magnetic drag of his presence like gravity or a vacuum. It was unopposable; her body bent in his direction no matter how she placed her feet or clung to an iron support. If he called her name in the middle of a crowded night, while cacophony raged above her head and voices vied with each other for volume, she would hear him; she would go to him; she would fight demons real and imagined to run to his side.

And so she would see him at three o'clock on this very afternoon, and she would learn if there was a reason to go on living.

The limo deposited her at the door of the Complex, but there were still many, many steps to take on a damaged ankle. She glided across the marble floors in the lower corridors, then stood panting in the closed elevator, willing the pain to subside. Her headaches were completely gone by now, and her wrist only required a simple, tightly wrapped bandage, but it seemed likely her ankle would never recover. She should have brought a cane.

The guard was new and did not seem interested in her arrival. A clock somewhere in the building was just chiming the hour as he unlocked the door, and she stepped into the apartment and into Jex's arms.

"Oh, Kit. Oh, I have been so worried," he murmured into her hair. He had gathered her against him much more carefully than was his wont, as if he actually remembered her bruised bones and battered head. She pressed against him, feeling, as she always did, a chemical need to soak up his scent, his textures, the rhythms of his blood. She had used to think, when she first loved Jex, that in time she would saturate; she would absorb enough of his essence to be satiated and content. And then she had realized Jex would never sit still long enough to allow her to perform that transfusion—she would never get enough of him. And then she had realized that it was not a resource that could be stored or archived; like food, like breath, it alchemized within her system, her body used it up. It constantly required more, which meant she had to be near him always.

And without this contact she was starved, as she had been starved for weeks, for months, as she might be starved for the rest of her life.

She pulled herself away—not too far away—and gazed up at his face. "Jex, what happened?" she asked in her most solemn voice.

He lifted his hands to either side of her face and gazed down at her with complete earnestness. His eyes were so bright they canceled the lamps in the room. "Kit, I did not plan the explosions in the Centrifuge six days ago. I swear that to you on my father's life. And had I known—had I known such a thing had been planned for that day—I would have found some way to ensure your safety. The second I heard the blasts—when I realized where you must be—Kit, I cannot tell you the agony I endured. I did not sleep for two days, until word came that you had survived. And even the news that you had been hurt—"

He seemed unable to find words dreadful enough to complete his thought. He dropped his hands, put his arms around her waist again, more urgently this time but still with a certain caution. Kit felt her whole body turn to smoke and vapor, weightless, unafraid. Of course, he could not, before Ariana Bayless's cameras, admit he had planned a bombing, but Jex was not the man to lie outright. He would not have sworn—on Chay's life!—to be innocent if he was not. And he had been sick with fear for her, and he had agonized until he knew her fate, and he loved her. The world was a spangled place, full of warmth and miracles, and Jex Zanlan loved her.

They sat for the next hour nearly immobile on the sofa, Jex cradling Kit's body against his own and murmuring endearments against her cheek. She thought surely she must be dreaming; Jex had never been so tame. They talked in soft, almost idle voices about Geldricht, the games they had played as children, the people they remembered from their childhood, things Chay had said to one or the other of them.

"Your father will not let you stay with me, you know," she said finally, something neither of them had ever said aloud. "He wants you to marry a gulden girl and have a family, and the sooner the better. And once you do that, I can't stay with you. I won't ever be able to see you again—it would break my heart."

"It's a long way off," he said in a faraway voice, stroking her arm with a slow, absentminded motion. "So much could happen before the day my father presents me with his chosen bride. Nothing we have to worry about now."

"Certainly, nothing we have to worry about while you're in prison," Kit said, laughing a little.

Jex tickled her briefly in the ribs. "Is that why you still come visit me? Because you know here I'm safe from other girls?"

"Oh, yes, I'm the reason you're still in jail. I told Ariana Bayless, 'Keep that man right there for the rest of his life. I want him all to myself.'"

More of this nonsense—sweet beyond telling—and the hour rushed to its impossibly rapid close. The guard was pounding on the door, calling "Time's up!" and they were still kissing good-bye. Kit did not think she would be able to tear herself away—literally did not think she would be able to unwrap her arms, shift her weight, see Jex's body as something distinct and separate from her own—but he came to his feet, and suddenly she was just herself again without her conscious volition.

"I don't know when I'll have another pass," he said, pulling her upright and giving her one final, painfully tight hug. "Where shall I send a note? To the charity bank or your cousin's?"

"I don't know. The charity bank. Maybe not. I don't know."

"I'll send letters everywhere. One of them will find you."

"Time to go!" the guard shouted through the door.

"I can't leave you," she said.

"I'll send you a message," he said, and helped her to the door.

And two minutes later, she was outside, and he was inside, and she felt like her body had been flayed from heel to temple. Dazed and disbelieving, she hobbled from the room, giving her head small, swift shakes to try to reorient herself. The elevator creaked slowly down its shaft, then deposited her on the bottom story. She made her way carefully across the marble floors, once more employing that cautious glide and shuffle, and pausing several times to lean against the wall and give her aching foot a rest.

It was during her third such break that a strange indigo man approached her at such a fast pace that she felt a moment's panic. She straightened against the wall and tried to assume a forbidding expression, and she was astonished when he grabbed her arm. His eyes were wild but hooded, as if he gazed at interior horrors; his face seemed ravaged by some disaster.

"Kitrini Candachi," he said, and it frightened her even more that he knew her name.

"Yes," she choked out.

"If you don't come with me now, I'll see to it that your gulden boyfriend dies. We have to leave instantly—you and I—for Gold Mountain."

CHAPTER TEN

The transmetropolitan trolley, which cut east-west across the city, could be caught three blocks from the Complex and deposited travelers half a mile from the West Two gate, nearest to the wealthy gulden residential district. From there, buses took travelers up and down the main residential roads. Oddly enough, there were no existing public transport routes—except the Centrifuge—which would efficiently take commuters from the north side of the city to the south, though Ariana Bayless was working on temporary ways to correct that omission. But, for the time being, the majority of business commuters who were stranded in the city were indigo.

Pakt had offered his house to any of the Biolab employees who wished to stay with him until the Centrifuge reopened—or bus routes were installed to the southern sector of the city. Cerisa, of course, who took a limousine to and from work, had no need of such offers; and since Melina and Varella lived within a few miles of Cerisa's home, the two young blueskin women had accepted transport service from her for the duration. A few of the other biologists had also found alternate places to stay or methods of transportation, but Nolan, Hiram, and Sochin gratefully accepted Pakt's offer.

Cerisa lent them all the use of her limousine so they could return home and pack enough clothes to last a week or so. "Though it will be a miracle if the Centrifuge is repaired by then" had been her dry comment. "But maybe Ariana will have buses in place by that time."

So for the next few days, they had what quickly began to seem like a camp out at Pakt's house. The guldman lived in an eight-bedroom house with his wife, three sons, and daughter. Even with three guests in the house, there was enough space for everyone who wished to have his own room. Nonetheless, the house was a bit crowded, though no one in Pakt's family seemed to mind, especially the boys. They were boisterous, friendly, and curious, and they appeared to welcome the upheaval the visitors brought to their household.

"Do you work with our father? Is he the smartest man ever?"

"What's that you're wearing? Is that a necklace? Men don't wear necklaces in Geldricht."

"I'm ten years old, and I can beat up all the boys in my class."

"Why is your hair that color? Is it that color everywhere?"

"Do you know how to save people's lives like my dad does? I'm going to be a bilololigist just like him when I grow up. Bio—bilo—bililo—"

"Biologist," Nolan said absently. He was trying to make neat folded piles of his clothes so he could find what he wanted quickly in this unfamiliar environment. Hiram, who had already unpacked in his room, was lounging in a chair nearby and listening. Sochin had merely dumped his clothes in his room and gone out searching for Pakt.

"Why is your skin that color? Is it that color *everywhere*?"

They were brawnier and more energetic than the indigo boys Nolan encountered when he returned home to visit relatives, so it was hard for him to gauge their ages. The ten-year-old, for instance, he would have pegged as twelve or thirteen by his size alone, though his conversation did not indicate such an age. He gave up trying to guess about the others.

"Yes, I'm blue everywhere," he answered. "Just like you're gold everywhere."

"Can I *see*?"

"No, you can't see, and that's a rude question to ask," Nolan answered tranquilly. Hiram, for some reason unmolested on the other side of the room, choked back a laugh.

"My father says it's important to ask questions or you'll never know the answers."

"Well, and your father is right, but some questions are asked only with great delicacy of people you know well, and neither of those conditions has been met in this instance."

It was said with his best high-caste hauteur, and it made the boys shout with laughter. Nolan could not help smiling. "Now, maybe you'd like to show us where your father is just now. I think I'm done here."

So an eager, dancing procession led them down the stairs and to a big dining room whose buffet table was already laden with steaming dishes. Pakt's wife, a middle-aged gulden woman, was arranging the plates of food as Hiram and Nolan entered, but she did not look up. A small, solemn girl stood by her side, apparently receiving instruction in a low murmur. Nolan could not catch any of this conversation. Perhaps it was in a gold-tongue.

Sochin and Pakt were already seated and talking casually when the boys descended on them like a gold-dust whirlwind. Nolan was not surprised to see Pakt greet each of his sons with a rough but obvious affection, faking punches to their chests and ruffling the bright hair with his big hands. They had spoken of their father proudly; clearly, he was a figure of dominant importance in their lives. But that they adored him was equally evident. Nolan could think of a good many indigo boys who respected their parents but did not love them.

The ten-year-old was clutching his father's arm with one hand and gesticulating with the other and chattering unbelievably quickly in goldtongue. Pakt held up his free hand.

"Ah—now—what have I told you? Speak in a language that your guest understands or you do dishonor to yourself."

The boy switched to indigo words. "Father, this one says his skin is blue *everywhere*! But he would not show me. Do you think he was lying?"

Pakt looked, for the first time since Nolan had known him, actually embarrassed. But both Hiram and Nolan were laughing, and so the guldman allowed a smile to come to his face.

"Just tell me the protocol here," Nolan said with a grin. "I told him it was rude to ask, but I don't mind giving him scientific evidence if you think that's better."

"I think it's better that he be sent to his room till he can learn to mind his manners with guests," Pakt said with a certain heat. "Nolan, I apologize on behalf of my son."

"He told us his father encouraged an inquisitive mind."

"Not in those words, I assume."

"No, but I wasn't offended. Don't send him away on my account."

Indeed, the young offender looked pathetically crushed, his eyes fixed pleadingly on his father's face, both hands now attached to Pakt's arm. "Let me stay," he begged. "I won't say another word."

Pakt glanced over at Nolan. "Ask the gentleman whom you have dishonored with your careless talk," he suggested. "If he allows you to stay at the table, you may."

Nolan resisted the impulse to say, "Sure, eat with us," since Pakt was obviously trying to make a point. He waited till the hangdog young boy took a few reluctant steps closer and bowed his bright head in a gesture of supplication.

"I did not mean to dishonor you with my stupid questions," the boy said in a serious voice. "May I still remain at the table for this meal? I will not trouble you again."

Nolan tried to keep his voice serious. "I'm not used to impertinence from children," he said. "But I'm willing to overlook it this time if you'll behave in the future."

Now the head tipped up and the green gaze met his somewhat fiercely. Where did they get such colors for their hair and eyes? "I *said* I would," he replied somewhat reproachfully.

"Wendt," Pakt said in a warning voice.

"And I will," Wendt ended, docile again.

"Then by all means, stay and eat with us," Nolan said.

That settled, everyone was happy again, and the boys and the adults arranged themselves around the table. Nolan noticed for the first time that there were only seven places set, and the men of both races occupied them all. The other two times Pakt had had coworkers to his home, they had had glorious masculine bacchanals, and it hadn't occurred to Nolan to wonder why Pakt's wife wasn't present. But he had expected her to preside over the routine meals that would take place while guests were in the house. Well, perhaps the woman (whose name he could not ever remember hearing) had fed the little girl earlier, and taken her own meal at the same time. Hard to know. He would follow Pakt's lead.

But it was even stranger than he had expected. Once the men were seated, Pakt's wife began to serve them—silently, almost invisibly—laying portions of meat and rice on their plates and sidling off to serve the next male. "Thank you," Nolan said when she served him, but she did not respond, and no one else at the table, not even Pakt, said a word to her. The boys acted as if she was not in the room, as if their food had appeared magically upon their plates, prepared by unseen hands, and no courtesies were due to the cook. Nolan could not believe it. Even in the Higher Hundred households, the servants were thanked or at least acknowledged. He would have expected a man as decent as Pakt to behave at least as well toward his wife, no matter what gulden custom might dictate.

But Pakt was cutting his meat and quizzing Wendt on a school problem. Hiram's glance intersected with Nolan's, and the other blue-skin shrugged. Sochin, like the gulden boys, appeared not to notice that anything other than a disembodied spirit had hovered near his head. He was laughing at Wendt's and Pakt's conversation, and eating his food with gusto.

And, indeed, the meal was delicious, though wholly unfamiliar to Nolan. These were not spices normally found in an indigo kitchen; he wasn't even sure the meat was something he could identify. And he was accustomed, on a blueskin table, to find a wide array of garnishes—plates of vegetables, fruit, bread, cheese—to supplement the main courses. But this appeared to be it. There was plenty of it, of course, and Nolan would not have complained even if there hadn't been enough, but still, it was unusual.

Or at least different.

After the meal, the boys ran from the table, yelling and laughing and seeming to be a dozen boys instead of three. Pakt and the indigo men rose and left at a more leisurely pace, though Nolan glanced behind him once. Would Pakt's wife now clear off the table and wash the dishes? Were there servants in the house that he simply had not noticed? Weren't there more important things she could be doing? He didn't believe Leesa had ever even handled a plate once it had been dirtied by food, let alone been responsible for cleaning it. He was certain his mother had not. He himself rarely ate in his own apartment because he so much hated the scrubbing that came afterward—but at least he knew how to do it.

The customs of the gulden were very strange.

Nolan followed Pakt and the others to a small, comfortable room gaily decorated with a marvelous assortment of colors and fabrics. A few of the pillows and wall hangings had deliberate, intricate patterns woven into them, and Nolan wondered if those were clan designations, or merely exuberant displays of color. He didn't ask. He was feeling very much like an outsider here, welcomed or not, and he did not want to pose questions that would make him sound as ignorant as Wendt.

"Anybody for choisin?" Pakt asked, pulling out a game board and pieces. It was an elaborate game of strategy and aggression that the guldmen had brought with them from Gold Mountain. About ten years ago, it had become the rage among the indigo and the albinos as well, with the result that every year there were all-race tournaments played throughout the city. Ariana Bayless was said to be a master at the game, and Cerisa and Pakt sometimes played on their lunch hours. Nolan had heard that they were evenly matched, which made him think Pakt must be at the near-genius level. He could not imagine Cerisa being anything less than ferociously good at any activity that involved competition.

"Sure, I'll play," said Sochin. Hiram murmured an assent.

"I doubt I'm quite up to your standard," Nolan said to Pakt with a smile.

"We'll play teams," Pakt suggested. "Pair up the best and the worst."

Sochin was laughing. "Then I'll take Hiram and you take Nolan."

"Just what I was about to suggest," the guldman said.

They teamed up and took their positions, Hiram and Nolan laying the counters on the board while Sochin and Pakt dealt themselves their opening hands. Actually, Nolan had never understood the appeal of choisin; he was not, in general, a territorial man. He owned a few material things, and he would never inherit any property. If a thief broke into his apartment this night and stole everything in sight, Nolan would lose nothing that had much importance to him. The only thing of value he owned was Leesa's medallion, and that had more sentimental than monetary worth. For the most part, what he cherished was the knowledge in his head, the education he had been given, the ability he had of analyzing certain kinds of complex data and applying them to practical, real-life situations. That kind of mind-set did not qualify him—even on a game board—to invade cities, annex land, and wage war with hostile nations.

"My opening, I believe," Sochin said, and the game was under way.

Playing pairs, in this instance, anyway, did nothing more than give Pakt the opportunity to move Nolan's pieces as well as his own. Hiram turned out to be a better choisin player than Nolan would have expected, though not nearly as good as Sochin, and Pakt was clearly superior to them all. However, luck was part of the game, and Sochin knew how to turn an unexpected card to his advantage. He was also ruthless; he was not afraid to forfeit whole armies of choifer soldiers (who littered the game board, as far as Nolan could tell, specifically to be sacrificed in this manner) in order to gain a slight advantage. Neither team had a decided edge by the time they agreed to call it quits for the night. They left the board in position so they could resume play the following night.

"If the Centrifuge is closed for long, we could have our own tournament," Sochin said.

"I think Pakt would win," Hiram said.

"But the fun is in the playing, not the winning," Pakt said, smiling.

"I'm not sure Cerisa would agree with you," Nolan said.

"No, she is rather serious about her choisin," Pakt admitted. "It is one of the keenest delights of my life to beat her at this game. A rare pleasure, but exquisite nonetheless."

Sochin and Hiram left the room together, talking amiably, while Nolan remained behind to help Pakt put away the slaughtered choifer troops. "What if someone comes in and knocks over the board while we're gone tomorrow?" Nolan asked, although he didn't really care.

"It won't happen. No one comes into this room but me and my invited guests," Pakt replied. "It is my *hoechter*."

"Your what?"

"My—sanctum, I suppose would be the best word. Every man who is a head of a household has one. It is a place where no one else can enter. A place no one else would dare intrude."

"Oh, like Cerisa's office," Nolan said with a grin.

Pakt smiled back. "Even more so. But that's the right idea."

"Well, you keep it pretty clean. If I had a—a hoker—"

"Hoechter."

"It would be a mess."

"Don't you clean your own apartment?"

"I have a service," Nolan answered. "Why—do you do all your own cleaning here?"

"Not me. My wife."

Ah, the silent woman in the kitchen who acted so much like a servant in fact was treated like one. Nolan thought he kept his expression neutral, but Pakt was regarding him with a gently ironic smile.

"I can see it troubles you, the way this household is run," he said softly. "But you are judging by your own standards, and not mine. And not my wife's."

"I didn't mean—that is, you are mistaken—I don't—" Nolan tripped over the words, unable to frame a coherent disclaimer.

Pakt waved him to silence. "Mine is a world where everything runs most smoothly if everyone's position is—not only *defined*, but *honored*. Running a household efficiently, raising healthy children, and seeing to the needs of the people under her care are considered great and grave tasks. A woman who performs them well feels a justifiable pride and has an envied place in her community."

"I'm sure that's true," Nolan said in a low voice.

"But you see the life as circumscribed. Valueless."

"Not valueless," Nolan said hastily. "Restricted, yes. There are so many other things a woman can do in this world—"

"More important things? Than bearing and raising children? I know the indigo think so, but how can that be? The female body has been designed with a capability the male body cannot possibly duplicate. You're a scientist, Nolan. Why would nature create a being with specific, unique abilities and then expect that being to function as if those abilities were not a part of its makeup? Why would nature create wings for a bird if the bird was not meant to fly? Or silk for the spider if it were not meant to spin a web? We are all, to some extent, defined by our biology. Why would we try to reverse or deny it?"

"Yes—true—only women can actually bear children, but that is not all their bodies can do," Nolan said, floundering a little. He could not believe he was having this debate, at close to midnight, in the house of a guldman who was his host. He had never attempted to think it through; he had never expected to have to defend what seemed to him such basic tenets. "You may as well say that since humans have mouths and digestive tracts, all they were designed to do is eat. We're all complex organisms, designed to perform a multitude of tasks. We shouldn't be defined by one aspect of our bodies or one function of our brains."

"Very well, then, culture reinforces biology," Pakt said. "And an organism must learn how to function within its society. A wild dog and a tame dog are both created with the same physical makeup and basic instincts, but the behavior of the two will differ radically depending on what is expected of them by the other animals in their pack or the humans who have adopted them."

"But that's my point," Nolan said. "You say a gulden woman is happy in a life where all she does is care for others, and that may be so. But not because she was *created* that way. Because she was *conditioned* that way. And if she had the chance to make a choice based on free will and not the dictates of her society, would she make that choice? Would she be happy with such a limited life?"

"But who among us ever makes a choice based wholly on free will?" Pakt demanded. "Did you? Are you going to stand there and tell me that, abandoned in some cave from the day you were born and raised all on your own, with no input from other human creatures who could teach you their system of values, that you would be the same person I see before me today?

Prejudices intact, all knowledge gained through personal observations? I doubt it! You may think you have come to many of your conclusions and deeply held beliefs all on your own—and perhaps you have—but my guess is that the very pattern of your thoughts has been outlined by the information you learned from your mother and your grandmother and all their ancestors before them. Heritage is just as hard to escape as biology—though you can throw off the effects of either one with varying degrees of success. But both of them go deeper than I think you realize."

Nolan put out a hand as if to ask for silence, and Pakt obligingly paused. But he could not think of another way to phrase his argument, and he could not be sure Pakt was not entirely right. "I have a headache," he said at last, and the guldman laughed.

"You are not used to thinking," Pakt said. "In your household, that little chore is left to women."

"That's not true," Nolan said with a small smile. "I think, but not about questions like these."

"I think about them all the time. And I concluded a long time ago that we are mostly what we have been made. It takes a cataclysmic event, I think, or great strength of will, to overcome our early training. And most of us are not burdened with either."

"Well," Nolan said, handing Pakt the box of choifer soldiers, "it's certainly been instructive talking with you, anyway."

Pakt smiled and took the box. "Go to sleep. The morning will come sooner than you expect."

And it did.

The next four days passed in much the same manner, days at the Biolab, evenings at Pakt's house. Hiram and Sochin, Nolan saw, began to enjoy themselves more and more at the guldman's residence. They showed in subtle ways how much they liked the idea of a submissive woman catering to their basic needs, one who was far more silent and sweet-tempered than most of the blueskin women of their acquaintance. They were never rude to Pakt's wife—they had far too much breeding for that—but it pleased and amused them to be lords over members of the gender they had, for most of their lives, been in awe of. Nolan saw them preening, almost expanding, in Pakt's male-dominated household; he saw their gestures grow broader and their opin-

ions more decided. The changes were so minute that he thought
Pakt might not have noticed, but for himself, he began to loathe
both of them.

He had taken to staying at the lab later and later just to cut
down the time he had to spend with the other blueskins at Pakt's,
and he hoped to be able to return to his apartment within a few
days. Ariana Bayless had managed to stitch together a mass
transit scheme that made the south gates accessible, but by all
accounts, the buses and trolleys were so overburdened with
commuters that the system wasn't really working yet. But soon,
he hoped. Soon.

Meanwhile, he tried to avoid Sochin and Hiram while he was
at the lab, and put in extra hours after closing time. Which he
might have done anyway, since he was on a new project that
he was having a hard time solving. It involved trying to come
up with a drug for an infectious disease that had mutated to the
point where it was no longer completely treatable by three existing medicines. Nolan's first task was to understand exactly
how it had mutated, and then to figure out how to nullify it. He
knew he would spend the first few weeks of his research bent
over his computer, learning and understanding, and the next few
weeks experimenting. At the moment, he was still learning.

"Are you still here?" Melina's voice demanded one evening
five days after he had moved into Pakt's house. "Why don't you
go home? Do you realize everyone else in the building is gone?"

He looked up at her with a smile, though for a moment her
face was blurry with images transferred from his electronic
screen. "That can't be true," he said. "Aren't there politicians
and security officers and even residents who are in the Complex
around the clock?"

"Well, you're the last one in this office. Go home. What are
you working on so hard, anyway?"

"The model for the mutated ARS-B virus. What's bugging
me is that I'm pretty sure there was a mutation between this one
and the model I've got. Isn't that when Cerisa concocted the
Moro-1 drugs?"

"Mmm, yeah, I think you're right. Two . . . three years ago.
Well, she must have that model on her computer somewhere.
Get it from her."

"She won't be back till next week, Pakt said. I don't know that I can wait that long. I basically can't do a thing till I have the intermediate model."

"So go into her computer and get it."

"Oh. Yeah. Like I could do that," he said with heavy sarcasm. He had not been joking the other night with Pakt; Cerisa's office was considered sacrosanct. No one went in there uninvited—and even then, they rarely went willingly.

Melina was laughing. "You could. No one else is here and *I'm* not going to tell."

"Even if I was willing to do that, you know she's got a password on her system."

Melina came a few steps closer. "Yes, but I know her password," she whispered.

Nolan sat back in his chair. "You do not! Why would she give it to you?"

Melina was grinning like a manic child let loose from the dungeon for the day. "Because once she needed something from her computer when she was away for the day. She called in from—I can't even remember where she was—and had me go to her office while I was on the linkline. Told me the password, what screen to call up next, exactly what information she needed. I didn't have a chance to sneak around in her other files—not that I would have, of course—because we were linked the whole time. But somehow I never forgot the password."

"I bet she's changed it."

"I bet not. She's careless about things like that. Besides, she trusts me."

"With good reason, obviously," Nolan said, sarcastic again.

"Oh, don't be ridiculous. What are you going to do, steal her precious medical secrets? All you want is one dumb model."

He still couldn't believe he was considering illegally opening Cerisa's files. "Come with me," he said.

Melina was scrawling something on a piece of paper. "Can't. I'm late as it is. Here. This'll get you in, this'll get you past the second security checkpoint. Then, it's just a matter of scanning files until you find the ARS-B virus. Couldn't be easier."

"Maybe you could stay late with me tomorrow night," he suggested, but she was already halfway out the door.

"*Nolan.* I *told* you. It'll be *fine*," she said in an irritable sing-song. "You'll be in and out in ten minutes. See you tomorrow."

And she was gone.

Nolan sat stubbornly at his own computer for another twenty minutes, pretending he was working, resisting the urge to break into Cerisa's files. If he was caught, he would be fired; no question. He should wait till the next day, get Pakt's permission, open Cerisa's computer with the guldman standing by to oversee. Except Pakt would refuse to do it. Pakt never deviated from strict protocol within the office. Well, then, neither should Nolan. He knew it was wrong, and he didn't need any guldman to tell him so.

But he honestly could not proceed a step farther without the previous model. It was a choice between a small misdemeanor that would harm no one and a week of wasted work. And Melina had practically ordered him to do it, and he had a long history of obeying the dictates of indigo women.

He came to his feet suddenly. All right. He'd do it. In and out in ten minutes.

Feeling a bit like a fool, he crept to Cerisa's office and turned on only the shaded desk lamp, so no telltale light would spill out the windows (should anyone from the streets happen to be looking). In the semidark, he settled himself before her computer and switched it on. The amber graphics on the screen seemed much more baleful than the friendly teal he mixed on his own monitor. It was hard to be in this room and not feel Cerisa's accusing presence all around him. It was hard to be at this screen and not feel as though her face was peering at him from inside the glass and circuitry. Hastily, he typed in the code that Melina had given him, and, when the screen prompted him with a new question, the second set of symbols she had written down.

And damned if he wasn't in. Who would have expected Cerisa to be so slipshod?

But that was not the only sign of negligence that he came across immediately. Her files were in no discernible order, and the directory was almost useless. Some of her projects bore recognizable names; others were coded with letters and numbers that must mean something to Cerisa but held nothing but mystery to anyone browsing through her data. Nothing bore the

ARS-B designation, or even Moro-1. He would have to open the files one by one and scan them.

Cerisa might be sloppy, but Nolan was methodical. He started with the first file listed, opened it, closed it, and went to the next one in the directory. His plan was to merely skim the opening words, looking for key phrases, and quickly put away anything that was not meant for his eyes. But curiosity got the better of him a couple of times when his searching led him to famous epidemics and well-known drugs that he hadn't even known Cerisa had helped formulate. He could not help himself; he sat and read the entire histories contained in two files, and began to pay more attention to the details of every new case that he opened.

The designation "GGP" meant nothing to him but, by the time he had reached the G's in the alphabetical listings, he had gotten into his rhythm. Open a file, scan the headers; if it sounded interesting, read on. If not, close it back up and move down the list. So he opened the file, ran his eyes over the reference line at the top of the page, and nearly fell out of his chair.

He read the reference line again, but it still said the same thing.

He read the introductory abstract, the paragraph outlining the project, its goals, its methodology, and its probable rate of success. He read the next twenty pages, describing the experiment as it was theorized and then enacted on a few carefully selected subjects. "One hundred percent success," Cerisa had written. Based on her limited control group, she could not guarantee the same results on a larger case study, but she thought the results of the test were so positive that they could risk going ahead with the project without further experimentation.

Which, in her addendum, she noted had been done.

Nolan read the whole thing a second time.

He felt his heartbeat slow to a rate that would barely sustain life; he felt his body cool to the degree of hypothermia. He felt like an iceman sitting before Cerisa's computer, a body so traumatized by shock that all its systems shut down. *Not possible. Not possible. None of this could be true.*

He read the report a third time, but by now that was unnecessary. He had memorized the whole thing, the analysis of the data, the cellular model arrayed in rotating 3-D on the screen. He could shut down Cerisa's computer, go back to his own, and reconstruct the entire file.

He turned off the computer and sat for ten minutes in the shadowy room, staring at the blank screen, body motionless and the clattering activity of his brain at a complete standstill.

Then, he suddenly leapt to his feet, ran down the hall, skidded into his office and punched keys to clear the images from his own monitor. He had aborted one file and called up another before he had even toed over his chair to sit down. His fingers scurried over the keyboard, desperately typing in data, calling up formulas, trying one speculative model after another and then running simulated tests. No; impossible; never work; no; maybe . . . maybe . . .

When he finally looked up from his screen, haggard and ferocious, dawn was coloring the windows of his office with a furtive spring gold. He had been here the entire night. Within two hours, the others would arrive.

He could not possibly face them. He could not tell any of them—Melina, Varella, Pakt—what he knew. None of it might be true. He felt lunatic and hallucinatory. Perhaps he had created this fantastic despair in his own disordered mind.

But what if it was real? What if it was true? What was he to do?

Shakily, he pushed himself to his feet and tried to straighten his crumpled shirt and trousers. In the men's necessary room, he scrubbed his face as if to soap away the whiskers and the proof of a disastrous night. In the mirror, he was astonished to see that his face looked ordinary as ever—blue, mild, unalarming. He looked tired, but hardly horrific. It was hard to believe.

He left a note for Pakt, explaining that he would be gone for a day or two, then took the back stairwell down. At street level was the corporate pharmacy where the biologists took all their experimental prescriptions. As he had hoped, the head pharmacist was already on duty.

"Have a little project for you," Nolan said in a casual voice. "Do you have time? I'd like the test pills generated by this afternoon. Two different sets."

"Let's see the scrips," the pharmacist said, and Nolan handed over his notes. "Sure, I think we can put these together. How many of each?"

"Hundred, I guess. I haven't narrowed down my subject field. I'm not sure exactly how many I'll need."

"Hundred. You got it. Be done by two."

"Thanks. I'll be back."

Nolan stepped out into the weak sunlight and stood stupidly on the sidewalk, trying to think. Sleep. He needed sleep. He needed fresh clothes. He needed a meal. He needed . . . he needed to turn the clock back a day and unknow what he had learned. But that took more magic than he could muster. Sleep first. Then he would figure it all out.

Half a mile from the Complex was a row of hotels that served politicians and other city visitors who had business with the mayor. Nolan stumbled to the nearest one and requested a room for the day. Five minutes after being shown across the threshold, he was lying facedown on the white bed, fully dressed, completely unconscious. He slept unmoving for the next seven hours.

When he woke, before he remembered anything of the previous night, before he even remembered where he was, he was conscious of a numbing sense of doom. Dread had riddled his heart and made it malfunction; his breathing was labored and unsatisfactory. And then memory leapt in him like a blaze through withered grass, and he scrambled to his feet, all his senses seared and jagged. What would he do, what would he do, what would he do?

He would tell Pakt. He had no other choice. The guldman would be able to advise him. The guldman would have the answer.

There was no answer. Pakt would be of no use whatsoever.

He didn't know what to do.

He showered, wished he could shave, donned his dirty clothes, and almost could not stand their texture against his skin. They felt contaminated by the knowledge he had absorbed last night, sticky with outrage and disease. He didn't have time to return to his own apartment or even Pakt's house to retrieve clean clothes if he was going to make it to the Biolab before it closed for the day. So, as soon as he had paid his bill at the front desk, he headed to the nearest men's clothing store and bought three complete new outfits, retaining only his shoes and Leesa's medallion. One outfit he wore out of the store, and as he passed a trash receptacle on the street, he tossed away his bundle of old clothes. The gesture—meaningless as it was— made him feel fractionally cleaner.

There was nothing else to do. He would return to the Complex and tell Pakt. First he would stop at the pharmacy and pick up his experimental drugs, and then he would tell Pakt. And together they would solve this insoluble puzzle.

At the pharmacy, his drugs were ready, big bulky pills stored in tough plastic containers. "That one'll pounce on the lining of the stomach," the druggist told him. "Tell your subjects to take it with food or maybe an antiacidic medication."

"That's what I thought," Nolan replied, though it had not occurred to him. He hadn't actually envisioned who might be taking these pills. "The other, though—"

The pharmacist shrugged. "Like a vitamin. If you're the type who gets a stomachache with drugs, take it with food. If not, don't worry about it."

"All right. Thanks."

Nolan tossed the containers into his shopping bag and stepped from the pharmacy into the Complex proper. This was the far end of the building, a city block from his usual entrance. He would walk very, very slowly to his accustomed stairwell and decide on the way what, exactly, he would say to Pakt.

And then he spotted her, leaning against the wall as she had been that first time he had seen her, in almost exactly the same place, though this time she looked a little less despairing. And on the instant, he knew what he must do. The plan blossomed in his head and crowded out every other thought and question. Before he could change his mind, before he could critique his theory, he crossed the wide hall at a near-run and grabbed her arm so she could not slip away. She looked first frightened and then quelling, but he did not care. She would do exactly as he said; she had to. He had no choice and neither did she.

"Kitrini Candachi," he said, and she gasped out an affirmative. "If you don't come with me now, I'll see to it that your gulden boyfriend dies. We have to leave instantly—you and I—for Gold Mountain."

CHAPTER ELEVEN

He was certainly a madman. Despite the expensive clothes, despite the cobalt skin that marked him a highcaste purebred, he was clearly deranged. They were in a public place; she was relatively safe. She had merely to scream and someone would come to her rescue.

But she did not scream. She said, "How could you hurt Jex?"

His hand tightened on her arm, and he gave her a little shake. "Never mind *how* I could hurt him," he growled. "Just know that it's in my power. And I will, unless you take me to Gold Mountain to see Chay Zanlan."

Kit felt an odd squirt of panic shoot through all the junctures of her bones. "Why would you need to see Chay?"

"Why are you asking questions? Don't you care what happens to your boyfriend? Don't you care that I have the power of life and death in my hands? Do what I say, and everything will be fine."

His speech had a bizarre, melodramatic quality to it; he delivered his lines as if they came uneasily to his tongue. As if he was not used to threatening people, as if his ability to deal in death was not one he relished. Of course, he was crazy. He had no such power.

But.

"Tell me why it's so important for you to see Chay," she said in what she hoped was a calm, sane voice. "Then I'll decide."

For a minute, his fierceness wavered. A look of utter desolation crossed his face and set ghosts to dancing in his eyes. Then his expression hardened, and he tossed her arm aside. He took one long stride away from her.

"Fine," he said over his shoulder. "I'm going to Ariana Bayless. And Jex Zanlan will be dead by morning."

"No, wait!" she cried, before she had even thought about it, before she had reminded herself that he was crazy. He stopped. "How can I possibly believe you?" she demanded.

"I don't care if you believe me," he said, and now he sounded weary beyond imagining, as exhausted as an old man who had viewed the random cruelties of the world for a century or more. "All I want from you is passage into Geldricht and an entree into the presence of Chay Zanlan. I won't harm you. I won't harm him. But I can promise you, on my life, on your life, on any talisman you care to name, that if I don't get to Chay Zanlan, he will die."

Another squeeze of acid into her veins. "Chay will die? I thought you said Jex would."

"Both of them."

"You don't have that kind of power," she whispered. "No one does."

"I do," he said, and he sounded so certain that, against her will and her rational judgment, she believed him. He could have them killed, one or both of them, and then what would the world hold for her? Her foot throbbed with a stabbing, insistent ache; her head was beginning its own rhythmic pounding; and she was afraid that, if she moved her hand away from the wall, she would lose her balance and tumble to the ground. But those were minor annoyances, nothing to be concerned about. Fear had ignited the rich oil of her blood so that every estuary of her body was on fire. She felt flames sparkle up through her pores. *Not Jex, not now, now that she was sure he loved her again.*

"What do you want me to do?" she asked.

"Take me to Gold Mountain. Leaving tonight."

"I have to get—clothes and money."

"I'll have money."

"And I'll have to write a note to someone and say I'm leaving. Otherwise—people will worry. I don't think you want that."

"I'll have to read the note."

"All right."

"Where are your clothes?" he asked.

"At my cousin's house. In the indigo residential district off of South One."

He shook his head. "No good. Too far away and too many people might see us. We'll buy you some clothes here in the city."

"How long will we be gone?"

"How long does it take to get to Gold Mountain?"

Kit spread her hands. "It depends on the rains. If the weather's been dry, the train will go straight through, but it will still take nearly two days. If there's been flooding and the tracks are washed out, it could be days longer."

"And that's the most direct way? The train?"

"It's the *only* way. Haven't ever been out of the city?"

"Not in that direction."

"This will be quite a journey for you then," she said, and despite everything, she could not keep the edge from her voice.

He responded with a hollow laugh. "The journey of a lifetime," he replied.

They spent the next two hours shopping. Everything about this encounter was so strange that Kit knew she should not be unnerved by the peculiarity of this, but she was. Such a friendly, casual, intimate activity—shopping for clothes with a friend—and here she was with a madman, picking out shirts and comfortable trousers and undergarments while he stood grimly by. She only had a bare minimum of cash on her, which she had told him, but he had waved that concern aside so she assumed he planned to pay for everything. Which made the whole event even more bizarre.

He had his own purchases to make, which included a couple of inexpensive suitcases so that they didn't have to carry their new clothes in paper bags. He also surprised her by stopping at a nondescript little drug store and buying a handful of medical supplies.

"You're limping," he said gruffly once they were back on the street. He led her to a bench on the sidewalk, and they both sat down. "You can wrap your ankle with that. And here's a couple of pain pills. I think you should take them."

Kit was not one to dose herself with remedies, and this was not a compound she was familiar with. "I'm—I don't like to take drugs. And I've never heard of this. What if it makes me loopy?"

He gave her a wintry smile. "This will make you feel a lot better. Trust me." He reached into one of his other bags and pulled out a big plastic bottle, rattling with capsules. "And here. Have one of these while you're at it."

He shook a pill into her hand, and she eyed it dubiously. "And what is *this* supposed to do for me?"

"Kind of like a vaccine. It'll protect you against any infectious gulden diseases that the indigo body isn't used to fighting off."

She tried to hand it back to him. "My body knows all about gulden diseases," she said. "I've lived in Geldricht half my life."

He closed her fingers around the pill. "Take it. You've been in the city how long now? A few months?"

"Six or seven months," she admitted.

"Long enough for you to lose your immunity. Take it. I don't want you getting sick on me just when I need you most."

She gazed at him resentfully. "Then why don't you take one?"

"I've already had mine. I'm protected."

She made him buy her a can of juice from a street vendor because the "vaccine" pill was too big to swallow unaided, and then she downed both tablets. What could she do? Maybe he was trying to poison her; maybe she would end up just as insane and hallucinatory as he was. But she felt she had no choice. She had committed herself to his fantasy. She had to exist by his rules.

"What's your name?" she said, when she had swallowed the second one.

"Nolan."

And she thought it sounded familiar, but she could not for the life of her decide why.

"Well, Nolan," she said, "I'm ready when you are."

They boarded the night train from the city. Twice a day, big sleek engines departed from the transit station at the southwest edge of the city, just inside the loop of the Centrifuge. Nolan paid for two round trip tickets, business class. Kit wasn't sure how he picked the fare—if he didn't know about the semiprivate cars or couldn't afford the rates, and if money was a problem, why he hadn't elected to take them tourist class. When she asked him, he said merely, "We're on business," which left her no more certain than before.

She had ridden this train more times than she could count, alone or with her father, so she knew all the tricks to making the journey bearable. "The back three cars are tourist-class," she explained to Nolan as they passed through one slim lozenge-shaped car after another. Nearly every seat was filled with tired gulden women, restless children, white-haired old men who pretended to be anywhere else in the world. The noise level was remarkable, somewhat like a midsized auditorium with badly designed acoustics. "The next three cars are business class, and past them are the private cars. We want to get all the way to the sixth car."

"Why?" he asked. He was taking quick, surreptitious glances at the passengers all around them, as if dying of curiosity but afraid to appear too rude by staring. She wondered what seemed so odd to him about these accommodations. She had traveled in the tourist coaches a good half of the time she had made this trip.

"Because most people are too lazy to walk through all the cars. They just take the first empty seats. So the cars farther up are emptier."

He nodded absently. "Good. Why do all these people have food?"

She glanced back at him as she negotiated a narrow aisle partially blocked by a protruding foot. "Because the journey takes two days or more. As I told you."

"But aren't there—I mean, I didn't bring any food."

"There are food stalls in a car between business and private. But the food's expensive. We'll make a few long stops tomorrow at stations where there will be vendors. We can stock up then."

He nodded, but for the first time he looked a little nonplussed. Overwhelmed, actually, by the sheer volume of details he did not know. Kit felt a small smug burst of satisfaction. Good.

The cars were linked by small, rubbery accordion-style chambers in which sound was peculiarly deadened and electrical smells had an alarming concentration. Kit always tried to pass through these as quickly as possible, particularly once the train was in motion. The next two cars had progressively fewer people in them, but the first car in business class was quite crowded. Here, most passengers were prosperous gulden men, business owners with operations in the city and homes fifty or sixty miles out in the one of the small towns that clustered around the train tracks. A handful of albino men were also traveling business class, and most of them sat bunched together in a few rows toward the middle of the car. A few of the gulden men were accompanied by their wives, well-dressed, well-groomed women who kept their eyes focused on their handiwork or novels. There were no children in business class; any rich man who chose to travel with his family booked one of the rooms in the semiprivate coaches.

The next car was not quite as packed, and the third one was more than half empty. Kit led them to the very back of the car, to two sets of high-backed green velvet seats that faced each other and created a small, imperfect cubicle of privacy.

"You sit here. I'll sit across from you. Put your suitcase in the empty seats. Now no one else will sit with us unless every last seat is taken."

He did as she bid but gave her a faint smile. "I would have thought you might want a leaven for my presence," he said.

She flicked him a look of scorn, though inwardly, she was puzzled. "It's not that I want to be alone with you," she said. "I just don't like to be thrown together with strangers."

"So what happens now?"

"Train leaves in about fifteen minutes. Stops about every hour for the first five hours. Then, it's every couple of hours, as we pass through the rockland where towns are scarcer. Then, we're in the valley, and towns are closer together again. Then, we go across the Katlin Divide, so it's very slow, but the train never stops. Then, another twelve hours, and we're at the foot of Gold Mountain."

"And how do you entertain yourself for a trip like this?"

Kit couldn't help a little smile. "Well, people who plan ahead bring books or work or perhaps some sewing project. Mothers with their children, of course, don't have to worry about entertaining themselves. Every once in a while, especially if you're back in tourist, you find some lonely soul who just wants to talk all night and all day. That's one of the reasons I try to find an empty car and pile up my seat with my luggage. I don't want to be stuck talking to a stranger for two days."

"I'll try not to annoy you with too much conversation," he said stiffly.

Kit felt a small shock of surprise run through her. For an instant, she had forgotten he too was a stranger, and a hostile one at that. How could she possibly have slipped into such an error? Perhaps because, aside from hers, his was the only blue face she had seen on the train.

Uncannily, he seemed to catch her thought. "I haven't seen any other indigo," he said. "Do they never go into Geldricht?"

"Sometimes. Not often," she said. "There are a few entrepreneurs who have business with the gulden, but they're more likely to want their partners to come into the city. If there are any on board, they're probably all in private rooms."

He nodded and looked out the window. They were still in the station, and there was little to see except a few passengers making the last-minute run for the train. But maybe this was an unfamiliar sight to him and therefore interesting. He was silent long enough that Kit finally asked a question.

"Why didn't you ask for a private room? Didn't the clerk tell you they were available?"

He nodded, still gazing out the window. "I thought you might be afraid," he said, "cooped up for two days in a small room with a crazy man."

Which astonished her so much that she couldn't think of another thing to say.

A few minutes later, the train lurched into motion. Kit, who sat with her back to the wall, facing all the other riders, saw every head bob in unison, side to side and front to back. Some of the riders, as if stubbornly awaiting this signal, leaned their heads against the chair backs and drifted to sleep. Others appeared oblivious to their surroundings and kept their attention on their books and papers.

"How long are we underground?" Nolan asked.

"Not long. But it will be dark soon. You won't be able to see much."

"What's the countryside like, then?"

"For the first hundred or so miles, rocky but you wouldn't know it. I mean, there's enough topsoil to grow houseplants and a few scrubby trees, but there's solid stone not far under the surface, and you can't really farm. Actually, nothing in Geldricht is really arable except the valley. They graze sheep in the mountains—and they also mine about a dozen products—and then once you get to the coast, it's mostly fishing and harvesting sea kelp. If you were asking about major industries."

"Just—I don't know much about Geldricht. Just asking questions. So that's what they live on? Sheep and fish and a few grains from the valley?"

"Well," she said dryly, "there's trade."

"With the blueskins?"

"More than there used to be, but about three-quarters of the trade is foreign."

That jerked his head around so he was staring at her. "Geldricht trades with foreign nations? Trades what?"

His surprise made her irritable. Hadn't he ever read a history book? "Gold, silver, copper, diamonds, coal. Those are the big ones. In return, they buy spices, some foods, some textiles. Almost all the silk you'll find in the city was imported by Geldricht. You didn't know that?"

"I never had a reason to ask about it."

"Well, what kind of industry did you think they had in Geldricht?"

"I didn't—I don't know. I guess I assumed they were all farmers or something."

"They're all farmers in Inrhio. That's where the fertile land is," Kit said tartly. "Remember? The indigo usurped the gulden cropland during their great march westward."

"That was hundreds of years ago."

"The races immigrated here hundreds of years ago," she corrected. "In roughly equal numbers. And both races first settled on the eastern edge of the continent. But gradually the indigo appropriated more and more of the land, until the Kaelian War and the resulting treaty which split the continent—"

"I'm familiar with the history," he said.

"Well, you don't seem to know too much about anything else, so I wasn't sure this was one of the things they taught you in your obviously inadequate school courses."

"We did focus more on indigo heritage," he admitted, "and the glorious achievements of the First Mothers of the Higher Hundred."

She could not help it; he made her smile again. "So anyway. Pushed to the western coast, the gulden adapted. They found metal, so they began to experiment with electronics. They found an ocean, so they sailed it. They found friendly nations on the other side of the sea, so they began trading. Actually, these days they don't trade in products so much as technology. Chay's cousin has set up an overseas operation in the country of Dournier where he's helping construct some incredibly complex transit system. It's going to make him the head of one of the richest families in Geldricht."

"Really?" Nolan said, and he sounded as if he was working very hard to grasp a concept so alien to him that he almost couldn't be sure it was possible. "I can't imagine that anyone would be that interested in new machinery. I can't imagine that anyone would be proficient enough at technology to be able to export it."

"You mean, that a gulden would be smart enough to be proficient," she said in a glacial voice.

He seemed surprised at her tone. "No, I—" He tossed his hands in the air. "I'm the first one to admit I don't know a thing about machines. Electronics. I couldn't begin to tell you how the Centrifuge works. And my computer back at the lab. I can turn it on. I can use it. I have no idea what went into it."

She relaxed again. "Gulden technology, most of it," she said. "But from what I hear, all computers are still pretty primitive. Compared to what the engineers hope to produce some day. But some of the existing technology truly is amazing. I mean, the Centrifuge. The cars are actually airborne. Do you think about that as you go diving through the lanes? How can you possibly be *flying*? But it's not true flight, or so I've been told. There's something about magnetic dissonance and an antigravity field that can only be used in a confined space. I've been told the real trick will be true flight in airborne vehicles that can cover hundreds of miles in a few hours."

Nolan nodded. "I've heard that, too. I used to work with a guldman who would go on and on about marvels like that. We all used to ignore him." He paused and seemed to brood a moment—remembering, perhaps, past conversations with that mocked visionary, and wishing he had been more receptive. "Well, he doesn't work there anymore, so I guess I can't ask him about any of this stuff."

"Where do you work?" Kit asked curiously. "When it comes to that, who are you?"

"I told you. My name is Nolan. Nolan Adelpho."

"Higher Hundred," she said instantly. Which made this little kidnapping escapade all the more unbelievable.

He nodded. "Spent my whole life in Inrhio till five years ago when I came to the city. I'll spend the rest of my life in-country once I'm married. You're making fun of me for what I don't know but—I know everything I was taught. Everything I needed to know for the life I was supposed to live."

"And aren't you living it?"

He glanced behind him at the carful of quiet guldmen. "I was," he said. "Until today."

He said nothing more so she prompted him again. "And you work where? Somewhere in the city."

He nodded. "Biolab. In the Complex."

That arched her brows. For all his talk of techno-ignorance, he was a scientist at heart. "That's where they make the new drugs, isn't it? I read an article about the Biolab just the other day, and it sounded pretty impressive."

"Yes, we produce the experimental medications. Some work a little better than others, but we've had some rousing successes."

She inspected him with a new eye, this man who had, almost with his opening sentence, offered death to the man she loved. "So, Nolan Adelpho," she said. "In fact, what you are is a saver of lives."

But something in that sentence made him turn his face away. He stared stonily out the window. "I used to be," he said, and had nothing more to add.

They rode for the next hour in silence. The blueskin man continued staring out the window at what had become the deep blackness of true night. Kit, who had not had time to pick up any diversions while they were shopping for clothes, had nothing to occupy her but her thoughts. Was it possible that, a few short hours ago, she had been lying in Jex's arms, content and at peace? How had she been wrenched from that idyll to this nightmare? What had possessed her to listen to this man? Why hadn't she called out for the nearest guard (the Complex was alive with security) and had this Nolan creature hauled away?

But he had threatened Jex. She had believed him. Oddly gentle though he seemed now, she still sensed truth and purpose behind his words. And how could she let anyone destroy Jex? Now that she knew he loved her again?

She resettled herself more comfortably in her seat and let herself relive that sweet hour in her lover's arms. He had been so worried, so affectionate, so solicitous. Of course, it was strange that he had, before she even accused him, denied any complicity in the Centrifuge bombing. But then, their last few conversations had been arguments about his violent activities, particularly the explosions at the Carbonnier Extension.

It was hard to believe there were two terrorist groups operating in the city, when until Jex's arrival there had been none.

However, Kit had not yet heard anyone say definitively that the explosions in the Centrifuge had been bombs—had been in any way deliberate. Perhaps they had been merely structural deficiencies, triggered by some combination of temperature, land shift, and electronic decay. Like Nolan, she had no understanding of the principles behind the Centrifuge; she had no idea what factors might contribute to a sudden combustion.

Though if the explosions had been due to natural disaster or human negligence, why had Jex been so eager to disclaim any involvement? If they had not been caused by bombs at all?

Her memory played back his words from this afternoon. "I did not plan the explosions in the Centrifuge six days ago . . .

And had I known such a thing had been planned for that day I would have found some way to ensure your safety. The second I heard the blasts—when I realized where you must be—I cannot tell you the agony I endured . . ."

But if he had not had knowledge that a bombing had been planned for the Centrifuge, why had he even bothered to worry about her? He knew that's where *she* was likely to be, yes, but how had he guessed where the explosives had been planted? Sound was an unreliable visitor—it wandered in from all directions. How had he sat in his cell in the Complex, heard the fearsome detonation, and instantly known the site of the devastation?

He had not known the explosions were planned for *that day*. He had known that his allies and fellow revolutionaries were laying the wire and setting up the blasting powder for some future strike against the city. And if he had known about it, he had no doubt been involved in the planning, because Jex was not the man to sit by and let his disciples decide a course of action without his input.

The timing had been wrong, somehow. But the action had been Jex's. So not only had he been responsible for the deaths of nearly three hundred people, he had lied to her; and he had lied so well that he had convinced her.

She should have let this Nolan Adelpho do his worst, then. She should have let him kill Jex Zanlan.

But maybe she was wrong. Maybe her reasoning was faulty. This was the man she loved beyond all sense of decorum or reason. How could she so easily condemn him, how could she so quickly believe such heinous things about him? She must return to the city, she must go back to Jex, ask him to his face very clearly what he knew about the bombing, how innocent he truly was. He would tell her. He might misstate the truth, he might speak in those indirections for which the gulden were famous, but at heart, Jex was not a liar. He scorned the need for subterfuge; he had never been afraid to take full blame for any of his words or actions. He would tell her, and then she could breathe again. As for now, her very ribs hurt with the soreness of her heart.

So bitter were her thoughts, and so completely lost in them was she, that she was sharply startled when Nolan spoke to her again. She jerked around to face him; she knew she must have appeared to jump in terror. "What? I'm sorry, I didn't catch what you said," she stammered.

"I said, do you want another pain pill? You look a little haggard. Is your foot bothering you again?"

It was, but she had not noticed that dull ache amid all her other, more fatal wounds. "A little. I don't think I want another pill now. Maybe before I try to fall asleep."

He nodded. "Are you hungry? I am."

Earlier, there had been a steady of stream of passengers past them on their way to the food stalls, but now the activity had slowed. Which meant the food car would not be too crowded. "Not very," she said, "but I'll go with you and show you how everything's set up. And maybe you could buy me a piece of fruit or something light."

He gave her a somber smile. "You're that broke?" he asked.

"No, it's just that a woman can't make a monetary transaction in Geldricht."

He stared. "You can't be serious."

"Quite serious. Unless she has a *kurkalo*, which I don't."

"A *kurk*—a what?"

"*Kurkalo*. It's a—well, basically an article of permission from her husband or brother or clan chief. It looks like a wooden stick attached to a bracelet. She just shows it to the vendors, and then they treat her as if she is an emissary for her clan chief. Which, basically, she is."

"I never heard of anything so ridiculous."

Her quick anger sparked again. "Oh? And what do you know about the structure of wealth and family in Geldricht? How do you think money should be apportioned? A man is responsible for the financial well-being of his household, which includes feeding and clothing his wife, his children, any brothers or nephews who are dependent on him, his servants if he has any, the unmarried daughters of the relatives who do not have connections of their own—everyone. Sometimes as many as a hundred people. If that money is spent frivolously by his wife or his daughter—or anyone else in the family—how will he have enough to buy all the necessary items to keep the household running? Someone must watch over the money. His wife and his daughters respect this. They only ask for a *kurkalo* when they have a need for something, or when they will be traveling somewhere without his protection. And then he is only too happy to provide for them. A man who does not provide for his women is a worthless creature, someone due no honor. Any woman engaged on legitimate business will have a *kurkalo*. The system works very well."

He leaned forward, a little riled up himself. "If it works so well, then why do we have an entire small *town* of gulden women who have run away from their fathers and their husbands, living in poverty on the fringes of the city? I must assume no one gave them any *kurkalo* to make *that* journey, wouldn't you agree? Or do you think they should have stayed in Geldricht, living in whatever conditions were so intolerable they forced the poor women to run in the first place? I don't claim to know much about the gulden lifestyle, or gulden men, but I know a fair amount about indigo men and women, and let me tell you, there are a few of them that I wouldn't want to be tied to for life with no recourse and no hope of escape. I would have to imagine there are plenty of gulden who make lousy husbands and fathers, and that there are plenty of gulden women who would rather die than spend another day in their company. And you're telling me that *that's* a system that works well?"

He had hit on it exactly; he had put into words much of what she hated about the feudal, patriarchal gulden society. He could not know how she spent her days, trying to empower those escaped gulden women. He could not know how slowly and carefully she had worked, when she last lived on Gold Mountain, to institute change and press for laws that would give gulden women some legal rights.

"You're right. The system is not perfect," she said stiffly. "And for just the reasons you state. But you should not so smugly discredit it when you do not know why it was set up in the first place and how well it works much of the time."

"I'm just amazed," he said, "that any woman would agree to such a situation. The women I know would poison a man in his sleep before they would agree to be chattels. Or—no—nothing so passive. They would demolish him in some much more public way. But they would not become dependents."

"The women you know grew up in a much different environment," Kit said quietly.

"There are some truths that seem so intrinsic—so instinctual, even—that I cannot believe they can be overcome by environment," Nolan said.

"Then you have a lot to learn," she said. "What you teach a man in the cradle he will carry with him to the grave. He may fight it—he may learn new truths that contradict and supersede the old ones—but he will not ever be able to entirely convince himself that what he learned first is wrong."

"That's terrible," he said, "if true."

She gave a mirthless laugh. "I'm sure it is true even in your own case! You appear to be a somewhat sophisticated man. You've lived in the city for five years—you've mentioned knowing at least one gulden man, and you talked of him as if he was a friend. But if you were brought up in-country on a Higher Hundred estate, I'll wager you were taught that guldmen were completely inferior, and even now you can't quite bring yourself to believe they're your equals."

He was silent for so long that she thought he might not answer. His face looked troubled, and he folded his hands tightly together before him.

"To a large extent," he finally said, in a slow, considering voice, "you're right. I was—my mother considered herself a liberal woman, and always taught us that we should treat people who were not of our own social level with—with dignity and respect. But firmness. We should not let them encroach. We should not let them get too familiar. This applied mostly to the mid-caste and low-caste servants who worked in the house. We were always taught that the world runs best when everyone knows his place—and stays in it.

"But that rule applied even more to the gulden. We didn't see many, of course—a few, probably brought into the towns specifically to do some of that electronic work you talked about. My mother was very clear on our behavior to them. Treat them with great gentleness but reserve, as you would treat some kind of afflicted child. The worst sin in her eyes was to be rude, but stepping out of your place in the social order was a pretty close second.

"Actually, my mother believed that gulden were about on a par with animals—fairly intelligent and occasionally useful animals, but no higher. I don't know that she ever used the word. I do know that that is how I viewed them myself. As primitive creatures. Without thought processes. Without refined emotions. Without—without any of the characteristics that distinguish men from beasts."

He paused a moment, squeezing his hands together even more painfully. "When I came to the city," he said, "I was—it's impossible to convey how profoundly I was shocked. Not only because there were so *many* guldmen, but because they walked around on the streets of their own free will, choosing which doors to open and which trolleys to catch. You understand, I had never seen a guldman—*never* seen a guldman—unattended before. The few I saw in-country were always being directed by some blueskin in some task. It didn't occur to me they could have independent motives and schemes. It hadn't crossed my mind.

"And then. The Biolab. I walked in that first day and discovered that half of my coworkers were guldmen, and my immediate supervisor was a gulden man. I couldn't credit it. That a guldman could be capable of the fine deductive reasoning and scientific research that had taken me so much study to achieve—well, it would be as if you told me a fruit tree could compute higher mathematics. I would not believe you. Not until I saw it work its own multiplication tables, writing in the dirt with its lower branches.

"Well. It took me the better part of a year to overcome my amazement. Pakt—he's my supervisor—he was very good with me. I think he must have known how I was feeling, and he allowed me to learn on my own how skilled and efficient a guldman could be. And I admire Pakt more than any man I've ever met—gold or blue. I truly do. But I have to admit—"

He paused again and looked down at his hands as if unsure of where they came from or to whom they belonged. The train clattered across an uneven section of track, making both of them sway in their chairs, but still he did not look up from his folded hands.

"You have to admit what?" Kit demanded, when it seemed he might not complete his sentence.

"That every once in a while, I slip. I see a guldman on the street, doing something, and I think, 'How can *he* manage that?' A guldman brushes up against me accidentally, and I recoil. The ones I know—Pakt and Colt and Dade—the ones I work with every day, seem intelligent and individual to me. The ones I don't know . . . I cannot entirely accept. It's not just that I don't consider them my equals. It's that, for a minute, I forget they're even human."

Kit smiled, though she felt completely humorless. "See, then? You have proved my point."

But Nolan hitched himself forward in his chair, leaning toward her with a frowning intensity. "But I think the fault is in me, don't you see? I don't blame my mother—her mother—all the blueskin women who over the centuries taught us that they had bred some master indigo race. I have a brain and a will. I should be able to overcome that training."

She was unexpectedly moved. "Well, give yourself time. Perhaps someday you will achieve unthinking parity."

He shook his head. "I don't think so. Parity would be not noticing—the very first thing I notice about a man!—if he is indigo or gold. It would be looking at a woman and thinking 'Isn't she attractive?' even if she was gulden. Some indigo men are able to do it. You see them, now and then, with the gilt girls on the city streets. I can imagine no situation in which I would allow myself to become involved with a gulden girl. But if I were able to achieve parity in my heart, would that be so unthinkable? I cannot help myself—I consider the mere thought a degradation. I don't believe I will ever overcome that bone-deep distaste. And I am lax by indigo standards. I see no hope for the races to ever come together in harmony."

This time, his words left her colder and colder. Kit had actually wrapped her arms around herself to ward off the chill of his confession. It shouldn't matter what he said. He was a lunatic, and he had practically abducted her; she should be glad to think they could not share an emotion in common. But she hugged herself tighter and thought, blindly, *What a terrible day.*

Suddenly, his voice changed, became less intense and more

. concerned. "Look, you're shivering. I have a sweater in my bag
here, would you like it?"

"No—no, I'm fine," she said.

"Maybe you'll feel better if you get something to eat," he
said. "Do they serve hot drinks? Something to warm you up."

Of course; moments ago they had been planning to fetch food.
Kit rose shakily to her feed. "Good idea. Let's eat."

The food car, adjacent to theirs, was practically empty. There
were four stands set up along one wall, each staffed by two or
three family members, mostly men. One vendor sold meat, one
sold fruit, one sold cheese and eggs, one sold beverages. The
contracts for these stands were lucrative and jealously guarded;
some gulden families had owned franchises for years.

"What do you recommend?" Nolan asked.

"Are you familiar with gulden food?"

"A little. I've eaten at some of the fashionable restaurants.
And I've been to Pakt's house, though he was careful what he
served."

"Then I'd stick with the things you know. Now is not the
time to get sick experimenting with native cuisine."

"All right, then. I'll get a meat pie and some fruit. What do
you want? Do I have to order for you, too, or just pay?"

"Order, too, though I suppose I'll have to translate."

"Will that be acceptable?"

"Oh, yes, as long as you appear to be making the decisions."

Ultimately, they chose an assortment from each of the stalls
and carried their purchases to one of the round tables lining the
other wall of the car. The train rocked steadily back and forth,
a hypnotic, soothing rhythm that lulled all the senses into a state
of serenity. Or maybe she was just tired, Kit thought. She had
been through such a broad spectrum of emotions this day that
it was no wonder she felt blank, purposeless, passive. She slid
into a chair and set down the food, cradling the more slippery
items to keep them from sliding off the table with the motion
of the train.

They ate in silence except when Nolan made a few brief
comments about the quality of the food ("This is better than I
thought it would be . . . What's this? I like the spices"). Kit's
foot was beginning to ache with a serious throbbing, and the

interior of her head felt as though it were expanding and contracting in time with the iron wheels below her. If she didn't sleep soon, she would die. Either alternative sounded equally peaceful and attractive.

An albino man had entered after them and was now carrying on a low-voiced transaction with the meat vendor. Nolan appeared to listen for a moment, though it was obvious he did not understand the goldtongue conversation. Indeed, as Kit watched him because she could not muster the effort to turn her eyes away, he shook his head in quiet admiration.

"I sometimes think the albinos must be the smartest ones of all of us," he observed.

"Oh?" Kit said, surprised she had the energy to speak.

"They learn one whitetongue when they're brought up, and then they learn bluetongue when they come to the city, and *then* some of them learn the gulden language as well. Think of all the translating that must go on in their heads for them to be able to talk to a guldman."

Kit felt herself staring in slackjawed stupefaction. "*What?*" she managed to scrape up the indignation to reply. "Do you honestly believe—hasn't it ever occurred to you that a man could just translate directly from whitetongue to goldtongue? That he wouldn't have to know the indigo language as well?"

He gaped at her—no, the thought had obviously never crossed his mind—and then he flushed so deeply that his cobalt skin turned purple. She wanted to rail at him ("You stupid, self-referential, unthinking fool!"), but she could not force herself to feel either enough anger or scorn. Instead, she put her hand over her face and leaned on her elbow, willing the world around her to simply dissolve.

The night passed, as it always did on the train, in a choppy blur of motion, color, and disorientation. The train's infrequent halts would jar Kit into a sudden moment of panic, as she woke from some fragmentary dream to wonder frantically where she was. The stations outside her window were a jumble of flashing lights, shadowed bodies and muffled cries of question and farewell. Ah. On the way to Gold Mountain. Then the train would ease forward again into its rhythmic, pacifying motion, and she would close her eyes and try to recapture her dreams.

Whatever drugs Nolan had given her had instantly mitigated the pain in her foot, but they had caused her brain to go loose and hazy. For she could not concentrate at any of the stops they made, could not marshal her thoughts and plan her strategy. How was it possible she was guiding this man to Gold Mountain, taking him straight to Chay's door, with no more information than he had given her? She must think what to say to the gulden leader. He would find her gullible and ridiculous; he would be incredulous to learn how quickly she had agreed to Nolan's proposition. She must find words to explain her terror and her subsequent actions, but she could not concentrate. Her mind fogged over. She was asleep again.

In the morning, she woke groggy and irritable, having slept poorly and feeling a dull pain start to chisel away at her ankle bone. Nolan, apparently, had visited the market stalls while she drowsed, for he had brought an assortment of breakfast foods back to their seats and was already munching on a pastry.

"Are you hungry?" he asked when she was awake. "Does any of this appeal to you? I could go back for more."

"Give me a moment," she said and struggled to her feet. In the women's necessary room, she cleaned herself up as best she could and tried not to be too horrified at the dull, slaty color of her skin. She could stand to go a day without washing her hair, but only if she braided it tightly back from her face, and she had nothing to tie it with. A murmured request to a gulden woman who eyed her with frank curiosity netted her a gaily striped ribbon that in no way matched her mood, but it would have to do.

"Thanks would I gladly give to someone who offers me such charity," she said formally, and the woman smiled and ducked her head.

When she returned to her seat she felt marginally more cheerful and quite hungry. She ate everything Nolan had bought her, but was less eager to swallow the pills he handed her to take with her meal.

"I think I'll skip the pain medication for now," she said. "It makes me too drowsy."

"Fine, your choice, but take the vaccine anyway."

"I thought I took one yesterday."

"You have to have it every day for ten days."

"Oh, that's ridiculous. I told you I'm immune."

"Take it anyway. Please. I don't think it will do my cause any good to have you arriving at Chay Zanlan's doorstep ill and fainting."

She took the tablet from his hand and gulped it down. "Don't think you'll do your cause any good to arrive with me telling tales of your threats of violence," she said as soon as she had swallowed. "Don't think I won't tell him everything you said to me."

He nodded soberly. "Oh, no. I know you aren't my ally. But it won't matter what you have to say once I've told him—" And he stopped, looked down at his hands, and then out the window, and clearly had no intention of adding another word.

They passed much of the morning in silence, though at least this day the view offered some distraction. They were approaching the low violet foothills that edged the valley with amethyst and provided a spiky, colorful, and ever-changing vista out the windows of the train. It was Kit's favorite part of the journey out, though mostly because she knew what was ahead: a two-hour layover at one of the massive refueling stations that was actually the largest city in this part of Geldricht.

At Krekt Station, you could buy an elegant meal, a change of clothes, fine jewelry or almost any other amenity. You could also, for a small fee, use the public showers and clean yourself from head to toe. It was a ritual Kit never failed to observe on the journey. Wash away Inrhio, present herself fresh-scrubbed to Geldricht.

Of course, the fact that she couldn't stand the grimy, clammy feel of going unwashed for more than a day had much to do with her appreciation of the public cleansing rooms.

As they pulled into the station, Kit arranged their luggage on their chairs to give the impression that all four seats were taken. Nolan watched her in surprise.

"You mean, we can just leave our things here? No one will steal them?"

Kit shook her head. "Very low crime rate in Geldricht. First, of course, the clan system ensures that almost everyone is taken care of, so no one needs to steal. Second, there are incredibly brutal punishments for theft, depending on the monetary value of the item being stolen. And third—" She laughed softly. "You can't get on the train without a ticket. Our things will be safe enough."

They climbed from the train and followed the crowd into the station. As always, Kit found it momentarily disconcerting to be on steady ground. Her body missed the constant, almost maternal swaying of the coach car. Her heels hit the pavement with an unexpected jar. The world seemed rocky and unforgiving.

She pointed out the various points of interest to her fellow traveler. "Men's showers—restaurants—clothiers, if you decide you didn't bring enough shirts and trousers with you—sleeping benches. But we only have two hours. Don't forget to watch the clock."

"Meet me back here as soon as you've washed up," he said. "We'll go together to get something to eat."

She was annoyed that he didn't trust her and irritated with herself for caring. "I've come this far with you," she said sharply. "I'm hardly likely to turn around now and run back for the city."

"Even so," he said, so she shrugged and acquiesced. They parted at the door to the women's necessary room.

Five minutes later, Kit was naked under the communal shower, reveling in the feel of hot water on her body and in her hair. If she had to pick one pleasure from the canon of human sensuality, it would be the act of getting herself completely, luxuriously clean. She would forgo food, she would forgo love, she would forgo the feel of silk against her bare skin all for the satisfying satin of shampoo rinsing away past her fingers. She kept her eyes closed and splashed water over her face again and again and again.

But it was a public place, and she had forgotten how very much she stood out in this environment. When she opened her eyes, she found herself the focus of sideways glances from the five or six other women also standing under the gushing sprays of water. She was the only blueskin here, of course. There must be no more than a dozen indigo women a year who passed through Krekt Station, and most of them would die before strip-

ping naked in front of their gulden counterparts in such a careless fashion. Kit was not so well-known outside Gold Mountain
that sheltered clan women this far from the coast would instantly
suspect her identity. And so they stared at her, and wondered,
and looked away when she tried to meet their eyes.

She didn't belong here. She knew she didn't belong in the
city, either, at her grandmother's table and in the ballrooms of
the Higher Hundred. There was no place that she truly fit in.

Even Chay would not be happy to see her. And Jex was a
refuge so dangerous she could not allow herself to consider him.
There was not a place on this entire continent that she could
call home.

It was in this bleak mood that she rejoined Nolan a few minutes
later. He too had taken the opportunity to shower. His black hair
formed wet curls at the collar of his fresh shirt, and he smelled
like disinfectant. No doubt she did, too. The soap in the necessary rooms was effective but hardly elegant.

"Well, I feel better," he said, sounding more cheerful than he
had since she'd met him. "How about you?"

Clean but outcast; she couldn't say that was an improvement.
"Yes," she replied anyway. "Are you hungry? Did you want to
shop?"

"I thought maybe we could stock up on snacks so we
wouldn't have to keep going back to the stalls," he said. "And
then—maybe a book or two? If we still have a whole day of
travel left."

"Or more," she said. "But I'm not sure you'll be able to find
anything to read."

He pointed. "There's a newsstand over there. Surely they
have magazines even if they don't carry books—"

She was giving him an ironic smile; she could feel it on her
face. "Ah. I didn't know you'd troubled to learn goldtongue
while you were in the shower."

"No, I—" he began before he realized her point. He looked
both angry and embarrassed. "I see. Nothing here in a language
I can understand. Of course. Well, then, let's just go look for
food."

There were maybe twenty-five different food stalls set up in one section of the station, in addition to two restaurants where passengers could go in, be seated and order a full meal. Nearly half the vendors sold fish in some form or another—raw, dried, fried, baked, laid between slices of bread—whereas there weren't many varieties of meat available. Of course, fish was not a common commodity in the land-locked city, and only a few of the in-country towns boasted river trout big enough to bother catching. Kit wondered if this sheltered blueskin boy would be brave enough to try food so foreign, but in fact he seemed drawn to the fishmongers' wares.

"So you like fish?" she asked him as he seemed to be considering the merits of fried and baked varieties.

"Yes. I've had it a few times at the city restaurants, and Pakt's wife served it twice. I found it very tasty."

"Do you know exactly what kind you ate?"

So she guided him through a few selections, recommending dried strips for travel, and then they headed to the fruit-sellers' stalls. It was a strange buying experience, Kit found, because naturally none of the vendors would sell to her directly, but she had to do all the translating for both parties. Nolan never made any pretense of speaking to anyone except her, but the vendors all stubbornly addressed themselves to the blueskin, despite the fact that he obviously didn't understand a word they were saying.

When they had bought enough to see them through the next couple of days, they sat at one of the broad, featureless tables set up near the stalls and had a quick meal. They had been done with their food for five or ten minutes when Kit's attention was caught by a pathetic drama enacted before one of the fish stalls.

A gulden woman perhaps a few years older than Kit was groveling on the floor before the stall, calling out in a piteous voice to the trio of men who were buying dried patties and laughing with the vendor. She was dressed in a ragged assortment of ill-fitting clothes, all of them filthy, and the hands she held up in supplication were covered with sores. She looked as though she might have crawled here all the way from Gold Mountain. Kit could think of any number of scenarios to account for her presence here, and they all turned her skin clammy-cold. This was the kind of woman who showed up every day in the Lost City—destitute, half-starved, brutalized. This one at least had no children clinging to her skirts, though perhaps she had hidden them in a corner somewhere, admonishing them to be silent, to draw no eyes, to run if they saw their father or their brothers coming . . .

Kit looked away. She could give this woman the address of the charity bank, but it seemed unlikely she would ever make it that far. Most of the refugees who arrived at Del's shelter had planned their escapes carefully for months. They had saved money, they had packed provisions. This one appeared to have left on a moment's whim, the one minute her husband's back was turned, and she might indeed have made this whole journey on her hands and knees.

Nolan's voice surprised her. She hadn't thought he had even noticed the desperate traveler. "That woman—what's wrong? She doesn't have a—a *kurakura*—whatever?"

"I'm guessing she's run away from her husband's or her father's protection," Kit said in an expressionless tone. "And she doesn't have food or money."

"Where can she go?"

"Not many places," Kit said. "The city. The ghetto. She'll find shelter there if she makes it that far."

"But if she doesn't have any food or money—"

"She might not make it," Kit said quietly.

He sat there silently another moment or two, watching the woman. Now she was begging before a tall, well-groomed businessman and his gaily dressed wife, both of whom looked past her as through an inoffensive ghost. "Will anybody help her?" he asked at last.

"Maybe. You see it in the younger men more than the older ones. One of them might buy her a meal or give her a few coins. If she doesn't get on a train before her husband arrives, though, she's essentially dead."

"Dead? You mean, literally? She'll be killed?"

Kit shrugged. "Brought back to the manor and locked in a room. Most likely starved to death. That's the typical punishment for disobedience. Sometimes, a husband takes pity on an errant wife or a father on a willful daughter. But it makes him look weak in the eyes of his neighbors."

Now Nolan looked at her, wrathful and amazed. "How can you talk like that?" he demanded.

"I'm only telling you the truth."

He was on his feet, and he was actually furious. "As if it doesn't *matter*," he flung at her, and stalked away. She was left sitting there, staring after him.

In a few quick steps, he had reached the side of the runaway. In his hands, he carried the bags of fruit and fish that they had just purchased, and now he bent over her, offering them to her with silent gestures of encouragement. The woman had reared back at his approach—*alien, blueskin, danger!*—but he dropped to a crouch beside her, possibly to look less intimidating. Kit continued to stare. This passed all her experience, all her wildest expectations. Now, he was reaching into his pocket, pulling out his wallet, thumbing out a few bills, though there would be precious few merchants who would accept money from a woman's hands. The gulden woman fell on her face before him, sobbing wildly, choking out thanks that he could not translate. Nolan rose to his feet and came swiftly back to the table where Kit sat.

"I think we'd better go," he said stiffly. He would not look her directly in the face, and Kit realized, with profound shock, that he was still angry with *her*. "Our train will pull out in about fifteen minutes."

She came slowly to her feet, trying to think of words. "Don't you want to get more food?" was all she could come up with.

He turned away from her and started walking toward the track. "I guess we'll just have to make do with what's on the train," he said. "Come on. We'll be late."

And she followed him, dizzier than she'd been since she first had her concussion, and wondered if she might, after all, be hallucinating now.

CHAPTER TWELVE

They traveled perhaps two hours in total silence. Afternoon tilted imperceptibly toward dusk. The white daylight hazed into apricot, individual particles of gold hanging suspended in the air. Nolan had, all this time, gazed out the window, unseeing, unmoving. Now he turned to Kit and began the inquisition.

"All right. Tell me about her."

"Apparently anything I tell you will just upset you."

"I want to *know*."

Kit shrugged. "Most likely she's married. Most likely her husband is violent, and she reached the breaking point. She's run away. Almost no one will take in a runaway wife. Sometimes, if her father is very powerful and loves her very much, he'll take her back and allow her to live in obscurity in his home for the rest of her life. Every once in a while, a brother will do the same thing. Rarely, though. You see, any man who takes a woman's side against another man is undermining the system that makes the whole society work. It often makes him an outcast in his own community. He becomes suspect. He loses honor."

"But that's—then, she has no recourse? A woman who has been abused or married into a violent household?"

"Very little. Except to run away. And her chances of making it to the city are slim. Maybe one in four. Less."

"And once she's there—she's not safe there, is she? I mean, you read those stories all the time, about some woman found slaughtered in the Lost City. A woman and all her children. And that's because she's run away from some cruel husband? He has the right to do that?"

"Ah. The slaughter of children is really a completely separate matter."

"You say it so casually!"

"I'm not casual" was her sharp reply. "I'm just trying to explain it to you."

"Then explain it."

"In Geldricht, paternity is everything. For a man, there is almost no point to life unless he has a son to whom he can pass on all his wealth, his possessions, his profession. A daughter is a bargaining chip for making advantageous deals that include marriage, but a son is the future.

"But a son is not a real person until he is twelve years old. Try hard to understand that, or none of the rest of this will make sense to you. Until he is twelve, he may as well not exist. He is cloistered with the women and the other children, and even his father rarely sees him. At least, in the more traditional households. There are some fathers who spend time with their children, but they are rare. When a boy turns twelve, there is a ceremony that marks his—well, actually marks the occasion of his coming into existence. He has legal rights. He can hold a position on his father's estate, he can inherit if his father dies. He is officially a man.

"It is those years before manhood that are dicey ones for a boy. If his father does not approve of the way he is growing up—if his father dislikes his looks, for instance, or considers that he is not intelligent enough, not manly enough, to follow in his footsteps, he can have the boy put to death. If he—"

"Put to death! Murdered! You can't possibly mean that!"

"Try to remember. Until he is twelve, the boy isn't a person. He has no rights. He's like—a dog, or a toy or—"

"You can't be saying this. No one could believe this."

Kit spread her hands. "In Inrhio, as I understand it, it's fairly common for a woman to abort a child before it comes to full term."

Nolan stared at her. "So? What does that have to do with anything?"

"Isn't it the same thing? Aborting a life before it becomes whatever you have determined is really an individual?"

"It's not the same thing at all! One is a—a collection of cells so small you can't see them unless you're in a lab with special equipment, and the other is walking around talking, breathing, laughing, playing—"

"Frankly, I think both practices are equally abominable."

"Then how can you talk so calmly? How can you defend something that you don't believe in?"

"How can you attack something that you don't understand?" she shot back.

He threw his hands in the air. "Fine! Finish your explanation! Nothing you say will make me view this as anything less than primitive and barbaric."

"And both of those elements exist in the gulden lifestyle. But unless you know why those elements are in place, and how deeply they are woven into the collective gulden psyche, you will have no hope of changing the fabric of that society."

"As if change were possible."

"It's possible. It's happening. But slowly."

"You can tell me about that later. Finish about the children."

"All right. So until a boy is twelve, his father can do with him what he wills. But if his father dies before he's twelve, his life becomes even chancier. When a man dies, care of his wife and family passes to his next of kin—father, brother, uncle, cousin—no matter how distant the connection. Most often, this kinsman does not want the responsibility of another family in his household, so his first priority is to marry off the widow. Though he only has a hope of doing that if she's still of child-bearing age, because no man wants to marry if he won't be able to produce sons. Does this all make sense so far?"

"In its way," Nolan said grimly.

"A man who wants to have his own children has no interest in raising another man's son. So, most often, a man who marries a widow with young children will have all the children killed. He may keep the daughters, if they are pretty enough to attract good husbands—"

"He *kills* them? Just like that?"

Kit nodded. "It is as if he—as if he were to drown kittens because there were too many in the litter. It happens all the time on in-country farms."

"I never drowned a kitten. I never killed anything in my life."

"You offered to see Jex Zanlan killed."

"I admit that's what I said. The truth is, I would not have been able to stop his death if you had not helped me."

She watched him with narrowed eyes. "If you do not have power over Jex's life," she said slowly, "then what am I doing with you here on this train?"

"You're taking me to see Chay Zanlan," he set in a set, stubborn voice. "Finish your story."

Kit resumed speaking in a subdued voice as if her mind, at first, was elsewhere. "So a widow with young children knows that her children have very little chance of survival if she is forced to remarry. And that is why so many gulden women immigrate to the city, looking for shelter. They know if they can all manage to stay alive until the oldest boys turn twelve, they are safe. To slaughter a twelve-year-old is to commit murder and be subject to a trial—and, very likely, severe punishment."

"So that's why there are all those stories of children killed in the ghetto," Nolan said. "It's all about inheritance and—and property values."

"You're less brutal about it in-country," she said softly. "But your laws are just as strict. For instance, you'll never be able to inherit property, will you?"

He shook his head slowly, dumbly. "Only through Leesa. I mean, there is property my mother will settle on me, but only when I marry. If I were to never marry, it would go to my sister or a cousin or one of their daughters."

"And what would happen to you?"

"My mother's estate would care for me the rest of my life. Or it would if I didn't have an income from my job, which is probably what I would choose to live on. So if I were, for some reason, cast out of my family, I could still live, though not as comfortably as I do now. But I wouldn't be on the street. I wouldn't starve. I wouldn't be hunted down and murdered by some avenging heiress."

"That must make you feel very secure."

"Don't mock me."

"I'm not mocking you! I just think you shouldn't allow the privileges and luxuries of your own situation to blind you to the realities that others live with—and live by."

"I'm not *blinded* by them. But they make me think—why can't these same options be available to others? A guldman doesn't want the responsibility for his brother's widow. Fine. Teach her skills, let her earn her own money, let her be an independent woman."

"Just because *you*—" she began, but he cut her off.

"Very few high-caste blueskin men have chosen to follow a career, as I have. And you're quite correct—if a blueskin man does not marry, he becomes a burden to his family. In the noble families, of course, it's easy to support half a dozen extraneous mouths. In the mid-caste families, so I understand, there's some tension when a man won't marry as he's bid. But more and more men are taking their educations seriously, so that they can choose to go to the city and work if they elect not to marry— so they aren't dependent on their families. I have to admit, the first time I heard a blueskin man tell me he was never going to return in-country, I was shocked. It had not crossed my mind that my sojourn in the city was anything more than—than an interval, a small recess in the planned course of my life. But the longer I am there, and the more I grow to love my job, the more I begin to think—why not? Why not stay here the rest of my life? I am productive and happy. Why should I have to give this up?"

"And why should you?"

He shrugged. "Because I am too deeply steeped in tradition to withstand the uproar that would create. Because I respect my mother and I do not want to hurt her. Because I love my fiancée."

"Interesting," Kit said dryly, "that you put the most important reason last."

Hot color flooded his cheeks; he looked away. "So I will live as my father lived," he continued, ignoring her interjection, "but perhaps my son will not. And if change can come to the indigo traditions, why can't it come to the gulden ones?"

"It is coming. I told you it was. The very fact that the Lost City exists is a sign of change. Fifty years ago, no guldwoman would have made it to the city. Simply no one would have aided her. And if she did make it that far, there would have been no one in the city to help her. And even if someone had helped her, her father or her brother or her prospective husband would have tracked her down. She would not have been able to live. And now . . . The Lost City isn't much, but it's a start. The children raised there will not be subject to the strict rules and rituals that have governed their ancestors. Like you, they will say, why not? And they will learn skills, and take jobs, and marry city girls who will not permit themselves to be dominated . . . But all that takes so much time. Generations, usually. And it is amazing the change has even been allowed to begin."

"Then why was it?"

"Chay's doing, mostly. He traveled a great deal when he was a young man, visiting some of the foreign ports where his father had established business contacts. He saw societies so grand he could scarcely describe them. He had never had much respect for the indigo, you know—none of the gulden do—but in the foreign cities he encountered women of great elegance and power who seemed to awe him greatly. And I think he began asking himself some of the questions you are asking. 'Why is my society this way? Who is benefiting and who is hurting?' But he has to proceed very slowly, of course. Chay is ruler only so long as those he rules respect him."

"I don't understand you," Nolan said. "Sometimes you seem to embrace this savage gulden lifestyle. Other times you seem to hate it. Which is it? How do you feel?"

Kit put her hands in the air and twisted her palms indecisively back and forth. "I love it, and I hate it. I love the structure, the symmetry, the definition. Everyone knows his role and does his best to fulfill it with grace and honor. When it works, it's beautiful. When you have a kind patriarch, a loving mother, children who strive to do well and please their parents and learn all the skills they need—then it is a peaceful and harmonious place. I love to walk into a house and know where the women will sit, what the children will be wearing, what the ritual greeting will be. I know I will be treated according to my station—which, since my father was a great friend of Chay's, is high. I know what is expected of me. There is great comfort in that."

She paused, took a deep breath, seemed to consider, and exhaled slowly. "But. So often the machine does not work quite so smoothly. A husband is abusive or merely stupid. A daughter rebels against her chosen husband and is dismissed onto the streets. A man dies, and his children cease to exist. These things appall me. As you say, if we could give them options, they could find a different way to function within the society. But the gulden have never been keen on options before this."

"I still don't understand you," Nolan said. "I don't know how you can have such patience with the gulden lifestyle and show such scorn for the indigo—which certainly is no worse!"

A small smile flickered across her face. "It's that obvious, is it? I do despise so much about the indigo. Maybe because my father did. Maybe because I think—with all their advantages—they really should be better than they are. You're right that they're no worse than the gulden. But they're almost as restrictive. They're not as violent to their own people, but they've been ruthless with the gulden. I expect them to be more enlightened, I suppose, and I'm furious that they're not. They're greedy and small-minded and obsessed with prestige, and I don't see how that makes them superior to the gulden in any way. And the fact that they *think* they are galls me no end."

"Then if you're so interested in change," he said, "why don't you work to change your own race?"

Now it was her turn to look out the window, letting the shadows of the passing landscape mask the thoughts behind her eyes. "Maybe I will," she said. "How do you know? Maybe I've been doing it all along."

They did not speak for another two hours, by which time it was almost full dark. They were in more densely populated territory now, and every thirty minutes or so they passed through another town. Here the streets were extremely wide and the houses were gigantic—huge, rambling structures in which additional stories appeared to have been grafted on at random, with no attention paid to previous materials or styles. They were built of a motley but somehow pleasing assortment of red brick, pastel granite, painted wood, dark marble, and white stone, with accents of copper, ceramic, and plaster. Every house, even the smallest, blazed with color against the twilight, and even the meanest lawn was freshly mowed and neatly trimmed.

Nolan pointed as their train eased through one such town. "Those houses are enormous," he said. "Who lives there? Rich people? How can there be that many wealthy people in one place?"

Kit shook her head. "Those are clan homes. Multigenerational. You might have as many as ten families living under one roof. Typically, that would be a man and his wife and his unmarried children—as well as his married children, with their spouses and children—and sometimes *their* children. Occasionally, two brothers will share a house, and all their offspring. Occasionally, a widowed woman will return to her clan home, if there has been no husband found for her elsewhere."

"And why are they built so oddly? As if they were just thrown together?"

Kit laughed. "Well, in a sense they were. Most of them were built over the course of a century or so. Even now, if a clan keeps expanding, new levels will be built above the old ones— or sometimes new additions will be built onto the back. A man likes to have a large, complex home. It shows that his family has many branches—that he and his menfolk have been virile— and that he is able to care well for all those who are his responsibility."

"Gulden houses aren't this big in the city."

Kit closed her eyes and leaned her head back against the seat. "No, they aren't. Just one of the many things lost to the city dwellers."

"What else?" Nolan asked, but she pretended to be asleep and did not answer.

At Klevert Station, there was another hourlong layover. They took the opportunity to buy more food, for they were both getting tired of train fare. Kit bought some magazines; Nolan browsed at the newsstand, pretending he could read the headlines. A pretty gulden girl walked in, saw him, and seemed to leap backward a pace, though in reality her feet did not move. Then she stepped forward again and bestowed a charming smile on him. When she addressed him in a quick, interrogative sentence, he spread his hands and shook his head.

"I'm sorry. I don't know your language," he said in bluetongue very slowly, as if by emphasizing each word, he could make her understand it. She repeated her question, disappointment clear on her face. "I'm sorry," he said again. The girl pouted, turned away, smiled at him again over her shoulder, and ambled from the shop.

Kit was at Nolan's side in seconds. Nolan turned to her with a bemused expression. "If I didn't know better," he said, "I'd say I'd just been flirted with."

"Oh, you were." She was laughing. "Take it as a compliment. It means she thinks you have money. Of course, almost any blueskin who comes this far into Geldricht *does* have money, but the *tikitiras* won't approach just anybody, you know. They have their standards."

"*Tikitiras?* Let me guess. In the city they're called gilt girls."

"Not exactly the same," she said. But before she could explain, the bell sounded, alerting them that it was time to board their train. They headed for the gate at a half-run, and it took them another fifteen minutes to dispose themselves comfortably in their seats and arrange all their new purchases.

"So," Nolan said finally. "The gilt girls. Or whatever."

"In the city, the gilt girls are mostly runaways, girls who elected not to stay and marry the husband of their father's choice, but who have no other skills through which to make a living. And some of them are the daughters of runaway wives, who choose this way to augment the family income. They don't consider it especially demeaning, because in Geldricht, being a prostitute is a reputable occupation."

Nolan snorted. Kit continued, "It's true. It's part of the system I told you about. Everyone has his or her place. A *tikitira* is usually a girl who has lost her parents and siblings and is taken under the protection of a clan leader. She has no connections, so he can't profitably marry her off, but he will provide her with a home and clothes and the basic necessities of life. In return she provides a—a service to the men of his clan.

"You see, marriageable women are very, very strictly guarded. I won't say none of them ever manage to have sex before they're married, but it's pretty rare. If they're discovered to have lost their virginity, they lose all hope of making a marriage, and they're generally summarily evicted. Occasionally killed, though that's rarer these days, though their lives once they're out of the clan home can be pretty grim. So young women must be virgins, yet gulden men are encouraged to have experience before they wed. Obviously, that equation won't work unless somewhere in the formula there are some willing women. Thus, the *tikitiras*. They'll never marry or have much status, but they do have their place, and they're treated well. It's not a bad life, all in all."

"If they're just for providing—services—to clan members, why did that one approach me?"

Kit grinned. "They're allowed to earn a little extra money on the side if they so choose. Indeed, *tikitiras* often have the nicest jewels and the most expensive clothes because they're able to splurge more than the other women in the clan. Every once in a while, it makes for a little hostility, as you might imagine."

"I don't think this is something I would ever, on my own, imagine."

"You have prostitutes among the indigo."

"Yes, but they're not something we're proud of! They're not something we've—we've set up as an institution so that other women can keep their place!"

Kit shrugged. "Oh, in a way they are. In Inrhio, only low-caste girls are prostitutes. They're the ones with no prospects, no hope of marrying for money, so they use their bodies like any other attribute to earn cash and get ahead.

"The mid-caste girls, now, they never sleep with a man till they're married, because it ruins their opportunities. They have a chance to better themselves through marriage, and they aren't going to lose that chance if it means losing their last hope of love. A man infatuated with a mid-caste girl marries her or wonders for the rest of his life.

"The high-caste girls do whatever they want. They'll have sex with their teenage sweethearts, they'll sleep with jahla girls, they'll marry, they'll take lovers. They don't care. It doesn't matter. They're the ones with the money and the land, and they know they'll be able to marry no matter what. And even if they don't marry, they still have the land and the power, so they can have the sex, too, if they want it."

Nolan gave a sigh of exasperation. "Why does everything have to go back to sex?"

"It doesn't. It goes back to power."

"So is that why you've been able to flout convention? Because you're a high-caste indigo?"

"I have never in my life traded on my mother's lineage," she said coldly. "I have flouted convention, as you say, because I have been brought up in the most unconventional manner possible. I was taught that the individual has the obligation to understand his society but the right to live outside it. But the only reason I was able to live by those convictions is that my father had a great deal of money, and he left it all to me."

"How's that? Blueskin men don't inherit wealth."

She gave a wintry smile. "He earned it himself. And then, under Chay's guidance, he invested it in gulden markets overseas. And the returns were quite impressive. He was careless with money, and he spent a lot of it before he died, but he left me enough to live on without worrying." She paused, laughed shortly, and continued. "It's much easier to be a rebel when you don't have to worry about where you're going to sleep and what you're going to eat. I often wonder exactly how passionate I would be about some of my issues if I was dependent wholly on my grandmother—or, in Geldricht, on Chay's good nature. I think I wouldn't be nearly so outspoken. Which infuriates me, but there you go. Wealth is freedom. And anyone who doesn't believe that is unimaginably naive."

He was quiet a few minutes, as if mulling that over. Then: "You never said. What exactly are you doing in the city? If you have money, I guess you don't need to work. How do you fill your days, then?"

"I do charity work in the Lost City."

"What kind of charity work?"

"There are places women can go. Gulden women. Where they can get food, and have shelter for a few nights, and find help getting settled into their new lives in the city. I work at a place like that. Mostly, I do fund-raising—I go into the city and ask wealthy merchants to help fund the charity bank."

"Gulden or indigo?"

"Both, but I generally have more luck with the indigo."

"That's odd."

"Not if you've been paying attention. The gulden don't approve of the Lost City."

"Well, blueskins aren't known for their kindness to the gulden."

"Ah, but blueskin women have a certain sense of—sisterhood, almost—with guldwomen. They like to think their meager contributions will lead to an overthrow of the patriarchy. And maybe they will. So some of them have been generous. But they don't like to deal directly with the gulden women—especially the poor ones in the Lost City—so I'm usually the emissary who approaches them. It makes them more comfortable, because they think I'm one of them. They don't realize how wrong they are."

He gave her a long, serious look. She became immobile under his scrutiny, neither looking away nor scowling to turn his gaze aside. He did not seem to be staring at her features so much as peering behind the worthless mask of skin and skull to pore over the brain below. Then he gave his head a small, helpless shake and shrugged.

"I don't understand you," he said again. And she made no answer. It was not something she knew how to explain.

CHAPTER THIRTEEN

True dark again. Nothing to see out the train's smudged window. Nolan stared out anyway, since it was all he felt safe doing. He was sick of this strange food, sick of the endless lazy rocking of the train, sick of his own thoughts of outrage and betrayal.

And electrified by this woman who traveled beside him, instructing him and mocking him by turns, revealing herself more with every word, confusing him more with every syllable. She looked every inch the indigo heiress, with that flawless blue skin, those aristocratic features, that turn of expression that could make a man feel like contaminated mud beneath the most expensively shod feet.

And yet she had rejected that pampered lifestyle wholesale. She had chosen to live among foreigners, adopting many of their beliefs—but challenging that lifestyle as much as she challenged the one that was hers by birthright. There did not seem to be a place for her either in the ordered scheme of the gulden world or the rigid caste system of the indigo. She was like no one he had ever encountered before. He could not get his mind to track with hers; he could not comprehend her motives or her values.

Why had she come with him? Why—since he had been the most lax of kidnappers—had she not fled from him at one of the stations they had passed through? Why had she not asked one of their fellow travelers for aid? Of course, given what she had told him about the gulden world, she may have had a hard time finding a champion. Traveling with him, she must appear to be under his protection, and in Geldricht, that relationship seemed sacrosanct. But she was a demonstrably resourceful girl. She could have escaped him if she would.

She must have her own reasons for returning to Geldricht, and to Chay Zanlan. There was no other explanation.

She was nothing to him—just a means, a key to a door that might be locked to him despite her—and yet he found himself, as the hours passed, growing more and more obsessed with her. What a passionate creature! So alive, so furious, so contradictory. For her, nothing came on faith. Nothing was immutable. Nothing could not be changed or overturned. Leesa would not have three words to say to her, and yet her heritage was every bit as rich, as impressive as Leesa's. Colt would hate her, instantly, comprehensively, and yet she knew as much about Colt and his upbringing as she knew about her own family. She was reserved and civilized, both in speech and manner, and yet her very existence was iconoclastic. She was a living dare to both of those insulated worlds, indigo and gulden. Her life said to them, "You may be well enough as you are, but you could be so much better."

He wanted her to talk forever; he wanted to ask her increasingly more intimate questions. She had not mentioned her imprisoned gulden lover, though he was the reason she had come with Nolan this far. She had not clarified her relationship with Chay. She had not asked Nolan to explain what possible reason he could have for dragging her so abruptly from her home, using her to gain entry into an alien society, offering violence to her loved ones.

(But did she love them? Did she truly love Jex Zanlan? She had scarcely mentioned him. But then, Nolan had mentioned Leesa only once. He had not felt much like talking about his betrothed.)

To love this girl would be to embrace fire and whirlwind and immolation. At least, that would be true for Nolan. Perhaps Jex Zanlan was flame and cyclone himself, and he would not notice how this woman churned through him, realigning his molecules, resurfacing his skin. For Nolan, she would be catastrophic, she would be upheaval on the grandest scale.

But he needn't worry. She was not intended for him, either by the fates or the dictates of his own society. Calmer things were in store for him, once this trip was over. He would never lay eyes on Kitrini Candachi again.

Kitrini. He had not even said her name aloud this whole time.

"Kitrini," he said now, almost without volition. He was still staring out the window, his face turned away from her, but she heard him anyway. She stirred, as if shaking herself awake, and looked his way.

"Yes?" she said.

He shook his head. "I was just wondering if you were awake. How's your foot? Still hurt?"

"A little. It's getting better, though."

"You want another painkiller?"

"Before we sleep for the night, maybe."

He turned to look at her, slowly, knowing (from his experiences the past day and a half) what a fresh shock it would be to see her face. Two eyes, a small nose, high cheeks, that familiar indigo skin—what was there about this collection of features to make his heart pause, actually shut down for three beats, and then gallop forward again at a clumsy, frantic pace? "You never told me," he said in a casual voice, "how you injured yourself."

An indescribable expression crossed her face. Nolan tried to catalog the swift emotions: pain, embarrassment, a lingering anxiety. "I was caught in the blast that shut down the Centrifuge," she said shortly.

Nolan's eyes widened. "You *were*? I thought nobody survived that."

"A handful of us only. No reason to it—the survivors were scattered over the whole area, our cars interspersed with the cars of the dead ones. Luck—fate—who knows? But it makes me feel very strange to have lived through something almost no one else survived."

"And most of them were indigo, weren't they? The ones who died?"

"Why would you say that?" she shot at him angrily, taking

him completely by surprise. "Gulden ride the Centrifuge!"

"I know—I just—since the explosion happened at South Zero—"

"They haven't discovered what caused it yet. Or at least, they hadn't by the time we left the city. There's no reason to think it was a bomb."

"I didn't think—did I say—"

"You implied that someone had set a bomb at South Zero to kill a bunch of blueskins," she said furiously.

Ah. Of course. The terrorist lover in jail. No wonder she was touchy on this subject. "I didn't mean to imply that," he said gently. "Frankly, I don't have a clue what started the explosion, and I haven't given it much thought. I do know that it disrupted my life most inconveniently."

"Well, Jex had nothing to do with it."

"I'm sure he didn't."

Now she gave him a look of renewed hostility. "And why are you so sure of that?" she demanded illogically. "He set off a blast in the medical center, after all."

Nolan spread his hands. She baffled him. "I just assumed he wouldn't be capable of something so—so horrifying."

"And why would you assume that?"

"Because you love him," he said softly. "And you don't seem likely to love a murderer."

Now she was the one to turn her face away. Her arms were wrapped tightly across her chest, and she had drawn her feet up to the edge of the seat, so that she sat in a small, folded position, looking as though she would prefer to disappear. "He told me himself," she said in a lost voice. "He swore to me that he did not plan for any bomb to go off in the Centrifuge. Why wouldn't I believe him?"

"Well, it might not even have been a bomb," Nolan said soothingly. "It may have been some electrical problem, I heard. Or a spark setting off some underground gases. They're looking into it."

"It was a bomb," she said, still in that frail voice. "You know some of the gulden have sworn they'll do anything to stop the Carbonnier Extension. This is one of the things they'll do."

"But even if that's so—Jex is still in prison, isn't he? How could he have had anything to do with it?"

"He *does* have visitors," she said in a strangled voice.

Nolan had a sudden vision of Colt, caught by Cerisa as he attempted to meet with Jex Zanlan in stealth. But surely Colt was not one of that band of terrorists. Colt had a fine disdain for all things indigo, but he was not a destructive man. He had chosen a career as a scientist, a preserver of life; he would not wantonly and randomly destroy it. And certainly he would not have risked the lives of his coworkers at the Biolab, many of whom rode the Centrifuge home at night, many of whom would have been at risk that fateful evening if Pakt had not kept them after hours with a meeting . . .

Nolan's mind came to a sudden dead halt. Such an evening meeting was rare. Not unprecedented, but far from common. Why had Pakt chosen that night of all others to discuss items even he had agreed could have waited till morning? Had Colt warned him about the bomb? Surely not, that could never be—Pakt would unquestionably have reported such information to Cerisa, to Ariana Bayless. But perhaps Colt had spoken more enigmatically—"There will be trouble tonight. Everyone will be safe if they stay in the Biolab until dark." That would not have given Pakt enough information to report, but enough to make him keep the others at his side. Perhaps Colt had not even said that much—perhaps he had merely told Pakt, "You'd better stay late at the lab tonight," and Pakt had taken it upon himself to keep them all safe. That seemed realistic. That seemed possible.

But then that would make Colt a terrorist. That would make Colt a murderer. That would make the man Nolan knew a monster that he could not recognize.

He shook his head, trying to shake away the vision. Melina would be able to clear it all up for him, if he ever got back to the city, if he ever had a chance to speak to his friends again. His whole life seemed so far away, unreal, something he had dreamed of in a fevered sleep. He shook his head again, more forcefully.

"What? You think he isn't allowed to have visitors? He is. I've seen him myself in his cell at the Complex."

Her words made no sense until he was able to recall what

she had said just before his brain descended into dark speculation. "No—I was thinking about something else—sorry, I wasn't paying attention," he stammered.

"Well, let's not talk about it anymore," she said.

"Tell me one thing," he said. "How does Chay feel about Jex? And some of his more—violent activities?"

"He hasn't told me," she said in repressive tones. "Why would he discuss his son with me? A man of honor would do no such thing."

"You must have formed an opinion," he persisted.

"I think—I think Chay has a very mixed reaction to Jex's strong opposition to Ariana Bayless," she said reluctantly. "On the one hand, he's proud of Jex for being so forceful, for following his convictions to the blind, bitter end. The gulden have always loved a man who was willing to die for a belief. And, in his heart, Chay agrees with Jex—he does not want to see the Carbonnier Extension. He does not want the indigo to take another inch of land from the gulden. On the other hand, Chay has rejected violence his whole life. He has preached negotiation and strategy—still forceful, but much less brutal. So he would not endorse Jex's methods even if they were successful. And I believe the parent in him fears desperately that Jex's methods will *not* be successful, and that Jex will lose his life in this endeavor. And Jex is Chay's only son. So you can imagine how deep such a grief would go."

"And you?" he said, before he could stop himself. "How deep would such a grief go with you?"

She gestured; a motion of helplessness. "He is my life," she said simply. "He has been since I can remember. How do you give up something like that? But I do not know that Jex will survive the course he has set for himself. And then—" She gestured again. Nolan made no answer. There were no words.

They were silent for another hour or two. Nolan was surprised when Kitrini was the one to speak next.

"Have you considered," she said, "exactly what you will say to Chay when you approach him?"

He looked at her dumbly. He could scarcely credit what he had to tell Chay Zanlan; he had not thought how to word it.

"No," he said. "Is there some way I should address him? Some title he goes by?"

"There are no titles among the gulden, but if you do not know a man, it is considered polite to refer to him by his full name every time you speak to him. As he will address you by yours. And do not come directly to the point. Make civil inquiries first. Ask about his health. Comment on the beauty of the landscape in Geldricht. These show you have an interest in the man, not just the issue."

"All right. But what I have to tell him is fairly urgent."

"He will have guessed that," she said dryly, "by your very appearance at his door."

"Does he speak bluetongue?"

"Fluently."

"Once we get to—to the issue—can I speak straight out? Or must I talk in that roundabout way that I have heard the gulden use?"

"No. If you are speaking in bluetongue, be plainspoken. If you were conducting the conversation in goldtongue, you would have to be more careful about how you phrased things, but in your own language, speak as you always would."

"Why is it," Nolan asked with a certain exasperation, "that the gulden always speak so obliquely? Do they do it just to be annoying? Because that's what it seems like."

Kitrini smiled faintly. "Well, sometimes they do. When they're dealing with blueskins. But their own speech is very circuitous—and that's because their language is mined with pitfalls. There is a certain case you use when you're addressing an inferior, a different one when you're addressing a superior, a neutral case if you're addressing someone to whom your relationship is not yet established . . . Very tricky. Thus, the syntax is designed to be indirect, so that no one is offended by the accidental misuse of a word. There are so many different ways to say 'you' in goldtongue that sometimes even I get confused, and I acquired the language as a child. It's so complicated it's almost impossible for nonnatives to learn it. Even if you know goldtongue, and you're conducting delicate business, you're better off using some other language, because it's so easy to make a mistake that will have you evicted from the room."

"Maybe you can stay and make sure I don't make any grave mistakes."

"I'm surprised you would ask for my help. You don't even know me. How do you know I wouldn't mistranslate on purpose?"

He looked at her a long time. "Because I trust you," he said at last.

"You have no reason to."

He spread his hands; a gesture of resignation. "But will you?"

"I will if Chay allows it. But you must have realized by now that women usually are not invited to conferences such as this. And besides—" She hesitated, then plunged on. "It may not do you as much good as you're hoping to be seen in my company."

"And why would that be?"

"Chay and I quarreled the last time I was in Geldricht. He may be far from happy to see me again. I spoke to him briefly when he was in the city, and he no longer seemed to be angry, but he will not have forgotten the quarrel."

"What did you argue about?"

"Things that don't concern you," she said frigidly.

He accepted the rebuke by bowing his head and appearing to think everything over. "I must say I'm getting a little nervous," he said at last. "What will Chay Zanlan do to me if he doesn't like what I have to say?"

She gave him a considering look. "And what are the chances that he *will* like what you have to say?"

"Not very good," he admitted.

"But you feel compelled to tell him something anyway."

"I have no choice."

"Then perhaps he will take that into account."

"But what will he do? How will he treat me?"

Kitrini shook her head. "I have no idea. I don't know how he will react to your arrival. I don't know what you plan to tell him. I don't know what else he will be in the middle of when we walk in. He has a lot to worry him right now, you realize. His son is in jail, possibly to be accused of murder. The easternmost edge of his land is under assault from greedy indigo imperialists. I happen to know that one of his most lucrative trading contracts is up for renegotiation and that he almost cannot afford to see it fail. How will he view your arrival? Not kindly, unless what you have to say is as important as the questions vexing him already."

"Oh, it is," Nolan said. "It makes everything else insignificant."

She looked at him wonderingly, but still she did not ask. Nolan almost thought he might tell her, if she asked. She said, "Then I'm sure he will deal with you with the respect and consideration you deserve."

Silence again, then sleep. Nolan woke several times in the night as the train came to a ragged halt, panted for a few minutes outside some garish station, then strained forward again till it hit its usual steady pace. Now his mind, which had been split into three equally desperate parts, subdivided again. Up till this point, his attention had leapt fitfully from horror at what he had learned, to panic at the thought of confronting Chay Zanlan, to infatuation with the girl beside him (a compartment of his brain that seemed to grow with each passing hour, despite the fact that the other two sections did not in any way diminish). Now, he had opened a fourth door and found another equally awful vista: the image of Colt as terrorist and killer. Like the others, it was too terrible to look upon for long—but anywhere he turned was a view equally as disturbing.

It was no surprise he could not sleep. No surprise that his skin felt as if it had been injected with acid, one single, liquid layer between the muscle and the flesh. It would be more of a surprise if he survived this adventure with any of his sanity intact.

And what then—?

He watched dawn idle over the landscape, spilling forward from behind them as they headed west. Now, they seemed to pass through nothing but city, one row of spectacular houses after another, a little more thoughtfully constructed than the country homes but still built with a pleasing motley and an air of self-satisfaction. They were in the heart of Geldricht, in the gentle foothills before Gold Mountain. Indeed, the sublime and jagged silhouette of the great peak dominated the land from every viewpoint, and they appeared to be headed straight toward it.

Chay Zanlan did not live *on* Gold Mountain, of course, though that was what everyone said. He lived in a palace at the base of the mountain—or at least Nolan had always assumed it was a palace. He'd seen pictures in the news monitors, and it looked almost as big as the Complex. Now, having traveled through the gulden countryside, he thought it might just be a larger version of the sort of building all the gulden called home.

Plenty of room there to incarcerate a visitor who came bearing strange news. No one in the world knew where Nolan had gone. No one would be able to find him if he suddenly disappeared.

He shook his head vigorously. Last night, Kitrini had told him that they should arrive at Zakto Station sometime after noon. A public conveyance would take them to Chay Zanlan's palace—and then who knew how long before the great leader would agree to see them? Nolan had thought Kitrini's company would buy him an instant entree, but she said no. Well, then. He would wait till he was invited in. All day, if necessary; all week.

And what then—?

Kitrini stirred, opened her eyes, and gave him one unthinking smile of recognition. Then—it was obvious from her face—she remembered where she was and who she was with, and she frowned quickly to mitigate the effects of the smile. "Where are we?" she said.

He pointed. "Within sight of Gold Mountain. I think we'll be at the station in a couple of hours."

"Are you ready?" she asked.

He shook his head. "Not even."

She rose to her feet, off to the women's necessary room. "Hold on to that thought," she advised.

When she returned, he had cut up some fruit and sliced bread from a loaf, and they ate for a few moments in silence. Then Nolan shook out the day's ration of pills for her.

"Oh, not again," she said impatiently. "I've told you—"

"And I've told *you*," he said. "You don't want to be sick."

"But I *won't* be sick. I have immunities."

Nolan looked at her seriously, willing her to believe. "Two

months ago," he said, "three blueskin businessmen returned from a visit to Geldricht. All three of them were sick with a fever the doctors couldn't identify. Two of them died. A week later, another blueskin died two days after he'd returned from Gold Mountain. Same symptoms. No one's been able to identify the illness."

"I haven't heard anything about this," she said, frowning.

"It hasn't been in the news. Ariana Bayless is afraid to create a panic. But if you worked at a firm that traded with the gulden, you would have received a detailed memo that outlined your health risks. And a prescription for pills just like these."

"If they don't know what caused the fever—" she began, but Nolan interrupted her.

"Wide-spectrum antibiotic," he said, shaking the capsules in their case. He was getting in deeper with every lie he told, but he did not think she knew enough about drugs to be able to contradict him. "Preventative. It's possible it won't protect you fully, but your chances become a whole lot better."

"Oh, all right," she said ungraciously and held out her hand for a pill. He watched to make sure she didn't just pretend to swallow it. That would be even more disastrous.

"How's your foot?" he asked.

"Feels pretty bearable this morning."

"Probably all this sitting the past couple days has done you good."

"Oh, I'm sure," she said, and there was a sarcastic edge to her voice. "This whole *trip* has done me no end of good."

So of course he had no response to that.

The train pulled into Zakto Station a little after noon. Zakto was huge, echoing, crammed with people waiting, running, shouting, eating, buying, staring. Nolan counted ten other gates leading into the station and asked Kitrini to have it confirmed: Yes, trains left from Zakto to points all over Geldricht. In fact, the line into the city had been the last one built. Nolan knew he should not be surprised, but he was. He had always thought the train tracks had been laid primarily to link Gold Mountain with the city. Now he learned the indigo had been merely an afterthought.

"I'm sure," Kitrini said, "that you would like to shower and make yourself presentable before you approach Chay Zanlan."

"Yes," Nolan said. "I don't have much in the way of clothing choices with me, but is there something I *shouldn't* wear? Some color or style?"

"No, but be sure and wear your fiancée's medallion so he can see it."

"All right, but why?"

"Because it's a symbol he'll recognize, and the gulden respect symbols. And it will do you no harm for Chay to instantly recognize you as a member of the Higher Hundred."

"Very well. Thank you."

They separated and headed for the showers. Nolan was getting used to the frank appraisal by the other men in the public rooms, though he still didn't like it. It was not just his blue skin that attracted their attention, he had realized that almost immediately. They appraised each other just as openly, noting body size, muscle definition, probable strength, and possible sexual prowess. This was not something Kitrini had warned him about—but then, perhaps women did not eye each other with quite the same agenda. He didn't know if it helped him or hurt him that he was slim, lean, and loose-limbed, whereas the naked gulden men in the showers beside him all seemed to be built of corded muscle wrapped around boxy bones. Would they be pleased that he offered them no physical threat, and thus leave him in peace, or would his vulnerability incite them to easy violence?

He made no conversation, no eye contact, and everyone left him alone. Oh, how he longed to be in the private, civilized world of Inrhio again.

He toweled himself off and dressed in the last clean clothes left in his luggage, wrinkled though they were. His hair had a tendency to spiral into wild curls if it wasn't rigorously dried, and so he spent ten minutes alternately combing it and rubbing his scalp briskly with another towel. He shaved carefully—this was not the day to be sporting a sliver of dried blood—and brushed his teeth twice. He slipped Leesa's medallion over his neck and took a moment to survey himself in the mirror.

Even to himself, in this place, he looked alien. How would Chay Zanlan receive him?

Kitrini was waiting for him when he emerged. She too had taken some effort with her appearance. She was wearing the most colorful of her clothes and a ribbon through her dark hair. Unless he missed his guess, she had also taken the trouble to apply rouge and mascara.

"Do you have enough money left to buy me something?" she greeted him. "There's a scarf in that little shop. Chay appreciates frills and bright colors, and I feel a little drab."

"You don't look drab," Nolan said, digging out his wallet.

"That's because you've grown to love the true radiance of my inner soul," she said with a quick flash of humor. "But Chay will like me better if I'm dressed in flame and scarlet."

"Then buy as many scarves as you like," Nolan said. "Because we certainly want Chay to like you."

Ten minutes later, they were seated in a narrow trolley similar to the vehicles that serviced the city. Kitrini sat in the back with the gulden women; Nolan sat as near to the back as he dared, so he could keep an eye on her and depart when she did. But most of his attention was on the sights around him. The streets were crowded with all manner of public and private vehicles— many more varieties than could be found in the city—and the trolley was constantly jerking to a halt or lurching forward in response to some break in traffic. The buildings lining the street were a gay mishmash of hues and styles, each bedecked with flags and ribbons and flowers. It all had a circus feel to Nolan, enhanced by the giddy sunshine and the bright clothes of the natives walking by. It seemed a happy, festive carnival.

This was not at all what he had expected.

They had ridden perhaps three miles when Kitrini swung to her feet and headed for the exit. Nolan was instantly behind her, hopping down the trolley steps with his luggage in his hand. They were standing before a huge, multilayered building built entirely of a warm, sandy granite. Its narrow grounds were flooded with flowers and edged with hedges. The white flagged walkway leading to the massive doorway was lined with pennants of every shape and color.

"Clan standards," Kitrini said, before Nolan had a chance to ask.

"Impressive," Nolan said.

"The flags or the building?"

"The whole presentation."

There were no guards outside, but once they had crossed the lawn and entered, they had to pass a number of checkpoints. There was an electronic search at the door (Kitrini had to explain to Nolan what it was; he didn't much care for the invasive tingle along his spine and groin). Then they were shown to a small anteroom, where a burly blond guard interviewed them briefly to ask their names and business. Kitrini translated, but she had made it clear Nolan must participate, so he spoke in a firm voice in bluetongue, and she said whatever she pleased to the guard. They were shown to another waiting room where perhaps thirty people were seated.

"Get comfortable," Kitrini advised, and settled herself in.

Nolan sat beside her. "Do you usually have to go through such an ordeal when you come to visit Chay?"

"I've never come before without an invitation or a *kurkalo*," she said. "I cannot come and go as I please. I did give them my name, and the secretary should recognize it, and that may get us in sooner than otherwise, but I don't know. Be patient."

Nolan nodded (he had never felt less patient) and looked around him. They were not, he was surprised to see, the only indigo in the room. There were two others, both male, sitting together hunched over what looked like blueprints. There was also an albino sitting on the opposite end of the room, as far as possible from both blueskins and guldmen. He was halfway through a fat book, and Nolan had a vision of him sitting here for days, weeks, months, slowly turning page after page until he had finished it. He wished he had a book of his own to distract him. Here, there was not even landscape to watch, nothing but the thoughts in his head to keep him glum company.

Kitrini had leaned her head against the back of her chair and appeared to be asleep, though Nolan suspected she was dissembling. More likely, she was reviewing what she would say to Chay Zanlan, before whom she was appearing so unexpectedly under such strange circumstances. Nolan wished she would share with him the contents of her introduction, but he was not used to demanding information from any woman, and he felt he had already used this one hard enough.

But no matter what Kitrini said, Chay would listen to him. He had to. This was news that could not be strangled.

Three hours passed. At long intervals, a guard appeared at the doorway, calling out a name, and that lucky petitioner rose to his feet and disappeared. But those hopeful moments were few and far between. Despite his anxiety, Nolan felt exhaustion, and the strain of the past few days begin to work their will. Like Kitrini, he closed his eyes and sagged back in his chair. Images flickered against his eyelids—gulden faces, gulden homes, gulden landscapes—in an exotic kaleidoscope. When he finally returned to Inrhio, would it look odd to him, stark and severe? It was hard now to call all its classic lines to mind, the clean blacks and whites he had lived with all his life, the lush in-country greens, the ordered homes and fields. Surely, once he stepped back inside those boundaries, they would become reassuringly familiar. He would not be in Geldricht that long.

"Nolan Adelpho and Kitrini Solvano," the low, gravelly voice announced, in accents so distorted that Nolan did not even recognize his name. Not until Kitrini came to her feet did Nolan realize they had been called. Suddenly panicked, he leapt from his chair, started toward the door, turned back for his suitcase and hurried after Kitrini out the door.

The guard stopped them both in the hallway, gesturing at their luggage. "We can't bring our bags into Chay's presence," Kitrini told Nolan. "In case we have weapons."

"Understandable. Will he watch them for us?"

"I'm sure he will."

There was another brief exchange of words, a young boy was called over to take charge of the baggage, and they were on their way. The inside of Chay's residence was airy and light, built of high arching ceilings, long hallways with many windows, and unexpected nooks featuring small gardens and fountains. Despite his worries, Nolan found himself responding to the architecture, relaxing a little, believing that nothing too awful could happen in such a pretty place.

But he snapped back to dread the instant they were ushered into a wide, formal room, and Chay Zanlan turned to gaze at them. The guldman was just as Nolan remembered him from those brief glimpses from Melina's window, only up close he was even more intimidating. He was more than six feet tall, broad-chested, stockily built, so leonine and so powerful that he appeared to radiate strength and energy. Even the faint sweep of white in the red hair, even the weathered lines around the intense gray eyes, did nothing to age or diminish him. He appeared to be a man in the prime of life, at the height of his physical and intellectual abilities, and for the first time Nolan wondered if he might be wrong.

If so, utter disaster. He was a fool beyond calculation. And he would deserve any scorn or punishment that could be meted out to him, either by this race or his own.

He stood stock-still, waiting. Kitrini had said he should allow Chay to speak first, though she had been uncertain whether the guldman would recognize her or treat her like a woman as invisible as any other. "Which would be a good sign?" he had asked, and she had given a hollow laugh. "I don't know," she had replied.

It seemed like a full minute that Chay Zanlan assessed them, his eyes flicking from one face to the other, but everything else about him immobile. Then he took three majestic steps across the room and enfolded Kitrini in a massive hug.

"Kit," the guldman said, and then a spate of other words that Nolan could not recognize. Kit? That was how she was called here? With so many other things to think about, Nolan's mind fastened on to that fact. Kit. He liked it. It suited her.

Chay Zanlan released her and addressed another comment to her in goldtongue. She answered in the same language, seeming entirely at ease, though Nolan sensed she was not. He continued to stand very quietly. Patience was the key here. That oblique speech. That indirect approach. He must remember to proceed as Kitrini had told him.

As Kit had told him.

Finally, after an interminable conversation in which Nolan had no part, Chay Zanlan gestured at his other guest and switched to bluetongue. He had a perfect command of the language, Nolan noted; someone had taught him well.

"So, Kit, I see you have traveled here in the company of a blueskin man," the gulden leader said casually.

"Yes, he was most interested in making your acquaintance."

"I am always curious to meet friends of my friend's daughter."

"I explained to him that you are a very busy man and do not have much time for idle talk."

"That is true."

"And he assured me he would not waste your time with insignificant matters."

"That is good to hear. In your journey here, did he explain to you what weighty topics he wished to discuss with me?"

"No, he did not," Kitrini said flatly.

Chay inclined his head. "That is well. A man should not debate such issues lightly with a woman."

Kit was silent. Chay appeared to consider. Nolan thought his tension must send him shrieking across the room. He clenched his hands till the nails scarred the palms. "And yet, some women have valuable insights into the hearts of men. My wife, for instance, can often tell me what it is I am thinking even when I have not resolved my thoughts."

Kit smiled faintly. "The lady Rell is wise in many ways."

"And you yourself are a woman of uncommon intelligence. Your opinion at times has been most welcome to me."

"I thank you for your respect."

"Then let me ask you. Do you believe this man, this indigo stranger, has any matters of true import to discuss with me? For I am in fact a busy man, and I will turn him away without a hearing if you advise me to do so."

Now Nolan's body was strung tight with astonishment. Nothing Kitrini had told him, nothing that he knew about the gulden hierarchy, had led him to expect such a turn of events, that his chance to speak to the gulden ruler would rest in the hands of a woman he had coerced into this venture. She had shown him a surprising tolerance, despite her moments of bitter scorn, but he had given her no reason to trust him, no reason to think him anything but a lunatic. A word from her now, and his opportunity would be thrown away; even if Nolan was dragged shouting and struggling from the room, Chay would not listen to him, would not acknowledge a single syllable. And Nolan could not believe her word would be a good one.

She seemed to hesitate a long time, weighing her response,

but Chay showed no impatience. Nolan, on the other hand, felt his veins stretch and coil around his bones; he felt his feet drift dizzily above the floor. He dug his nails more deeply into his skin and said nothing.

"I believe," Kitrini said slowly, "that he had a compelling reason to make this journey. It is not a thing lightly undertaken, to leave your familiar home to travel to a place where you have no friends. He is not a man to do such a thing on a whim. Whatever news he brings you must be momentous indeed."

"And should I believe him? For blueskins have lied before to guldmen. He may have a great cause, but it may be great only to his nation. Will he speak to me in honest words?"

Again, she seemed to struggle with her reply, searching her soul before she formed the words. "I will not lie to you," she said, and Nolan went limp with fear. "I did not come here of my own free will. This man induced me to accompany him through threats and offers of violence. But I would have found a way to divert him, or a way to warn you, if I had not come to believe he had a message that you must hear. I would not put you at risk. I would have led him to the edge of Gold Mountain and pushed him into the sea rather than bring him to your door."

"And yet my door is precisely where you have brought him," Chay said. "So tell me plainly—does this mean that you trust him?"

"I trust him," she said in a low voice, and Nolan had to stop breathing to hear her. "I cannot tell you why. I can only judge him by my heart, and my heart has been wrong before. But I believe he is a good man. I believe he has been steeped in kindness. I would be willing to see my life forfeit if he were able to do you harm."

Nolan stared at her, everything else washed away by stupefaction. When had she developed this opinion, or could she possibly be lying? She was gazing unwinking at Chay Zanlan, her face set and serious, her expression almost fierce. She looked like a true believer. Chay, who had never once glanced at Nolan since this conversation began, gazed back.

"As it would be," Chay said softly. "Which you knew when you walked in here."

"As it may yet be," she whispered. "I know."

Chay watched her a moment in silence, and then nodded once, sharply. "So. Tell me his name."

Nolan's limbs had all turned to yarn and rubber. He felt himself bobbing like a puppet as both of them turned to look at him. "Nolan Adelpho," Kit said. "A respected member of his race's nobility."

Now Nolan looked into those fierce gray eyes, and it was like stepping off a cliff. He felt very much as if Kit had actually shoved him off a precipice on Gold Mountain. "Nolan Adelpho," Chay repeated. "I understand this is your first visit to Geldricht."

Small talk, idle conversation. Even now they must spar and establish rituals. "Yes, Chay Zanlan, it is," Nolan replied.

"And what do you think of it?"

"What I have seen from the train windows is fascinating and complex," he replied. "I had many questions to ask of Kitrini Candachi. She was an excellent source of information."

Chay nodded regally. "It is a good sign when a man is interested in learning," he said.

"I think I have a great deal more to learn, even so," Nolan said. "I found your land rich with color and ritual and beauty, just from my window. I am sure it would be all that and more if I had time to study it."

Chay permitted himself a smile. "A gracious comment," the guldman said. "Your land, I know, has its own riches and beauties."

"Yes, and I love it with most of my heart," Nolan said. "But I see now that a man must reserve a portion of his heart with which to appreciate things outside his immediate experience."

"I confess," Chay said, "my heart was not much won over by your metropolis. Perhaps I did not stay there long enough."

"The city is not the true measure of Inrhio's beauty," Nolan said, wondering when all this pointless talk would end. "It is the countryside, so unbelievably green and fertile, which holds the affection of most indigo."

"Well, then, perhaps one day I will be fortunate enough to travel there. But since I have returned from the city, I have found myself weary and disinclined to travel again anywhere, at least anytime soon."

Nolan infused a faint note of concern into his voice. "I hope your health has not been troubling you?"

"A slight cough merely. I so rarely suffer any illness that even the smallest one takes me completely by surprise."

"A cough?" Nolan said casually. "Did you fall ill while you were in the city? A place so crowded with people breeds disease, you know."

"Perhaps I contracted something while I was away from home," Chay conceded. "It is not a matter I am concerned with. What I would rather talk about is your reason for traveling all this distance to see me."

"In fact," Nolan began, but Chay held up one large hand to suspend him.

"But is this an issue that can be discussed freely before a woman? You are the one who traveled here in secrecy. Do you desire Kitrini to overhear your words?"

"She may hear them," Nolan said bleakly. "I did not tell her because I thought this was news you should hear before any other."

"Then she may remain," Chay said. "Speak. Tell me."

Nolan took a deep breath. He had rehearsed it a hundred times, a thousand times, and it always sounded horrific. "In fact, my reason for seeking you out directly concerns your health," he said. "I believe that on your visit to the city you were, at the behest of Ariana Bayless, deliberately exposed to a dangerous virus that is fatal to gulden unless treated. Not only is it fatal, it is highly contagious, and you and everyone who has come in contact with you since you returned from the city could be dead before the year is out."

CHAPTER FOURTEEN

The silence in the room was complete. Nolan could feel Kit's eyes on him, marveling, disbelieving, but Chay Zanlan's serious expression did not change while he considered the pronouncement.

Finally, the gulden leader said gravely, "Do you have more information? How was the virus administered? For I was very careful about the foods I ate and rarely took anything from the hand of a blueskin."

"There was a banquet one night. At a gulden restaurant. A place where you would not be suspicious."

"And I was exposed then? In my food?"

Nolan shook his head. "It wasn't mixed in your food. You were seated at a table with a number of high-ranking indigo. Including a woman named Cerisa Daylen. You might not remember her. She's about the same age as Ariana Bayless—"

"I remember her. She is the head of a scientific laboratory."

Nolan nodded. "That's her. She brought the virus in a vial of some sort—a perfume bottle, perhaps. Something she could open at the table and seem to accidentally spill so it splashed on you. I wasn't there. I don't know how she accomplished it."

"She said it was medicine," Chay said. He spoke very calmly, precisely, as if recalling an episode that held no particular significance for him. "She poured it into her dinner drink. But she miscalculated, and some of it dripped on me. She was very embarrassed."

"That would be it, then," Nolan said.

Chay spread his massive hands. "But I saw her sip from the drink. Surely, even to kill me, she would not be so reckless?"

"You don't understand. It's a selective virus. It strikes only the gulden. The indigo can eat it, drink it, rub it all over their faces, and it will have no effect on them. It was tailored."

Chay nodded. "Ah. How did she know that such a brief contact with the virus would infect me? For of course I soaked up the spill immediately."

"But I'll wager your sleeve was wet. Or your trousers." Chay nodded. Nolan went on, "And this particular germ thrives in a damp, warm place. You were probably at the restaurant another hour or so, while the sample festered against your skin."

"Yes, as I recall, you're correct. But I did not begin feeling ill for another two or three days."

"And you probably won't start feeling really bad for another few days. The virus has a slow gestation period, but it's replicating and settling in throughout your body. In your lungs. In your liver. In your blood. Once you start to get very sick, you have a very short time to live."

"I take it that this disease has been observed in other gulden, then?"

"Yes. At the prison. There have been several deaths among gulden men, all attributable to this virus. The disease followed a virtually identical course with each man. Between inoculation and demise was a matter of three to four weeks."

"And were these men, too, deliberately infected?"

"From what I've been able to determine," Nolan said, "yes."

There was another profound silence in the room. Kit still had not said a word. She might as well have been turned to ice or stone; Nolan could not even feel the weight of her stare upon him anymore. He dared not do more than risk a sideways glance at her, for all his attention was focused on Chay Zanlan.

Who at last spoke again. "If this is true," said the gulden leader, "it is a crime so heinous as to be almost incomprehensible."

"I know," Nolan said. "It took me a long time to comprehend it myself."

"For what it appears has been attempted—if the disease is as virulent as you say—is nothing less than the complete elimination of the gulden race."

"Yes," Nolan said. "That is how it appears to me as well."

"I am interested in learning several more things," Chay said, still with that preternatural calm. "One is how you discovered this abomination. Or were you part of the team that created the pestilence?"

"No." The single word broke from Kit's mouth as if uncontainable by will or muscle. But she said nothing else, and Chay did not so much as glance her way.

"No," Nolan echoed. "My guess is that no one in the world except Ariana Bayless and Cerisa Daylen knew of the scheme."

"Then how did you come across it?"

"By accident and by stealth. Alone in the lab one night, I needed information I could only find in Cerisa's files. The results of the prison test were there. The basic molecular formula for the disease was there. Your name wasn't mentioned, but there were detailed notes about introducing the infection to a 'new subject' and how that could be accomplished at a venue where Cerisa would also be present. I pieced the rest of it together. I admit I did a lot of guessing."

"And is it possible that I have not been infected?"

"It's possible. You'd need to be tested. But if you're rarely sick and you've developed a persistent cough—which is the first symptom of the disease—I would say you've contracted it."

"And everyone who has come in contact with me has also contracted it? Everyone? The list numbers in the thousands."

"It's possible they have not all gotten sick. In some cases, it takes multiple exposures. But many of the people who work with you or live with you will have caught the disease. And many of them will have passed it along to their own family members. There is no telling how many people may now be infected."

"You said," Chay said, "that it was fatal if not treated. Does that mean there is a treatment available?"

Nolan swallowed hard. "Again, I am only guessing," he said. "But I think so."

"That requires more explanation."

Nolan nodded. "In my work at the Biolab, I have become something of a specialist in diseases that affect the gulden. I have personally formulated two antidotes that reined in epidemics. This virus has much in common with those two diseases, and so I could use parts of my old drugs to create a new one. It has not been tested. I have not used it on any live subjects. Based on scientific theory, it should work. But theory has been ineffective in the past."

"And have you brought with you copies of this hypothetical formula?"

"I have brought actual samples that I had made up at the pharmacy before I left."

Chay arched his thick eyebrows. "That was foresighted."

"I was thinking overtime. I was trying to account for everything." Nolan reached into his pocket and pulled out the second bottle of pills, the untouched container, and he laid this and a sheaf of folded papers on Chay's desk. "There. That's everything. My notes, my models, my drugs."

"So if I take these—samples—of yours, I will be cured? Assuming I do in fact have this dread disease?"

"I don't know," Nolan said, and he heard the strain scraping through his voice. But he could not continue like this, carrying on this dispassionate cool debate. His blood was shrieking in his veins, his body was dancing with adrenaline. "They may have no effect. They may have a miraculous effect. You may not be as sick as I think. Your constitution may be stronger than that of the men in prison. I have given you the information as I know it. I have brought you the only tools I could fashion. It is your choice to believe me or not. I am finished."

Again, Chay watched him with that unwavering regard, weighing him, dissecting him. Nolan wondered wildly what this stranger could possibly discover behind his mild eyes and innocuous face that all his friends and family had never been able to discern, for not one of them would have pictured him in this place, on this mission, with these companions.

"Not quite finished," Chay said. "I have one more question.

Why are you here? Why did you bring me this information?"

"How could I not?" Nolan cried, no longer able to maintain his calm demeanor. "To know that genocide was being committed and I had the key to preventing it? How could I sit quietly in my chair and let it happen? But who else could I tell? Cerisa Daylen had designed the disease—could I run to her for help? The very woman who controls the city devised the plan—should I have gone to her? I didn't know what to do! Until I saw Kitrini." Nolan's voice came to a dead stop as he fought to regain control. He watched Kitrini a moment, but she was still silent, still immobile. When he spoke again, his tone was quieter. "And I remembered that she knew you. And I thought her company would find me a way into your presence. And I thought you were the one who needed to know."

"You have done a great act of bravery," Chay said, "or a great act of betrayal. For your own people will look at this as such."

"Some of them, maybe," Nolan said in a voice barely greater than a whisper. "Not all. Not all of them are so unenlightened and afraid that they would wish to see an entire nation dead."

"You realize, of course," Chay said, and his voice had become brisk, almost businesslike, "that I cannot take any of what you say on faith. Despite what appears to be an act of heroism, I must consider that every word you say could be a lie."

"And that the pills I have brought you are in fact poison," Nolan said. He nodded. "I did realize that. But your own doctors and scientists should be able to duplicate my experiments. There is nothing here so abstract they will not be able to follow it."

"And I must be tested, and my associates must be tested, and the results must be analyzed. This all takes time."

"Yes. I am prepared to wait."

Chay stepped backward and touched a dial on his desk. Nolan heard nothing, but presumed it was a signal to call a guard. "You must be prepared to wait under arrest," he said. "I will make your quarters as comfortable as I can, but I must treat you as highly dangerous."

"I understand."

"You will not be allowed to leave your quarters without an

escort and my permission. You will not be permitted to see anyone except the guard."

This time Nolan risked a full glance at Kitrini. "May I be allowed to speak to Kit from time to time? If she will see me?"

"Oh, yes," Chay said, "for she will share your quarters."

Nolan was still looking at Kit, so he saw her start forward, suddenly wakened from her frozen state. "Share exile with him," she said. "But I had nothing—I did not know—"

The door opened, and two guards walked in. They were both at least six and a half feet tall, burly and uncompromising. Chay addressed Kit as if they were the only two in the room. "If this is a war," he said, "you must choose your side."

"I choose yours," she said instantly.

Chay shook his head. "Your blood chooses for you," he said. "Your face. Your heritage."

"But I love you," she whispered.

"There is no love in a war," Chay said, and turned away from her.

The guards were between Chay and the visitors. Nolan did not resist as one of the men took him none too gently by the arm and marched him from the room. Behind him, he heard no more protests from Kit. It was a struggle to keep up with the rapid pace down the sunny granite hall, past dozens of doorways, through a maze of corridors. Nolan just concentrated on not falling flat on his face and having to be dragged by his heels down the endless hallways.

In perhaps ten minutes, they arrived at their destination, and they were forcefully pulled through the doorway into what appeared to be a suite of rooms. The guard holding Kit snapped out a few sentences, to which she replied with one numb word, and then both of the gulden men tramped out. Nolan heard the lock turn in the door and footsteps fall away down the hallway.

It took almost all his strength to briefly take stock of his new residence. They were in what appeared to be a sitting room, gaily furnished with bright tapestries, rugs, low chairs, cushions, and short-legged tables. One large grilled window let in light and air, though it clearly would not permit a chance to escape. Doorways led off of either end of the main room, most likely to separate bedrooms. Somewhere, Nolan could hear water playing. It did not look much like a prison.

But to Kit, clearly, it was a dungeon in the base of hell. Her face had a smudged, stricken look to it; she appeared to be on her feet only because she was too rigid with shock to crumple to the floor. Her eyes darted from one corner of the room to another, as if seeking the hidden exit, as if looking for the clue, the key, the retraction. Her lips trembled as if she was on the brink of speech, but the audience she required had not yet made its appearance. Nolan had never seen anyone so wretched in his life.

"I'm sorry," he said to her in his gentlest voice. "I did not realize he would bracket you with me. I did not realize he would consider you guilty of my crimes."

She looked at him blankly, as if she heard the sound of his voice but could not translate his words. Nolan tried again. "I thought he might throw me into a jail of some sort. He'd be a fool not to! I thought he'd want to test the information and the drugs I gave him. I knew it would take time. But I didn't think he'd make you suffer with me." He glanced around. "Though I have to say these are better accommodations than I had hoped for. He must think there's a chance I'm telling him the truth."

"He believed you," Kit breathed. "Or you would be dead."

"In any case," he said, "I'm sorry you're guilty by association."

"Is it true?" she said, still in that small, almost soundless voice. "Is it true he's going to die?"

"I believe he's been inoculated," Nolan said gently. "I believe my drugs can save him. But all of it is out of my hands."

"Because," she said, and now she seemed to startle into life, now she wrung her shaking hands and began to pace through the room. Nolan turned to follow her motion. "Because a world without Chay is a world impossible to contemplate. He loves me more than he loves his own daughters, you know. He has told me that many times. And when I was a child at night, I used to lie awake asking myself, 'Who do you love more? Your father or Chay Zanlan?' And sometimes I answered the question one way and sometimes I answered it another. When my father died, I remembered all those midnight conversations, and I hated myself for having doubted, even for a moment, even as a child, that my father was the most important person in creation. But now when I think of Chay dying I think—I think—if I had the choice of bringing my father back or allowing Chay to live, I would keep my father in his grave. And Chay will die anyway."

"We all die," Nolan said. "What matters is not having that life taken away from us a second sooner than absolutely necessary."

"What matters is that we do not lose the love of those we cherish," Kit said, still kneading her hands. "That we remind them every day that we love them. That we do not quarrel, and part in anger, and never have a chance to reconcile."

"Are you thinking of Jex?" Nolan asked stupidly, and she rounded on him in a weeping fury.

"No! I am thinking of Chay! Who loved me once, but sent me from his home more than six months ago, and has not told me again to my face that he loves me! And now he may be dying, and he does not trust me, and how can I go forward in the world with that burden on my heart? That Chay Zanlan did not forgive me? How can I survive?"

There were no words to assuage such a heartache. Without conscious volition, Nolan crossed the room and took her in his arms. She shook so dreadfully that he tightened his embrace, trying to placate the traumatized nerves, trying to squeeze the flailing muscles into submission. She did not resist him, but she could not be comforted. She rested her face against the front of his shirt and sobbed with all the abandon of a child.

After that outburst, Kit slept for ten solid hours. Nolan had guided her at random to one of the bedrooms and laid her on the bed, and she had followed the promptings of his hands as if she had no will of her own. He wished he had a sedative with him, but stress was its own tranquillizer. She closed her eyes and slept, and did not emerge for the rest of the night.

Nolan used the last of his energy to inspect their quarters. As he had guessed, it was composed of the sitting room, a shared necessary room, and two bedrooms. The fountain was playing off a small balcony that looked from the window of his room. Here, the bars that kept him from the outside world were a decorative verdigris that did not block the sun at all, but they were thick, sturdy and sunk in stone at both their top and bottom edges. There was no escape here.

He didn't want to escape. He had put himself willingly and unreservedly in Chay Zanlan's hands. He would not have tried to leave the compound if he had been given free run of the place.

And anyway, he would never have been able to leave Kit behind. Not tonight, certainly; not ever, perhaps.

But this was impossible. How could he have fallen in love with this blueskin girl, this fierce, strange creature who cared nothing for the life Nolan prized, who had rejected every doctrine and canon he had grown up believing as absolute truth? Putting aside the fact that she could never care for him—a man who had abducted her from her home!—putting aside the fact that he was not free to love anyone, how could he have fallen for her? He had only known her two days. And she was nothing like his picture of an ideal woman. And she was in love with another man.

And yet he knew it was true. And he did not know how to change it. He had no serum for this particular disease. He might have vaccinated himself in advance, if he had known the malady was lurking, but he had no cures for it now. And he would suffer with it until he died.

Two hours later, guards brought food and the luggage Nolan and Kit had surrendered when they entered the palace. There was, in addition, a pile of silks and cottons thrown onto one of the tables. The guard pointed and explained, but Nolan merely shrugged. Kit would have to translate in the morning.

However, sifting through the pile once the guards had left, he learned that Chay had sent them clean clothes, which seemed a favorable sign. At first, Nolan was unsure of which items might be intended for a man and which for a woman, for in Inrhio, only women wore color; men dressed exclusively in black and white. Yet here was a tunic much like the one Chay had worn that afternoon, and these were the sorts of leggings Nolan had seen on the commuters at the various train stations. Surely, they had been intended for him.

So he showered and changed, and took a moment to study himself in the full-length mirror. The royal purple of the tunic turned his face a sultry midnight blue; the bones of his cheeks looked longer and heavier. His hair shone with azure highlights. He did not look at all familiar.

He ate the food—now cold—then wandered back and forth between the sitting room and his own chamber, not sure how to pass the time. Perhaps, if Kit was awake when the guards returned, she could ask if the palace boasted any reading material in bluetongue. If not, and she would not speak to him, he would be reduced to doing mathematical equations in his head. It was how he had convinced himself to fall asleep when he was a boy; sometimes it still worked. Only he was not quite ready yet to seek his bed.

But. The thought of running formulas through his mind gave him an idea. He had paper and ink in his suitcase. He could find a way to profitably use his time.

Accordingly, he dug out a notebook and a pen and made himself comfortable on one of the low chairs. The hours passed, and he barely noticed. He did get up twice to check on Kit and make sure she was still breathing. Other than that, he did not stir. He merely experimented with numbers, X'd out impossible combinations, refigured models, and tried again.

When he finally went to bed, numbers and symbols danced before his eyes, and it was a long time before he could quiet his questing brain. But he had time. It would be days, maybe weeks, before Chay's physicians and pharmacists verified Nolan's data. He could play with these new numbers as long as he wanted.

In the morning, Kit was awake before him, looking pale but calm. Guards had brought breakfast while they were both still sleeping, and she was eating a pastry when Nolan emerged from his room. He was delighted to see her, but kept his greeting grave.

"How are you feeling?" he asked.

"Somewhat savaged," she admitted. "I'm sorry I made such a scene last night."

"Don't apologize," he said swiftly, seating himself on a sofa across from her. "Not to me. I'm the one who brought you to this."

She gave him one lengthy, unfathomable look. "You're the one who may have saved Chay's life," she said. "If it can be saved."

He longed to ask her one simple, direct question: *Did you really mean what you said to Chay, about my goodness and my kind heart?* But he could not bring himself to voice the words. "I hope it can," he said. "So! What did they bring us to eat?"

They munched in silence for a few minutes, Nolan casting about for something else to say. "I'm not sure what we'll do to entertain ourselves," was the best he could come up with. "Maybe Chay could be persuaded to bring us books. Do you think he's got anything in bluetongue in his library?"

She rose to her feet and began opening doors to cabinets and shelving units. "There should be a monitor here somewhere. Chay has every electronic toy invented . . . Ah," she said in satisfaction, as the door of a small bureau slid back to reveal a square green screen. "Let's see what kind of programming we have today."

She turned it on and began flipping through channels. Most of them appeared to be showing news events, much like the ones broadcast in the city, though Nolan saw no hard copy attachment. A few of the stations she came across offered music, and one of them sounded as if it might be a theatrical production.

"Any of that interest you?" she asked, her back still to him.

"Well," he said, smiling, "I can't understand a word."

She turned to face him. "Of course. Perhaps I should teach you goldtongue."

"Actually, if you have the patience, I would like that very well. Then perhaps I would at least be able to greet my host in his own language."

"Your jailor," she said.

Nolan shrugged. "I am in his hands. Either way."

She watched him a moment, looking as if she wanted to say something dangerously important, but then she shrugged and forced herself to smile. "I like your new outfit," she said lightly. "You should dress in colors more often."

"I feel very dashing," he said. "They've brought clothes for you, too. In that pile."

"Good. I guess I'll bathe and change." She crossed the room and picked through the blouses and trousers. "Meanwhile, why don't you look through the rest of these cabinets? You may find a few more diversions."

So he searched while she showered, and he turned up a few prizes: a pack of unfamiliar playing cards, two board games he'd never seen before, and a box of choisin pieces. He laughed silently. Enough days in a prison cell with no other diversions, and he might yet become a champion at the game.

Kit, it turned out when she rejoined him, enjoyed choisin. "Though I can't say I'm very good," she added. "Jex is a ferocious player, and he would always beat me unless I had someone on my team. And not many guldmen will play a game like this with a woman."

"How did you learn, then?" Nolan said, setting out the pieces.

She was silent a moment. "My father taught me," she said. "And Chay would always let me play beside him."

"Well, I'm lousy at it," Nolan said cheerfully. "So I'm sure you'll do a splendid job."

As it happened, they were about evenly matched, which meant the game was fairly dull. Then again, there was little else to do, so they continued playing in a halfhearted fashion. When she corrected him once ("No, you can't move your choifer there") he picked up the offending piece.

"How is this called in goldtongue?" he asked.

"Choifer. Same word. It's a gulden game."

"Then teach me something else."

"Do you really want to learn the language?"

"It seems more productive than anything else I could be doing."

"All right. Let's see. I've never taught anyone words before . . . *Kokta, Braeta*. Man, woman. Can you say that?"

He repeated the words back to her, then the words for all the other objects in the room. Then she tried colors, but he began to get confused. There were ten synonyms for red, and nearly as many words for all the other hues. And who needed to know those things?

"Teach me verbs," he said. "And then important sentences. Like 'How are you this morning, Chay Zanlan?' and 'Have your scientists analyzed my reports?' "

"Those seem a little complicated," she said.

"How about 'Thank you for the purple tunic'?" he said, growing facetious. "Or teach me to say, 'I am so pleased with my guest quarters. I am learning choisin so well.' "

" 'I am an honest man,' " she said quietly.

He paused, all the silliness leaving him, and shrugged faintly. "That, too," he said.

"I will teach you only true things," she said. "That way you can never lie in goldtongue."

"I rarely bother to lie anyway," he said.

"I know," she said, and he wondered how she knew. "But this time you will have no choice."

CHAPTER FIFTEEN

Kit had never tried to teach anyone anything before, not language, not math, not manners. She couldn't tell if Nolan was a quick study or not. He seemed to be. He seemed genuinely interested in learning. He listened closely to her syllables and her inflections, then parroted back whatever she said.

"I am," she taught him. "He is. We are."

"I am. He is. We are," Nolan said gravely.

Her brain wildly completed the sentences, in both of the languages she knew. *I am completely intrigued by him. He is like no blueskin I have ever met. We are strangers, and yet, and yet . . .*

Why had he come here, burdened with a murderous knowledge, risking his own safety to tell an unfriendly stranger the most explosive secret? She could not imagine Jex doing the same for Ariana Bayless, had the situation been reversed. No, Jex would have been more likely to commission the virus that would destroy the blueskins; he surely would not have tried to save them.

But that was a terrible thing to believe about the man she loved. Jex would never conceive of such an awful thing.

But he had been involved in plans that caused the deaths of any number of blueskins. What was the difference here, except in scale?

A huge difference, of course.

Enough of a difference—?

"I see," she said to Nolan in goldtongue. "You see. He sees. We see."

She saw, but she tried not to see. She had been shocked, upon first returning to the city, to learn that Jex had set a bomb in the medical building. "No one was hurt," he had said impatiently, when she tried to question him, but she could not see that that made a great deal of difference. Someone could have been hurt. Even if he had scouted his location thoroughly (which she knew he had not; Jex could be unbelievably careless)—even if he knew that on most days the building emptied out by nightfall, this one evening could have been different. This one night, someone could have worked late, stayed in his office to write a letter, had a fight with his wife so he did not bother to go home . . . and that one person could have died in the colorful blast that brought down the whole pile of stone and mortar. It was luck that no one was killed in that first explosion, not intent; and if you could not trust a man's intent, what could you trust?

"I know. You know. He knows. We know."

Jex was not a good man. She had not judged him by such criteria before; it hadn't occurred to her. He was brilliant, gifted, charismatic, a man of light and motion. He had allowed her inside his vortex, and she was shocked into new life. She had not questioned his goals and desires. She had even believed in them. But she had not realized he would kill to achieve his ambitions, and once she had realized it, she had continued to love him. What did that say about her? What did she know about her own heart that she was afraid to examine?

"I want. He wants. You want. We want."

He was Jex. She loved him. She desired him with a physical addiction that went beyond thinking, beyond volition. She could not change him. Was she allowed to judge him? If she judged him, and he failed her criteria, must she leave him?

Of course she could judge him. Of course he had failed. Of course she must leave him.

"I think. I thought. I have been thinking."

She could think of a dozen guldmen who would have done what Jex had done, if they had had the nerve and the skills.

More—she could think of twenty, of fifty. But she knew other guldmen who would never condone the terrorist acts Jex had engineered. Jex was a product not only of a violent society, but a reckless personality. He had learned courage and discipline from Chay, but he had also been much indulged; he knew that anything he wanted, he would eventually be able to get. He had not been above much scheming, as a child, to get his way. He was still scheming, but the stakes were so much higher.

She could not forgive him just because she loved him. She could not forgive him just because she understood him. She could not forgive him just because he was a guldman, and his race had been abused by the indigo, and he had some reason for his anger and his attitudes. There was still no justification for his actions.

"I hope. I hoped. I have been hoping."

But was he any worse than the indigo, when it came to that? What had Ariana Bayless done—conspired to destroy the entire gulden race? Jex's random slayings seemed insignificant in comparison. Could Kit, after all, judge Jex and abandon him when there was so much greater evil in the world—and in power?

But how many blueskins would condone Ariana Bayless's actions? Not Sereva or Granmama, certainly. They would rise up in horror and denounce her, they and all the Higher Hundred. They had no love for the gulden, but they would never endure such inhumanity. For so long, Kit had been used to thinking of the blueskins as violent and the gulden as victimized, but she could see now that it was not always so. The races each had their own crimes and their own criminals, but it was not their skin that made them behave so. It was the individual brain that made the individual choice; it was the heart that outlined its own dictates. She could not just embrace the one race and reject the other. It was going to be more difficult than that.

"I fall. I fell. I am falling. I have fallen."

And then to judge a man on his own merits, you must consider everything about him. What he believed, what he was taught to believe, and whether he examined those teachings with the cold searchlight of adult reason. How he behaved when it was easy, how he behaved when it was hard. When he was cruel. When he was thoughtful. Whom he valued more than himself.

She could not even catalog all the criteria. She had not even realized how many items were on the list, that she herself had put there, when she was not aware of it. But she knew that the man before her would meet all her requirements, would embody them, would be her standard for the next time she would love.

Because she didn't count this time. He had risked his life to save the gulden, but he had made it clear he had a distaste for the race. He could be kind to them, but he could not love them. And she had been brought up in their houses, consorting with their sons. That was not something he would be able to overlook. She would not expect him to. But he had taught her that the ideal man existed, and she had not even known she had been searching.

"I understand. I understood."

Oh, if only it were true.

A guard came for her in the afternoon. She had not allowed herself to hope for this favor, but of course it had crossed her mind that Chay might send for her. She had chosen, from the pile of clothing he had provided, the prettiest blouse and the most flattering skirt. She had taken some care with her hair, brushed color on her eyelids. Just in case.

Nolan had come to his feet when the guard entered, and he watched her with shadowed eyes. "Will he send you back here, do you think?" he asked, and she had no way of knowing if that was something the blueskin would welcome or despise.

"I imagine so," she said coolly. "He's made it pretty clear that he is not treating me like a daughter this time. He may just want to question me further. This may not be a good sign at all."

"Well, I hope it means he has forgiven you," he said.

Not *I hope it means he will listen to me*. Not *I hope it means I am safe*. Just a hope that her own life would be eased. Did this man ever think of himself at all?

"Anything you want me to tell him?" she asked casually.

Nolan shrugged. "I have told him what I came here for. You

could ask him if he has anything I could read to pass the time. Otherwise, I can't think of anything."

Again, amazing. She shook her head slightly. "I'm sure I'll be back later," she said, and left.

The guard did not hold her by the arm; that was promising. Kit followed him through the bright corridors, trying to compose her thoughts. This might mean a rapprochement. It might mean an interrogation. She had no choice. She would follow Chay's lead.

The guard took her to Chay's *hoechter*, a sybaritically well-appointed room near the main living quarters. That was a positive sign, and an even better one was when he left her there unattended. A small table was set for a light afternoon snack, and there were only two places laid.

Chay entered a few moments later. As always, she was momentarily overwhelmed by his bulk and radiance. He filled any room like a small sun that had tumbled in, throwing off heat and light. He was speaking to someone behind him, but no one followed him through the door, and when it shut behind him, they were alone together.

"Kit," he said, and crossed the room to hug her. She closed her eyes and leaned into that embrace. It was like falling into safe sleep, coming to rest after long and troubled passage. They had been at odds six months and more, and she had not been sure he would ever forgive her. She was not sure he had forgiven her now. She rested against him until his arms loosened, and then she pulled away.

"Chay Zanlan," she said formally, speaking in goldtongue. "How can I help you?"

He gestured at the table. "Sit for a while and talk to me. I'm famished. I haven't eaten since dawn. How about you? Have they been feeding you well?"

"Very well, thank you. And thank you for the clothes."

"They look very nice on you."

She permitted herself a smile. "The lady Rell must have selected them for me."

He laughed out loud. "Well, she did. But I was busy. And has Nolan Adelpho seen fit to don gulden attire?"

"Yes, and he seemed most grateful for the gift."

"An unusual man."

"Very."

She would not say more without a cue; she did not know why she was here. Chay had cut himself bread and meat and was eating heartily, but Kit had no appetite. She poured herself a little tea and sipped it.

"It has been a long time since we have talked, you and I," the guldman said presently, when the edge of his hunger had been blunted.

"I saw you a few weeks ago, when you were in the city," she reminded him.

He waved a hand. "A few words exchanged in the street. Merely greetings. It is a long time since we have talked as friend to friend. And that last time, we were not pleased with each other."

"You were not pleased with me," she said tranquilly. "I am always happy to be in your company."

He smiled slightly at the mannered compliment. "And yet I do not believe you followed the advice I gave you at the time," he said. "Which was to avoid the company of my son."

"No," she said. "I did not."

"I cannot change my mind on that, you know," he said in a serious voice. "There is much I have been able to do that runs counter to traditional gulden thinking, but I could not countenance a marriage between my son and an indigo woman. It would not be acceptable to any of the clan leaders—and it is not acceptable to me."

Kit took a deep breath. "I do not desire to marry your son," she said. "And I am willing to renounce all ties to him except those caused by the affection I feel for you."

Chay's gray eyes narrowed; he watched her with a close attention. "Then I must suppose it is true," he said quietly at last. "That my son was responsible for the explosions in the Centrifuge."

"As far as I know," Kit said, "they have not yet determined the cause of those explosions."

"They have now," Chay said. "Two bombs. A third one was supposed to go off but somehow it malfunctioned. They found the whole of it in the rubble."

"That is terrible news indeed," she said. "But how can you think they will look to Jex? He is still in an indigo prison."

"Do not be coy with me, Kit," he said, switching to the more forceful indigo language. "Jex has friends, and many of them are in the city. They all would carry out any request he cared to make. If he asked them to, they would destroy the world."

"He swore to me that he did not plan any bombing for that day. And Jex does not lie."

"But Jex knows how to carefully select his words. He is only as honest as it suits him to be."

"A fine opinion to have of your own son."

"I have loved him even longer than you have," Chay said, and his voice sounded tired. "And I know him far better. Tell me truly, Kitrini Solvano. Do you believe he caused those bombs to be set that killed all those blueskins in the Centrifuge?"

She was silent a long time. She had never heard Chay ask his wife's opinion, or his daughters'; she had never heard any gulden man consult with a woman on any important topic. She was different—because of her blue face, because of her father, because Chay loved her—but she was still a woman. He must be powerfully uncertain and disturbed to ask her such a question, and to wait with such strained intensity for her reply.

"I do believe it," she said quietly. "And it has broken my heart."

Chay nodded slowly and turned his hands palm outward, as if absorbing the poison of her words through the porous membrane of his skin. She did not know how he would react to this lethal dosage, the second one he had been administered in a few weeks. She did not know which one might kill him the quickest.

"Will they execute him, do you think?" he asked next.

"It's possible, though I think it's more likely they will keep him imprisoned, as long as Ariana Bayless believes she can still use him to bargain with you."

Chay smiled thinly. "It is my guess," he said coolly, "that she does not expect to have to bargain with me for very much longer."

Kit digested that a moment in silence. "So your physicians have completed their tests."

Chay nodded. "And I am well and truly infected with the virus."

She felt a stab of fear plunge from her stomach up through her throat. "Can it be treated? Arrested?"

"They aren't sure."

The air was unbreathable; the sunlight had failed. "You mean—they think you are—it's possible you could be dying?"

Chay nodded again. "They are experimenting with the prescriptions your friend brought. I am already on a regime of drugs. But we might not have caught the disease in time. It will be a week or more before we know."

"But Chay," she said, and could not find any words to complete the sentence.

He gave her a faint smile. "I know," he said gently. "And there is worse news."

"How is that possible?" she breathed.

"For Nolan Adelpho was right. The infection is highly contagious, and many of those I have spoken to in the past weeks have begun to develop its symptoms also."

Now her body was alive with panic; her veins jumped with adrenaline. "And those they have spoken to—and those—?"

"Yes. It is a chain without an end, and its links spread in all directions. There is some hope that the drugs your friend brought us will arrest the disease in its early stages. We cannot know yet. And there is also a slim chance of good news."

"What news?" she whispered.

"Among the papers he brought us was the formula for a vaccine. A preventative pill. My doctors are preparing quantities of that even now to duplicate and distribute throughout the nation. If we can inoculate everyone against this disease, we will have thwarted Ariana Bayless's main ambition."

"But if you die," she said, still in that whisper, "the world may as well come to an end."

"Not true," he said briskly. "I can think of five men I would trust to take my place. I have no fears for Geldricht, but I have some concerns for my family. With me dead and Jex in prison, my nephew Girt would become head of the Zanlan clan, and he is not always the wise patriarch I would wish."

Kit thought of the family slaughtered in the Lost City a few weeks ago. "He is not a thoughtful man," she said. "And he is steeped in the oldest and most violent of Geldricht traditions."

"And he is even now in the city, doing the bidding of my son," Chay added. "Which means his own life may be forfeit before long. In which case care for my family will fall into other hands."

He was so calm, as he had been yesterday when Nolan had told him the dread news. He had always been a man able to meet trouble with an unmoved demeanor, but Kit marveled at his control now. Catastrophes beset him from every side; it was hard to choose the most wretched circumstance.

"What will you do?" she asked, because she could not help it, because she herself could see no way out of the mess. Any of the messes.

"I will wait," he said, "for the pronouncement of the doctors."

"And then? How will you confront Ariana Bayless, how will you revenge yourself upon her?"

"The survival of the gulden nation would be revenge enough, I think," he said. "But I will consider my other options."

She stared at him, struck by an unexpected insight. "You aren't going to tell anyone, are you?" she asked. "About the virus. About its creation. You're just going to say—you got sick in the city. You aren't going to say how."

"To spread that information," he said seriously, "would be to light a match to tinder that will burn to ashes. There would be no way I could stop the clans from arming and storming into the city for murder. There would be a civil war that would destroy all of us. Not a gulden man or woman would be left standing. I have spent my life avoiding that. I have yielded land that I could have defended. I have suffered insults that no one has overheard. I have preached concession when every man around me wanted aggression. And why? Because Geldricht would lose that battle. We have technology that the indigo do not have, and we could make bloody inroads on their people and their land. But they have the numbers, and they have the geography, and they have the land. They cannot be starved out—they cannot be attacked on any front but one, and that one can be guarded till the world ends—and there are twice as many of them as there are of us. Civil war would annihilate the Geldricht nation as surely as this disease could. And my entire goal, my entire life, has been the survival of the race.

"No, I am not going to inform the gulden of Ariana Bayless's treachery. If I could, I would tell the indigo, for I think they would rise up in fury and oust her from power. But they would not believe me, guldman that I am."

"Then I'll tell them," she said swiftly.

"They would not believe you, either. Your very name makes you suspect. Possibly there is no one they would believe. I must find some other way to punish her—perhaps by managing to live. After that, I will see."

This meek retreat ran counter to everything she knew of Chay, everything she knew of the gulden, so fierce and quick to defend their honor. Yet she was wise enough to see that it took more strength to resist the reprisal, more courage to stay silent and endure. He was even stronger than she had always believed—and he might be dying.

"You are a great man, Chay Zanlan," she said in a low voice. "The world was enriched the day you were born, and it will be a much poorer place the day you die."

"That is good to know," he said. "But do not eulogize me yet. I have a great deal of energy in me still, and a great deal left to do."

He rose to his feet, and she followed suit. "When will they know if the drugs will help you?" she asked.

"In three days, I believe they said."

"Will I be allowed to see you again?"

"If my schedule permits. It is a rare pleasure for me to talk with you, daughter of my dearest friend."

"And yet, yesterday you consigned me to my own race," she said, somewhat daring.

He smiled briefly. "And there I will return you. What I said then is still true. You can flirt with another culture, but you will always return to your own."

"It has been more than flirting," she said with some indignation.

He took her hand in his huge one; it was like being enveloped in friendly flame. "It has been true love," he said. "But that changes nothing. You belong with your own."

"That is not the way to change the world," she whispered.

"You're right," he said, and kissed her fingertips, then released her. "But this is not the day the world will be changed."

When the guard showed her back inside her quarters, Nolan looked up quickly. He was seated on the sofa facing the door, poring over notebooks which appeared to be filled with mathematical equations.

"Well?" he asked hopefully. "What did he say?"

But she could not speak. There was too much to say. She headed straight for her room, closed the door, and sobbed away the rest of the afternoon. And then, because she could think of no other escape, she closed her eyes and slept.

It was dark outside when she woke, feeling sodden and generally achy. What had shaken her from sleep was a knock on her door, and a minute later it was repeated.

"Kit? Kitrini? Are you awake? Kit?"

She sat up in bed and reached for the light. "What is it?"

"Can I come in?"

"What's wrong?"

"I just want to see if you're all right. Can I come in?"

She must look frightful. Her cheeks were tight with dried tears, and her hair fell in knots around her face. "I'll be out in a minute."

But he opened the door and peered in anyway. "Are you all right? You've been quiet for so long. And you missed dinner."

"I'll be fine." She sat up straighter in bed, smoothing her hair down with her fingers.

He came all the way in, carrying a tray of food. "I saved you the best pieces," he said in an encouraging voice. "Some fruit, and some dried fish, and some really wonderful bread. You must be hungry."

"I ate with Chay," she said.

"That was hours ago," he said firmly, and set the tray on a nightstand beside her bed. Then he pulled up a chair and sat beside her. "You'll feel better if you eat. I promise you."

"Oh, all right," she said ungraciously, and picked up a fork. The food was all cold, of course, but it had come from Chay's kitchens, and so it was marvelous. She did actually feel a little more cheerful as she ate the last bite. Impossible that mere food could make any difference against such a sea of troubles.

"*And* your vitamins," he said, handing her one of the pills he had been dosing her with for the past three days. She didn't even bother to argue this time, just swallowed it with a sip of tea.

"And your foot?" he asked. "Does it hurt? Do you want a pain pill?"

"Actually, it feels pretty good today. I think I'm fine."

"Good. Now tell me what Chay Zanlan said."

"All bad news," she said quietly. "He is in fact infected. He's taking the antidote you brought, but his doctors aren't sure they've caught the disease in time. And they've already found it in many people that he's dealt with in the past few weeks. It's as contagious as you said."

Nolan nodded gravely. "But they can spread the word about it, can't they? Convince the whole race to get inoculated? He found the papers I gave him, didn't he, with the formulas for the vaccine?"

"Yes. And the gulden have a marvelous information network—and a fanatic loyalty to their leader. If Chay says everyone should take the vaccine, everyone will take it. They should be able to contain the virus."

Nolan sat back in his chair, smiling and pleased. "That's it, then. That's success. That's the best news you could hope for."

"No," she said. "The best news would be that there was no fear of Chay dying. The best news would be that such a virus did not exist."

"I meant the best news in the real world," he said.

She shook her head because she had nothing to say to that. "So, how did you entertain yourself all day while I was gone—or sleeping?" she asked.

"I watched the monitor a little. I picked up a word here and there, but I couldn't really tell what they were saying. And I worked on a project of my own. Something I should be doing at the lab, but I thought I could get a start on it here."

He fell silent a moment, thinking about something, and then he looked over at her with a smile. "Though it's hard for me to imagine going back to a job at the lab," he said. "Working with Cerisa as if nothing had happened. Living an ordinary life. It's as if the door has closed on the past and there's no way back to it."

"You might feel differently once you're in the city."

"Maybe."

"Or maybe not," she said, with assumed energy. "Maybe now's the time to marry your fiancée—what's her name?"

"Leesa."

"And move back in-country. Forget the city. Forget Cerisa. Forget that you were ever in Geldricht."

He gave her a small smile that seemed full of pain. "That seems even harder to imagine," he said.

"Forgetting Geldricht?"

"Marrying Leesa."

She was silent because her heart ballooned up, squeezed aside her lungs, choked off the passages to her throat. She merely looked at him, arching her brows as if to ask the casual question.

Nolan shrugged, smiled, glanced away, glanced back. "For so long," he said, "she was the epitome of everything I wanted. We were betrothed when I was fourteen. I had known her my whole life. She is exactly what any high-caste boy would dream of. She's beautiful. She's charming. She's sweet-tempered— which is a rare thing among indigo women, as you may have noticed. And she loves me. She's the only woman I've ever been with. She's the only woman I wanted to be with. Until—"

"Until?" Kit managed to ask.

"Until recently. The past few months. She wants to be married later this year and go live on her grandmother's estate. That means I would leave the city forever. Be just like any other blueskin man, happy and anonymous. Raise our children, scheme to see our daughters marry well. Once that was the only life I could dream of. Now it frightens me."

"So what life would you prefer," she asked, "in a perfect world?"

He shrugged. "I haven't thought about it. I didn't realize there were other options. I guess I'd want to do something worthwhile with my life. Continue my work at the lab. Study to become a doctor. Do something that mattered."

"Marrying and having children matters," she said.

"Having children matters, if you do it right," he agreed. "If you raise them to be honest citizens with kind hearts and uncompromising ethics. Otherwise, you've made the world a worse place, not a better one. But marrying? I don't know that in and of itself it's something that improves the world."

"But love always improves the world," Kit said. "It—it loads the scale on the side of good. It's a counterweight to all the sadness and deceit and just plain evil that make the world so wretched."

"If you marry for love," Nolan said quietly.

She had no easy reply to that. "So what will you tell Leesa," she asked at last, "about your adventures in Geldricht? What will she think?"

"I don't know that I'll tell her any of it," he said. "I don't think—I really don't think—she would condone the genocide of the entire gulden race. But I don't think she would seriously consider it a bad thing if the whole nation died out through some mysterious, innocent infection. And she wouldn't understand why I found it important to save Chay if I could. She would not have harmed him herself, you understand, but she would not have considered it her responsibility to warn him, either. It would not seem important enough to her."

"That will be a very big secret to keep from her the rest of your life," Kit said gravely.

He shrugged and smiled. "From everyone, I imagine. At least if I want to attempt to try to live any kind of normal life."

Kit shook her head. "How strange. Here I am, wanting to shout of Ariana Bayless's treachery to the whole city, and you and Chay are thinking of how to conceal it. Is she to be allowed to get away with this, then? Perhaps to try something worse another time? Is no one going to bring her to justice?"

"I thought Chay would do all that."

"He says not. He wants to avoid civil war."

Nolan closed his eyes and passed a hand over his eyes. Kit took the opportunity to study the lines of his jaw and cheekbone.

He was such a common-looking man, attractive enough but un-distinguished. How had his features come to seem so extraor-dinary to her? How was it she could close her own eyes and call up the exact shade of his skin, delineate the double scallop of his brows? When had he become so familiar, when had he become so exceptional?

"Well, I'll have to think about that some more," he said, and he sounded tired. He dropped his hands to his knees.

She wanted to reach over and comfort him. She wanted to say, *You have done enough. Let someone else take up the ban-ner*. But she sat where she was, clasping her hands in her lap, and said nothing.

He seemed to brood a moment, studying his own curled fists, then looked up at her with a smile. "So, are you bored?" he asked hopefully. "Would you be willing to play a round or two of choisin? Or teach me some more vocabulary words?"

She smiled and rose from the bed. "I'd be glad to," she said. "Take your choice."

The next two days were essentially a repeat of the first, except that Chay did not again call for Kit. She tried to persuade herself it only meant that he was busy, not that he had grown suspicious of her again, not that he was feeling too ill to see her. He had not forgotten them, that was certain. Delicious food was deliv-ered to their door on a regular basis, as well as fresh clothing and, occasionally, flowers and other gifts. She had neglected to ask Chay about reading material for Nolan, so the next morning she asked a guard, and that night, a stack of novels arrived with the evening meal.

"I'm astonished," Nolan said, browsing through the choices. "I really wasn't expecting him to have anything, but these are classics."

"Gifts from my father, I would guess," Kit said, for she rec-ognized titles that she had been encouraged to read. "My father always said cultural literacy is essential if you want to interact with another nation, and he would spend hours—days—telling Chay some arcane point of indigo history. But Chay may have read these on his own without my father's encouragement. Chay knows five or six languages besides goldtongue, and he probably has sampled major literature in all of those languages. He is nothing if not informed."

"Any of these you particularly like?" Nolan asked. "I haven't read these since—since my schooldays back in-country."

"*A Wanderer's Tale*, by Lorella Tibet," Kit said, smiling. "That was one of my favorites when I was growing up."

"I don't think I've read it. Heard of it, of course. Leesa and my sister each read it about a dozen times."

"Well, it is sort of a young girl's adventure book," Kit conceded. "You might not like it."

"But I might," Nolan said. He settled onto the couch and gestured for Kit to sit across from him. She did, wondering what he planned now. He opened *A Wanderer's Tale*, glanced down at the first page, and began reading aloud.

"Prologue. 'Hetta stood at the garden gate, one hand on the latch, and wondered if this was the day she would finally slip through the ornamental fence, leave behind the manicured lawn, and escape into the rough country just visible beyond the borders of her mother's house. Behind her, she could hear her sister calling her name, but though her sister came nearer with every step, somehow her voice seemed to grow fainter and farther away. The trees on the other side of the fence, however, appeared to move closer the longer Hetta watched. They squirmed and wriggled where they stood, shaking their long trailing branches at the young girl watching, inviting her over to partake of whatever mystery and excitement they had discovered on the other side of the gate. "Hetta!" her sister called again, but Hetta almost could not hear the voice, so faraway had it become. She lifted the latch and stepped outside the fence, and into another world . . .' "

He read for about an hour. When he stopped to fetch himself a glass of water, Kit took the book and read the next few chapters. Hetta had been her idol, back when she had first encountered this book. That had been during one dreary, interminable summer she had spent with Granmama, when her father had not come to visit her once for six endless weeks. Like Hetta, Kit had longed to escape the neat lawns, the formal houses, the regimented days. Of course, she had known that a completely different world existed, and she was determined to make her way back to Geldricht, not the mythical kingdom that Hetta eventually stumbled upon. And she would not make Hetta's mistake, oh no. She would not, at the end of her own tale, forsake the bright kingdom in favor of the familiar green lawns of Inrhio.

Or would she? Chay had made it clear that her position here was precarious, certainly not permanent. She did not know how long she would be permitted to wander within the brilliant, dangerous boundaries of the alien kingdom. That was a bitter lesson Hetta had not been forced to learn, that sometimes you are not welcome where you most desire to be.

"I like this," Nolan said, when Kit laid the book aside once she got tired of speaking. "But if all the girls of Inrhio read this when they're children, why are they all so conservative and traditional once they grow up?"

Kit laughed. "And I suppose, after you read *Corbin Heather, Trewillin Soldier*, you joined the crew of a merchant ship and sailed off to fight in foreign wars? Because I read all the boys' adventure books, too, and they're just as full of intrigue and daring as the girls' books. And yet I never did meet an indigo man who confessed to having been a pirate."

"No, I suppose I should have been reading *Corbin Heather, Lab Scientist*, but I never came across any book like that," Nolan said with a smile. "Maybe that's why children are always so disappointed with real life when they grow up, because all the adventures only exist in fiction."

"Were you disappointed?" Kit asked curiously.

"A little. When I began to realize how my options were narrowing down. Or worse—how I didn't really have any at all. The course of my life was set when I was fourteen, and at that time it all sounded pretty exciting. At twenty, it seemed a little dull. But then I got accepted into the state university and invited to work at the Biolab, and some of the excitement returned. A different kind of excitement, though. Tempered. That's when I realized that this was as good as it was ever going to get. No piracy on the high seas. No sword fights with evil barbarians. No adventures."

"*This* is an adventure, in its way."

He nodded, serious again. "But this one I would have forfeited," he said.

The third day, Chay sent for Kit again. She was elated as she hurried down the hall after the guard—but as soon as she saw Chay, she was alarmed. Three days ago, he had looked as healthy and energetic as ever. This day, he looked weary and pale, and he coughed incessantly. He had again invited her in for an afternoon snack, but this time they were not left alone. One of his personal assistants stayed in the room the whole time, coming forward every time Chay's cough grew more insistent to offer a soothing drink or a cloth to spit in.

She tried to hide her concern, for it was not acceptable for a woman to show that she thought a man was weak, but she was so worried that it was impossible to conceal that completely. "How long have you been this ill?" she asked him, when he had recovered from a particularly severe fit.

"Yesterday and today," he said, breathing heavily. "I had been better this afternoon, or I would not have sent for you."

"What can I do? How can I help you?"

He shook his head. "I just wanted to have the pleasure of your company another hour. To assure myself that you are well and being treated with courtesy."

"Yes, every courtesy," she said impatiently. "What have the doctors said? Your cough is so wretched—surely this is not a good sign. Have the drugs helped you at all? What do they know?"

"They know very little," he said, then paused to cough again. "Time is the only physician who can give us the answer."

"I thought you said you would know something in a few days."

"Now it appears to be a few days more."

"And the others? Who have caught your infection?"

"All of them seem to be responding well to the treatments."

"Then it is only you," she said slowly.

"Then it is only me. Which is good news indeed."

She gave him a look of silent protest, but he only smiled. "Do not despair yet," he said. "I am a strong man, and a determined one. I will live if I possibly can."

"I'll ask Nolan," she said suddenly. "He may have a new

formula. He may realize he left something out of his old drugs. He'll come up with a fresh cure for you."

"You have great faith in this unconventional blueskin."

"I think he is the most amazing man I have ever met," she said honestly. "I think he is—so pure of heart that he makes other, ordinary men seem wicked by comparison. I think he is so generous that my own thoughts shame me by their selfishness. He is so kind that he makes me search my soul to find new ways to be compassionate to others. And brave. Not one man in ten thousand would do what he has done."

"You must wish your father could have met him," Chay said.

"*You* have met him," she said. "That is almost as good."

The guard practically had to drag her from Chay's presence. The guldman had broken down several times into an uncontrollable asthmatic wheeze, and the last time, Kit had flung herself across the room to kneel at his feet, begging him to stop coughing. He had waved to the attendant, who pulled her none too gently to her feet, but she couldn't stop pleading with Chay to take a drink, breathe deeply, feel better, be all right. When the bout had passed, he lay back weakly in his chair for a moment. His face was so pale that the gold sheen of his skin seemed to lay across his features in a layer so distinct that she could peel it back to reveal the blood and muscle underneath. His hair was dark with sweat, and the breath shuddered into his lungs. He did not look strong enough to stand.

"Chay—" she said desperately.

He opened his eyes, looked at her, and summoned a smile. "If this should be the last time you see me," he said, "remember me any way but this."

"Chay, don't say such things!" she cried.

He heaved himself to his feet, wavered, but seemed to gather strength. "But I do not think it will be the last time," he said more cheerfully. "If I allow you to hug me, will you promise to release me?"

"I promise," she whispered, and he signalled to the guard to free her. But it was a lie, because she couldn't let go, and Chay had to detach himself with some force.

"Now go," he told her, putting her into the hands of the guard, who held her with a grip there was no gainsaying. "I will see you again in a few days if I am able. Study patience. For there is nothing worthwhile bought with any other coin."

"Chay—" she begged, but he turned for the private door, taking his assistant's arm. "Chay!" she called, but she was being pulled out the other exit, guided down the hall, and there was nothing she could say, nothing she could do, nothing that would change anything.

But when she was deposited inside her own quarters, she turned on Nolan in a frenzy. To his casual query of "How's Chay?" she responded with a frantic, "He's dying! You must do something."

"Dying! But two days ago—"

"He's so sick—he can't stop coughing—and he looks so exhausted. Nolan, you have to fix him. You have to come up with some better drugs. Something more concentrated, maybe. You know, Chay is very strong. He can withstand dosages that might kill other men. You can mix up a medicine just for him."

"Kit, I can't. I only know one formula, and it—"

"But you have to!" she exclaimed. "There must be something else you could try, something you left out because it was too dangerous. Talk to Chay's doctors! They'll tell you what he can endure. They'll help you come up with a new prescription."

He put his hands on her shoulders and tried to calm her with the persuasion of his touch. "Kit. I have done what I can. There is no magic in me to fix Chay. I have no other cures."

She wrenched away from him and began pacing the room. "If it was an *indigo* lying in there dying, you'd be working at your lab books hard enough, trying to come up with answers . . . If it was Ariana Bayless, you'd try new formulas."

"I doubt it," he said dryly.

"If it was your Leesa—oh, the sun wouldn't set on any day that you hadn't come up with at least three new drugs to try and save her—"

"I would do for Leesa what I have done for Chay—try my best."

"It's because he's gulden!" she said furiously. "You won't help him because of his gold skin—"

He looked thunderstruck. "How can you possibly say that to me?"

"You told me! On the train! You said how you despised the gulden, you thought of them as less than human—"

"It is true that I have had to work to overcome my prejudices," he said, seeming to fight for calm. "And I consider it a great personal flaw that I have at times looked on gulden as— as not quite equal to me. But that doesn't mean—"

"You can't stand them," she accused. "You don't care if Chay dies. If any of them die."

"I have spent most of my time, these past few years, coming up with medicines to cure the gulden," he said in a low, steady voice. "I personally—me, Nolan Adelpho—I found the drugs that stopped two epidemics before they had time to become disasters. I worked overnight at the lab more times than I can count, putting together those formulas. I didn't rest until I found the cure, the combination. It is not because Chay is gulden that I cannot help him. It is because this is all I know. I have done my best. If it is not good enough, then I am not good enough. You cannot change that by cursing."

"You could try," she whispered, suddenly turned supplicant, clasping her hands together to plead for the favor. "You could look at your old formulas and try to come up with something new—"

He gestured at the notebook even now lying open on the sofa. "What do you think I've been doing the past three days? I've been going over my math. I've been reviewing my chemistry. Without a computer and a fully equipped lab, I can't do any actual tests, but I haven't been able to devise any new patterns that I'd like to try, anyway. Do you understand me, Kit? I have done what I can."

"But you're killing him!" she wailed.

"He may die, but I didn't kill him," Nolan said in a grim voice. "I have done everything I can to save him."

"I hate you," she said.

He said nothing for a moment, then nodded and shrugged his shoulders. His face had grown unbelievably tired. "Your privilege," he said, and turned away.

She crossed the room in four swift strides and caught his arm.

"No—no, I didn't mean that," she said, turning him back to face her. She was swamped with a whole new set of unbearable emotions—remorse, fear, self-loathing. "You of all people I could never hate."

He stood passive in her grip but would not meet her eyes. "You have no reason not to," he said bitterly. "After I threatened Jex's life and practically abducted you. Why wouldn't you hate me? I expect nothing else."

She gave his arm a little shake. "Nolan, don't say such things. You're the kindest, the best man I know. I would trust you with my life—with Jex's life—Chay's. You are such a good man! It makes me ashamed of myself."

He looked at her now, sideways, tentative. "That day we first arrived," he said shyly. "When Chay asked you your opinion of me. Did you mean it? All that about trust and your heart."

She nodded, her eyes fixed on him, willing him to believe her. "Don't ask me when it happened," she said. "Maybe when you fed the runaway wife at Krekt Station. Maybe when you said you had not taken a private car on the train because you didn't want me to be afraid of you. Maybe before that—maybe in the city, when you made me take the pills. You seem so concerned about everyone. Willing to care for everyone. That's a trait I haven't seen in anyone before, man or woman, blueskin or gold. It's not in me, certainly."

He shook his head. "I don't. I don't care for everyone. Sometimes I wonder if I love anyone as much as I should. I want to be a good son—a good husband—a good father, if the time ever comes. I try to be a good friend. But most of the time that just consists of being agreeable on the surface and keeping my thoughts to myself. That does not make me a kind man. It just means I manage to stay pleasant to most people most of the time."

"Oh, Nolan," she said, and she could not stop herself. She lifted one hand to trace the wide curve of his cheekbone. The color of his skin was so intense that she could almost feel its sultry heat, distinct from the pulse and fever of his body. The nubbed texture of his whiskers felt like spiky linen under her fingertips; his lips were an inset panel of satin. "I hope Leesa deserves to marry a man as wonderful as you."

He had not moved since she touched him; he had transmogrified to granite. His eyelids had half-closed, as if the spell that had changed him to stone had caught him mid-blink, mid-swoon. When he spoke, his lips brushed against the palm of her hand, still laid across his mouth. Not another muscle in his body changed position. "I will not be marrying Leesa," he said.

She pressed her fingers harder against his mouth as if to push the words back in. "Don't say such things," she said. "Of course you will. She will never learn of your visit here—and if she did, she would love you anyway."

"No matter what happens here—no matter what she learns, or does not learn—I cannot marry her. This trip has changed me too much."

Kit dropped her hand. "If it has made you a better man, that is no reason not to marry."

"It has made me an inconstant man. And I cannot marry her if I do not love her."

He had not moved; but now Kit took a step backward. "What makes you think you have stopped loving her?"

"Because I have started loving you."

It was as if buildings crashed, bells clamored, sirens rose like demonic voices, and yet the room was absolutely silent. Kit could hear water playing from the other chamber. She could hear Nolan breathing. She could hear her own heartbeat.

"What?" she said faintly.

His feet were still nailed to the floor but he made one cautious movement, spreading his hands in a gesture of helplessness. "You. How can you think I am so wonderful when you are— you are—this incredible, complex, passionate, loyal—ideal— woman? I can't think when you're in the room. When you're not in the room, I can't think of anything *but* you. I marvel that you could exist, that such a world as ours could produce you. You have changed me in ways I can't even describe."

She backed away with every phrase he uttered, shaking her head, holding her hands before her in a protective, warning gesture. "Don't say things like that," she said. "You'll regret them. You'll be sorry."

"How could I be sorry? For you to know how I feel? Oh, I know you can't love me back. I know your heart is given elsewhere. I'm not asking for anything from you. But I wanted you to know. I love you, and I can't unlove you, and when the world ends, I will love you still."

Now she stood half a room away, still shaking her head, but she had folded her arms high across her chest so that her hands clung to their opposite shoulders. "You wouldn't love me if you knew," she whispered. "There are things about me that would turn you away—"

"Nothing," he said.

"Everything!" she cried. "Do you forget? You hate the gulden so much, and yet half my life has been among them. They have been my lovers, they have been my closest friends—"

"I don't care," he said. "Do you think I'm afraid that you have been tainted—corrupted? You? One look at your face and anyone could see how pure your heart is."

"One look at my face, and you would think I was a high-caste indigo heiress," she said tensely. "But that is exactly what I am not."

"I have known my share of the Higher Hundred," he said quietly. "And what I love about you is that you are nothing like them at all. You're unique."

"I'm alien," she said.

"Exotic," he amended.

"But I'm not for the likes of you," she said. She made her voice hard, though it took all her strength. Inside she was shaking like wine held in an unsteady hand. "You are on foreign soil and stirred by unfamiliar sensations. When you're home again, this madness will pass—you'll look back on this entire episode as some kind of crazy dream. You'll want your usual friends and playthings around you then. You'll be shocked to think you could ever say you loved me."

"If I thought that was true," he said, "I would stay on Gold Mountain the rest of my life."

"You would not be welcome here. You are an outsider, you do not belong. You belong with your own people, your own family, and the girl you have loved your whole life. Go back to them and forget me."

"I may go back. I won't forget you."

"Once we leave this place, you'll have no reason to see me again."

"Every reason," he said. "I love you."

"Not in Inrhio," she whispered.

Now he finally moved, three paces toward her, bending forward a little as if to peer at her face from a far height. "And if, once I return to the city, I find you are still in my blood like some kind of shadow heartbeat?" he demanded. "What then? Would you believe me if I came to you then and said I still loved you? Would you trust me, and be willing to try and love me in return?"

"It will not happen," she said.

One step nearer. She was against the wall, she could retreat no farther, but the stern look in her eyes stopped him where he stood. "And if it does? Can I seek you out? Convince you?"

She had once more folded her arms across her chest, this time to try to control her fevered shaking. "I don't know—I don't know—it would be wrong," she stammered, losing the ability to put her argument in words without telling him everything, without saying the worst—what he would perceive as the worst, anyway. "You will not want to see me, let it go at that. When we're in the city—"

"When we're in the city," he said firmly, "everything will be different. But you'll see how much things are the same. I have changed for the last time—this is the man I will be till I die. And that man loves you."

And because she still had no answer for that, she turned and ran from the room. One more time to fling herself on this bed and cry as if the world was ending. She used to think she was a woman who seldom cried. Strange how one trip had changed that, changed her perceptions of herself, of the people around her. Changed everything.

CHAPTER SIXTEEN

The next three days passed in fragile silence. Their quarters were too small to allow Nolan and Kit to avoid each other completely, and Nolan made no attempt to. He had no wish to stop seeing her; for him, nothing had changed. Speaking the words aloud had not made him any more sensitive to her presence, or any less, or altered what he felt or what he wanted. His bones still crumbled the first time he saw her every day; his brain momentarily shut down with the shock. But that had been true for days now and was not actually unpleasant. The enforced intimacy was no hardship on him.

Kit kept to her room as long as she could in the mornings, but hunger eventually drove her out. She managed to be civil to Nolan, though hardly warm, and he kept a respectful distance. He didn't badger her with questions or repeated assurances of his love. He merely repeated to her whatever news he'd been able to guess at on the monitor, told her if the guards had left any message with the breakfast tray, and went back to work on his formulas.

But he felt sorry for her. She clearly felt trapped, desperate, anxious for Chay and wary of her fellow prisoner, and there was nothing she could do about any part of her situation. Midway through the second day, just to offer her a distraction, Nolan suggested they continue reading *A Wanderer's Tale*, and she gratefully acquiesced. She didn't seem up to reciting the text herself, but she sat slumped in the chair, hand supporting her chin, and listened as Nolan read. It pleased him that he could do something for her, even something so small.

When the book palled on both of them, they took up choisin again, Kit playing with far more concentration this time. Two hours passed without either of them saying a word except to request a card or a turn at the dice. Nolan tried to remember some of the strategies Pakt had used, just to make the game a little more exciting, but he still could not get his mind around the tactics, and so Kit won handily.

"Another game?" he asked, but she had risen to her feet.

"I don't think I could bear it," she said. "I'm going to bed."

It was barely past sunset; she couldn't possibly be tired. But maybe she was one of those people who possessed the knack of retreating into sleep when the world became too much to cope with. He had never had that skill and, until now, had not envied it.

"Tomorrow, then."

"Oh, I imagine so."

They finished *A Wanderer's Tale* the next morning and moved on to *Corridor of Fire*, a stately and tragic story of one man's slow dissipation. This one had never come Nolan's way, either, and he found the subject both depressing and distasteful, but the language was so beautiful that he kept pausing at the end of sentences just to recover from the intoxication of the words. It was strange to him that he would be reading one of his culture's literary masterpieces while being held under guard in the palace of a foreign dignitary. But no less strange than anything else that had happened to him in the past few weeks.

On the morning of the fourth day, Chay sent for them.

When the guards appeared at the door, Kit was unprepared. She had dressed in some of the laundered indigo clothes she had purchased in the city, and she had not troubled to style her hair. "How do I look? Am I all right?" she asked nervously, though Nolan could not tell if she directed the questions at him or the guards.

"You're fine," he said.

"Maybe if I put a scarf on—"

"He's not calling us in to inspect your clothes."

They followed the guards down the sunny corridors, Nolan happy to be out of his quarters for the first time since their arrival. Kit seemed so tense that he wanted to take her hand just for reassurance, but he had no illusions that she would find this a comfort. The guards had said they were taking the prisoners to see Chay, but Nolan wondered. They could be heading straight for execution. He tried to summon dread but could not. On this trip, he had become a fatalist. What had been set in motion, even by his own hand, could not be altered now by his words or desires. He strolled through the passageways and felt remarkably calm.

Once they entered Chay's living quarters, they had to pass through a series of anterooms and sitting rooms, all of them empty. The last chamber they came to was airy, colorfully decorated with tapestries, rugs, and flowers, and clearly set up as a sickroom. For there was Chay, half-reclined on a lounge chair, bundled in robes and blankets against the slight chill of the outside air, and pale unto death. Despite the open window, the room smelled of potions and sickness. Even Chay's gray eyes seemed siphoned of color, almost transparent. His golden skin seemed diluted, mixed with opaque white. His gestures were those of a man whose bones had grown frail.

"Kitrini. Nolan Adelpho," he greeted them, waving toward a set of chairs. "Sit down."

Kit sat, but she looked as if she would have preferred to fling herself to the floor before him. "Chay," she said in a pitiful voice. "You do not look well."

The guldman smiled faintly. "No, and I have very little strength. But the doctors tell me I have stabilized for the moment. They do not know if I will next become much better or much worse, but they expect no change at all for a day or two."

Nolan sank more slowly into the chair assigned to him. "I would think it is a good sign to have arrested the development of the disease," he said. "Are they hopeful?"

"They do not want me to die," Chay said, turning that smile on Nolan. "Therefore, they seem very hopeful indeed. They were interested in your information about the possible length of the recovery period."

Nolan shook his head. "As far as I know, no one *has* recovered from the infection before. So I don't have any idea."

"Yes, that's what I thought you had said before."

"What about the others? Who else has fallen ill, and who else is taking the drugs?"

"As far as we know, about forty others have caught the infection. None became as sick as I did, and most of them seem to have recovered already."

"Excellent!" Nolan exclaimed. "And the vaccine? It has been distributed?"

Chay nodded. "Here and in the city. I am a little concerned about the population in the city, in fact. So many of the gulden there have divorced themselves from utter fealty to me. They will listen to the news, but perhaps not act upon it quickly. And our system of disseminating information among the city gulden is not as good as it is on Gold Mountain."

Nolan's hands tightened on the arms of his chair. "Possible epidemic," he said.

Chay nodded. "We have alerted the gulden news media. The hospitals. The health-care workers. But we are worried."

"Surely, if someone falls ill and seeks out a doctor, the doctor will recognize the symptoms—" Kit said.

Chay nodded. "We hope so. If the person seeks a doctor in time. He might not realize he is at risk."

"Every gulden in the city is at risk!" she protested.

Chay nodded again, but his eyes were on Nolan. "Tell me, Nolan Adelpho," he said. "Does an individual have to be a full-blooded gulden to be affected by this disease? If a child is half-indigo, for instance, or even one-quarter, might that keep him safe from infection?"

Nolan frowned. Beside him, Kit grew very still. "I'm not sure," he said cautiously. "I wouldn't think it would be a major problem. There are so few interracial couples that mixed-breed children are almost nonexistent."

"But there are some," Chay said. "And if they can catch the disease, or spread it—"

Nolan nodded. "Well, the infection attacks a specific combination of molecules in the gulden bloodstream," he said. "There's certainly a one-in-two chance that a mixed-breed child would carry those molecules. So then I would say, yes, those individuals are at risk. But the same antidotes and the same vaccines would keep them safe."

"Then we need to make sure the media and the hospitals have that information," Chay said. "I will see to it."

"Once news of the epidemic becomes public knowledge," Nolan said, "Cerisa will have to react in some way. She will at least have to pretend to be looking for a cure."

"We have informed the doctors and the news media that our own pharmacists have come up with medicines. I hope this does not disappoint you."

Nolan laughed. "Certainly not! I'd rather not be given credit for this particular breakthrough."

"Though if you are willing," Chay added, "I would be interested in hearing from you about Cerisa Daylen's reaction. What she says and how she behaves."

"In hearing from—but I—am I to be sent back to the city, then?" Nolan stammered. "I thought—you seem to be so dangerously ill—and you said before—"

Chay nodded. "I have reconsidered. If I die while you are still here, your life will be instantly forfeit. No matter what orders I leave to the contrary, I am afraid you will fall under suspicion and mysteriously disappear. Even if your drugs do not save me, it is clear that they will have saved countless others—a whole nation—and I do not want to repay your generosity in such a dishonorable way. Therefore, I am sending you back to the city on tonight's train."

Nolan came to his feet. "But I don't want to go back," he said urgently. "I want to stay here—and do what I can for you— and for any of the gulden. I want—"

"There is nothing else you can do for any of us," Chay said. "And now I want you safely away."

Nolan turned to look at Kit, sitting carved and immobile in her chair. Her gaze was fixed on Chay; she had not moved or spoken for the past several minutes. "Does Kit come with me? If you die, I don't want the wrath of the gulden to fall on her."

"I want to stay," she said instantly.

"Kit, I believe, is safe," Chay said, as if she hadn't spoken. "She is too familiar to my family and my people to be at risk."

"Well, I am not so certain of that," Nolan said stubbornly. "I would feel much better if she was allowed to return to the city with me."

Chay smiled, and this smile was both stronger and edged with malice. "I realize that," he said, "and that is why I want her with me. I still do not entirely trust you. Forgive me for that."

The words made little sense. Nolan glanced at Kit, then back at Chay. "What?" he said.

Chay spread his hands. "You have brought us timely warnings. You have brought us miraculous cures. Even I may live. For that we are profoundly grateful. And yet, this disease may turn on us still. Your cures may not be effective. Your vaccines may be useless. All the gulden may still be at risk. I think we can trust you more if we know you have left behind with us something you value greatly."

"He does not value me," Kit said quickly.

"Oh, yes, he does," Chay answered. "It is obvious the man is in love with you. It was clear to me the day you arrived on my doorstep. I will keep you at my side—not because I adore you as I do not adore my own daughters—but because he will not do anything foolish while you are in my power and at risk."

"You just told me," Nolan said in a low voice, "that she was safe here. That your family and your friends would guard her. Do you tell me now that you lied? A man of honor such as yourself?"

Chay smiled; he seemed to appreciate Nolan's inept attempt to use the gulden's chief weapon against him. "Not at all," he replied calmly. "She is safe from physical assault. But is she safe from your manufactured disease?"

"*Chay!*" Kit cried, and leapt to her feet, her hands balled into fists, and her whole body strained with protest.

Chay ignored her and continued speaking. "Because you said, did you not, that anyone with the smallest percentage of gulden blood was susceptible to this illness?"

Nolan nodded, not even breathing. Kit, though she had once more turned to stone, seemed to writhe in acid agony within her marble shell.

Chay's smile widened. "Anton Solvano's father took a gulden woman to wife," the guldman said. "That he was allowed to do so was a high mark of favor from my father. But Anton himself appeared to be a pureblood indigo, a fact which amused him and which he learned, at a very early age, to use to his advantage. Very few people, I was told, knew of his mixed ancestry. Or am I wrong?"

"No," Nolan breathed.

"So you see," Chay said, reaching out a hand to Kit, who moved forward like a sleepwalker to take it, "if your drugs are not as effective as we hoped, the woman you have fallen in love with will die. You go. She stays. Only you know how confident you can be."

Kit was staring down at Chay as if she had never seen him before. "You used me," she whispered. "You called me to your side these past few days merely to expose me to the virus. Knowing I was unprotected. Knowing I could die. How could you do such a thing to me?"

"Because it is a war," Chay said in a very gentle voice, "and I have almost no weapons to hand."

Kit turned to Nolan, who had not moved, not even to yank her hand away from Chay's, as he so desperately wanted to do. He had traveled all this way, gambled his entire life, to save this man; and now all he wanted was to claw out the guldman's heart with his fingernails.

"I'm sorry," she whispered to Nolan. "I'm sorry for everything. I didn't want to hurt you this way. I didn't even want you to know."

"I knew," he said, his voice no louder than hers.

There was a moment's complete silence. Chay, startled, had dropped Kit's hand. She stared at Nolan with disbelieving eyes. The room seemed to have been sucked clean of air.

"I knew," Nolan said with renewed energy. "I heard the story of Casen Solvano's life among the gulden. I wondered who he had found to bear his only son. There are not many indigo who would follow such a man to Gold Mountain—Roetta Candachi might be the only one in sixteen generations. So who was Anton Solvano's mother if not a gulden woman?" He pointed an accusing finger at Kit, who stood with one hand pressed against her mouth, gazing at him. "I knew all along you were gulden, if that's the secret you were afraid to tell me. It made no difference to me. I fell in love with you anyway."

"Nolan," Kit said through her fingers, and shook her head.

Chay recaptured her hand and did not look likely to let it go anytime soon. The look on his face was part anger, part determination. "Then we have no secrets between us anymore, which is best among civil men," he said in a voice far less genteel than his words. "She is still my hostage to your medications."

Nolan laughed, surprising even himself. "Kit won't fall ill, Chay Zanlan," he said scornfully. "How stupid do you think I am? She's had a full course of vaccines in the past nine days. I started dosing her before we left the city."

Kit's hand spasmed in Chay's hold, as if she would jerk herself free. The guldman's grip tightened; the hostility in his gray eyes was impossible to miss. "Then she is only as safe as the rest of us," Chay said. "And you, Nolan Adelpho, must be the judge of just how safe that is."

"As safe as I could make her. As safe as I could make any of you," Nolan said. "I have no fears for her on that score. But I worry about her safety in the hands of a man who could use her as a choifer in such a mortal game."

"You have been playing choisin," Chay said.

"It is not a pastime I care for, frankly," Nolan said. "I have no heart for attack and counterattack. I have no taste for betraying my longtime allies. I am a straightforward man, and a simple one. I have done what I can for you and your people. Now let Kit go. Let her return to the city with me."

"No," Chay said.

"Then I will stay and wait out your illness with her."

Chay gestured, and two guards entered the room. "No," Chay said again. "Your luggage is in the hall. You will be escorted to Zakto Station within the hour. You will be accompanied on your journey back to the city, and for that trip you will be quite protected. But enter Geldricht again without an invitation, and I do not believe you will go unmolested. My people have been told that the indigo grow treacherous, and they will look with suspicion upon any of your race."

The guards had hold of Nolan by both arms. He would not let them drag him from the room. He would walk out with what dignity he could manage. But he backed out slowly, his eyes never leaving Kit's face. Chay he ignored; Nolan had spoken his last words, given his last aid to the guldman.

"Kit," he said, coming to a halt at the threshold. "I love you. Come to me when you return to the city."

"She may choose not to return," Chay said.

Nolan ignored him. "I love you," he said again. "Come to me."

"Nolan," she said, and not another word. The guards pulled him from the room, and the door shut between them. The march down to the front gates took nearly twenty minutes. In the grand hallway, his guards collected his suitcase, and they were on their way to the train station. Back to the city. Back to Inrhio.

Back to a world that no longer existed.

CHAPTER SEVENTEEN

As far as traffic was concerned, life in the city was almost back to normal. The Centrifuge was still under reconstruction, but a fleet of buses and trolleys had been installed to carry traffic to every possible destination, and so the daily commute was again possible. Nolan assumed he would find this very handy if he still had a job.

He had been gone from the city nearly two weeks, and away from his apartment for even longer. Entering it now, mid-afternoon on an uncomfortably hot day, he found that it smelled dusty, stale, and unfamiliar, but not as bad as he had thought it might. No rotting trash, no unfortunate plumbing leaks left un-attended too long. Still, there was something peculiar about it, stranger than the smells of emptiness and neglect, and he moved from room to room trying to identify what.

Color.

He had been too long among the gulden, first at Pakt's merry house, then in Chay Zanlan's glorious palace. His eyes had be-come accustomed to riots of blues and purples and passionate pinks. He expected tapestries, rugs, stenciled walls, painted mouldings. Here everything was neutral, subdued, elegant, and sterile.

And *sound.*

Pakt's house had been alive with children laughing, voices calling, furniture being shoved from one side of the room to the other. And in Geldricht he had only been alone for those brief times when Kit had been called away to Chay Zanlan's presence. Of course, there had been many times during those days when she did not speak to him, but still, she had been a presence there, moving about in the other room, her personality so compelling it had seemed to shout to him even through her determined silence.

But here there was nothing. No commotion, no signs of life. Nothing to remind him that he was not alone in the world.

He went out at dark to forage for food. He bought prepared meat and dried fruit at the corner grocer; he didn't think he could remember how to cook a meal. There were half a dozen other young men about his age picking out menu items in the other aisles. He recognized all of them by sight, even knew some of their names. A great loneliness washed over him, and he felt an almost irresistible desire to go up to one and say, "Hey, come back to my place for dinner. You wouldn't believe the adventure I have just had."

But with whom among his friends or acquaintances could he share this story? Not even those closest to him would understand or approve. He left the store by himself, having exchanged only three words with the clerk. He wondered if he would live in unbroken silence for the rest of his life.

Back in his apartment, he consumed his meal while standing over the counter, flipping through his mail. Bills, magazines, letters from his mother and Leesa, notices about neighborhood sales and citywide events. He would have expected something more drastic, after such a long absence, but none of these missives stirred him to frantic action. He did sit down and write quick notes to Leesa and his family, blaming the Centrifuge and the disrupted city life for his failure to respond more quickly.

There would be more, at some point, to tell Leesa. But he could not envision how that conversation would go. He could not, at any rate, put what he had to say into a letter.

That night he lay in his own bed for the first time in weeks, staring at the well-known patterns on the walls and ceiling. Nothing could have felt less familiar. It was as if his body, not his heart, had undergone the radical change, so that shadows fell with unaccustomed harshness on his foreign eyes, and the fibers of personal items rubbed on a borrowed skin. He did not belong here. This was not his place. These were not his things. He was the imposter.

In the morning, he rose, dressed, and headed for the lab as if he had been doing just that without interruption for the past two weeks. He had no idea what he would say to Pakt. He had no idea if there was still a job awaiting him. He could not imagine how he would explain his absence or return. He just could think of nothing else to do instead.

He arrived early, the first one there except for Pakt himself. Taking a deep breath, Nolan traversed the hall, knocked on the guldman's door, and entered.

Pakt, who was seated at his desk poring over papers, looked up and then grew motionless. Nolan waited a moment for a greeting and then said, "Good morning."

"I'd been wondering if you were still alive," Pakt said in a neutral voice.

"I left you a note."

"Not a very helpful one. Not too specific about dates and causes."

"I wasn't too sure about dates myself."

"And causes?"

Nolan raised his hands as if they would help him shape the words, then dropped them and gave his shoulders an infinitesimal shrug. "I don't know if I'll ever be able to talk about the causes."

Pakt leaned back in his chair and gestured Nolan to a seat. "Problems with Leesa?" he asked gently.

Nolan sat on the edge of the chair, arms on his knees, hands clasped before him. "Well," he said slowly, "ultimately I guess it will come down to that."

"I went by your apartment a week ago," Pakt said. "But no one was there. No one had seen you."

"I've been gone," Nolan said.

"Let me know when you can talk about it," the guldman said.

Nolan looked over at him. "You're the only one I think I *could* talk to about it," he said. "But I'm not sure—even you—" He let the words trail off.

"So. Are you back?"

"I'm back," Nolan said. "If you still want me here."

"We've all missed you."

"What did you tell them? Cerisa and the others?"

"That you were having family problems. I pretended I knew something. I don't think anyone will ask too many questions."

Nolan rose to his feet because he couldn't think of anything else to say. "Well. Thanks for that."

Pakt stood, too, concern crossing his face. "Are you all right?" he asked with some urgency. "You look like you're sick."

Nolan felt a hollow laugh whuffle through his cheeks. "That would be ironic," he said. "No, I'm fine. Is there something on my desk for me to do? Or should I go back to old projects?"

Pakt was frowning, looking even less reassured as the conversation progressed. "Old projects for now, I guess," he said. "I'll let you know if something new comes in."

Nolan nodded and left his office.

It was midmorning before anyone came in to check on him, although he knew the others were all aware of his return. He could catch their voices in the hallway: "Nolan's back!" "Did you see? Nolan's in his office." "Where's he been?" "What did Pakt say?" "Hey, was that Nolan?" It was standard lab procedure to try to determine what was happening through indirect methods (gossip) before proceeding to more direct approaches (interrogation), so Nolan was not surprised at the whispering. In fact, it comforted him a little. Made him feel at home.

When he had been working at his computer for a little more than two hours, there was a knock on his door, and Melina entered. "Hey, Nolan, good to see you," she said with studied breeziness.

He swiveled in his chair to smile at her. She had been letting her hair grow, and now it stood up in tufted spikes all over head. There was nothing she could do to make herself look unattractive; in fact, the coiffure gave her a waifish charm that was quite appealing.

"Good to see you, too," he replied, and meant it. "What's been going on here?"

She leaned against the doorway. "Well, let's see. Varella's betrothed."

"She is! To Roven?"

"No, it's such a shock. Someone she met in the city. He's a high-caste man, so no problem there, but *not* someone her mother approves of. It's kind of been a scandal, and I think her grandmother's threatening to divert her inheritance."

"That would be pretty severe."

"She says she doesn't care. Says she's going to live in the city the rest of her life, anyway. And her fiancée is a doctor over at the East Side hospital, so between them they ought to be fine in terms of income. But what a surprise, huh? Varella never seemed like much of a rebel to me."

"You're just jealous because you didn't think of it first," Nolan scoffed. "Refusing the man your family had picked out for you."

She smiled and squirmed against the hard doorframe to achieve better comfort. "I did do it, but I was seventeen, and they've been afraid to matchmake for me ever since," she retorted. "Now they're waiting for me to get over my infatuation with Julitta before they introduce me to eligible men."

"I think you should follow Varella's lead and find your own man."

"Maybe I would," she said softly, "if I could figure men out."

Nolan assumed that was a veiled reference to his own behavior and decided to change the subject. "Any other news? How's Cerisa?"

"Like you care."

"Just curious."

"She's been gone a lot. Speculation is that Ariana Bayless is considering reconfiguring the Biolab and Cerisa's been there a lot advising her. That, or they're involved in some torrid affair, because they are together *all* the time."

"I could see that. Cerisa Daylen and Ariana Bayless."

"Anyway, she hasn't been around much, which of course has made the rest of us just as happy as bugs in the springtime. Hiram thinks maybe she's considering resigning, but Pakt says that won't happen till the world ends. But we talk about it a lot."

"That *would* make her happy."

"So what about you?" she asked. "You okay?"

"Okay."

"Don't want to talk about it, I guess."

"Not really."

"Would you want to have lunch, though? You cannot talk about it while we eat."

"That sounds good. I'm hungry already."

Over the meal, she filled him in on other small events that had transpired in his absence. As she spoke, the world began to resume some of its normal shades and contours; it was as if, with her words and details, she applied color and depth onto his flat, gray perspective. Now and then she would mention the name of someone whose existence he had literally forgotten, and he would reinsert that person into his interior landscape, until gradually it became populated and lively again. Sometimes he became so engrossed in remembering these newfound friends that he missed a few of her next sentences.

"I'm supposed to go to my mother's this summer, in fact, for at least a month," she was saying once when he fugued back in to the conversation. "Coleta Templeton—you remember the Templetons?—is introducing her youngest daughter at a birthday ball, and my mother is just adamant that I return for it. And of course the summer is the high social season at my mother's house, because that's when we celebrate *her* birthday, and my *grandmother's* birthday, and *my* birthday, and so I know if I once set foot in-country, I won't get away for weeks."

"Will Julitta go with you?" Nolan asked.

Melina sipped her drink and looked quizzical. They had been gone from the lab for nearly ninety minutes, and she showed no signs of wanting to return. Nolan assumed she had cleared this all with Pakt ("I'll take him out to lunch and see how he's doing"), so he had not bothered to glance at his watch since they sat down.

"Julitta wants to go, and my mother has invited her, but I don't think I'm really supposed to bring her," Melina said at last with the air of one making a confession. "I think I'm supposed to be meeting Steffel Templeton and Ronan Baner. I think my mother wants to parade the candidates before me, and that would be a little harder to do with a jahla at my side."

"So," said Nolan, toying with his silverware, "in fact the infatuation has already waned."

"No," Melina said seriously. "No. Every time I think to myself, 'I'm going to have to give this woman up sometime,' I feel my heart stop. I find myself bargaining for more time. I tell myself, 'Another year. I won't even think about it until next spring. Next summer. Next fall.' I don't know what I'll do when it actually comes down to it. When I have to marry and move on."

"Then don't do it," Nolan said.

Melina spread her hands. On her face was a hurt smile. "I'm the oldest daughter. I owe my family something—I owe them everything. What else can I do?"

Nolan rose to his feet, too filled with a sudden rush of restless energy to sit quietly for another moment. "Let the land pass to a younger sister or a cousin or a niece. Let it fall into fallow ruin. What will it matter? Don't let them marry you off to some stupid clod just to get yourself a daughter. How can you turn your back on love? If you had ever had it once and let it go, you wouldn't even be able to talk about it now."

She gaped up at him, seeming too stunned to move. "You've broken your engagement with Leesa," she said.

He had turned to go, so he answered her over his shoulder. "Leesa," he said, "is the least of my heartaches right now." And he walked out of the restaurant without even glancing back to see if she would follow.

The next two weeks passed at an almost languorous pace. Nolan was aware of the unfolding of each minute, second by second. He watched time array itself before him as he would have watched the blooming of a flower through stop-motion photography. Small events jogged his memory, reminded him how it felt to be human, and indigo: *This* was the exact scent of summer asphalt in the city; this was the precise taste of homemade holiday bread. It was as if all these details had been wiped away by the invasion of the gulden lifestyle, and now his brain and his body had to relearn their most basic components.

But none of the recovered knowledge erased what he had acquired on Gold Mountain. The two sets of memories coexisted, side by side and antithetical; he could not make them meet inside his head. He was like a planet circling a single sun, so that only half of his surfaces were illuminated at any one time. But nightfall did not obliterate one nor daylight make the other paramount. He watched the revolving scenery in his mind and wondered when he would succumb to madness.

He tried over and over to plan a trip to Inrhio, but he could not bring himself to make the travel reservations. It was not that he was afraid to see Leesa, wracked with worry over the pain he would inflict on a kind and innocent soul—he should have been, but he was not. What held him back was this surreal lassitude, this inability to fully function, this strange detachment that, despite his best efforts, allowed him to slip weightlessly through his own life. And yet it was unfair to Leesa to fail to tell her how signally her life had changed. Even in his dreamy state, he recognized that.

She forced the issue by arriving in the city one evening only twelve hours after she had alerted him that she was coming. "I've taken a hotel for the first two nights, because I have no idea what you've planned these days," her note informed him. "If you're free, come to me this evening. If not, send me a note. Can't wait to see you."

So he dutifully presented himself at her room as soon as he finished work for the day. She seemed pleased to see him, but preoccupied. She had come to the city on business, and not all her transactions had proceeded smoothly.

"I'll have to run these figures by mother, because she's much better at numbers than I am, but I don't think this is the yield we were expecting," she told Nolan, still frowning down at some papers. She was dressed in a flowing summer frock of froth and aqua, and she looked like some sea goddess who had drifted in on the evening tide. Nolan could not help thinking how beautiful she looked, but the thought was distant; it chimed in his head like some faraway bell.

Eventually she laid the papers aside and smiled at him across the room. She was seated behind the massive, impersonal desk. He had draped himself across a flowered sofa. "I'm sorry," she said. "I haven't seen you in so long, and here I am going on about unimportant things. How have you been? I've heard practically nothing from you this past month or so."

"Busy," he said. "Odd things have been happening."

She crossed the room to come sit in the chair beside him. She took his hand and held it on her lap. "What odd things?"

He shook his head. He had never, with all his mental preparation, come up with a good lie to tell Leesa. "Among other things, I've been thinking over what's going to happen in my future."

She smiled again and squeezed his fingers. "Silly. Your future is marrying me and living in a beautiful house and having marvelous daughters. They'll have my face and your brains, and everyone will adore them."

"I wish that were so," he said seriously.

"Why wouldn't it be? I know we've waited a while to marry, but we're still young enough to have children. As many children as we want."

Nolan sat up in his chair, and his strange detachment took this moment to fall away. Suddenly, everything seemed hyper-real—every distinct color in the room, every individual bone in the hand that held onto his, every breath he painfully drew into his lungs. "I don't think so," he said in a low, firm voice. "I don't think that is the future I want after all."

Leesa's dark eyes grew darker, shadowed from within by sudden doubts. "Then—what is it you do want? You've never mentioned any other plans. And we've talked about this often enough."

"Sometimes, I think you don't realize how important my work is to me," he said. "Sometimes I haven't realized it myself. I can't move back in-country with you to live on your grandmother's estate. I can't turn my back on the life I have so carefully fashioned for myself here. I can't give up everything I've worked for to become your husband and the father of your children."

"But—you never said—if it matters that much—well, we could find a way," she said. Her face was both frightened and hopeful. She looked like a child trying to reason her way out of a nightmare. "Lots of families have homes in the city and homes in the country, and they move between them—if you only had to work four or six months a year—"

"It's not just the work," he said as gently as he could. "It's the life. Nothing about it matters to me. All that talk of who marries whom—what heiress has received what property—it's central to your existence, but I don't care about it. I don't like those people. I don't want to be with those people."

"You don't want to be with me," she whispered.

"Up until a month or so ago," he said, "I was the right man for you, and you were the only woman who had ever mattered to me. It had not occurred to me those things could change. It's not just that we want different things. It's that I have become a different man. To marry you—to live with you—would be false. To both of us. You deserve someone who comes to you with a whole heart."

"You've fallen in love with someone else."

"That's only part of it," he said.

"That's the only part I need to know." All this time, she had kept his hand in hers, but now she released him, in a gesture both stately and final. She came to her feet, and he followed suit, feeling as if there had not been enough sentences between them for him to explain what he truly meant.

"There's so much to tell you," he began, "but so much I don't know how to put into words."

She held up one hand as if to enjoin silence and moved back from him a pace or two. Her face was so stony he was sure she was holding back tears, but she moved with all her usual grace and dignity. "At times like this," she said, "words are the most harmful things in the world. The less you say, the less I'll have to remember."

He stood still a moment, trying to think of a response to that, but it was clear all she wanted from him was an exit. He made a small bow, a quaint acknowledgement of her unexpressed desire, and moved toward the door. On the threshold he paused, and turned back toward her.

"Yours is the spirit that formed me more than any other," he told her. "When I think of the last fifteen years of my life, everything will be colored by you. You taught me only the sweeter aspects of love. I never knew, till others told me, that love also can be careless and cruel. What I have become is something you would not want, but I did not become that because of anything you have done. Had I been given a choice about it, I would have remained who I was, and faithful to you. And I will always love you for the beauty you brought to my life."

She listened, but nothing about her softened. "None of that helps," she said in a forlorn voice, and turned her back on him. He waited a moment longer in silence, then left the room. That would be, he thought, the last time in his life he would ever see her.

He told no one about his farewell with Leesa, but somehow everyone knew. He received a letter from his mother, filled with baffled recrimination, and one from his sister, filled with some of the harshest language anyone had ever addressed to him. At work, he caught a few sidelong glances of pity or rebuke from his indigo coworkers, depending on their own level of happiness in their relationships, and Melina took him out to lunch again.

"I won't pry," she said, "but you could at least tell me how you're feeling."

"Like I've been pummeled and battered, every day, every night."

"Well, then!" she exclaimed. "Go back in-country—make up with her—I'm sure she'll listen to your excuses."

Nolan shook his head. "Can't," he said. "It feels like the wrong thing to have done, but I know it was the right one."

"Maybe in a few weeks you'll feel differently," she suggested.

He shook his head again and declined to answer, merely taking another bite of his casserole. Melina sighed loudly and turned her attention to the hard copy she'd purchased on their way in. She had said she was looking for news about the grain export levels, but she appeared to be reading even the most obscure items with equal interest.

Suddenly, she let loose an indistinct exclamation of surprise. "I can't believe it! They've released Jex Zanlan!"

Nolan's food turned to rubble in his mouth. He swallowed carefully and said, "What did you say?"

She pointed at the paper. "Jex Zanlan. They've let him out of prison. Yesterday morning, apparently."

"I don't believe it," he said.

"Well, it says so right here. But isn't that strange? I mean, everybody assumes he's the one behind the bombing of the Centrifuge, not to mention the troubles at the Carbonnier Extension and the medical building, so why would they—Nolan? Where are you going? Nolan?"

For he had jumped to his feet, flung money on the table, and headed toward the door. If Ariana Bayless had released Jex Zanlan, that could only mean one thing.

He waited till nightfall, and then he took the cross-town trolley to West One. This time, the colorful houses along Elmtree looked less strange to him, more inviting. He imagined the daily routines inside, the fathers and sons going off to work every day, the mothers and the daughters preparing the food and working in the gardens, each member of the household knowing his place, oiling one component of the domestic machine. Not the life Nolan wanted, no, but with its own symmetry and peace. Sometimes, lately, he knew he would be happier living a life in which his role was defined, his every movement forecast and expected.

Well, he had had such a life, and he had given it up. Now, till the end of his days, he would be guessing.

The men on the bus glanced at him and glanced away, but Nolan didn't care. They would not challenge him without a reason, as long as he did not disrupt their ancient patterns. He remembered the street much better than he had thought. He rose for his stop the block before it arrived and swung easily off the bus. Yes, this little cluster of gaily decorated shops was exactly as he had recalled. And here was Cloverton, and he would walk until he arrived at 1811.

At the striped house with the slanted copper roof, he paused a moment before summoning the courage to knock. It was certainly possible Colt was not here, or would disbelieve him. Nolan had no idea what he would do next if that were so.

The door was answered by the same gorgeous, terrified young woman who had opened it to Nolan when he was here with Melina. "Colt," Nolan said, firmly and slowly, and then remembered a few of the words Kit had taught him. "See Colt. I see Colt."

The woman responded with a rapid flood of interrogative phrases, but Nolan just shook his head. "I see Colt," he repeated. It crossed his mind, a wild thought, that Colt was dead and the woman thought Nolan must be hallucinating, but he had no other language with which to make his request known. Kit had not even taught him the word "please." He had asked for it, and she had laughed. "Guldmen never use it, so you have no need to learn it," she had replied.

The guldwoman before him answered again in a spate of unintelligible words, then suddenly ducked behind the door and disappeared. Nolan just waited. Perhaps she would fetch the young interpreter; perhaps he would be standing here the rest of his life. But no. Those were footsteps, and then the door was flung open, and Nolan was suddenly confronting the large blond man he had not seen in more than a month.

There was a moment's dead silence. Nolan found himself wishing he had remembered how big Colt was, how deadly looking. Weeks of outlawry had intensified the underlying ferocity of his features, honed his reckless edge. He had always appeared dangerous, at least to Nolan; now he appeared lethal.

Colt spoke first. "You," he said in that familiar mocking voice, "are the very last person in the city I expected to find at my door."

"I was here once before," Nolan said. "We left you messages."

"Anyone could have guessed that that particular visit was Melina's idea, and not yours," Colt said. "But here you are, all on your own. I guess I have to ask you why."

There were considerations of honor here, and Nolan did not want to make false accusations. But he had not mastered the indirect complexities of the gulden tongue, and so he plunged right in. "Cerisa fired you," he said bluntly, "because she thought you had associations with Jex Zanlan. And I'm here because I hope you do."

Colt did not look angry; he looked incredibly amused. "And if I do? You expect me to admit this to you and tell you all about our rebel meetings?"

Nolan shook his head. "I want to tell you something, and give you something, and I want you to pass them both along to Jex."

"And I'm sure the son of the chief of Geldricht would be interested in any message you have for him," Colt said in a silky voice.

"Jex is dying," Nolan said flatly.

Colt raised his eyebrows and leaned against the doorframe. "And how would you know this? Have you even laid eyes on the man?"

"First he had a cough, nothing too bad. Then a severe cough. Now he's exhausted, and growing weaker every day, but the cough is gone. Have you read the papers? Have you heard about the new gulden virus that's spreading in from Geldricht? The hospitals are aware of it. Has he seen a doctor?"

"The doctor said his symptoms were not those of this mysterious virus."

Nolan nodded impatiently. "That's because he's gone through the first three or four phases. He's in the final phase now—it doesn't look anything like the first few. It doesn't matter. It's a disease that can only be treated up to a certain point, and he's crossed it. They wouldn't have released him unless they were sure he was beyond the power of the drugs to cure."

"How do you know this?" Colt demanded.

"Because I have studied the disease and the drug."

"It's new—a few weeks old. You cannot have learned much."

Nolan smiled grimly. "I learned it all in a day. There's not much to know about it, except it is fatal to gulden, if untreated, and it was created by Cerisa Daylen."

Now shock made all Colt's features go slack. "Created by—"

Nolan nodded. "Manufactured. Specifically. To kill. The gulden."

In the space of seconds, Colt had assimilated the information, recovered from stupefaction, and grown calculating and cold. "You can't prove this," he said.

Nolan shook his head. "I can't. But you know Cerisa, and you know me, and I think you will believe me."

"Oh, I do. I am determining now how to kill her."

Nolan shook his head. "Let her live until I see her," he said. "For, trust me, her life is about to become worthless."

Now Colt looked amazed and stared down at Nolan as if he

had never seen this particular indigo before. "You? What would you do to her?"

Nolan handed Colt a sheaf of papers he had fished from his pocket. "I'm giving you the tools to strike back. You're the only guldman I know who will be able to read them, understand them, and use them. And I will tell her what I have done, and why."

Colt opened the folded papers and scanned them, then gazed back at Nolan with a marveling eye. But all he said was, "Tested?"

Nolan shook his head. "Lab work."

"Antidote?"

"Still working on it."

Colt laughed suddenly, a harsh, brutal sound. "Shall I let Jex make the decision?"

"That is what I assumed."

A moment more of silence, and then Colt suddenly thrust his hand out to shake hands with Nolan. It was the first time Colt had made such a gesture in the five years they had known each other. Nolan felt his bones protest under Colt's hard grip.

"You're a man of honor, Nolan Adelpho," Colt said. "And so I will tell anyone who asks."

The long trip back into the city by bus and trolley, by starlight and streetlight. Nolan was still numb, both physically and mentally. He moved as if propelled by unseen and insistent hands, surprised at himself but not surprised enough to resist. He had not even taken a moment to plot his strategy. He had known, apparently for weeks, what he must do. And now he was merely doing it.

It was a couple of hours before midnight when he walked into the offices of the gulden news media. There were about fifteen people working there, most of them men, but one or two, unexpectedly, were women. The place appeared to be one big, stark, brightly lit room filled with a jumble of desks, people, monitors, and electronic equipment. Nolan stood there for a moment, getting his bearings. He was not sure whom to approach or how to get anyone's attention.

However, within three minutes, one of the workers came up

and civilly asked what he needed. The reporter was a gulden male about Nolan's age, with long curly hair and intelligent eyes. His bluetongue was perfectly unaccented.

"I want to get a story into the gulden press," Nolan said.

The reporter nodded, his eyes fixed on Nolan's face. "And why?"

"Because it's a story that affects the gulden. And the indigo media wouldn't carry it."

"What makes you think we will?"

"If you believe me, you will."

"Do you have anything that will make us believe you?"

"I think so," Nolan said. "You have to. Because it's true."

He spent three hours at the media office, going over facts, dates, chemical formulas, and medical information. He waited while the reporter—now augmented by half a dozen coworkers, editors, and lawyers—called two of the gulden hospitals to confirm facts. Chay had deliberately kept news of the virus at a very low-key level, so that the medical community knew of the disease but not its origin and not its ramifications. As the magnitude of the event began to sink in, the members of the gulden press grew more and more grim.

"This will dissolve the city," said one of the lawyers who had been called in for consultation. "This is civil war."

"Then should we rethink?" asked a reporter. "Not run it?"

"Have to run it," was the brief response of the man Nolan assumed was the managing editor. He seemed to be in charge of the whole group. "We would be just as guilty as Cerisa Daylen if we didn't. People will live or die because of this story."

"The city will go up in flames," the lawyer said, shaking his head.

"There's more," Nolan said. "Maybe worse."

"That's hard to believe," the managing editor said.

"Jex Zanlan has found a weapon with which to fight back."

"What kind of weapon?" the lawyer asked. In a slow, clear monologue, Nolan told them. There was a long blank silence once he had finished speaking.

"You're right, it's worse," the managing editor said faintly.

"It's not a war, it's a complete meltdown. We could have a ghost city in three days."

"That's why I thought somebody ought to know," Nolan said.

The lawyer was staring at Nolan strangely. He was slight of build, for a gulden, with pasty skin that bespoke too much time spent indoors, snatching food at random. "But why tell us?" he demanded. "Why tell anyone?"

Nolan rose to his feet. He was weary beyond telling, and he still had one more stop to make this night. "Because it was the right thing to do," he said.

"I don't know that I would have done it in your place," the lawyer said.

Nolan turned to go. "Then Cerisa Daylen and Ariana Bayless have already won."

Out into the cool dark of the deserted city. He was in the central district, not six blocks from the Complex, and limos for hire were cruising the streets, looking for passengers. It would be a tidy sum to ride from here into the residential neighborhoods on the southern edge of town, but Nolan flagged one down anyway. All he could think about was sleeping, going to bed and forgetting everything about this evening, everything about his life. He would dream, insignificant and anonymous, and if he was lucky, he would wake without remembering who he was.

He had never been that lucky.

The limo moved quickly through the empty streets and was so comfortable that Nolan almost did fall asleep. He jolted to full alertness as the driver stopped before a large, shuttered house that showed no gleam of light at any door or window.

"Looks like they're all asleep in there," the driver remarked.

Nolan counted out a few bills and handed them over. "Not for long," he said with dry humor. "Be the last time anyone in that house sleeps for a good long while."

On the porch, he sounded the door gong repeatedly to send the sense of urgency through the house. Even so, the limo had disappeared before lights came on in the front rooms, and a tousled male servant opened the door.

"The *hela* is sleeping," the servant said. "What message may I convey to her in the morning?"

"No message," Nolan said, brushing by him to step into the hallway. He had never been inside this house, but its opulence for a moment stopped him—black-and-white marble in the foyer, a curved stairway sweeping up to the second floor, glimpses of rooms off to either side filled with massive antique furniture. "Tell her I must see her tonight."

"I do not wish to disturb the *hela*," the servant said a little more forcefully.

A voice spoke from the top of the stairs. "It's all right, Coto, I've already been disturbed." It was Cerisa, speaking with her usual acerbic aplomb. "Well, Nolan, your behavior has been increasingly erratic of late, but this may be your most outrageous episode yet. Coming to my house in the middle of the night."

Nolan gazed up at her. She had never been a beautiful woman, but her patrician features and haughty bearing always made her arresting. Even now, startled from sleep and in no good humor, the colors and contours of her face spoke a strength of will that was almost unopposable. He had been afraid of her since he had met her—they all were, even Pakt. But tonight, she inspired in Nolan not the slightest tendril of panic or alarm. Her hold on him had been broken irrevocably.

"It's the last time I'll trouble you," he said. "But I think you'll want to hear what I have to say."

"If it's to tell me you're resigning, you could have left me a note," she said. "I prefer my histrionics at one remove."

"I'm resigning," he said, "but you are, too."

The dark brows arched over the black eyes. "You *are* mad," she said calmly. "Shall I call the servants?"

"Call them if you want," he said. "But I think you'd prefer to hear me out first."

"There is nothing you could say to me at this hour that I would be interested in hearing."

"Nothing?" he said softly, still staring up at her. "Can you think of nothing you might have done that I could have discovered and would be willing to tell the world?"

"Coto," she snapped. "Show this man to the study and bring a tray of refreshments. No one is to disturb us. I'll be down in five minutes," she added to Nolan, and disappeared.

It was more like fifteen minutes before Cerisa joined Nolan

in the small, plush sitting room whose walls were filled, floor to ceiling, with shelves of medical texts and journals. Nolan had already helped himself to the food and wine Coto had brought in. He was starving. A stress reaction, he supposed, the body using up all its reserves as it launched itself into combat. The food was delicious. He took another bite and watched Cerisa shut the door behind her.

"Now, Nolan," she said in a smooth, dangerous voice. "Why don't you tell me what you think you know?"

No need for games and subterfuge. Nolan swallowed his last mouthful. "On Ariana Bayless's orders, you developed a virus fatal to the gulden. You exposed Chay Zanlan to it when he was in the city visiting his son. Apparently, you also administered it to Jex Zanlan, because he's been released from prison to die in the arms of his cohorts and infect the lot of them. And your purpose was to destroy the gulden completely. Plague. Genocide."

She didn't deny it; she didn't even look concerned. It occurred to Nolan that she was planning to have him kidnapped from her home, taken away somewhere and quietly disposed of. It was probably within her means and definitely in character. "Even if that were true," she said, "I don't see what you could do about it."

Nolan actually laughed. "I can do a lot!" he exclaimed. "In fact, I've done it."

"Really? And what exactly have you done?"

He counted off the items on his fingers. "I worked late to modify some of my general gulden formulas to counteract the virus. Same with existing vaccines. I traveled into Geldricht to share the drugs with Chay Zanlan. Who was pretty sick when I left, by the way, but stabilized. He may recover. At any rate, we've heard no news of his death, which I consider a good sign."

Cerisa preserved her calm, but her eyes had taken on an icy intensity. "You're right, that is quite a lot," she said. "I'm impressed by your industriousness, but—may I say it?—disappointed at the direction your conscience has taken you. Has it occurred to you that Ariana Bayless and I may have had perfectly legitimate reasons for constructing such a virus?"

"No, not really," Nolan said. "What would those reasons be?"

Cerisa rose to her feet. "The preservation of the indigo race! It is an assault on us from all sides by the gulden! They attack our buildings and our institutions, so that the city is not safe for innocent people to live in. They thwart our attempt toward progress, denying us the right to expand and grow. But worst—and don't tell me you haven't seen this!—they have begun to intermingle with our people. Twelve years ago, when my own daughter was approached by a gulden man, our government knew what to do to stop such outrage. But now? What do you see on the streets every day? Gilt girls walking hand in hand with well brought up blueskin boys—it makes me sick to my stomach to see it. There were fifteen interracial marriages in the city last year, did you know that? Fifteen! The year before that there were only three, and the year before that, one. Before that, none! It wasn't to be thought of! But now, they grow bold and fearless. They think they can be just like us. They think they are as good as we are. They think they can make *us* just like them. But they're wrong. And they must be stopped."

"You're the one who has to be stopped, Cerisa," Nolan said. "You and Ariana Bayless and however many dried-up old fanatic hags there are like you in the city. If there's two of you, there must be more. I hadn't thought about that before. I guess I'll figure out how to deal with the rest of them later, when I know who they are."

She gave a laugh of pure disbelief. "Deal with *them*!" she exclaimed. "How do you think you're going to deal with *us*?"

He took a moment to study her face. He had always thought she was the quintessential Higher Hundred matriarch, with the bone structure that had been copied over and over again onto the faces of all the women he knew. But now, he was relieved to see, he could note subtle differences. There were angles and secrets in her face that he had never seen in Leesa's, never seen in his mother's. She was not the prototype. She was the aberration.

"I've already dealt with you," he said softly. "I've told my story to the gulden press. Your name and Ariana Bayless's name will be on every monitor in the city tomorrow morning."

For the first time, he had shocked her. She reared back in

horror, and her blue face turned dark with anger. "You didn't," she said.

"Oh, I did. Names, dates, places. And a hard copy printout from your computer for proof. The GGP file. Gulden genocide plan."

"You're lying," she said. Her hands had clutched, clawlike, on the arms of her chair. He took a brief moment to reflect that a mortal threat brought out the animal characteristics of even the most sophisticated woman.

"No, I'm not," he said, still in that easy, unconcerned voice. "I expect tomorrow will be an interesting day for both of you."

Now he had silenced her; she stared at him as if he were the face of evil itself. He waited a few minutes for her to speak, then shrugged and climbed to his feet. "So, that's what I thought you'd be interested in hearing," he said, ambling for the door. "Aren't you glad I came by?"

"Get out of here," she whispered. She was still clinging to the chair which looked, by some amazing alchemy, to have swelled around her to twice its original size. Or perhaps she was shrinking, her bones contracting and her flesh drawing itself close for protection. "You—you—"

He paused at the doorway. "Oh, and one more thing," he said casually. "I gave Colt the formula for a new virus. But this one attacks indigo only. And so far I don't have an antidote."

Her mouth opened but no words came out; she had been robbed of the ability to speak.

"They might ask you to stay on at the lab until the cure is found," Nolan continued conversationally. "Or they might like the irony of asking Pakt to find the antibiotic that will save the indigo. Although he might not be too keen on the task. He might be one of those who hopes we all succumb to infection and die wretched deaths. To save the gulden, you know, from our dreadful indigo taint."

"You have betrayed your race," Cerisa breathed.

Nolan opened the door. "No, Cerisa," he said. "You have." And he walked out the door, down the elegant stairway, and out into the spangled night.

CHAPTER EIGHTEEN

Kit stayed in Geldricht for ten days after Nolan left, no longer as prisoner but as favored guest. She was not deceived, of course. She knew that Chay's guards followed her anytime she left the mansion grounds, but she took every opportunity to leave anyway. Chay, who had always spoiled her, had given her a substantial gift of money. So she browsed the markets for a few days, mostly buying clothes, because she was heartily sick of the few outfits she had been revolving for the past weeks.

She also bought gifts for Rell and Chay's daughters, and spent many enjoyable evenings with the women who had loved her even better than her own family had. Rell was wise, and the girls were loving, and Kit felt at ease with them as she felt with few people in the world. Not that she told them anything of her recent adventures. Not that she told them of Jex, or Nolan, or Chay. What Rell knew, Chay had told her, and the guldwoman would want to learn nothing important from any other source. So they talked of clothing, and the girls' prospects for marriage, and the changes that new construction had brought to Gold Mountain, and the hours passed peacefully.

Kit had no desire to see Chay, and he did not send for her.

She knew he was recovering, because Rell told her so, tears of happiness running down her fair cheeks. Once Kit would have cried like that, too, so joyous she could not express her emotion any other way, but not now. Not for Chay Zanlan. Not for the man who would have sacrificed someone he loved deeply merely to gain an edge with his enemy.

Or perhaps he had never loved her. How was it ever possible to tell when emotion was genuine, when it was false, and when it was summoned for a convenient purpose? It wasn't just Chay whose feelings she doubted. Her own had been in such severe flux for so many weeks that she questioned the authenticity of any surge of passion.

Her love for Jex Zanlan, which had consumed her for so many years, had burned itself out in the inferno of horror. She could remember every contour of his body, every timbre of his voice. She could call up with an almost sensual detail the way her heart had reacted the first time he kissed her mouth. She had forgotten nothing, she would deny nothing; this was a man she had adored. But no more. That white-hot fever had charred itself to ashes. There was nothing left to rekindle.

Her love for Chay, always such a powerful, comforting thing, had chilled overnight to frost and shadows. He had deliberately risked her, and not to save himself, not to save anyone, merely to hurt someone else. He had always been a superb tactician— that had been his great strength as a leader—but she had not realized until recently how ruthless that had made him. She guessed now that, when he had been in the city making deals with Ariana Bayless, he had been willing to sacrifice his son to the communal goals, and that realization froze her soul even more. She could not live like that; she could not love like that; she could not forgive such calculated betrayals.

And yet these were two of the people she had loved most in the world. How then was she to trust her heart? It fluttered now like a shy, rapturous bird, caged with uncertainty but breathless with hope, and she could not help but believe she would be a fool to follow it. This same heart had taken her down grand, giddy paths before, leading her straight to devastation and despair. Why was she to think it was any wiser now? *She* was not one who could differentiate the noble character from the base; *she* could not discern the black lie threaded through the gaudy truth. She could not love again; there was no safety in her judgment.

She would not seek out Nolan Adelpho once she returned to the city.

Nolan had been gone for ten days when Chay finally called for Kit again. The guard escorted her to one of the staterooms, so she knew before she saw him that he must be much improved. And indeed, once she stepped into his presence, she saw that he had begun a slow recovery. He was still unwontedly pale, and he seemed to have lost a good deal of weight, but the vibrancy was back in his eyes, his voice, his skin.

"Kit. You're looking well," he greeted her, gesturing for his guard to leave and for her to seat herself at a table laden with food. They both complied. Chay took a chair across from her. She thought that he had chosen this room for the audience because of its rich amber walls, which reflected extra color onto his cheeks and brow. He was still far from completely well.

"As are you, Chay Zanlan," she said formally. He had spoken in goldtongue and she followed suit.

"And you have been well entertained in your visit here? My lady wife and my daughters have helped you amuse yourself?"

"They are, as always, charming and delightful."

Talk continued for a while in this vein, the careful social indirections for which the gulden were famous. They each served themselves platefuls of food, and took small bites, and continued chatting, and nothing of importance was said for at least twenty minutes.

Finally, laying his napkin aside, Chay leaned forward a little in his chair. "We must talk, you and I, Kitrini Solvano," he said.

She raised her eyebrows. "I thought we were talking," she said serenely.

He smiled. "We can converse in bluetongue, if you prefer," he said, switching to that language.

"Only if, in such words, you can tell me outright what you want me to hear," she said, matching him again.

"It is a language made for plain speaking," he said. "At times I envy it."

"Then speak plainly," she said.

"It is time for you to leave Gold Mountain," Chay said.

She nodded. "I am glad to hear it."

"And I would wish you to leave not hating me."

Again she raised her eyebrows; this time she was truly surprised. "I would have thought that a man who could behave as you did would not care who hated him and who did not," she said bluntly.

"It is one thing to behave a certain way. It is another to disregard the consequences."

"At first," she said, "when you bargained with Nolan Adelpho for my life, I was hurt to the core of my being. I thought, 'He would never have betrayed his own son and daughters this way.' And then I realized that—had it been expedient—you would have treated them just as badly, or even worse. What bargain did you make with Ariana Bayless when you sojourned in the city? Once I realized that any of us—all of us—are choifer soldiers on your game board, I stopped being hurt. I realized it was not that you loved me any less. It was that I had always been wrong in believing you were someone who deserved my affection to begin with."

"I understand that you are angry, but I am surprised as well," he replied smoothly. "Did you learn nothing from your father? He abandoned a family, a history, an entire culture, on principle. To prove a point. He made you a misfit in your natural environment as a sociological experiment. To see what the result would be. How is that any different from what I did, which was to use you as a shield to protect my own life?"

Kit came to her feet, not caring if he was ready to dismiss her or not. "My father believed indigo society was truly evil and that the only way to protect me was to raise me outside its boundaries. The difference is, he was trying to save me, and you were trying to kill me."

"Not trying to kill you, Kit," Chay murmured.

"Willing to," she amended. "Just as bad."

"I always thought you had a large and generous heart, Kit," Chay said, now returning to the delicate, nuanced goldtongue. "But today it seems to have grown hard and knotty."

"Perhaps I do have a small heart, Chay. It is too full of other things to have room for forgiveness."

"Perhaps, when you eradicate the anger, there will be a space yet for such a sweet thing."

"When I dig up the anger and toss it from my heart, I will plant other flowers in that garden," she said. "And they will blossom, and they will be beautiful, but they will not be for you."

He had not risen when she did, and now he seemed to slump backward in his chair. But he raised his hand in a ceremonial benediction and spoke still in that same calm, affectionate voice.

"Then take your small heart, and leave me," he said. "Travel in safety, live in health, rejoice in happiness. If I do not see you again, remember these as my last words to you."

She wanted to, but she could not leave with a bitter farewell. She did not want to have to return someday merely to quiet her conscience with an apology. "The mirror catches all those wishes and returns them to you in silver," she said, giving him the traditional gulden reply. "Be well, Chay Zanlan. I will not forget you."

And she left him. And she found, not at all to her surprise, that the guards had already packed her clothes for her and purchased her a ticket for the evening train. There was time to say goodbye to Rell and the girls, but Kit did not attempt it. She wanted to leave Gold Mountain without crying.

This time.

But in the city, there was cause enough for tears. While Kit had been gone, her grandmother had died, and the whole family was in disarray.

It was the first thing Kit learned when, weary and travel-stained, she showed up on Sereva's doorstep two days later. The butler merely gaped when he saw her on the porch, but Kit heard Sereva's voice from the upstairs hall.

"Is that the lawyer?" Sereva called.

The servant did not answer, so after a pause Kit raised her voice. "No," she said. "It's me."

"What? Kit? Is that you?" Sereva demanded, and came hurrying around the corner of the bannister to stare down from the upper landing. She was dressed in a gown of severe burgundy, the indigo color of mourning. Kit felt her stomach lurch with warning. "Where have you been? Are you all right? Why have you been gone so long?"

"It's a complicated story," Kit said, brushing that aside and running lightly up the stairs. Seen at a close range, Sereva looked as exhausted as Kit felt, though infinitely calmer. "What's happened?" Kit asked. "Why are you dressed like that?"

Sereva stared at her. "You mean you don't know? It's been in all the media."

"Granmama," Kit guessed. "No, I hadn't heard . . . What happened?"

"Her heart. She was fine one day. The next morning, she was dead. The servants have been hysterical. It only happened two days ago, so all of us are still in shock. I thought you must have seen—I thought that's what brought you back."

Kit shook her head, her throat too tight to allow words to pass. Two days ago, she had been leaving Chay Zanlan's bright mansion. One week sooner, and she would have had another chance, a final conversation, a word of farewell for her mother's mother. Yet one more charge to level against Chay, another reason to despise him.

But Sereva was mustering up some anger herself. "What am I saying? Of course that wouldn't have brought you back. You didn't care about Granmama, anyway. You hated her and everything that mattered to her. So why would you care if she died?"

"Sereva!" Kit choked out in protest.

Sereva turned away, pacing down the hall. Kit followed her to Sereva's private study. "Well, it's true," her cousin said. "I can't count the times you complained about her obsessions with bloodlines and family connections—"

"Yes—I know—there was a great deal we disagreed about, but—Sereva, could you stand still for a minute? She was my grandmother. I loved her. She irritated me. I made her frantic. We were not always on the best of terms. But—but—if she's dead—"

And suddenly it all caught up with her, the trip, the dreadful revelations, the sense of loss piled high upon loss, and she started sobbing. She put her hands over her face to muffle the sound, to soak up the tears, but nothing could stanch this terrible weeping. Sereva turned to stare at her in astonishment, but only for a moment; only for that long did her coldness last. She ran

the few paces back to Kit and pulled her into her arms, hugging
her and murmuring endearments. There was no safety in this
world—Kit had learned that over the past few weeks—but this
felt like comfort. This felt like home, and a place to rest. Kit
turned within the circle of Sereva's arms, and cried till her body
held no more tears.

But it was hard, Kit discovered, to try to recount the events of
the past few weeks. Sereva called to postpone the lawyer's visit,
and the two of them locked themselves away to talk for the next
three hours.

"What I tell you," Kit said, "you're going to find hard to
believe."

"Your adventures always are."

"And you can't talk about it with anybody."

"Again, your escapades are rarely things I want to repeat."

"Oh, my part in the story is the smallest part of all."

At first she could not think how to begin ("Ariana Bayless
has tried to destroy the gulden!"), but finally she started with
her visit to Jex and Nolan's first wild approach. Sereva gasped
in fear, but Kit laughed.

"Save your outrage," she advised. "Nolan's actions are the
least frightening thing that happened."

It was not hard to draw a compassionate picture of Nolan; it
was harder to make him sound merely human. Kit could
scarcely conjure up now that first wave of fear and desperation
she had felt, when she had actually believed he had the will—
and the ability—to destroy Jex. Now he seemed omniscient,
virtuous, brave, magnificent. Those opinions were harder to conceal.

At first Sereva did not believe the story. Could not believe it.
"But Ariana Bayless—Cerisa Daylen—I know those women.
Such a thing is not possible," Sereva said more than once. But
she looked a little less certain each time she said it. Kit guessed
that she was remembering casual conversations, offhand re-
marks, maybe even whispered comments that she had heard over
the years, small details that dove-tailed with the accusations Kit
was making now.

"And haven't there been stories," Kit pressed gently, "alerting the gulden to a virus spreading through the city? Nothing too alarming, just a warning to seek out a doctor if certain symptoms appear?"

Sereva nodded, deeply troubled. "I heard something about it, but I didn't pay much attention. There are no gulden in my office, so news like that rarely trickles in. I didn't think—" She shrugged. "It wouldn't have occurred to me—"

"It wouldn't have occurred to anyone," Kit said. "Not even Nolan. Even when he came across proof, he didn't believe it at first."

But she had pronounced that name once too often. For a moment, Sereva was able to shake off her profound unease and concentrate on matters closer to hand.

"This Nolan," she said, watching Kit closely. "You seem to have grown fond of him. During this trip. I admit, if he did what you say, he must be an amazing man, though it's still hard to believe—So tell me about him. What's he like? What's his family?"

Kit couldn't help laughing. "Adelpho," she said. "Fine enough even for you, I would think."

Sereva's eyes widened. "That's Higher Hundred," she said. "Yes."

"Not only that—" Sereva searched her memory. "If he's the branch of the family I'm thinking of, one of them is betrothed to Analeesa Corova. They're to be married this winter."

"That would be Nolan," Kit said quietly.

Sereva's eyebrows rose. "As usual," she said dryly, "you show your exquisite taste in hopeless men."

Anger seemed the safest response; Kit let hers fire up. "What's that supposed to mean?"

"Well, if I didn't know you were in love with the terrorist son of Chay Zanlan, I'd say you'd fallen hard for this quixotic young indigo man who has just done the most incredible thing."

Kit came to her feet, too agitated to sit calmly. "Jex is—I'm not in love with Jex anymore. I am—he is—there is too much about him that I cannot love, that I—that I actually abhor. I know he was responsible for the bombs in the Centrifuge, I *know* it. And—there are other things. I never thought I would be able to cut him out of my heart, but he has done the cutting for me."

"Making room, then, for this Nolan."

"Who loves someone else," Kit said. He had said he did not, but he could have been mistaken; Leesa might be more a part of him than he realized.

"But if he did not? If Analeesa Corova discovered his crazy adventure and said she wanted no part of him? What then? Would you marry him, if he asked you? Would you love him?"

Kit spun around to face her. "How could I do that?" she demanded, almost in tears. "I have spent my whole life denying the importance of, the *existence* of, the Higher Hundred. I have fought against prestige and family connections—I have disdained everything the high-caste indigo stood for. How could I suddenly say, 'I've changed my mind. This is what matters to me after all. I want to be safe within the society I have mocked.' I don't think my conscience would let me do that, no matter what my heart desired. It would be like, after all this time, letting Granmama win in the end."

"Do you really think," Sereva exclaimed, "that Granmama would be pleased to see you marry a man so outrageous that he would investigate the leader of his own city, collude with the ruler of the gulden, and threaten your life—all before breaking his engagement with a wonderful girl merely to take your hand in marriage? Do you think she would consider a man like this an *improvement*? She wanted you to marry some boring, brainless high-caste second son who fit her notions of propriety and decorum. This Nolan person would not have pleased her at all. Don't let the fear of Granmama's approval keep you apart from a man you love."

The sarcasm made Kit blush; she was not used to such a tone from her cousin. "He still represents everything I have consciously rejected in my life," Kit said defensively. "It is not Granmama's approval I have to worry about, but my own opinion. I swore I would never marry an indigo man, and my reasons were good. How can I break that promise? How can I allow myself to change so much?"

"Well, if you plan to marry—or not marry—for political reasons, then you are just as bad as any blueskin heiress who plots with her grandmother, looking for a mate," Sereva said flatly. "I thought your high ideals would save you from that mistake, at least. No one who marries for love marries for her principles at the same time."

Kit turned away, feeling suddenly exhausted and shrunken. "You don't understand," she said in a small voice.

"I understand, all right," Sereva said. "You're afraid."

Kit laughed shortly. "Of everything you can think to name," she said over her shoulder. "That at least shouldn't make me unique."

Sereva came up behind her and gave her another hug. "And you're tired. And your way has been very strange. Go to bed. We'll talk some more in the morning."

But the morning brought its fresh shocks. Or the afternoon, really, since Kit could not manage to drag herself from her room till well past noon. She had slept and woken, slept and woken, so many times that she lost all sense of time and could not tell if she had been in this bed for days or merely hours. When she finally rose, she was starving, but she felt so grimy that she had to take a long, thorough bath before she would let herself go downstairs in search of food.

One of the servants met her in the dining room, inquired what she wanted for a meal, and added that *hela* Candachi wanted to see her as soon as she was ready. So Kit ate quickly and joined Sereva and an unfamiliar woman in Sereva's sitting room.

"Good morning, Kitrini. I was beginning to think you wouldn't be among us again until tomorrow," Sereva greeted her. "Angeline, this is my cousin, Kitrini Candachi. Kitrini, this is Angeline Marcosa, Granmama's lawyer."

Angeline Marcosa nodded and assessed Kit with one quick glance. She was a middle-aged, self-possessed woman who looked efficient and professional; mid-caste, Kit guessed, but intelligent and hardworking enough to make herself both powerful and dangerous.

"We were just going over the terms of your grandmother's will," the lawyer said in a cool voice. "She was, as you probably know, quite fanatical about the upkeep and disposal of her property, and she rarely let a month go by without consulting me on some small change or bequest she wanted to make."

Kit nodded tranquilly. None of this mattered to her since not an acre of her grandmother's property would go to her. A personal bequest, that would be nice, maybe even a small legacy, but the bulk of the property would go to Sereva and the rest to a few other relatives.

"Granmama liked to keep her hand in," Kit said equably.

Angeline Marcosa consulted her notes. "About three months ago, when she called me in, she made a few substantial changes in regards to two of her smaller properties. The last time I saw her—which was only two weeks ago—she went over every item in her will again and approved them each individually. So it is my professional opinion that this final will stands as the last record of her intentions."

"Sounds reasonable," Kit said.

"Kitrini, she left you Munetrun," Sereva broke in.

"She what?" Kit said faintly.

"And the city house," the lawyer added.

"She left me Munetrun? But that's her—I mean, I know it's small, but that was her favorite property. She told Bascom. I heard her."

"Munetrun, the city house, and enough annual income to keep them both up in handsome style," Angeline Marcosa said. "Appearances always were important to her, you know."

"Yes . . ." Kit said absently. She was staring at Sereva. "But why would she do that?" she asked wonderingly. "We never had five words together without getting into an argument. There was nothing about me—nothing!—that made her proud or happy. I wasn't even good to her. I never thought—Munetrun!"

"There's more," Sereva said gently. "A bequest. An annuity to your charity bank in the Lost City. A pretty good sum, too."

Angeline Marcosa examined her papers again. "Well, the exact annual figure can't be known until we've calculated the death taxes and the city taxes and—"

"But a lot," Sereva interrupted. "I think that answers the question of whether or not you ever made her proud."

"But I—" Kit said, and then shut her mouth hard. She couldn't speak, couldn't think about it, or she would start crying again. These days, it seemed that the unlikeliest people loved her and the obvious ones did not care for her at all. How would she ever sort it out, how would she ever learn whom to trust and whom to love?

"Yes, well, the disposition of Munetrun and the city house are really the smallest details of the will," said Angeline Marcosa briskly. "There's Govedere and Fairenen and Glosadel, as well as the farmlands, and I think it would be just as well if we went over those now."

"Of course," Sereva said, and Kit nodded, but she didn't pay any attention to the rest of the lawyer's words. In fact, she might as well not have been in the room at all. She was remembering the wild green tangle of woods that formed the southern border of Munetrun, the dense interwoven branches that built a mysterious, inviting castle of living forest. She had spent one whole summer there, when her father left her without explanation with his dead wife's relatives. She had been miserable when he left, inconsolable, actually, until Granmama took her to Munetrun. But she had loved that verdant estate, overrun with wildlife and impossible to tame into any semblance of lawn or garden. She had loved it, and so had Granmama, and now it was hers. She shook her head and tried to listen to the conversation again, but her thoughts would not stay on the spoken words. Another strange twist to her life; this was not a map she would have sketched in no matter how wild her imagination. Quietly, so they would not notice, she began crying again anyway.

Sereva wanted Kit to journey in-country, to look over her new property as soon as possible. "I'll go with you," Sereva said. "I can help you make an inventory. I don't even know how many servants there are on the place, though I'm pretty sure the steward is reliable. Well, he must be, or Granmama would not have left him in charge for so many years."

"I'll go," Kit said. "But in a week or so. I'm so tired of traveling. I need some time to rest."

"Munetrun is the most restful place I know," Sereva said with a smile.

"Yes," said Kit, but she still made no plans to travel.

She made no attempt to return to the charity bank, to take up the threads of that life. She refused to go with Sereva to the

various social engagements her cousin attended during the next
few days—"banquets, balls, and breakfasts," as Kit scornfully
termed them—even though Sereva assured her she'd be welcome.

"You're now a woman of property," Sereva said with a laugh.
"Think how well you were received at Corzehia's party when
you had nothing to recommend you but your bloodline. You
would be so popular now!"

"Maybe next time," Kit said, knowing that nothing would
induce her to attend another such event. She did not care for
parties; she did not care for the trivial interactions of these
wealthy and vacuous indigo. Truth to tell, she did not care if
she saw another gulden again as long as she lived, either, so
what was the point in seeking out any society at all? She would
be better off immuring herself in Munetrun, hiding there the rest
of her life, seeing no one, speaking to no one, beating down her
memories with ruthless fists until they could trouble her no
longer.

She should leave the city, but she could not, and she could
not have said what tethered her there. Almost as if she was
waiting.

The letter came a week after Angeline Marcosa brought news
of Kit's inheritance. She instantly recognized Jex's handwriting,
though his letters were usually terse and this envelope felt thick
and heavy. The gulden boy who delivered it stayed only to put
it in her hand. When she tried to ask him a question, he shook
his head and darted off the porch.

Jex did not expect a reply, then.

She retreated to her room to read the letter, closing the door
so no one would disturb her. The goldtongue words seemed to
have been written with care—not Jex's usual hasty scrawl—and
she read them as slowly as she imagined they had been committed to the page.

Kit:

    *Since your last visit, I have not had an opportunity to
send for you again. My jailors have been whispering*

amongst themselves, and for a while I suspected they were plotting to find some ingenious way to dispose of me and then claim an accident had resulted in my death. I have been very careful of stray knives and unfamiliar foods, you can be certain! But now it appears that they had other gossip to convey to each other.

I had a visit this morning from Ariana Bayless herself, telling me she has decided to set me free. I'm afraid I was very cool and insolent with her, which probably made her want to change her mind, but I cannot be otherwise with such a smug and self-satisfied blueshi. So I said, "I see your sense of justice has finally triumphed over your desire for vengeance." But she is very cool herself. She said, "You are a choifer in a game much more complex than you know, and it suits me to release you." Arrogant, yes? So I said in my turn, "We learn that no mere mortals know the position of every player on the board, and last time I checked, you were still one of them." She actually laughed. I cannot recall anyone I have ever hated as deeply and unwaveringly as I hate her, but I have to confess I laughed as well.

So—amazing news, is it not? I had begun to lose some of my usual optimism, for I have been here so long and heard no news. And I do know that much of the recent violence in the city has been laid at my door. Perhaps Ariana Bayless thinks I will be calmer once I am free again and that I will direct my efforts to more peaceful negotiations. What I know is that I will be more careful once I am released.

And being more careful means restricting myself to the smallest possible group of confederates. I must not let anyone know where I am staying—not even my father. I have thought and thought, and I have been unable to devise a safe way to have you brought to me. I think it is possible that we may never see each other again.

So the great love that has sustained me for so long comes to an end in this fugitive way. I tell myself that the times may change—governments may change—the world itself may change—and you and I will one day be together

*again. But my future looks blurred and uncertain, and I
do not believe any of my own words. What can I say
except that I will always remember you and always love
you? You cannot reply, but I tell myself that you would
say exactly the same words to me.*

Jex Zanlan, of the clan Zanlan

For an instant, Kit could not breathe for the pain in her chest.
She had told Sereva just the other day that she no longer loved
Jex Zanlan, and yet this letter pierced her with arrows of longing, regret, and memory. She had tried to imagine what she
would say to him the next time he sent for her—how she would
tell him she could not accept his careless brutality and ruthless
zeal—but in those mental conversations he had been the bloody
revolutionary and not the tender lover. How had she believed
she could so easily put aside those sweet memories, those desperate passions, the hurt and delight and confusion that were
her relationship with Jex?

And to never see him again? To not have a chance to say
goodbye? To receive only this letter and then, for the rest of
her life, to wonder where he was and how he fared? Who would
know of him? Who would speak of him to her? Even if Jex
communicated with his father, there was no guarantee that Chay
would relay any information to Kit, if Chay himself lived,
though it seemed he might—

And then Kit had a thought that stopped her heart completely.

She read the letter again. *I had a visit this morning from
Ariana Bayless herself, telling me she has decided to set me
free.* Why would Ariana Bayless make such a visit? Why would
she come to such a decision? What master plan could she hope
to accomplish by freeing Jex Zanlan?

What other odd visitors had gone to Jex Zanlan's prison cell
in the past few weeks? What other strangers had come bearing
remarkable gifts and seemingly joyful news? He laughed about
being careful of weapons and meals, but Nolan had explained
how easy it was to inoculate someone with this dreadful virus.
Who had come calling at the Complex prison, and what had
they used to infect the inmate?

For Ariana Bayless would never release Jex Zanlan, healthy and vengeful, to wreak mayhem on her orderly city. But a dying Jex Zanlan, polluted with a disease he did not know about—now, that man she would be happy to set free among the city gulden. And he would surely be dying; the mayor had learned her lesson with the prisoner's father. She would have kept him in his cell until the disease was uncontainable, beyond the reach of any fabulous antidotes. And then, for a few brief days, she would give him back his life.

Kit sank to the floor, the letter still clutched in her hands. He was dying, and he did not know. He was dying, and she could not go to him. He was dying, and she could not save him. He was dying. Jex Zanlan was dying.

No matter how often she said the words, she still could not bring herself to believe them.

For the next three days, Kit watched the news media with an obsessive attention. She rose early every morning to journey into the city and find one of the gulden monitors (there were none to be found anywhere near Sereva's neighborhood). The indigo media, she was sure, would not cover the news she was interested in, the news she was most afraid of hearing: that Jex Zanlan was dead.

The gulden monitors did carry the first piece of information she watched for, the fact that Jex had been released. The item was the lead story on all the monitors, though she noticed it did not make it into the indigo media until the following day. She expected the streets to be filled with outraged citizens, blueskins storming the Complex to protest, but she appeared to be the only one in the city who had noted that particular paragraph, who cared at all about the fate of Jex Zanlan.

He must be well and truly on the path to death, or Ariana Bayless would not have risked releasing him. Kit knew she must scan the monitors every day to glean what information she could.

But the next morning, what she read on the gulden news screens was an article about the other man she loved. And it was even more shocking.

• • •

"Kitrini, what's wrong? Are you sick?" Sereva demanded as Kit staggered into her cousin's office, clutching a hard copy of the story. "Sit down. What happened? Claressa, go get me some water," she directed at her secretary before flying back to Kit's side. "What's wrong?"

Kit held out the hard copy, but Sereva merely glanced at it impatiently. "What is that? I can't read it."

"Article," Kit whispered. "Nolan's gone to the gulden media with the story of the virus."

"What?" Sereva demanded and snatched the paper from Kit's hand as if she had miraculously summoned up the ability to read gold-tongue. "What does it say?"

"Everything. Ariana Bayless. Cerisa Daylen. Chay Zanlan. Everybody is named. And—" Kit shook her head. She couldn't swallow. The words were caught in her throat, hurting her, cutting off her air. "And—"

Sereva was studying the paper again. "Is this him? This picture? This is Nolan?" Kit nodded. "So it names him, too. The stupid man, he's just ruined his life. He's ruined *their* lives. I can't imagine—what in the world can come of this—?"

"It's worse," Kit said, still in that hoarse, constricted voice. "He's made up another virus. For blueskins."

"A virus for the indigo? A—you mean, a *disease*? He's created a disease for his own people? Why would he do that? Why would—and how would the gulden papers know about that?"

"He told them. And he told them that he—he gave the virus—he gave it to the gulden—"

The papers fell from Sereva's hand; her dark face grew darker with disbelief. "He *what*?"

"To make everything fair. To give them power over us like we have over them. To make sure no one else does what Cerisa has done. But he—but he—he gave the virus to Jex Zanlan, or one of his friends—"

"But Jex Zanlan will instantly use such a weapon!" Sereva cried.

Kit nodded. She was exhausted, empty, dull with terror. And these were the two men she had loved most in the world. "I know," she whispered. "I know."

•   •   •

The city was in a frenzy for the next seven days. Sirens split the air with warning; loudspeakers broadcast unintelligible updates; quarantine made the streets ghostly during what should have been the busiest hours. Schools were shut down, houses were shuttered against airborne germs, and only those who absolutely had to venture out could be found hurrying fearfully down the deserted sidewalks.

But they had to have news. The media, both indigo and gulden, had expanded their broadcasts and set up remote communal monitors in neighborhoods where the residents could not afford to buy their own screens. The wealthy homeowners had their own screens and could watch the stories unfold from the safety of their fortresses, but the poor and the transient collected in small uneasy groups on the sidewalks of their neighborhoods to follow the progress of the crisis.

Ariana Bayless and Cerisa Daylen had committed a double suicide in the mayor's home. Their bodies were discovered shortly after the indigo media translated the gulden news item and incorporated it into their noon coverage. They were dead; their offices were in utter disarray; and Nolan Adelpho was nowhere to be found.

At the Biolab where he had worked, however, the activity was at a fever pitch. De facto laboratory head Pakt Shoiklin gave terse interviews that boiled down to: "We are aware of the problem, and we are working on it." Indigo journalists wanted to know how they could trust a gulden to find a cure for a blueskin disease, and the man smiled.

"A blueskin infected the gulden, and a blueskin found the antidote," he said. "Why shouldn't a guldman find the cure for the blueskin poison? Thus each race will have cause to be grateful to the other."

"You would save the indigo?" a blueskin reporter asked with obvious skepticism.

The man named Pakt smiled somewhat menacingly. "Even if I would not," he said, "I have biologists on my staff who would. Does that satisfy you?"

But he would not allow the journalists in to interview his workers, saying, "They're too busy, and if I were you, I would not want to distract them from work that might save my life."

Reporters camped out in front of the lab doors, waiting for workers to come and go, but none of the scientists left the building, a news item in itself, which was duly reported. Not a day went by in the next week in which there was not some broadcast from "the shadowed halls of the city's Complex, where brave and diligent scientists are hard at work racing to solve the mystery of disease."

Kit watched them all—the features about the individual scientists at the Biolab, the bulletins about what form the disease might take, the updates of hysteria at the hospitals, the speculations about the whereabouts of Nolan Adelpho, the broadcast debates among city leaders about his ethics and his actions. "Hero or Traitor?" one of these panels was named, but there was very little actual question: hero to have attempted to save the gulden, traitor to have developed the formula that could destroy his own race.

"Unforgivable," pronounced one of the panelists. "Evil," said a second one, and two of the others nodded.

"But don't you think," said another woman, a small mousy blueskin who looked to be mid-caste and held some hard-won position in one of the governmental offices, "don't you think he did the only thing possible to dramatize the barbarity of Ariana Bayless's action? Don't you think that otherwise we might have been shocked, but in a comfortable sort of way, because we didn't feel at risk? If you yourself aren't afraid to open the door and saunter down the street, how can you empathize with someone else who is?"

"Don't be ridiculous," said an older, turquoise-skinned woman—a member of the clergy, Kit thought, if she remembered the identifications correctly. "I don't have to be on the point of death to comfort my parishioners who are dying."

"Don't you?" was the mousy woman's unconvinced reply. "Don't you have to experience hunger to worry about whether the poor are fed?"

"*I* don't," one of the other panelists said virtuously.

"And how much have you given to charities in the past two years?" the mid-caste woman asked him.

"Well, I—my own family is my first concern, and I direct my

money and my energy to making sure *they* are not hungry," he said stiffly.

"Not a penny, then. Is that what you're saying?"

"How is this relevant?" the moderator broke in impatiently. "We were discussing the unspeakable actions of Nolan Adel- pho—"

"He wanted to get your attention," the woman replied softly. "And he wouldn't have gotten it otherwise. I think he did the right thing."

But that opinion was vociferously voted down, and Kit never saw the woman on any other news panels.

Sereva had to drag her away to eat meals and interact with the family, but Kit was reluctant to be in any room that didn't have a monitor. At what point would they find Nolan, at what point would they discover Jex had died? She could not miss those announcements, either one of which would rend her in two. Sometimes, Sereva had meals brought to her in the study where Kit spent most of her time; sometimes, she sent Marcus and Bascom in to try to distract her. Kit played choisin with her nephews and helped them with their lessons (Sereva had de- signed a study plan for them during the quarantine), but she kept the monitors on. She couldn't miss anything.

Thus, she was watching late one evening when the reporters waiting outside the Biolab were rewarded with a glimpse of one of the scientists. The exhausted woman who stepped through the door looked vaguely familiar to Kit, though at first she couldn't say why. The reporters clamored about her so loudly that Kit missed any mention of her name, though they did calm long enough to let her speak.

"We think we've made some progress," she said in a tired but calm voice. "It helped that Nolan's notes were so complete."

"Nolan's notes—Nolan *Adelpho's* notes?" one of the report- ers demanded.

The woman nodded. "Yes. Two days after we learned of the indigo virus, we received a package from Nolan with a molec- ular breakdown of the disease and his theories on an antidote. We can't be sure it's effective, of course, until we have an actual human subject. But his notes are pretty thorough."

The reporters seemed unable to grasp this entire concept.

"You mean, Nolan Adelpho designed his own cure?" one of them finally asked. "And he told you how to make it?"

"That's exactly what I mean."

"But why would he do that?"

The woman searched the crowd for the speaker, her tired eyes suddenly gone dark and angry. "Because he is not Cerisa Daylen! Because he does not want anybody to die! Because Nolan concocted this virus to make you—all of us!—stop and think about who we are, what we're capable of—"

"Murder and betrayal, that's what he's capable of!" one of the journalists shouted.

"Look," the scientist snapped. "None of you understands what has happened here. Cerisa Daylen was not the only biologist clever enough to create a lethal virus—but until she did it, no one else thought to try it. We think we've stopped her epidemic—and we think we can stop Nolan's. But there are gulden biologists who are fully skilled enough to design new germs, new diseases, that we'll know nothing about until they begin to destroy the indigo race. *That's* what Nolan did. He reminded the gulden that they have a weapon every bit as sophisticated as ours—and he warned us that the weapon was already in gulden hands."

She began to push her way through the crowd, but the reporters kept shouting questions at her. "Which gulden scientists can manufacture such a disease?" "Do you really believe we've reached an age of biological warfare?" "One more question about Nolan Adelpho—" But she ignored them all, answered no more questions and finally made her escape. When she had finally disappeared from view, one of the broadcasters turned to the screen and announced, "That was Melina Lurio, a scientist at the Biolab for almost four years. She first joined Cerisa Daylen's team the summer the *tiseese* virus was sweeping through the albino community—"

Kit stopped listening. Melina. Now she remembered. She had met Melina at Corzehia's ill-fated party, and they had talked of pointless things, but the indigo woman had been kind. And Nolan had mentioned her name to Kit with great affection; they must be close friends, she thought. She could not remember him mentioning anyone else's name—except for Leesa's—and the media had already established that Analeesa Corova had no clue as to Nolan's whereabouts and would not willingly speak to him if she had. They had also discovered he was not at his city apartment. His family, while maintaining a stony silence on his behavior, had proved to the satisfaction of the authorities that Nolan was on none of the Adelpho properties.

But perhaps this Melina Lurio might know where Nolan was. Kit fetched Sereva's copy of the city directory and looked up Melina's name. Yes, just as one might expect from that skin color and that chic appearance: She lived in one of the trendier indigo neighborhoods, deep in the city itself. It would be no trouble at all to find her.

Accordingly, the next morning, Kit left the house early and took the limo to the city. A few of Sereva's servants had volunteered to run errands and pick up groceries and, in general, brave the infectious perils of the world, so Kit had begged a ride from one of them. The streets were eerily deserted, only a few hardy souls walking the lonely sidewalks, cloths around their mouths to filter out germs and shoulders hunched to ward off unspecified dangers. It took the driver almost no time to cross the empty roads and deposit Kit on the doorstep she had requested.

Melina Lurio lived in a modern three-story building with classical lines but unusual decoration in a neighborhood of houses that similarly mixed the traditional with the avant-garde. A hush hung over the whole street, and no one appeared to be stirring, either inside or out of the modish apartments, but that didn't stop Kit. She boldly climbed the three steps to the front entrance hall, located the interior door that matched the number she had found in the directory, and knocked imperiously.

After a long pause, during which Kit knocked twice more, the door was opened by a slim blueskin woman who looked mid-caste, tired, and irate. "Yes?" she said shortly.

Kit stepped so close she was almost over the threshold, though this put her practically face to face with the woman at the door. "My name is Kitrini Candachi. I need to see Melina Lurio."

"You can't. She's sleeping. She's been very busy this whole week working at—"

"Yes, I know, she's a Biolab scientist," Kit said impatiently. "Doing important work. I need to see her. I need to ask her about Nolan."

"Nolan!" the woman repeated sharply. "Do you know him?"

"Yes. Do you?"

The woman shrugged and shook her head in an indeterminate motion that was supposed to convey "no" but looked unsure enough to be "yes." She said, "Melina has talked of him. In the past."

"Does she know where he is now?"

"Why would she?" the woman asked with an attempt at belligerence. She didn't have true animosity in her, though; it came off more as apprehension.

"Because somebody must. I need to find him."

"I'll tell her you came looking. I can't wake her up now. She needs her sleep."

"I'll wait here till she wakes."

The woman tried to close the door, but Kit had rested her shoulder against it and did not budge. "You have to leave now," the woman said with a somewhat pathetic attempt to be severe. "It's too important that Melina be allowed to get her rest—"

But there was a small commotion behind them and a weary voice from the other side of the door. "What's the problem, Julitta? Is it the reporters again?"

Julitta turned her head to answer and Kit tried to push the door wider but succeeded in gaining only an inch. "No, it's some woman who says she needs to find Nolan."

"Nolan!" the voice exclaimed, and suddenly the door was flung open to reveal the Melina of the news monitor. She looked younger but scarcely more rested, dressed in a nondescript bathrobe and rubbing the exhaustion from her eyes. "How do you know Nolan? What do you want from him?"

"I want to know where he is. I want to know if he's all right. I remembered that you were a friend of his. I thought you might be able to help me find him."

Melina was studying her with those quick, expressive eyes that seemed so thoughtful and, even at this hour, compassionate. "I know who you are," she said slowly. "You're Kitrini Candachi."

"We met at Corzehia Mallin's party," Kit said formally.

Melina nodded. "But I'd heard of you before . . . And we saw you once, in the Complex. Nolan and I. But he didn't know who you were then. Why should I believe you're a friend of his now?"

Kit spread her hands. Was she really a friend? What, exactly, was she to Nolan Adelpho? "I took him to Gold Mountain to save Chay Zanlan's life," she said quietly. "I didn't know him before that journey, it's true. But on the trip—we became friends. I want to help him now if I can."

But Melina had heard something in Kit's explanation that was not in the words themselves. "So you're the one," she breathed. "He didn't tell me your name."

Kit's spirits lifted with hope. "He told you about the trip?"

Melina shook her head. "I don't think he told anyone—until he told the reporters. But it was clear something had happened. It was obvious he had fallen in love with someone."

Kit felt her face color with heat. "Do you know where he is?" she persisted. "I'm worried about him."

Melina stepped back and motioned Kit inside. Julitta closed the door behind her as Kit stepped into the spacious living room. She glanced around briefly at the colorful wall hangings and imaginative sculpture, then turned all her attention back to Melina.

"I'm worried about him, too," the scientist said frankly. "Half the city wants to kill him outright, and I'm not sure he'd be safe if he was spotted on the streets. I've tried to persuade him to go back to his mother's but he says he isn't welcome there, and he's probably right. My grandmother wouldn't let me cross the threshold of her house if I had done what he's done."

"It was the noblest thing in the whole world!" Kit cried.

Melina nodded. "Oh, I agree. But stupid and dangerous and incendiary nonetheless."

"I think he did the right thing," Kit said in a low, stubborn voice. "And I want to find him before somebody else does— and lynches him on the spot."

Melina shrugged. "How can you help him? Do you have some safe place where he can hide out for a year? Or however long it takes?"

Kit put her chin up. "As a matter of fact, I do. And I'm willing to take him there tonight if I can find him."

Melina met the challenging gaze with a cool, measuring one of her own. No fool, this woman; she was used to grappling with contrary entities, puzzling out their secrets, and rendering them powerless. But she could also tell which alien life-forms posed a threat and which might exercise a beneficial effect.

"Julitta," she said without taking her eyes from Kit, "I need the keys to your apartment. Give me a minute," she said to Kit, turning away, "I have to get dressed. I'll be right back."

It was a thirty-minute walk from Melina's trendy neighborhood to the commonplace, featureless high-rise complex where Julitta had her small lodgings. But there was only sporadic public transportation running, and Melina didn't want to hail a public limo driver, "who might remember something if my face ever appeared on the news next to Nolan's." Kit thought that very unlikely, but did not bother to say so. She was in an agony of excitement, uncertainty, and anticipation. She was on her way to see Nolan.

"So he's at your friend's apartment?" she asked, just to have something to say, words to occupy her mouth, if not her mind. "How did that come about?"

"He came to my place in the middle of the night. The night he went to the media, I guess. Told me what he had done. I knew—*he* knew—the instant his name was released that there would be no safety for him anywhere in the city. I thought about taking him out to my mother's, but she watches the monitors, she knows what's happening in the city. He wouldn't have been safe there, either. All I could think of was Julitta's place. She hasn't lived there in more than a year, but she's kept the lease. In case she ever gets mad and decides to leave me, I guess," Melina added with a small smile.

"Have you checked up on him? Made sure he has food—hasn't gotten sick?"

"I haven't been out of the lab till yesterday," Melina said gently. "I don't know if he's even still there. But I don't know where else he could possibly go."

They entered Julitta's apartment building and, in silence, took

the elevator to the fifteenth floor. Kit had lost the ability to
speak; her lungs had shrunk to the size of fists. Her veins ran
with ground glass, spiky and fevered. She would see Nolan
again . . .

Melina knocked on an unmarked door down a long hallway
of identical doors. Kit moved to one side, out of direct line of
sight, and tried to persuade herself to breathe.

There was a muffled noise behind the door. "Yes?" said a
man's voice. Nolan's voice.

Melina put her mouth to the door. "Nolan, it's me. Melina.
I've brought—" But before she could complete her sentence,
the door flew open. Nolan stood there, ragged from sleep but
otherwise whole. He did not look haggard or haunted or riven
with regret. He did not appear to be suffering. Kit felt herself
relax just the slightest bit.

"Melina! What's wrong?" he exclaimed. "You shouldn't be
here."

"You don't need to tell me that," she said with a quick smile.
"But I've been worried about you. I wanted to see if you were
all right. And I wanted to bring you—"

"I'm fine," he interrupted. "I've gone out a few times. I cover
my face with one of those masks, just like everyone else, and
no one has recognized me. So far, anyway."

"You should leave the city."

He raised a hand as if in acknowledgement of an argument
lost a long time ago. "When I think of a place to go."

Melina took a deep breath. "There may be a place," she said.
"I've brought someone to tell you about it."

And before Melina could turn to wave her forward, before
Kit could take a step, Nolan's eyes lifted and found her. He did
not move a muscle, but his whole body reacted; he appeared to
leap forward, to glimmer with incandescence. His hand on the
doorframe tightened till Kit could actually sense the protest of
the wood.

In the silence, Melina's voice sounded strained and artificial.
"She came to my place looking for you. I believed her when
she said she knew you. But if you don't want—if you—say
something, Nolan. Let me know if you want me to take her
away again."

"No," he said, and nothing else.

There was another moment of complete silence, while Kit and Nolan stared at each other and Melina waited for instructions. "Well, then," Melina said finally, "I guess I'll be going. If you leave the city, Nolan, please let me know where you go. I'm glad you're all right. I'm glad you—" Her voice trailed off. No one said anything. Melina's laugh came, soft as a whisper. "I'll be on my way, then. Goodbye, Nolan. Goodbye, Kitrini." And she edged away from them and down the hall. And they were left alone, face-to-face.

CHAPTER NINETEEN

"Nolan," Kit said.

He nodded, the first time he had moved since he had glimpsed her. "Come in," he said. "No one's supposed to see me."

She crossed the threshold and glanced around blindly before her eyes went back to him. "You've been all right? You've been safe here?"

"So far. But I've watched the monitors. People are looking for me."

Kit nodded. "Reporters."

"And some government authorities. And angry indigo who would like to see me murdered in the street."

"Melina's right. You should go away. Hide someplace."

He shrugged, then smiled, making no direct answer. "How did you find me?" he asked. "How did you find Melina?"

"Saw her on the news. I remembered that you'd mentioned her name. I thought she might know where you were."

"And why did you want to know that?"

"Because I wanted to tell you—"

He waited while she searched for words. "Tell me what?"

She spread her hands; all-inclusive. "Tell you everything," she said at last. "Jex is dying, I think."

"I know. They would not have released him otherwise."

"And the whole world has changed."

"I know," he said again.

"And Chay is not the man I thought—and you are not the man I once thought—and even my grandmother is different than I believed—"

"Would you like to sit down?" he interposed. "I could get you something to drink."

She shook her head. She had crossed her wrists and drawn her fists up to her collarbone; she was having difficulty with the very concepts she was trying to put into words. "I don't know how you ever know what to cling to," she said at last. "How you ever know what to believe in. How you ever know if what you're doing is the right thing and if who you're loving is a good person. How do you know that?"

"You make your best guess, and you act on it," Nolan said. "And if you find out you're wrong, you try to make amends. I'm not saying it's easy. I've just done it for the first time myself. And almost everyone in the world will tell you I was wrong."

"I think you're the bravest person I know," she said.

"Is that why you came here?" he asked. "To tell me that?"

"No," she said. "I came to offer you sanctuary."

He smiled, genuinely amused. "Last time I heard anything about it," he said, "you didn't have much of a haven for yourself, let alone anyone else."

"I've become a woman of property," she said. "My grandmother died."

"I'm sorry."

"I'm sorry, too. But she left me a legacy—a house in town, and an estate in-country that is so isolated no one can find it without directions. I think you should go stay there. You'd be safe."

Nolan looked at her for a moment, unmoving, then turned sharply away to pace the room. "I can't run away from what I've done," he said over his shoulder. "A great thing—a monstrous thing—however it's judged, I did it, and I would do it again, and so I must stand by my actions. Leaving the city would not change that. I cannot hide away for the rest of my life. I don't want to."

She watched him closely. "Not the rest of your life. A few months—a year—however long it takes for the maelstrom here to die down. Soon enough, you'll be needed back at the Biolab, haven't you realized that? Do you know what demons Cerisa Daylen has unleashed? Your friend Melina said that to the reporters yesterday. Now that we know how to kill each other with disease, what other powerful viruses might we invent? What other kind of invisible wars might we learn to wage on each other? On the albinos? On foreign nations? We have entered a new era. And you are one of the few people who understands how to navigate through its mazes. They'll realize that soon enough. And then you'll have to return. But for now—"

He stopped striding around the room and passed one hand over his face. He looked suddenly exhausted. "For now," he said quietly, "I would so much like a place to rest. A place to sort out my thoughts. A place to recover."

"Munetrun," she said. "We can be there tomorrow night."

"We?" he repeated. "You would come with me?"

"You wouldn't find it on your own."

"And then? Would you leave, or would you stay with me there?"

Kit looked at the floor, a neutral collage of tiles in an uninspired pattern. "What does Analeesa think of what you've done?" she asked in a low voice.

"I have not spoken to her since shortly after I returned from Geldricht. When I released her from our engagement and told her I was not the man for her."

"That must have been hard for her."

"It was hard for me, too. But I could not in good faith pretend to love her when I love you instead."

Kit looked up. "Is that still true?" she whispered.

"What could have changed me?" he demanded.

"Why does anyone change?" she countered. "Once you loved Leesa, too."

"Leesa was part of a way of life I loved. The only way of life I knew until now. And I have left that life behind. You are—you embody all the things I have come to admire and respect. Wondrous things and difficult things. Things I cannot put into words. I don't know that I could ever have loved you before, being who I was then. Being who I am now, I don't think I can ever stop. I don't want to embarrass you or frighten you or make you angry. But I don't want you to doubt that I love you."

"I have loved Jex Zanlan my whole life," she said, in a slow, halting voice. "Both because of who he was and—and, I guess, because of what he represented. But I learned there are no boundaries in Jex. I learned that we do not have the same view of right and wrong—of good and evil. And I learned that I could not love a man who did not value the things I prize most. But it is hard to let go of an old love. And it is hard to trust yourself when you think you love again."

"Those things are both true," Nolan said gravely.

"Let me come with you to Munetrun," she said at last. "I'll stay as long as you like. I'll teach you goldtongue. We'll play choisin. We'll read. We'll talk. We'll find out if we have really learned to read each others' souls."

"All right," he said.

"I think I do love you, Nolan," she said. "But I want to make different mistakes this time. Let's stay in Munetrun until the city has forgotten about you—until we've forgotten about our old lovers—until we're sure of everything."

"The world will end before we're sure of everything," he said with a slight smile. "But I will agree to stay until you're sure of me."

"When can you be ready to leave?" she asked.

"Anytime. Now."

"I have to tell Sereva where we're going and arrange for a car to take us in-country. And it's probably better if we leave at night."

"I can meet you somewhere. At the East Zero gate, maybe—that's right on the road to Inrhio."

Kit thought it over a moment, then nodded decisively. "Good. Wait until full dark before you leave here. I'll be there about an hour after nightfall."

"I'll be waiting."

She turned toward the door, hesitated, and turned back. He stayed where he was, waiting. She took three quick steps to cross the room and kissed him lightly on the mouth.

"Tonight," she said, and not another word. But even as she left the room, he was with her; walking the silent streets, she felt him beside her. She saw the city, heard her own footfalls, with his senses; and she knew that would be the way of it from this day forward, no way to disentangle, no need to, no desire. The closer she came to Sereva's house, the faster she went, till at the end she was almost running. It was not the distance she was trying to shorten, but the time. Nightfall was half a day away, and she could only endure the sluggish drag of the minutes if she whirled into frenzied activity. She must pack; she must arrange for transportation; she must secure funds, close the city house, talk to Sereva. Much to do and little enough time. She flung herself toward the appointed hour.